The
LOST
DIARY

ROSE ALEXANDER

The
LOST
DIARY

bookouture

Published by Bookouture in 2023

An imprint of Storyfire Ltd.
Carmelite House
50 Victoria Embankment
London EC4Y 0DZ

www.bookouture.com

ISBN: 978-1-83790-718-2
eBook ISBN: 978-1-83790-717-5

A Flower Given to My Daughter

Frail the white rose and frail are
Her hands that gave
Whose soul is sere and paler
Than time's wan wave.

Rosefrail and fair – yet frailest
A wonder wild
In gentle eyes thou veilest,
My blueveined child.

— JAMES JOYCE

*

It is estimated that 60 million people were displaced by the Second World War, including 12 million German citizens. Both the flight of those Flüchtlinge across the continent of Europe and the Long March, in which 30,000 Allied POWs were forced to walk through Poland and Germany in appalling winter weather conditions, are historical facts.

This book is based on the true stories of family members during the Second World War who participated – however unwillingly – in these momentous and cataclysmic events, and many of the scenes described come directly from their memories.

Throughout the text, place names, dates and times have been changed to protect identities and in the interests of the narrative.

PROLOGUE

BERLIN, 1945

The bus wheels trundled along the street, still rubble-strewn and riddled with potholes. Bomb-blasted buildings stood like fractured teeth, the pleading arms of splintered sides reaching heavenwards.

The woman in the smart new conductor's uniform leaned against a seat for balance as the vehicle turned a sharp corner. The next stop was approaching.

'Alight here for Cumberland House,' she said, as loud and clear as she could.

She marvelled every time she spoke out loud in English, heard her own tongue forming the unfamiliar words. She must be doing it right because everyone seemed to understand, and often they asked her supplementary questions. *Which way for Spandau? What stop for the Kurfürstendamm? How far to Tiergarten?* She'd memorised the street atlas in order to be able to respond to any enquiry, however obscure.

Two women in the front seats prepared themselves to disembark. As the bus ground to a halt, brakes screeching, doors flapping creakily open, they stood, smoothed down their skirts, adjusted their hats over precisely coiffed hair, straightened their pristine gloves on their perfect English hands and moved towards the exit.

'Thank you,' they said to the driver, and 'thank you,' they called back to the conductress.

'You're welcome,' she replied.

The British were lovely, everyone agreed. So well-mannered, fair in everything, thoroughly decent people. They could not be more different to the Russians. When first the city began to be divided, those in Charlottenburg hardly knew how fortunate they were to be in the British zone. Now, after all that Berliners had endured throughout the war and during its aftermath, they thanked their lucky stars every day.

As the two women descended the steps to the pavement, a man jumped on, in the distinctive blue garb of the Control Commission. The conductress took no notice of him; the buses were free for members of the British administration. She busied herself with taking tickets from civilian passengers, making her way from front to back, the calculating machine that hung from her neck whirring and groaning and spewing forth stiff paper tickets as she went.

She reached the seat where the man was sitting. There was no one left to pay, so she paused, fiddling with one of her dials that was playing up. As she did so, she became aware of being watched. Slowly, she looked up, wondering if she were doing something wrong, if this uniformed man was going to report her. Her job on the buses was so new and so precious, with the salary it brought, and the sense of purpose it gave her. She'd worked hard for it, studying the English grammar and phrase book she'd been given at the interview, taking care to learn every possible way to give directions, tell the time, comment on the likelihood of rain.

Her eyes met his.

Instantly, she had a sense of recognition, that feeling of knowing you've seen someone before but not being able to place them. She wrestled with her memory for a few moments.

And then it came to her.

A gasp sprang involuntarily from her throat and she clutched her hand to her chest as if to still the sudden, erratic, staccato beating of her heart.

'Sorry,' the man apologised. 'Really sorry. I didn't mean to startle you, staring like that.' He paused, took a deep breath. 'But it's you, isn't it? You're the woman. The woman with the...' His voice tailed off as if having second thoughts. He had been going to mention the baby, she was sure, probably wondering if it had survived. In these desperate days, it was always a strong possibility. Life hung by a thread – for the youngest, the thinnest thread of all.

The woman fought to overcome the tidal wave of emotion that threatened to engulf her.

'Yes,' she replied. She felt dizzy, light-headed. 'Yes, you're right. I am.'

Silence followed. Not even the noisy rumbling of the bus, waiting at one of the newly reinstalled traffic lights, broke the hush.

Suddenly, the colours changed and the vehicle lurched forward, taking the conductress by surprise, causing her to stumble. The man put out his hands, steadied her. His touch, in the short moments before he let her go, was electric, a charge shooting through her veins.

He had not once taken his eyes off her.

'I can't believe it,' he said, wonderingly. 'That you're here. That you survived.' He paused. 'I can't believe I've found you so soon.'

The woman nodded, though she didn't really know why. What did he mean by 'so soon'? Or by 'found', which implied a conscious act of looking? But she said nothing. She didn't know how to, in a way that would be polite, or appropriate.

The man grimaced, his forehead furrowed, his expression one of trepidation. 'And – the baby? What... How is the baby?'

A group of passengers noisily boarded.

'I need to go,' said the conductress. 'I have work to do.' But she stayed put, ignoring her new customers.

'Of course,' replied the man, hastily, anxiously. 'But...?'

'The baby is fine.'

There was another pause.

'I...' he began, but his voice faded, leaving just the single word hanging in mid-air.

The moment was too big. Neither of them knew what to do with it. The woman made as if to move away, get back to the task in hand.

'I'm getting off soon,' said the man, speaking so quickly she struggled to understand. 'I'm supervising some building work, such a need for accommodation...'

'Of course.' She understood. He needed an excuse to end the encounter, to call a halt to it.

But then he spoke again, more urgently.

'Where do you live?' he asked. 'I've got tinned meat, cigarettes, chocolate, soap – I could bring them round for you and the little one.' He hesitated, gave a short, awkward laugh and then went on, 'Well, the cigarettes not for the baby, obviously, but...' He held her gaze, willing her to agree. 'No obligation, no... Look, this isn't going how I planned, but you know what I mean. I have things you might need; I could help you out. After all,' he made a wide, expansive gesture with his arm towards the broken city rolling past, 'there is so little food.'

The woman's stomach rumbled spontaneously at the mention of the word. She was always hungry. Everyone was.

She nodded. 'Thank you. That would be kind.' She told

him her street and house number before she moved off down the aisle.

The bus jerked to a halt, the man jumped down and the bus swayed off.

I'll never see him again, thought the woman. The realisation was accompanied by a dull numbness. She no longer felt sadness, nor any emotion really. All such feelings had been beaten out of her by hardship and hunger and horror and heartbreak. It was enough just to exist, now. To survive.

She turned back to the passengers she'd neglected – a family group, a man, a woman and two children, who were arguing intently amongst themselves. When they saw her hovering, they stopped abruptly.

'Which stop for the park?' they asked.

'Third from here,' answered the conductress. 'Don't worry, I'll tell you.'

CHAPTER ONE

The mantelpiece was truly a monstrosity, I thought, as I watched the workmen hack at the mortar that stuck the huge wooden structure to the wall. It was far too big for the proportions of the room and the varnish, darkened by age to an ugly shade of treacle-brown, was now splintered and cracked, jagged fissures revealing the cheap pine beneath. Within its wide embrace, tiles in varying shades of sickly green surrounded the gas fire that, at one point in history, had had a boiler behind to heat the apartment's hot water.

The block was old and showing its age, full of idiosyncrasies such as external wiring and Bakelite light switches, not to mention the incredibly dated serving hatch between the kitchen and the sitting room. Throughout my childhood, my mother, Katja, had usually been on one side and my father, Lou, on the other, exchanging cups of tea and pleasantries – or sometimes, because we are all only human, sharp words and arguments.

But my father was long dead and my mother recuperating from a major operation at my house, a chalet bungalow next to

Hampstead Heath, so while the flat was unoccupied, I had arranged for a complete overhaul to try to bring the place into the twentieth century. My mother had been resistant at first, reluctant to spend the money. Eventually, I had persuaded her that putting in a combi boiler, central heating and a washing machine would not only make life easier but also enable her to stay put, living independently, for much longer. That last point had sealed the deal; independence was my mother's middle name. Agreement achieved, the first thing that I was waging war on was that hideous fireplace.

With a final blow, the builders wrenched it out. A shower of plaster shavings and flakes of paint rained down onto the floor, while dust rose up in a thick cloud that momentarily obscured everything. When it cleared, a little collection of items that had lain trapped for decades was revealed: a hairgrip, two or three buttons, a few ancient and tarnished coins. And a piece of folded paper, which must once have been white but was now yellowed with age.

Curious, I picked it up. It was filthy, caked in a layer of dirt that felt horrible against my fingertips and made my skin crawl. I thought about putting it straight in the bin. But then my inquisitiveness got the better of me. It might be of nostalgic interest: a bill showing prices in pounds, shillings and pence, for example, or a shopping list that harked back to some previous era, reminding the shopper to buy Vim, condensed milk and sugar cubes.

The workmen left the room, hefting the mantelpiece along with them, manoeuvring it through the apartment's narrow hallway and out of the front door. In the hiatus that followed their departure, I unfolded the paper. As I did so, a small explosion of desiccated plant matter flitted across the grimy surface. There, encased in its paper wrapping, was what remained of a dried flower, that had presumably once been pretty and colourful but was now bleached of all colour and brittle with age. Time had robbed it of any possibility of identification and it was so delicate I barely dared to touch it.

As I stared, I saw that there was something written beneath where the flower lay. With utmost care, I let the flower head slide across the paper, revealing the words that had been hidden. Just two of them, so it turned out. *Für sie.*

I knew what the words meant by virtue of having a German mother. *For her.* For who, though? As I stared at it, questions tumbled through my mind. Who had made this gift of a once-beautiful flower, and who had they given it to?

Mystified, I folded the paper protectively back over the flower and tucked it into the inside pocket of my bag. It must belong to my mother, I thought – such a memento was far more likely to be kept by a woman than a man. What part of my mother's past did it relate to?

A sharp ring on the doorbell disturbed my thoughts. Assuming the builders had managed to lock themselves out, I went into the hallway and pressed the entry buzzer, then opened the door. But instead of the burly workmen, the person who appeared was petite and female.

'Emma!' I exclaimed in delight at the sight of my daughter, my eldest child. 'How lovely to see you. How did you know I was here?'

Emma swept in, giving me a quick hug as she passed through the door. 'The builders are having a fag on the doorstep, by the way,' she grinned, before going on to answer my question. 'I called your work and your colleague told me you'd left and you were heading here, so I thought I'd pop in. I was at a meeting just down the road. It's looking...' Emma briefly surveyed the part-dismantled kitchen and then walked into the living room, where plaster dust still hung in the air. 'Well, it's not looking great if truth be told – but I'm sure it will. Eventually!'

I had to laugh. Emma's comment was so typical of her –

pulling no punches and telling the truth but always in an upbeat way.

'We'll get there,' I said, confidently. 'I have faith in the team – even if they do spend a lot of the time outside smoking, as you've just observed.'

Emma smiled and went to the window. 'It feels strange without Grandma,' she mused. 'I don't think I've ever been here when she's not.'

'She'll be back,' I replied, reassuringly. 'But not until I've got the place shipshape,' I added, hastily, lest Emma think I was going to neglect her precious grandmother. 'Anyway, any news on the wedding?'

Emma was in the process of planning nuptials that some-times alarmed me, as they seemed to be getting more elaborate – and expensive – by the day. I had to work hard to hide my doubts about the whole shebang. Emma was only twenty-three, which I felt was too young to be tying the knot in this day and age. I wished she would wait a while – five years or so. But I knew better than to voice my concerns; it was not my place to interfere, and anyway, the last thing I wanted was for Emma's betrothed to cast me in the light of judgemental mother-in-law. And even if I had said anything, Emma would be unlikely to take any notice, given that she had had determination as a central character trait since birth.

Added to which, she would not hesitate to cite my own early marriage as a case of leading by example. Which would be ironic, given that mine and her father's was a shotgun wedding because I was pregnant with Emma, and even more ironic now that Ed and I had separated and were in the midst of getting a divorce.

At the thought of my own parlous marital situation, my heart jolted in my chest and unwelcome tears pricked behind my eyes. Blinking them back, I hid my struggle to compose

myself behind a tissue I hurriedly unearthed from the depths of
my bag.

You're not even that upset about the divorce, a voice in my
head hissed at me.

And I wasn't... was I? Of course not. The marriage had run
its course and that was that.

I forced my mouth to form the brightest smile I could
muster and turned back to Emma. 'How are the preparations
going?'

The noisy reappearance of the builders at this precise
moment was providential, offering a momentary distraction
that meant my daughter didn't see my smile falter. Who was I
trying to kid? I was devastated that the union I had sunk everything into, had thought was for better or for worse, had simply
crumbled into nothing. But the last thing I wanted was for
Emma to see me broken. She might be a grown-up, but, in
common with all children, she still needed to believe her
mother invincible. And I didn't want her to know that I was
unhappy, in case it made her unhappy, and then that was just
more unhappiness in a world that had far too much of it
already.

My demeanour restored to equanimity, I turned to Emma
as she pulled a sheaf of paper from the handbag slung across her
shoulder. 'Well,' she began busily, 'the lists are getting longer
and longer, as you can see, but I think it's under control. G's no
use whatsoever, but then again I didn't expect him to be, so
that's no surprise.' She gave a brief laugh of resignation. 'The
most important thing for you to remember is that I've got a dress
fitting two weeks on Saturday, 3.30 p.m., so make sure you get
there on time.'

I grimaced apologetically. 'Noted,' I responded, with a mock
salute. Some might accuse Emma of being a bit of a bossy boots,
whereas I knew that it was just her natural habit of being forthright, and I loved her for it. With Emma, you never had to

wonder if she was secretly offended or upset or aggrieved; she would tell you straight out if that were the case.

'And no muddy wellies!' she added, with a roll of her eyes.

'OK, got it,' I laughingly agreed. 'I'll be there, suitably attired and punctual to the second.'

Emma was right, though: I would have to remember to change my shoes. She, like all my family and friends, knew that, when I was not at work at my dull job in administration for the local council, I would always be found in my garden, which meant that, oftentimes, my footwear of choice was a pair of trusty wellies.

'I can't wait to see the dress,' I said. 'I know you're going to look marvellous.'

'Great,' replied Emma, looking and sounding relieved. 'Thanks. Now, before I go – I brought this to show you.'

She thrust a copy of the *Evening Standard* under my nose. It was open to a half-page advert for a citizen journalist project, asking Londoners to record, on paper, Hi8 or cassette tape, their experiences of the Second World War in preparation for the fiftieth anniversary of VE Day, which would be celebrated next year. There were plans for an exhibition at the Imperial War Museum, as well as special features in the paper and on Channel One Television.

'What do you think?' Emma was peering closely at me, gauging my reaction. 'I thought it might be a nice project for you and Grandma, while you're being forced into each other's company. Give you something to do together – mother and daughter time.'

I smiled faintly. Though, of course, I loved my mother and would always look after her, our relationship had had its up and downs. She was often prickly and lacking empathy – not always, if truth be told, that maternal. And she was notoriously tight-lipped about the past, particularly about the war years. Her reticence to speak of that period in her life – together with the fact that my father, Lou, had died when I was sitting my O levels, long before I had acquired the maturity to understand the value of the older generation's memories – meant that I knew almost nothing about my parents' wartime experiences.

'Umm, maybe,' I said, hesitantly. I took the newspaper, folded it and tucked it under my arm as I gathered together my coat, bag and the flat keys. 'We'll see.'

Emma and I left the apartment together and said our good-byes. Sitting on the bus on my way home, I fumbled in my bag for the folded paper containing the flower and examined it anew. *Für sie.* For Katja? But, in that case, why not 'For you'? That would surely make more sense.

Outside the smeary windows of the bus, the spring sunshine was bright, but with the particular harshness that the light can have in late May, and the air, now it was rush hour, was heavy with traffic fumes. My life, at that moment, seemed similarly weighed down by all that was happening, events that seemed to have a life of their own and over which I had no control: my impending divorce, my mother's health concerns, my eldest child's marriage, my son Evan's university placement on the other side of the world in New Zealand, where he was learning to be a winemaker.

Everyone else was moving on, but I was stuck where I was, literally and metaphorically. I felt suddenly, inexorably, over-come by a desperate need to know. Not just about the flower, with its cryptic message, but about all of it. About my mother's past, and my father's, about how, exactly, they had met, and where, and what had happened next. I knew that, in the imme-diate aftermath of the war, an English ex-airman named Lou had met a German girl from Berlin called Katja. They had got together, had me in 1946 and come to London in 1949. I also knew that my mother had been married before, to a German army officer who had died on the Eastern Front. But more than that had never been shared.

How was it possible, I pondered now, that, after almost half a century on this planet, I still had so few facts? Perhaps this was what had been missing all these years, this understanding of my origins, the exact circumstances of my birth. The newspaper that Emma had given me rustled as my arms rested heavily on my bag. It seemed to offer the perfect pretext to start a conversation that had been waiting in the wings for so long. Far too long.

The bus slowed to a stop. As I stepped down onto the pavement, the sun burst forth from a partial covering of cloud, bathing the city streets in a flood of bright light. At that moment, I knew. It was time.

Time to talk about the war.

CHAPTER TWO

Picking up the boiling kettle, I filled the teapot with water and placed it on the tray for Saturday elevenses. Next to the pot, I put the newspaper, folded open at the advert that Emma had so delightedly shown me. I had left it until the morning to broach the topic with my mother, thinking that we'd both be fresher earlier in the day.

As I was about to lift the tray up, I remembered the note with its dried flower. Fetching it from my bag, I wedged it between the two cups, then took the tray to the downstairs bedroom, where my mother was ensconced for the duration of her stay. My spaniel, Springer, always my shadow, followed closely at my heels.

Opening the door, I saw that my mother was awake. Gently, I rearranged the pillows, solicitously patting and plumping them before helping her to a sitting position. Now she was in her late seventies, she had lost all trace of her once shimmering, silken hair, the deep brunette replaced by grey, but she was still a good-looking woman, with high cheekbones and a delicate mouth.

The hysterectomy, which she had resisted for so long, had

taken its toll, though, and she looked washed out, a result of the severity of the procedure and the after-effects of the anaesthetic still coursing through her system. The last thing she would ever want was my pity – or anyone's pity, come to that – but nevertheless I felt sorry for her, hating her to be in pain, to be frightened. My way of dealing with it was to look after her as best I could during her convalescence, but given she abhorred fuss as much as she abhorred illness, that was proving to be pretty tricky at times.

I poured the tea and passed my mother her cup, then settled down in the chair next to her with my own.

She took a sip as she eyed the tray suspiciously.

'What's that?' she demanded, gesturing towards the newspaper.

I suppressed a smile. My mother might be getting old, as well as recuperating from a major operation, but she was as sharp as ever. There was no point trying to pull the wool over her eyes; never had been, never would be. I decided to go straight in, without preamble.

'It's something Emma found,' I began, knowing that any mention of her adored granddaughter would be guaranteed to soften my mother's heart. 'They want ordinary people's Second World War stories for next year's commemorations. I doubt they'll get many from the German perspective, so we thought you might want to take part.' The judicious use of 'we' was intended to ensure that Mum knew Emma was behind this plan – another ploy to predispose her towards cooperation. 'You never know,' I concluded, airily. 'You might be famous.'

A tiny light sparkled in her eyes at my last words. She had always loved attention. But then, just as suddenly as it had appeared, the light dimmed.

'I don't know why anyone wants to remember those times,' she muttered, grumpily.

There was a short pause while I considered her reply.

'Because it's important, I suppose,' I finally came up with. 'History is important. Otherwise what do we learn, how can we make society better?'

She harrumphed dismissively. I suppressed a sigh.

Perhaps a change of tack was in order. Glancing around for inspiration, I saw the paper containing the flower.

'By the way, Mum,' I said, carefully picking it up. 'I found this behind the old mantelpiece – it must have fallen down there years ago. I wanted to show you – I thought you might know what it is.'

Reluctantly, she took the proffered item and stared at it intently. I was sure I saw a glimmer of recognition in her eyes, but just as soon as it had arrived, it was gone. Slowly and deliberately, she put the folded paper down.

'I don't know anything about it,' she said, bluntly. She stared straight ahead of her, not looking at the flower. 'Perhaps it's something you did,' she continued, eventually. 'You always loved nature. You squashed all manner of plants in that little flower press you had – dandelions, daisies, forget-me-nots. Probably why you're so keen on gardening now.'

My forehead furrowed even as I nodded my agreement to my love of the natural world.

'What about the writing?' I persisted, gently. '*Für sie*. What could that refer to?'

'Poof!' She swept her arm in front of her in a gesture of dismissal. 'Just some note, something scrawled on a piece of paper then reused. We didn't have nothing to just throw away.'

Mum's English grammar went a little off kilter, as it was wont to do, especially when she was tired or stressed. But why would a dried flower cause stress? It didn't make any sense.

'We reused everything in those days,' she continued. This was a well-worn theme of hers and not one I wanted to pursue at that moment. If I had hoped that seeing the long-lost possession would trigger an outpouring of memories, I was plainly wrong. It wasn't going to be that easy. And I had to be careful not to push. Pushing my mother never worked.

'I'll get rid of it, shall I?' I said, assuming that, if my mother could remember nothing about it, and believed it to be of no significance, she wouldn't want it lying around. 'It'll only gather dust here, like it was—'

'No.' Her voice cut across mine. 'No, don't throw it away,' she went on, more quietly now. 'I want... I mean, it might come to me. What it is. What it was for.'

I smiled. 'Of course. I'll pop it in here for now.'

I pulled open the drawer, which always stuck slightly on one side. 'It's probably glad to have been rescued from all the dust behind that hideous fireplace,' I said, as I stowed it away.

'I never liked that thing either,' she remarked. 'I thought it ugly – though, over time, I got used to it. One can get used to anything, over time.' She paused after this enigmatic statement, then sighed heavily before continuing. 'When we first moved in, we were grateful to have a place to live at all, thankful that they let us share with them – your father's mum and dad, and his dad's mum and dad. There were seven of us in a flat meant for four, no privacy whatsoever. We didn't know the meaning of the word.' She punctuated this statement with a dismissive snort at the very thought that *anyone* would know the word privacy's meaning. 'There was such a housing shortage back then. No one expected to have their own place – not like young people nowadays. And that flat was considered luxurious because it had a kitchen and indoor bathroom. Where I had lived in Berlin, accommodation was much more basic. We had a toilet there, but the only way to bathe was in a tin tub in front of the fire.'

My mother was on familiar ground here, talking about the realities of everyday life: how many people to a room, how little space, the deprivations of existence in cities such as London or Berlin, bombed from end to end and exhausted after nearly six years of war. Her favourite topic of all was the 'the younger generation don't know they're born' line of argument.

But this, I recognised with a sudden clarity, was the problem. Whenever my mother did talk about the past, she focused exclusively on the superficial, the basic facts, the commonplace and mundane aspects, not the details, never the emotions. I had always assumed that was just the way my mother was, the way she'd been born. But maybe there was more to it than that.

Reasons that I could not even imagine.

'In Berlin, after the war,' she resumed, 'so many were homeless, left to live on the streets. Your father and I – we considered ourselves lucky.'

'It all sounds so difficult,' I sympathised. 'So much hardship everywhere.'

At that moment, the four sheltering walls of my own beloved house seemed to wrap themselves closer around us, my mother and I, keeping us safe and comfortable.

'But,' I began again, 'that's why it would be great if you took part in the project. To preserve your memories for future generations, so that they never get forgotten.' *And so that I know*, I added internally to myself. *So that I understand.*

As I spoke, I kept a wary eye on my mother to see if she would take the bait.

Eventually, she rolled her eyes skywards, sighed, then started to talk again. 'We just had to survive,' she muttered, 'that's all we had to do. You say that people need to know about history so that they can learn – and what they must learn is that it must never happen again. *Never again.* Those were terrible years. Terrible.'

I leaned forward and patted her knee comfortingly. 'Why so terrible?' I asked, gently encouraging. 'What happened to you, Mum?'

She shook her head, her face contorted as if with pain. When she answered, her voice had a plaintive, pleading tone.

'No one who wasn't there can understand what it was like. The risks I had to take, the constant, debilitating fear after...' She stumbled to a halt, then eventually resumed again, but not to finish the previous sentence. 'How could I ever explain what I'd gone through, how far I had sunk, to keep us alive?' she concluded, grimly.

I regarded my mother's white hair and liver-spotted hands, on the backs of which the veins stood out like tangled ropes as she clutched the bedsheets under her chin. This was the challenge of opening up the memory bank: you did not know what would be thrown up, high and dry, to face the light of day. A flash of pity seared through my veins. Suddenly, I understood what haunted my mother's past; I'd always known there was something but had never been able to put a name on it. Now I could. It was shame, that most powerful of human emotions, one of the few that we share with other animals that live in social groups.

My mother was ashamed of her past. But why? My desire to know immediately became a desperate need – a need that had to be fulfilled.

'So why don't you tell me what happened?' I asked, simply.

'Where shall I start?' For a moment, my mother looked helplessly at me, her lips wavering, her eyes bewildered, unsure.

'At the beginning?' I suggested.

There was a pause and then my mother drew herself upright, shaking her head emphatically. 'I don't know exactly when the beginning was. Perhaps, for me, it really began in the middle of the war, November 1943. Horst was gone, off to fight. Oh, it was bad, Jo. Terrible bad. When the bombs came, they brought the buildings down with them and caused infernos to rage like the fires of hell.'

My mother's sudden eloquence took me by surprise. After all the years of silence, to hear her giving such passionate voice to these long-buried memories took me by surprise. Like anyone else, I knew of the difficulties and horrors of war from books and films but this was different, this was lived experience. And not just anyone's. My own mother's lived experience. This was nerve-wracking, given that it was already clear the story wasn't for the faint-hearted. But it was also encouraging. Because it meant that I was right and that now was the time. The right time.

And so my mother began to tell me, in dribs and drabs, with interruptions and many stops and starts, what happened to her as the Second World War burnt itself out in blood and death and hatred and starvation.

As she talked, I wrote, sometimes as she was speaking, but oftentimes afterwards, when, on my own, I would type up her words, struggling to capture the essence of my mother so that potential followers of the history project would truly feel that she was a real person who they knew, and for them to understand what she had endured.

The more she talked and the more I wrote, the more I knew that this was a tale the world needed to hear.

CHAPTER THREE

The shop bell chimed to announce the arrival of another customer, the umpteenth of the morning. Groaning inwardly, Katja took a few moments to summon the energy to haul herself to her feet. She'd only just sat down for the first time since 6 a.m., and she felt drained.

As she stood, the baby kicked, strong and forceful. Katja winced. Her belly was huge now, her time for confinement nearly upon her. And she was all alone – no one to help her in the shop, bar the young girl who cleaned at the beginning and end of every day, and no one to help her at home.

Katja and her husband, Horst, had thought he would be safe from the call-up, as he was already in his mid-forties – over fifteen years older than her. But, lately, the papers had been arriving for men of all ages. She'd waved him off just six weeks earlier and had received only one letter since, telling her he was on the Eastern Front. Katja had no idea when she would see or hear from him again.

Leaning on the shop counter for support, Katja eyed the

latest customer. She was a woman, around thirty Katja guessed, but she moved like a much older person. Katja watched her make slow progress towards the counter. The woman appeared cowed, as if frightened of something, but what could be intimidating about the grocery store, with its comforting aroma of freshly ground coffee, Katja could not imagine. She waited patiently for the woman to approach. As she did so, a kerfuffle from outside caught her attention.

She turned her gaze away from the woman and out of the huge plate-glass shop window where a gaggle of children were gathered, waiting outside while their mother was making her purchases. Two of them seemed to be in some kind of altercation, while the tallest child, presumably the eldest, held the handle of a huge pram and rocked it back and forth with a detached expression on her solemn face. From under the pram's black hood, Katja glimpsed two pairs of bright eyes peeking out.

Including the twins in the pram, Katja counted seven children. Seven! Instinctively, she laid her hand on her baby bump. *Imagine doing this – being pregnant – six times*, she thought, *and having such a brood to care for*. Katja shuddered.

While she had been looking and counting, the woman had gone to the window and was now making a threatening gesture through the glass. Reluctantly, the fighting pair ceased their quarrel and all five lined up in order like perfect doorsteps, each one a head shorter than the next, bearing testimony to the regularity of their appearance in the world. Katja had never considered how many children she wanted to have, was just delighted to be having this one, the first. But she decided then and there that two or three would be more than enough.

The customer cleared her throat, drawing Katja out of her reverie. She turned to face her and summoned a welcoming smile.

'How can I help?' she asked, encouragingly. The woman did seem to be very nervous.

The woman's eyes flicked to and fro, as if checking there was no one else around. She leaned conspiratorially towards Katja and, when she spoke, her voice was so low that Katja struggled to hear.

'I've no ration book,' she whispered. 'The boys,' she gesticulated beyond the glass, 'tore it up and threw it on the fire during a quarrel. The authorities say I can't get another one until next month. Even if I could, the babies had a fever and I've no money left after paying for the doctor. We've got nothing to eat and I don't know what to do.' She paused, coughed, gave Katja an anguished look. 'I wondered...' The woman broke off, unable to continue as tears threatened.

Katja's heart went out to her. How awful, to have a houseful of hungry mouths to feed and nothing to give them, no means to provide for them. Times had often been hard in her own childhood, but there had always been food on the table. She pursed her lips, deep in contemplation. She knew instinctively what the woman had been trying to ask. It was irregular, but she could cobble something together to help her out. There was a time for going by the book and time for compassion, and this was definitely the latter.

As Katja ran through the options, the poor woman's stomach rumbled loudly. Katja grimaced at her sympathetically. Her need was clearly urgent. There were potatoes out the back that were past their best, plus some carrots in the same condition, and several tins of a type of bean that had proved unpopular and not sold well. She also had nearly stale black bread. And even though they were scarce and expensive, she'd add in some eggs, meat and butter. After all, growing children needed protein.

'I'm sorry,' she murmured, quietly. She hated to see another woman – a mother at that – in so much distress. 'But don't worry and please don't cry. I'll see what I can do.' Thankfully, no one else had entered the shop since the woman came in. 'Wait here a moment,' Katja said. 'I'll be right back.'

In the storeroom, she found an empty box and filled it up with the groceries. She heard the bell chime twice as she did so, which made her hurry even more. She didn't want to draw attention to what she was doing as there were those who would frown on it. Rules were rules and all that. Handing out rations without a book, giving supplies to someone who didn't have the correct paperwork – that was punishable. Quite what the punishment might be, Katja was a little hazy on. But the fact that there could be unpleasant consequences was incontrovertible, a fine at the very least and, more significantly, the authorities being aware of her. Watching her. That was something no one wanted in these dark and dangerous times.

Lifting the heavy box with a stab of pain, she struggled back into the shop, her progress impeded by the size of her belly. With a sinking feeling, she saw that the new customers had formed an orderly queue by the counter and were waiting expectantly for her.

And, even worse, that one of them was a policeman.

Fear seared through Katja, chilling the blood in her veins, almost making her drop the box. Struggling to keep her composure, she knew she had to think quickly.

'Well, well, here we are,' she blustered, her voice high and loud with fake cheeriness. 'Everything you ordered, and as I've already taken payment and taken your coupons, we're all sorted.' Katja laughed and pointed to the window. 'You can get one of those strapping lads of yours to carry the box for you.' She glanced at the police officer, who was watching with far too much interest. 'It'll get him into practice for when he's old enough to join the *Wehrmacht*, fight for the Fatherland,' she chuckled, with a brightness that was utterly false.

The policeman's expression remained impassive, his piercing gaze unwavering. Katja's stomach turned over. She had really misjudged this. He was completely unconvinced by her attempt to cover up what she was doing. Far from it; he could read her guilt like a book – it was written all over her.

And then something in Katja flipped. Why was she doubting herself? Her actions were entirely selfless, to help a poor woman feed her hungry children. She should not have to apologise for that, or be punished for it. What was a ration book when lives were at stake, young ones at that? And as for the money, well, it was her business if she didn't charge someone for their goods.

Meeting the officer's gaze straight on, she suppressed her defiance with a smile. 'What can I get for you?' she asked. Silently, she willed the woman, who was visibly trembling, to get going, get out of the shop right now, before it was too late.

'One minute,' the police officer replied.

For an awful moment, Katja thought that was it. All of her faked brash bravado deserted her. He was going to confiscate the food as evidence of Katja's wrongdoing, march her straight down to the police station, lock her up. What would happen to her own baby then, most likely condemned to being born behind bars, wrested from her at an early age... Her mind ran away into panic and desperation. To lose her own child because she'd tried to help someone else's – that would be the most terrible irony.

And then the police officer spoke again, and it wasn't a command or threat. Instead, 'Allow me,' he said, most courteously. Picking up the box, he swept towards the door and went outside, placing it into the arms of the oldest boy, who Katja reckoned was about eight. The mother, managing to overcome her own fright, cast Katja a glance that was laden with almost palpable gratitude and scuttled after him. Once she'd gone, Katja found that she was quivering with relief and the release of pent-up emotion.

She had just about enough time to compose herself before

the officer returned and began putting in his own order. Her hand trembled as she measured out the coffee beans, put a tin of condensed milk and two-hundred grams of sugar into a bag, took his coupons and his money, rang them up on the till.

When he'd finally gone, she almost forgot there was another person waiting, an elderly woman nearly bent double over her walking stick. Katja managed to serve her before collapsing down onto the chair, grimacing as the baby began a renewed bout of kicking. Far from being able to relax, her mind kept returning to the police officer, how scared she had been. This was what life had become since the war began; everyone always fearful of putting a foot out of line, of looking unpatriotic. All around, all day long, Katja heard the cries of 'Heil Hitler' and the fervent praise bestowed upon their leader, the armed forces, the Gestapo. Most people seemed genuine in their belief in the rightness of the war, their support of the cause. Katja supposed that she always had been, too. Just that, lately, she had begun to wonder. Why was the country at war, purely for the purposes of expanding the German empire? Did it need to be any bigger? What would be gained, at the end of it all? Katja didn't understand. She hadn't had a high-school education; her parents could not afford it for her. But, nevertheless, book learning or no book learning, she felt that something wasn't right. And what had happened today had increased that feeling of unease, that sense that perhaps things weren't quite as simple as they were often made out to be.

CHAPTER FOUR

It was early evening and Katja lay on the bed in her silent apartment, watching a trapped bluebottle beating its wings against the window. It was a few days after she had helped out the shop customer with the brood of children. Katja had wondered if she'd come back when the food ran out, but there'd been no sign of her. She wished she'd made it clearer that she would do whatever she could to make the poor woman's life easier. But there was nothing she could do about it now, and anyway, she'd have to shut the shop for a few days after the baby was born, which could be any time now. The government was supposed to be sending her a mother's help, as was the norm, but this was unlikely to happen due to the war – girls, even those still teenagers, were needed in the factories and on the land, not to work as nursemaids.

Katja sighed, rolled onto her back and then immediately onto her side again. She simply couldn't get comfortable, whatever position she was in. The bluebottle fussed and hummed, every now and again breaking off from its futile battering and resorting to flying around the room, its irritating, whining buzz slicing through the stillness. She should get up and let it out of the window, but she had no energy to do so.

The baby had hiccups now and Katja smiled at the sight of her belly rhythmically rising and falling. It was a moment of light relief amidst the anxiety and apprehension. She had not imagined herself alone when the baby came, and it wasn't as if Horst would have played any part in the birth, but at least if he were still here, everything wouldn't be down to Katja alone. And, to make matters worse, every time she saw her neighbour, who lived across the landing, Renate regaled her with stories of how awful labour was. It had got to the point where Katja didn't dare walk out of her flat without first spying through a chink in the door to make sure Renate was nowhere in sight.

Now, though, encumbered by her huge size, swollen ankles and constant exhaustion, even Renate's lurid tales couldn't stop Katja wishing that the baby would come soon.

TEN HOURS LATER, as she screamed and writhed in childbirth, she wasn't thinking that any longer. If truth be told, she wasn't thinking anything at all, except when would this agony be over. Her cries competed with the sound of air-raid sirens that streamed through the windows, and that Katja simply had to ignore. She felt like having this baby was going to kill her anyway, and you could only die once. So bombs were not a concern at that very moment.

As planned, Katja had stumbled across the landing to rouse Renate once the pain had become unbearable, and Renate had sent her oldest daughter to fetch the midwife. But there'd been a delay and Frau Wolf had only arrived half an hour ago. Katja felt as if she'd been screaming and struggling for a lifetime by the time the woman showed up.

Finally, in the early hours of the morning, a baby boy slithered into the world and Katja's torment was over. The sirens were still wailing, but Katja was beyond caring about anything except that the torture was over and her baby was all right. Taking hold of the precious bundle, Katja kissed his head and stroked his tiny hands and wondered how on earth she was going to look after him, all on her own and in the middle of a war.

By mid-morning the next day, the joy had almost evaporated to be replaced by deep despair. After hours of trying, worn out from the birth and increasingly agitated by her failure, Katja still hadn't managed to get her baby son, who she'd named Hans, to latch on and feed. Now, as the baby screamed tearless cries of furious hunger, Katja also sobbed, and between the two of them they were making so much noise that she only just heard the rapping at the door.

Hauling herself from her bed, she half walked, half crawled down the corridor, yelling, 'I'm coming, I'm coming,' as she went.

The door swung open to reveal the homely figure of her upstairs neighbour, a matronly widow with hair rollers and a well-worn apron over her day dress.

'Gerta,' said Katja, surprised. She had expected it to be Renate, or someone come to complain about the noise. 'What do you want?' She wasn't in the mood for visitors, was not ready for congratulatory words or cooing well-wishers. Just then, she couldn't see that she ever would be.

'I met Renate on the stairs and she told me you had the baby.'

Katja shrugged as if to say, 'Of course.' She should say sorry about all the crying, the infernal noise the baby was making. But what was the point? She had no idea how to stop it. She didn't know how to calm her child, or how to make him feed. She assumed that, at some stage, he'd cease his fussing and fretting and get on with it. She assumed he knew how. Because if he didn't know, she most certainly didn't, and where that left the two of them, she had no idea.

'Is everything all right?' Gerta's tone was one of genuine concern, not censure.

Katja shrugged again, but the tears that sprang from her eyes and flowed copiously down her cheeks belied her diffidence.

'Oh my poor lamb,' soothed Gerta, taking Katja completely by surprise. Katja didn't know her well, but Gerta had always seemed to be a no-nonsense kind of woman rather than someone brimming over with empathy. Maybe Katja had had her wrong all this time. 'You've no one to help you, you poor mite,' Gerta continued. 'Let's get you inside, make you a nice cup of coffee and something to eat.'

Taken aback, Katja allowed herself to be led back to her bed. She watched silently while Gerta puffed pillows and straightened sheets and then obediently climbed back in.

'That baby is starving,' Gerta stated, bluntly.

Katja nodded miserably. Of course he was. He just didn't seem interested in what she had to offer.

'Loosen your nightgown,' ordered Gerta. She grabbed Hans, waited until he had opened his mouth for an almighty scream and, in a flash, rammed him onto Katja's breast. There was a second's pause, and then a sharp pain seared through Katja and she was the one howling.

'Keep going,' urged Gerta, a wary hand hovering protectively behind Hans' tiny body in case Katja pushed him away. 'It soon stops hurting. You just have to stick with it.'

In her agonised, befuddled state, it crossed Katja's mind how Gerta knew all this. But she had no opportunity to ask until later, when, at last, Hans was sleeping in his crib and Gerta was closely watching as Katja slurped her way through a bowl of delicious beef stew that her neighbour had fetched from her flat.

'Thank you for your help,' she said, between greedy mouth-fuls. 'I don't know what I would have done without you. The midwife didn't have many ideas. Or useful ones that she was prepared to share with me, anyway.'

Gerta smiled grimly. 'As I saw.' She sighed and put her elbows on the table, sinking her head onto her hands. 'Having little ones is hard. I had twins – double trouble, that was...' Her voice tailed off.

Katja let her spoon drop to the bowl in astonishment. 'I didn't know you had children,' she blurted out. 'I've never seen them.'

The comment was awkward and potentially rude, but Katja was too tired to excuse herself. Despite the stew, she felt light-headed from lack of sleep.

'No, you wouldn't have done,' replied Gerta, her eyes suddenly misted with memory. 'They were identical twin boys – both were lost in the Great War, and their father, too.'

On hearing that Gerta had had not just one but two chil-dren taken from her in the previous conflict, Katja's heart broke for the woman's incomprehensible loss. Though so small and new, she already loved Hans with a ferocity and intensity that she had not expected and could not have put into words. Gerta must have felt that way about her boys, too.

'That's terrible,' Katja murmured, inadequately. 'I'm so sorry.'

Gerta nodded and sniffed and then turned to the stove, where she fussed unnecessarily with a pan for a few minutes. A knock at the door made them both start. Gerta bustled off to answer and Katja shut her eyes, hoping Gerta would be able to deal with whoever it was and that they'd leave her alone.

When Gerta returned, she was on her own. But as soon as Katja saw the older woman's face, blanched quite white, and her eyes, wide and staring, she had a terrible sense of foreboding.

'Wh-what is it?' she asked. And then her gaze fell to Gerta's hands and what she held in them. A telegram.

There could only be one reason for the receipt of such a missive.

With trembling hands, Gerta handed the white paper over to Katja.

There was no point in putting it off. Slowly, she opened it up.

Sehr geehrte Frau Schmidt, Ich habe die traurige Pflicht...

Dear Frau Schmidt, I have the sad duty...

After the first few words, Katja's eyes glazed over and she was barely able to read to the end. It was obvious what it was going to say. Her worst fears had been realised.

'Horst is missing presumed dead,' Katja announced, eventually. There was no easy way to put it.

Gerta inhaled sharply, involuntarily clutching her hand to her chest. 'Oh my dear. My poor dear.' She shook her head as tears bled from the corners of her eyes. 'I'll take care of you and the little one until you're back on your feet, don't you worry.'

Katja felt her shoulders sag. It was so kind of Gerta, and she definitely needed help. She wasn't, if truth be told, that devastated about Horst. It hadn't been a love match, rather a marriage of convenience. She'd been brought up by her grandparents after her parents had died of influenza, but they were very elderly and couldn't support her forever. So, as soon as she was old enough, she'd left their village near the Dutch border and come to Berlin. She'd had to work, to pay her own way. After a stint labouring in a laundry and then a bakery, she'd got the job as assistant at Horst's shop. It wasn't long before he had invited her to move out of the backroom and into the flat with him and the relationship, unremarkable as it was, had moved on from there.

Marriage and pregnancy had quickly followed, possibly not in that exact order, but, in the midst of war, who was counting?

But even though Katja was sure she hadn't been in love with Horst, she had welcomed the security he offered, and now she had lost even that, right at the time when she needed it most.

Gerta's offer of companionship was the best she was going to get and she was grateful for it. Over the next few days, with Gerta's assistance, Katja gradually began to get the hang of feeding her baby, though Hans still cried a lot.

'He's just getting used to the world,' Gerta comforted her. 'He'll soon settle down.'

But in the midst of a raging war, Katja wondered how likely that was.

At night, when the air-raid sirens blared, Gerta would insist that they went down to the basement shelter.

'You can't take risks,' she would say. 'You've a child to think of now.'

Staggering down the steep stairs, dizzy with sleep, still aching and bleeding from the birth, Katja wanted nothing more than to stay in her bed and hope to wake up in the morning, but Gerta would not allow it.

The night of the eighteenth of November was particularly bad. Cranky from being woken, Hans cried and screamed and the other unwilling inhabitants of the cramped cellar shot Katja increasingly hostile stares.

'Can't you shut that child up,' shouted one elderly man.

No, I can't, thought Katja, sobbing silently and desperately. It was only a week since he'd been born and she'd hardly had a wink of sleep. *I don't know how.*

But Gerta knew and stepped in once more, tightly swaddling Hans until finally he quietened and slept.

The thud and thump of mortar shells continued intermittently through the night and into the morning. When they stumbled back up above ground, it was astonishing to find the building still standing.

Gerta made coffee for them both and they drank it as a rosy

sunrise streaked the sky pink and red and the noise of the wakening city rose up to them through the blown-out kitchen window in Katja's flat. The two women, who until so recently had been little more than strangers but had now been united in their care and love for newborn Hans, sat in silence for a while, until finally Gerta stood up to get on with some chores.

Four nights later, the RAF bombers came back, and this time, all hell was let loose.

CHAPTER FIVE

It wasn't late when the sirens started to sound, only about a quarter to eight in the evening. Katja was heating milk for a drink of cocoa. When the familiar wailing began, her first reaction was annoyance. Not again. Memories of just a few nights ago, the horrible experience of being stuck in that stuffy, claustrophobic cellar with a bunch of rude and complaining people, flooded her mind, making her shudder. She'd really rather stay up here in the flat, take the risk.

Katja poured the milk into her cup and stirred. The sirens continued to wail and suddenly they were joined by a much closer howling. With a sigh, Katja realised that Hans had woken. It was inevitable with such a racket going on. Wearily, she went to the bedroom and scooped her son out of his crib. Perhaps if she fed him, he'd settle back down and go back to sl—

Her thoughts were cut through by a violent hammering at the door and then a voice, calling her name.

'Katja! Katja!'

It was Gerta.

Letting her in, Katja was shocked by her state of dishevelment, nightgown hanging awry, hair loose and wild, eyes wide with fear.

'We must go to the cellar. The bombers are almost overhead.'

Seeing Katja hesitate, Gerta grabbed her by the wrist.

'Now, Katja. I looked out of the window and there are hundreds of them. Hundreds, I say. Quick!'

Infected by Gerta's distress, fear gripped Katja's heart. Clutching Hans to her chest, she nodded, then cast her eyes around the hallway, searching for her shoes.

'There's no time, I tell you,' insisted Gerta. 'We need to get down there now.'

Gerta was already back outside the apartment door, frantically gesticulating to Katja to join her. Grabbing the pram blanket from the hall table as an extra layer for the baby, Katja gave up on warm clothes or shoes for herself.

As she followed Gerta down to the cellar, the entire stairwell was filled with noise; not just the air-raid warnings but also the sound of aircraft engines – low, constant, terrifying. The rumbling was loud, and getting louder, so much so that it began to drown out the sirens. Ever greater terror seared through Katja's veins and stayed there, holding her in its icy grip. Gerta was right, there must be many scores of bombers up there.

As they descended, they caught up with other, older and slower inhabitants of the block. Katja willed them to hurry up. She was still waiting to get through the cellar door when she felt the first impact. It was enormous, as if the whole city was shaking, as if the world was ending.

Screams erupted from all around and Hans, who had quietened somewhat during the trek down the stairs, began to cry, loudly and insistently. Katja's heart felt as if it was going to explode like the bombs, it was beating so wildly.

'Hurry up,' she muttered under her breath. 'Please, hurry.' It was clear that this was going to be the mother of all raids.

She jolted forward as someone almost fell on top of her, nearly losing hold of Hans.

'Careful,' she yelled, 'I've got a baby here.'

'Get a bloody move on then,' came a voice from behind, muffled by the jam of people all trying desperately to enter the cellar.

Katja pressed forward, following in Gerta's wake, negotiating the narrow, steep steps that led down into the gloom. She was halfway down when another almighty sound rose up all around and, once again, the building shook. A moment's silence and then more screaming, crying, shouting, coming from behind her, from those pushing and shoving their way to the relative sanctuary of underground.

A hand on Katja's back sent her slipping down the last few stairs. Clumsily, she managed to right herself and, holding Hans tightly to her, stumble towards one of the benches that had been placed against the walls. She had just sat down when another blast struck nearby, then another and another. On the final one, the lights went out and the entire cellar was plunged into darkness.

Wailing and crying resumed from those crammed in the cellar, but gradually quietened. Everyone was too terrified to move, to speak, to utter any sound. Only Hans cried on, and on, and on, as the building rocked and the ground shook and the sonic booms filled the space, and it was clear that, if they got out of here alive, it would be a miracle. Even Gerta could not calm Hans. The poor mite was inconsolable.

'Get that child to stop its infernal noise, won't you,' shouted someone, eventually.

Katja recognised the same voice that had previously chastised Hans for the crime of being a baby.

A chorus of approval followed from those nearest to Katja and Hans. Inwardly, despite the fear and the distress, she fumed. How could they be so heartless and lacking in understanding? She knew that the man must be tired and frightened – but so were they all. That was no reason to pick on each other like animals in a pack.

Gerta tried to work her magic on the fractious baby, but to no avail. Hans cried and cried and cried until, energy spent, he fell into a deep sleep. Though that provided some small relief, Katja found she could not relax. She was permanently on edge, waiting for the crying – and the complaints – to resume.

Time lost all meaning in that cellar on that dreadful night. Katja had no idea how long they had been in there, waiting for the building to collapse on top of them, waiting for fire to rip through the entire structure. Waiting to die.

She began to wonder if it would have been better to stay above ground. The thought of a bomb dropping directly on the building, burying them all alive, paralysed her with fear. She felt she couldn't breathe, was already suffocating, as she would when the house, with all its bricks and wood and tiles, was on top of her, pressing her down.

Katja held tight to Hans and prayed to a God she wasn't sure she believed in that, when the end came, it would be quick. And that, whatever happened to her, Hans would be saved.

All that mattered was Hans.

Eventually, the noise abated, the explosions ceased and the city fell silent. With no idea whether the bombers would be coming back that night, no one dared leave the cellar, despite the discomfort of the hard benches, the cramped, dark conditions, the frayed tempers. It wasn't until the one person with a watch announced that it was 7 a.m. that people felt able to resurface. The planes rarely came over by daylight; it was too risky, too easy for them to be shot down.

Creeping out of the darkness and into the light, Katja was amazed to find that, once again, the building was still standing. Back in her flat, she left Gerta in charge of Hans while she headed out. She had not opened the shop since Hans was born and wasn't sure when she would again, but there was no fresh bread or milk left, so she needed to buy some.

Stepping out onto the pavement, the first thing she saw was encouraging. She'd had the huge shop window boarded up in case it blew out and allowed looters in, and that had been a smart move because the glass had completely shattered. But as Katja moved through the streets towards the shopping district, what she saw became ever more horrific.

Fires burned on all sides, and countless buildings lay in ruins, walls ripped off and ceilings fallen in, parts of rooms teetering on the brink of collapse. An apartment block had had the entire front wall ripped off so that the insides were revealed like a doll's house, the details of strangers' lives on show for all to see: their floral wallpaper, their mismatched furniture, their curtains, ripped to shreds. Katja watched as a dining table in the top-floor flat slowly slid across the sloping remains of the floor and descended into the precipice below, landing with a resounding crash on a heap of rubble.

People wandered around, seemingly aimlessly, looking distraught and confused. And then Katja saw something that at first she could not work out. It was a man who seemed to be smothered in candle wax, stumbling and staggering along the broken pavement. Katja walked towards him, wondering if she could help. And then halted abruptly, bile rising in her throat as both the realisation and the stench hit her. It was not wax that was dripping from the man's torso but his own skin, hanging in sheets from his terribly burnt body. And soon Katja saw that there were others like him, many of them, some walking but most lying and writhing in agony.

Her head spun and she stumbled and swayed, almost falling over, so macabre and awful was the sight. There was nothing she could do to assist any of these people. Shopping forgotten, Katja ran as fast as the cracked pavements and piles of rubble allowed back to the apartment, to Hans and to Gerta. This was a living nightmare.

And it was far from over.

The next night, the bombers returned, and yet again another two nights after that. By the end, huge parts of the city were destroyed, including much of Charlottenburg, where Katja lived, and the nearby areas of Tiergarten, Schöneberg and Spandau. The Neukölln Gasworks took a direct hit, leading to the biggest fire of all. Thousands died, hundreds of thousands were left homeless.

These devastating attacks on the German capital brought the brutality of the war into stark reality. It was no longer something being fought a long way away, and Berlin citizens could no longer think of their city and their country as impregnable. The impact of this sapped the souls of Berliners, Katja included. Why was this happening, this terrible conflict that was ripping lives apart? Katja could make no sense of it.

On the twenty-seventh of November, feeding her baby at dawn, Katja could hardly see the sunrise. It was obliterated by the smoke and dust that filled the air, the entire sky grey, the world dark. Looking at her son's perfect face, his beautiful, trusting eyes, Katja wept. What did the future hold for this little innocent? At that point, it was hard to imagine that anything good would ever happen again.

CHAPTER SIX

When my mother finished speaking, there was a long pause.

'Mum, it sounds awful,' I finally managed to utter, inadequately. 'Unbelievably terrifying.'

I wanted to say something about Hans, the brother I had never met and knew so little about, to delve deeper into his desperate start in life, but found that I couldn't. I thought instead of the bombs, those instruments of destruction raining down from turbulent November skies and my mind travelled back many years to an interactive exhibition at the Imperial War Museum that I had gone to with Emma's year four school class.

In a special sensory room, an audio installation delivered up the scream of the air-raid sirens, the thud of falling ordinance, the staccato firing of anti-aircraft guns – a spine-chilling soundtrack to a life-or-death experience. I shuddered at the memory. I had been frightened enough, Emma and most of her classmates utterly petrified. Sweeping the children up, the teacher and I had led them out, through the brightly lit museum hall, into the sunshine, where the terrors had ebbed away and the fake bombing was soon forgotten. How lucky we were to be able to do that. My poor mother, so young and vulnerable, stuck in an underground cellar with a tiny, helpless infant, had been unable to escape.

But alongside the pain I felt on her behalf, I couldn't help but wish she had told me this before, when I was younger. If she had, then maybe I would have understood her better, her hard edge, her occasional outpourings of bitterness. I might not have felt so dejected when she didn't show me much sympathy when I suffered some minor injury – a cut or a graze on falling from my bike or tripping on a paving stone. I might not have secretly thought her a little crazy when she put sandbags against the door of the flat whenever there was a National Front riot or other disturbance on the streets of London.

Only a couple of years ago, the IRA bomb at the Baltic Exchange had caused a blast so big it had been clearly heard at my mother's place in Camden. I had raced straight round to find her sitting under the kitchen table, shaking with fear. Thankfully, I'd decided to stay the night, so had still been there when the second bomb, placed in a van at Staples Corner, went off. It had taken days for my mother to stop trembling.

'It was horrendous,' she agreed, quietly. 'But we endured it. We had to.'

I shook my head. 'I'm so sorry you had to go through that,' I murmured. 'So, so sorry.'

'Thank goodness I had Gerta,' she mumbled, gripping the bed cover for dear life as if clinging to her upstairs neighbour. 'If not for her support, I don't know what I would have done. Everyone seemed to be against me, down in that dreadful cellar. There were other children there, older ones! It was as if all their mothers had forgotten that they were once infants, too, and how would they have behaved in the same circumstance?' My mother's voice rose in vexation, shrill with the recollection of injustice, which I felt too on her behalf. 'We were petrified all the time, Jo. Convinced we were going to die.'

She stopped, unable to speak as she exhaled a huge, juddering slough of air. It was clear and understandable that bringing these experiences to the surface was affecting her deeply.

I squeezed her hand. 'You don't have to carry on if you don't want to.' I had so badly wanted to hear all of this. But perhaps I was demanding too much.

In the distance, the snapping of a heavy vehicle's air brakes on the steep incline of the road to Highgate village was clearly audible and I saw a flash of visceral fear cross my mother's face.

Once the fear had faded, she spoke again.

'And then the miracle happened,' she murmured, a distant expression on her face. 'Out of the blue, amidst the chaos.'

'A miracle?' I prompted. 'What miracle?'

'The miracle that took us from the horror of Berlin to a faraway place, a beautiful place.'

I smiled gently. It sounded like the beginning of a fairy tale. As I listened, I realised that perhaps that was exactly what it was.

'Gerta made the coffee,' my mother continued. 'She set it on the table and then she said, *I know somewhere we could go. Somewhere with no bombing, in the mountains, a long way from here, but where everyone speaks German. I have my pension and you'll have your war widow's allowance, so we'd have plenty to live on. The baby would be safe there. Let's just shut up the shop and go.* I could hardly believe it. *Where is this paradise?* I asked. *The Sudetenland*, she replied. *We can get there by train. It will be easy.*'

CHAPTER SEVEN

THE SUDETENLAND, 1943

It took a few trips up and down the stairs before Katja and Gerta had all their luggage gathered together on the ground floor.

Horst had had the apartment door reinforced with steel, wanting Katja to be safe while he was away. Katja made sure it was double-locked and then checked the shop door, too. When this was done, the two women stood for a few moments, looking at each other. It was as if, now the moment had come, neither was entirely sure that they wanted to go through with it.

Katja gazed at their worldly possessions, spread out on the pavement. She'd left a trunk with Renate; it would be collected and sent on later. Even so, they seemed to have a lot of things to carry: clothes, shoes, Hans' nappies, big coats for when winter set in.

'We should go, if we're to make the train in time,' said Gerta.

Katja nodded, but it was a few more minutes before either of them moved. Then Katja picked up one of the rucksacks and slung it on her shoulders. Gerta followed suit with the other.

Hans began to cry and Katja snatched him out of the pram and held him tight. It was as if the infant knew that he was leaving his home and had no way of knowing whether it would still be there when they returned.

If they ever returned.

With a lurch of her heart, Katja took in the reality of the moment. This might be it. No more Berlin. For a second, she thought about not going through with it, telling Gerta she'd decided to stay after all. And then she remembered the bombs and the cellar, the horror of it all.

'Katja.' Gerta's voice was urgent now, interrupting Katja's reverie. 'We need to go.'

Katja laid Hans back in the pram. 'Right,' she said. 'Let's get moving, then.'

As if in a trance, Katja began to slowly walk away from the building which held her flat and shop, her livelihood and her home. It was the right thing to do, she told herself. For Hans. It was the right thing for Hans.

THEY ARRIVED in the Sudetenland in the afternoon, as the fading light of dusk smudged the landscape into a misty blur. Tumbling wearily from the carriage, Katja carrying Hans and Gerta lugging the pram, they looked around for a porter to help them with the rest of their luggage.

Katja had a sudden panic. They hadn't brought cooking pots and pans, crockery, utensils. Would they need these? She had no idea. Looking at the rucksacks, and thinking of the trunk that was to follow, it all seemed very paltry. They had packed what they thought they would need and could carry. But what if they were away for years? There would be no nipping back for anything that had been forgotten. All those years, building a home in Horst's flat in Berlin and now she had left it all behind.

Hans stirred in his sleep, his tiny eyelids fluttering, his lips making a sucking motion. A rush of love subsumed Katja as she remembered who she was doing all this for. Mustering all her resolve, she stood up straight, pushed her shoulders back and indicated to Gerta that she was ready to go.

The two women and Hans made their way out of the station into the tiny town of Meindorf, where the air was suffused with the aroma of burning pinewood, and plumes of smoke from all the many chimneys stained the slowly darkening sky with shades of purple and grey. Their footsteps rang out into the still silence that surrounded them.

'It's so quiet,' breathed Katja.

'No more sirens,' extolled Gerta. 'No more bombs.'

They walked past houses with steeply pitched roofs, built to withstand the winter snows, and pretty gardens with picket fences. Everything was so neat and tidy and perfect, it was like being in toy town. At either end of the main street stood a church, one Catholic, one Lutheran, and behind them rose high hills, darkly shrouded in dense forests of pine, oak and birch.

Katja felt a thrill of contented excitement run through her. They had done the right thing, coming here, to such an idyllic and peaceful place. Hans would grow up breathing fresh mountain air and eating good country food. That latter thought was matched by the most delicious smell of roasting meat emanating from an old coaching inn, making Katja salivate. It was a long time since they'd eaten, but she'd have to wait to sate her appetite. First, they needed to track down their new home.

Gerta's resourcefulness was both impressive and faultless. Somehow, she'd found out about a house with rooms to let. She'd sent a telegram and arranged it all. Rocking Hans in the pram, Katja watched as Gerta, address clutched tightly in her hand, stopped to quiz a passer-by about how to find their lodgings.

Eventually, after a few wrong turns, they reached the lodging house, an ancient building that lay on the edge of the town at the foot of the mountain. Beyond it, the road petered out to a stony track that led up and up into the forests that cloaked the slopes. The house was owned by a man called Richard Wagner.

'No relation to the great composer,' he joked, as he welcomed the two women and the baby inside. He had two rooms to let to them, plus use of the kitchen and bathroom. In the former, Katja was pleased to see a huge, green-tiled *Kachelöfen* with built-in seating to the side. That meant the room would be cosy when the cold weather truly set in. 'In a few weeks' time,' said Herr Wagner, as if reading Katja's mind, 'there'll be ten metres of snow up there.' He gesticulated towards the hills behind the house.

Katja shivered. She thought of Horst, of his body cold and abandoned on some battlefield somewhere. He'd died not even knowing that he had a son. Katja wasn't religious, but she wondered if Horst were up in heaven, looking down on her and Hans. She would make sure their son knew about his father. The German state would have it that Horst had died a *Heldentod*, a hero's death, but Katja would not tell Hans that. That felt like a story to her, told to soften the blow of the losses that so many families were experiencing.

Without doubt, there would be many other women receiving telegrams as Katja had done. The fighting was fierce, brutal and unrelenting all along the Eastern Front, the Soviet beasts using every dirty tactic available to them. Or, at least, that was the story cobbled together from the hushed discussions that were all anyone dared to have. The newsreels proclaimed nothing but German victories even though, to ordinary folk, nothing felt particularly victorious right now.

OVER THE NEXT FEW DAYS, as they settled into their new life, Katja discovered that Gerta had been right and that Meindorf's

population was partly made up of Germans, families who had
been settled there for generations, and partly of Czechs. Since
Hitler's annexation of the Sudetenland five years previously,
the Germans had taken the upper hand in everything. Grateful
though she was to have found this place of refuge, and much as
politics bored her, Katja felt a pang of something – guilt?
Sorrow? – when Herr Wagner explained that the German
owner of the next-door property had been evicted after refusing
to divorce his Czech wife. His house had been given to a
German soldier, posted here from Cottbus, who lived there now
with his wife, Monika, and their four children.

Neighbours aside, their isolation in the house by the mountain meant that Katja and Gerta spent most of their time alone
together. Much as Katja appreciated Gerta's company and
everything Gerta had done for her – helping with Hans, telling
her about the Sudetenland, coming here with her – the older
woman did get on her nerves sometimes. Gerta believed every
piece of propaganda that came her way and Katja had to bite
her tongue and refrain from snapping back that, if everything
was so wonderful, why were men still being called up in their
droves and why was there still no sign of an end to this war?

But these occasions were rare. Most of the time these days,
Katja simply forgot about the conflict, which barely intruded on
their day-to-day lives in their new sanctuary. It felt so very far
away, and now that everyone either she or Gerta cared about
was already dead, there was no one to worry about except themselves and, above all else, Hans.

For the first few months, until the spring of 1944, Katja
contented herself with settling into the house, caring for her
child and exploring their new surroundings. But once Hans had
started on solid food and the novelty of pushing the pram up the
steep path on their daily walk had worn off, Katja began to
champ at the bit like an impatient horse. She had always
worked six days a week and inactivity sat uneasily on her shoul-

ders. Gerta was more than happy to babysit Hans, so Katja had the opportunity to go out and look for a job. And before too long she had found one – in the nearby town of Stahlbach, a few stops along on the little railway branch line that wound along the valley. A huge old house, complete with turrets and towers and a red-tiled roof, that had once belonged to a Bohemian count had been requisitioned for use as a Waffen-SS officers' convalescent home and they always had need of women to help the nurses with their important task of restoring the men back to health.

Though many of the officers in the hospital had suffered terrible injuries, Katja loved spending time here. The jobs she was given to do, however mundane, made her feel important and wanted, busy and useful. Helping the patients with their meals, mending their uniforms, reading to them from the classics of German literature, singing (for she had a good voice) if there was someone in their number who could play the piano or the violin – all of these tasks she set about with enthusiasm.

If truth be told, her work was a welcome break from the endless cycle of feeding and changing and boiling nappies and hanging them out on the line, where, in the cold of winter, they would freeze stiff as boards and never get truly dry. She loved her son with an incalculable adulation, but caring for a baby involved countless hours of drudgery alongside the moments of joy. Her time with the young men was light relief compared to her many daily duties as a mother.

In Meindorf and in Stahlbach, many hundreds of miles from the front, time progressed unremarkably, until, in the early summer of 1944, something happened that stirred Katja's quiet life. A pilot arrived at the convalescent home, one Karl Hausmann. His presence quickly gave Katja's visits a new purpose, and a new urgency.

Entering the building one day, suppressing a shiver as she went from the warm sunshine outside to the chill of the huge stone-flagged hallway, her heart leapt and her stomach flipped over. There he was, her new favourite patient, limping out of the dining room and across the triple-height hallway. Katja rushed towards him to offer help, but then hesitated. The last thing Karl wanted – the last thing any of the men wanted – was to be treated like the invalids they were. For each and every one there was a single goal – to get fit and back into the sky to win this war.

Composing her face from an expression of wild excitement to one of demure professionalism, Katja approached Karl.

'Good afternoon, Hauptsturmführer Hausmann,' she said, speaking as modestly as she could. 'Let me find a chair by the window for you so that you can enjoy the sunshine.'

'Thank you, Fräulein Schmidt.' Karl flashed her a brilliant smile that made the butterflies already buffeting Katja's insides even more agitated. He always addressed her as Fräulein – Miss – even though he knew she had been married and had a child. It didn't feel disrespectful – far from it, she liked it, especially the way that he said it, slightly teasing, accompanied by a wry look in his eye as if they were sharing a secret joke. And anyway, she was still young enough to be a Miss, no doubt about it. 'But please,' continued Karl, 'no more of the Hauptsturmführer – just call me Herr Hausmann. Or Karl, if you prefer.'

This request took Katja by surprise. Rank and hierarchy was everything to these men, understandably. After all, they'd earned their stripes undertaking dangerous missions over enemy territory. They deserved their bravery to be acknowledged and recognised by their countrymen and women. But, despite this, Katja was more than happy to drop the formalities. This must surely mean that Karl liked her, mustn't it?

She accompanied Karl into the day room and stood at his side as he lowered himself painfully into a chair.

'You look well today,' Karl said. 'And I feel warmer already. You've brought the sunshine in with you.'

Katja blushed. 'I don't know about that,' she replied, bashfully. 'But all of us here do our best for our...' She paused, unsure how to continue. She didn't want to say 'patients', which made it sound as if the men were weak and frail, rather than strong German men in the prime of their lives, just needing a little recuperation time before they were back on their feet again. 'Our airmen,' she settled on, eventually.

Karl smiled at her as if aware of her struggle to find the right word. 'Your efforts are much appreciated,' he responded. 'By all of us. And how is your little one, Hans? Behaving himself, I hope.'

Katja rested her eyes upon Karl as they chatted. He was so good-looking, with chiselled features, blond hair and shrewd green eyes. He had been transferred to the convalescent home from a hospital in Germany; anti-aircraft fire had penetrated the cockpit of his plane and pierced his scalp, shattering the bone and leaving a deep and painful wound. Because of this, his hair had been shaved off on one side of his head, while on the other, in complete contrast, it remained thick and lustrous. Other injuries sustained when the battered aircraft had crash-landed included a leg broken in three places, fractured ribs and a punctured lung.

Despite all his damaged parts, his splintered skull, his pronounced limp, there was something vital about Karl Hausmann, something reassuring in his quiet air of confidence, that enabled Katja to temporarily forget her animosity towards the Führer, with his harsh, high voice that was full of hate, and believe that, whatever happened, it would be all right.

Every day that she nursed him through his debilitating injuries, Katja fell more in love with the handsome airman, swept up in his stories of heroism and bravery, beguiled by the steady authority of his uniform and his demeanour. The war had shown her how fragile life could be, but Karl made her feel safe, and safety was a precious and valuable commodity.

At twenty-eight, Katja was good-looking and knew it; she was also vibrant and very much alive. Horst was gone. There was nothing to stop her loving Karl. And if there was love to be had, in this cruel, cold world, why should she not take advantage of it?

Katja took a seat next to Karl, seizing the opportunity to extend their chat before someone gave her another job to do. He was talking about a book he had recommended to Katja.

'So the conclusion I came to,' Karl said, 'is that the author's intention is to encourage us all to see that the greater good is always more important than our own individual wants and needs.' He looked directly into Katja's eyes as he spoke, his gaze steady, his demeanour open. Katja had a sudden feeling that there was something more beneath his words, a hidden message, that she was meant to understand and yet did not.

'Oh, well, yes, I-I'm sure you're right,' she stuttered in reply. She had told Karl she'd read the book and it hadn't been a lie – she had taken it to bed with her every night for a week and looked at the pages, but the truth was that little had sunk in. She was so tired at the end of each day that she was incapable of focusing on what she was reading. Admitting that to Karl, though, was out of the question. He clearly – mistakenly! – thought that Katja was his intellectual equal, even though nothing could be further from the truth. But she was happy to let him believe that she was as educated and literary-minded as he. He would be the first person who had ever thought such things about her and it was a nice feeling.

'Tell me,' Karl said now, reaching out and placing his hand upon hers. 'Are you a church-goer, Fräulein Schmidt?'

Katja was taken aback; she hadn't expected this question. Did he want the answer to be yes or no?

'Well,' she replied, slowly, hedging her bets. 'I go when I can, but with the little one it can be difficult – he's not so good at sitting still and staying quiet...' At this, Katja remembered, with a flash of horror, the nights in the bomb shelter with Hans bawling his eyes out.

'You will go,' interjected Karl, ignoring her babbling protestations. 'I'd like you to. Attend the 10 a.m. service at the Lutheran church in Meindorf this Sunday.'

Katja looked at him, questioningly. Why this sudden interest in saving her soul?

'It will be good for you,' Karl continued, as if in answer to her unasked question. 'And please pay careful attention to the sermon so that you can tell me about it on Monday. I am not able to go at the moment,' he continued, glancing down at his leg, 'so you shall go for me.'

'Right,' answered Katja. 'I mean, yes of course, if that's what you want. And I'll try to remember everything.'

Karl smiled once more and this smile was different again – a smile of gratitude mixed with satisfaction, as if Katja had been given a test and passed, just as Karl had known she would. Katja glowed inwardly, basking in Karl's approval.

But as she was leaving the building later that evening to catch the last train back down the valley, a sense of unease accompanied her. Was Karl challenging her? Assigning her a mission? If so, could it really be a religious one? Katja didn't get the sense that what Karl wanted was to save her soul. There was more to Karl's request, she was sure, something she didn't fully understand, a mystery. The feeling of intrigue lingered, hanging about her, as did the condensation from her breath in the cool night air.

CHAPTER EIGHT

In my little house by the Heath, the ticking of the grandfather clock in the hallway was clearly audible in the sudden heavy silence. It was the first I'd ever heard of this man, Karl; I'd obviously never met him, nor I presumed ever would. I had the precipitous, awful feeling that perhaps my mother had loved him more than my father.

At the thought of my dad, my heart turned over. When a parent dies, you get used to the loss, but you never stop missing them. I regarded my father's photo, standing proudly on the bedside table, where I had placed it after bringing it from my mother's flat so that she would always have him nearby during her recuperation.

My father was not really handsome, I thought, as I picked up the photo to study it more closely, not the way my mother described Karl, but, nevertheless, there was something attractive about his buoyant smile and laughing eyes. He was my dad, after all – I was bound to see his good points. I pondered how coincidental it was that he was an airman, as well as this marvellous Karl person I was hearing about. With a frisson of jealousy, I focused on the impressive medals that adorned my father's uniform. How many did the magnificent Karl have? I wondered defiantly. Though my father's authority and masterfulness, it had to be said, was somewhat diminished by the way his ears stuck out from under his cap.

'What's so funny?' asked my mother, seeing the smile spreading over my face.

'Dad's ears,' I replied. 'Look at them!'

'Oh yes,' she laughed, 'terrible ears he had. I think he should have had them operated on, pinned back or something, when he was a baby. But it didn't never happen.'

My mother's grammar, gone awry again. How ashamed I had been of that in the past. I'd spent many hours chastising and berating her failure to obtain a perfect grasp of the English language, for not becoming, in effect, a native speaker. I hated myself for that now.

At least, over the years, I had tried to make up for being so critical in the past, ensuring my mother was fully integrated into my grown-up life, that she spent oodles of time with her grand-children, with all of us as a family. I was grateful for that, and also that I was able to continue to do so now, demonstrating my love for my mother by nursing her through her recovery.

I looked back at the photo. 'At least I didn't inherit the ears,' I joked.

My mother looked momentarily confused, her forehead furrowing. 'Well...' she began, then stopped, falling silent for a moment. 'No, you didn't, you...' she faltered again, casting her eyes around her as if searching for the right words. 'Do ears even get passed to the next generation?'

I shrugged and laughed. 'I've no idea.' I replaced the photo-graph, but continued to regard it. 'Though, if eye colour is hereditary, I don't see why ear shape wouldn't be,' I mused, as I repositioned myself on the side of my mother's bed.

I paused. How had we got diverted onto the heritability or not of facial features? There were so many other, more important, things I needed to find out. Fortunately, my mother seemed ready to provide the answers.

'I'll always remember that day we arrived in Meindorf, which seemed to us like the promised land.' My mother's voice had sunk to a murmur, her tone reverential, as she thought back to that long-ago past. 'And the first time I saw Herr Wagner's house. You turned the corner and there it was, like a gingerbread house in a fairy tale. My little boy, Hans, loved Herr Wagner, treated him like the grandfather he didn't have, and the old boy loved him back. I think, in truth, he was lonely. We were all lonely. Me and Gerta, and Herr Wagner. Two lonely widows and a widower.'

A wave of sympathy swept over me. I had no experience of war, but I certainly had of loneliness. I'd been lonely as an only child and, often these days, I looked back and wondered if I'd also been lonely throughout my marriage. Perhaps loneliness, once so firmly embedded, could never be shaken off, but became inherent, a character trait that never leaves.

I rubbed my hands across my eyes as if I could wipe away the forlorn vision of myself, growing old as a lonely divorcee, that had come to join the picture in my mind's eye of the three lonely people my mother described.

'If it was so easy to get to the Sudetenland,' I asked. 'Why didn't everyone from the big cities go?'

My mother shook her head and smiled ruefully. 'I don't know,' she replied simply. She shifted in the bed and I leapt up to rearrange her pillows. 'I felt guilty at the time... for getting out, for getting away. Later, those feelings changed. Later, it stopped looking quite so clever. Well, they say hindsight is a wonderful thing, don't they?'

I nodded. I burned with questions but did not want my

mother to feel under interrogation. Best to let the story emerge gradually, at her pace.

'At first, Meindorf seemed too good to be true,' she went on. 'But scrape beneath the surface and it really wasn't. I turned a blind eye to much of what went on there.'

'Such as?' I had no idea what she meant. Whatever we had learnt in history class at school, it had not covered this.

'Germany's annexation led to so much hardship for the Czech people,' she replied, her voice tinged with guilty sadness.

I sighed and nodded. Germany's treatment of these folk had no doubt been abominable, but it wasn't my mother's fault.

'Herr Wagner's next-door neighbour, for example,' she continued. 'That German woman, Monika, who got the house – why did she deserve it?' She shook her head and shuddered at the memory. 'Sometimes we would chat over the garden fence or on the path as we went back and forth to the town, but there was something about her I didn't like, and not just because she was living in a home that didn't belong to her. She was a terrible gossip, poked her nose into everybody's business. Her children were awful, too – four of them there were, terrible bad-behaved, never did nothing she told them.' My mother's grammar failed her again as she expressed her strong disapproval. 'She assumed I'd be her friend because I was German, too. But I thought she was a bully.'

'She sounds awful,' I agreed, as a jolt of nausea surged in my stomach. I knew all about bullies. My mother and I had never discussed it, but our German-ness – *my* German-ness – had been the cause. There was little love spared for Germans in London in the late 1940s. The victimisation had begun small and got bigger and bigger as I myself grew taller and older.

To counteract it, I'd invented narratives about myself – I was actually Italian (because that equalled exotic, desirable, though was hardly credible, given the red hair and freckles), or I'd been adopted and my real mother was English and Katja was just my stepmother. I felt my stomach shrivel inside me as I recalled that now. How could I have been so cruel as to want to deny my own parentage? But children are cruel when they experience cruelty and I had had that every day, day in, day out, at school.

Even now, every time my mother called me *liebchen*, I felt a jolt of the animosity that term of endearment had always engendered in me during my school years for revealing our secret, mine and my mother's true identity. Back then, my mother's pronunciation of my name, which she always began with a 'y' sound, never having mastered the English 'j', was a particular source of ridicule.

'Yo-Yo, Yo-Yo, where you going, Yo-Yo,' the bullies would chant as I made my way to class along lino-floored corridors with the shiny, anti-graffiti paint. Sometimes they threw things at me – rubbers, pens, bizarrely once, penny chews and Black Jacks.

In class, we studied the poem with the words 'No man is an island'. I tried to convince myself that I was an island. That's what I would tell myself as I slunk past the groups of my assailants. *You're an island, Jo*, the voice inside my head would exhort me, *an island in the middle of a big, wide river. No one can touch you. You are an island, inviolable, intact.*

But, of course, I wasn't. And even if I had been, the bullies had boats.

My mother's deep sigh brought me back to the present. When she spoke, her voice was as quiet as the whisper of a breeze. 'I'm sorry I gave you that heritage, Jo.'

It was as if she had read my mind and, for a fleeting second, I felt a closeness to her that I'd rarely experienced before. I had spent so long wrapped up in my own suffering that I had not seen how much she, too, had suffered.

She pushed her frail shoulders back against the headboard and took a deep breath. I saw that she was trying not to cry. 'We were not wanted here,' she said, 'were we? It was only because of your wonderful father that we got by.'

Outside, in the tall trees at the back of my garden that marked the boundary with the churchyard beyond, a rook cawed, a harsh, discordant note tinged with melancholy. Overcome with emotion that I hadn't expected and didn't know how to deal with, I seized up the plate of biscuits and offered it to my mum. I had arranged the custard creams and slices of Battenberg in well-behaved rows, in the way she would have done, not haphazardly in a pile as would be more my natural style. My mother thrived on everything being neat and tidy, exemplified in the way she would hang socks out to dry already in their pairs for easier sorting later. I had always thought it was the German in her; chaos neatly ordered in the small things. But now it suddenly occurred to me that it was something more, an attempt to control anything that could be controlled because there was so much that couldn't.

I watched as she plucked a custard cream from the dish. Perhaps I had misunderstood my mother for all these years. Perhaps her indomitability, her frequent lapses of empathy, had all been a facade, built to withstand the horror she had lived through in Germany and the animosity she had endured in London. The thought was shocking, irrevocably leading me to ask the question of myself: what if everything I thought I knew about myself, my parents, my past, was wrong?

'You're probably getting fed up of me rabbiting on,' my mother said, with a brief laugh. 'Goodness, how I had to listen to that old bird, Gerta! I grew to love her like my own mother, but she never was quiet.'

I poured more tea as she took a bite of her biscuit and I selected a piece of cake.

'We didn't have anything like this for so long,' she mumbled between mouthfuls. 'We craved it – sugar, sweetness. They call them empty calories now, don't they? Hah! How can something be empty when it's so delicious?'

She finished the biscuit and dabbed at her lips for the crumbs.

'You know,' my mother went on, 'there were so many things – bad things – happening, but we all just went along with it. What did I do about Monika being given that poor man's house? Nothing.'

Pensively, I took a mouthful of cake and ate it, smoothing the counterpane beneath my hand as I did so. 'That's how totalitarian regimes work,' I mused. 'They make dissent impossible. They normalise the atrocious to make it acceptable.'

'Well, I'm sorry for it now,' my mother rejoined. 'I regret it. As I regret lots of things. But there's something I can't regret.' She paused, and when she spoke again her voice was suddenly stronger and louder. 'Perhaps it was the only truly good thing I've ever done.'

CHAPTER NINE

After Karl's request that she attend the Sunday service, Katja had to think of a reason to give Gerta for her sudden attack of religious fervour. She thought about it long and hard and then finally came down on the side of keeping it simple.

'There's a war on,' she stated, when Gerta questioned where she was off to dressed in her most respectable clothes, including her much-prized fur jacket. 'So I reckon we might need God's help. And I want to bring Hans up with knowledge of the church.'

Katja looked down at her son, dressed in a sailor suit one of Monika's horrid children had grown out of. Despite her dislike of the previous owner, Katja was not too proud to accept hand-me-downs. And Hans looked unbearably cute in it, with his white-blond hair and cherubic face.

'You won't mind if I don't come with you, will you,' Gerta replied. 'There's so much washing to do, and then I'll try to make an early start on our meal. I thought—'

'Yes, of course,' interrupted Katja, anxious to be off. 'See you later. We should be back around midday.'

With that, she picked Hans up, plopped him into the pram and set off at pace towards the Lutheran church which lay at the far end of the high street.

The interior of the church was cool and still, the air expectant somehow, though of what, Katja could not tell. Awaiting the presence of God, perhaps?

As she took a seat at one of the pews, she looked around her. It was a long time since she had set foot in a church and she'd almost forgotten how peaceful such places were. The essence of Lutheranism was simplicity; there were no bleeding statues of Christ or overly sentimental depictions of the Virgin Mary here. Instead, the interior was painted plain white, unadorned apart from the glorious colours of the stained-glass windows. There was nothing to detract from a focus on the Lord and Katja tried hard to do just that. It was not easy, though. Her mind buzzed with all she had to do when she got home. Gerta had said she would start on the washing, but their rooms desperately needed cleaning, as did the windows... The list of chores was never-ending.

And then there were the thoughts of Karl, constantly infiltrating her mind. What was the real purpose he had sent her here? She'd fallen for him so heavily and hoped, though she knew she probably shouldn't, that perhaps something could come of their burgeoning relationship, in some dim and distant, hazy future. But though she was in love, she was still in control of her faculties. She wasn't blinded by her feelings for Karl like some women might be. So how was it that she had not questioned him, just immediately agreed to his request? Katja was unclear herself about exactly what was behind her ready acquiescence, just presumed that, when the time was right, Karl would enlighten her.

The church was gradually filling up, each new arrival wearing Sunday-best outfits that had seen better days. Despite the local cobbler's efforts, shoes were in particularly bad condition; no one had had a new pair for years. Only Hans looked relatively smart; even though his outfit was second-hand, it exuded quality. Clearly Monika – or her husband – had ways to get her hands on items that were out of reach for ordinary citizens. *I wonder how she does that,* thought Katja wryly.

A slight rush of air alerted Katja to the pew behind her becoming occupied. She glanced over her shoulder to see a young woman settling down, rearranging a green scarf that she had loosely tied around her hair. Katja reckoned she must be about the same age as her, but this woman was not just ordinarily pretty like Katja but stunningly beautiful, quite mesmerisingly so. As their eyes met, Katja smiled but did not get a response. Chastened, Katja turned back around and distracted herself by ruffling Hans' hair.

The service was longer than she had expected and it was so difficult to keep Hans from making a noise and disturbing everyone that Katja almost forgot about Karl's instruction to listen carefully to the sermon. When the minister mounted the steps to the lectern and began to speak, she tried her best to pay attention, but it was hard to concentrate fully. She hoped Karl would be happy with what she was able to relay back to him – something about faith, and how much was necessary, and that sometimes a small faith was as good as a huge one. It would have to do, but her distraction with Hans meant that if Karl asked her what the sermon meant, she would be truly stumped. *Let's just hope he doesn't,* thought Katja as she gathered up her bag and Hans' coat.

Swinging Hans up into her arms, she joined the file of people making their way towards the exit. The beautiful young woman from the pew behind appeared by her side and Katja tried the smile again. She didn't come across many people her age and she craved company other than Gerta, Herr Wagner and her frightful neighbour, Monika. Perhaps the woman could become a friend and they could go for walks in the mountains together, even take the train to Stahlbach to the cinema one evening, if Gerta would mind Hans for her.

But, once again, the smile went unreciprocated and Katja's spirits sank. It seemed that it wasn't going to be that easy. It occurred to her that maybe the woman only spoke Czech. She may have heard Katja speaking to Hans in German and immediately realised that the two of them would not be able to communicate. Then it would make sense for her not to be too friendly, as nothing could come of it. Though why the woman would have come to a German church service if she couldn't understand a word of it was a mystery Katja couldn't solve.

Unencumbered by a small child, the woman passed Katja. Katja noted how glamorous she looked, even from behind. For a moment, Katja was tempted to follow her, see where she lived, so she could perhaps pass by in future and just happen to bump into her, make friends that way. Then she sternly told herself off for being so ridiculous. That was the behaviour of a mad person. Instead, Katja put the woman out of her mind and didn't think about her again.

She wasn't due back at the convalescent home until Wednesday and the time chafed at her. Karl came often to her thoughts, and as she scrubbed the tiled kitchen floor one afternoon, she found herself pausing, sitting back on her heels, and letting her mind drift. When the war was over, it would be possible to start again. At some point, Horst would be declared officially dead, rather than 'missing in action', and then Katja would legally be a widow and free to remarry. Did she dare to dream that Karl would... Katja checked herself. *Don't get your hopes up*, she told herself sternly. And then added, even more strictly, *and how can you be so uncaring about Horst? Show some respect.*

Hans, crawling, appeared at her side. He planted a chubby hand on his mother's shoulder and a fat kiss on her forehead. Laughing, Katja pulled him towards her and buried her face in his neck. While her love for him was absolute, it wasn't worry-free. She'd saved him from the bombing and protected him so far. But an uncertain future still lay ahead. And there was another thing. What if Karl wanted her but not her son? Having acknowledged the possibility of this scenario, Katja swiftly pushed it away. She would not dwell on it. There was no doubt about where her chief loyalties lay – to Hans, of course. But the idea of having to make that choice made her stomach feel hollow and dried her throat.

She stood up. '*Komm,*' she said to Hans, sweeping him up into her arms. It was a dull day outside, but at least the rain of earlier had stopped. She'd take the little boy outside for half an hour to get some fresh air and tire him out before bedtime.

Unfortunately, Monika was also taking advantage of the weather and was in her garden with her brood. Katja had no choice but to engage in a stilted conversation across the fence with her.

'How is the little one?' asked Monika, pointing at Hans.

It's not as if she doesn't know his name, thought Katja, crossly.

'Hans is fine,' she replied, with emphasis. 'And yours?' She wasn't going to use their names if Monika couldn't be bothered to use Hans'. But Monika ignored the question and simply asked another one of her own.

'Have you been out much lately?' Her voice was sharp and abrupt.

'No, not really,' Katja answered, trying not to let her antipathy to Monika show in her voice. 'Nowhere to go, is there, apart from when I go to Stahlbach to work. It's rather dull.'

Monika sniffed, nodded. 'I find myself entirely occupied by my children,' she said, primly. 'No other entertainment is necessary if one is devoted to being a mother, bringing up healthy children for the *Vaterland*.'

Katja bit her tongue and swallowed down her anger. The woman was so self-righteous. Everything she said to Katja was either a criticism or a rebuke. Monika bent down to one of her children and, while her back was turned, Katja stuck her tongue out at her. The childish gesture was satisfying, making her feel a bit better. She picked Hans up and took him back indoors, calling out goodbye over her shoulder.

It was an insignificant encounter in the great scheme of things, she knew, yet nevertheless it unsettled Katja. There was something about Monika that not only irritated but also unnerved her. Monika clearly had none of Katja's own doubts about the rightness of this war and sometimes Katja worried that she'd been sent here to spy on Katja. But that was nonsense. Monika had moved in next door to Herr Wagner weeks before she and Gerta had arrived, and couldn't possibly have known they were coming. Katja was letting the woman's unquestioning patriotism unnerve her. She resolved not to let Monika get to her in future, and focused on counting down the hours until she would be back at the convalescent home again.

When she finally arrived there at midday on Wednesday, Katja was seized by a sudden apprehension that she would be unable to live up to Karl's expectations of her – whatever those were. For a moment, she hoped that she would not see him today. But her wish was not to be granted. The senior nurse on duty sent her straight to the day room to clear up the morning coffee cups and there, in his usual chair, sat Karl. Katja saw how he was looking expectantly at the door as she entered and how, as soon as he saw her, he smiled in delight.

Despite her apprehension, Katja found herself smiling broadly back. Suddenly relaxed, with that feeling of safety that

Karl always imbued in her, she went over to him. 'Would you like more coffee, Haupt— Herr Hausmann?' She opened her mouth to add something about her visit to church but something stopped her and she shut it again, abruptly. An innate sense told her to wait, to let Karl take the lead.

'No, thank you.' Karl watched her as she picked up the cup and saucer from the side table next to him and put it on the tray the nurse had given her. 'Before lunch, would you mind escorting me around the garden?' he asked her. 'My leg is feeling much better these days and I need to start strengthening it up. The sooner I'm fit, the sooner I can get back to my base.'

A sharp clang rang out. Apologising, Katja bent down to pick up the teaspoon she had dropped, turning away from Karl as she did so in order to hide her face from him. She did not want him to see her quivering upper lip and incipient tears. It was only natural that he was desperate to resume active duty, but that didn't make it any easier to think of him being gone, and what felt like so soon. Too soon.

Bracing herself, she stood back up. 'Of course, we can go to the garden. It will be my pleasure.'

Karl fixed her with his steady gaze and she understood something he was silently communicating to her. That her report from the church sermon should wait until they were alone together and far from prying eyes and listening ears. But why were the words of a preacher so secret? Katja had no idea.

Twenty minutes later, she hoped she was about to find out.

Offering Karl her arm to lean on should he need it, the pair of them left the house through the large doors that led from the music room into the garden. They barely spoke until they reached the path through the rose garden. The first flush of flowers was over and the plant stems bristled with sharp thorns that could easily dig into the flesh. Katja had caught her arms on them before; she kept well clear today.

'So – tell me what you learned.' Karl's voice was calm and

even as always, but Katja thought she detected a hint of apprehension behind it. This made her even more aware that she had been set a test, but one that she did not know the rules of, or how it would be marked and judged.

'It was very interesting,' she began, with more confidence than she felt, before going on to relate what she had heard.

When she had finished, Karl said nothing. Katja looked up at him, his square jaw and perfect profile. *Oh please God* (it was all right to invoke the Almighty now that she'd been to church) *let him feel for me the way I do for him*, she thought.

Karl led her further down the winding path to where a large linden tree stood sentinel at the property's boundary. There he paused and turned to face Katja, reaching out for her hand. Katja held her breath. She found herself longing for Karl to take her in his arms, kiss her, hold her, declare his undying...

'And you saw someone there, I think.' Karl's statement cut through Katja's dreams. 'An... acquaintance of mine.'

Katja hesitated. At first, she wasn't sure what Karl meant, but then it dawned on her that maybe it was the beautiful woman. Was she a friend of Karl's? That was far from good news. Could the two of them be more than friends? A wave of jealous nausea rose in Katja's stomach and she forced it down.

A gust of wind rattled the linden's branches, and a rook, black as night, cawed, shattering the silence that had descended between them after Karl's last words, robbing the moment of the expectation of romance.

Before Katja had time to think of how she should answer, Karl was talking again.

'Her name is Laura,' he said. 'This Sunday, you will see her again. She will smile at your son and ask you how old he is. You will tell her the answer.' He reached inside his pocket and pulled out an envelope. It had nothing written on it. He handed it to Katja. 'And then you will give her this and leave. Do you understand?'

It was clear what answer Karl expected.

'Yes,' Katja replied, slowly and hesitantly, 'of course I do.'

She didn't. She had no idea what this was all about, but it felt serious. And Karl needed her to do it, so she would. She wondered fleetingly again if they were lovers, Karl and the beautiful woman, but something told her that they weren't, that this was not a love note that she had been entrusted with. It felt much more important than that. Much more serious than a matter of the heart.

She put the letter in her coat pocket, thrusting it down so as to make sure it would not fall out.

'Thank you,' said Karl.

'Um, wh...' Katja faltered, took a breath, started again. 'What is it?' she asked, her voice scarcely more than a whisper. 'What is this all about? What should I know?'

Her questions seemed to hang in the air, buffeted to and fro by the gusting of the wind. Katja looked at Karl. His expression was grave and he seemed to be weighed down by something. The weight of her expectation? Katja couldn't tell.

Then Karl shook his head, slowly and meaningfully. 'I can't tell you now, Katja my love,' he answered.

Katja's heart stood still. This was the first time he'd used such an endearment, or her first name. She suddenly felt closer to him than she'd ever felt before.

'Please just trust me. And help me. When the time is right – then you shall know.'

A million other questions formed in Katja's mind. But before she had a chance to articulate any of them, Karl leaned forward, put his arms around her and drew her close. And then he was kissing her, hard and passionate, and Katja forgot all her doubts and worries and queries as the world stood still.

· · ·

THE FOLLOWING SUNDAY, everything went exactly as planned – except that Katja had to bite her tongue to stop herself from questioning Laura. She wanted to ask her what this was all about, but, as well as Karl's reluctance to tell her, Laura's presence itself was so mesmerising, so regal, that Katja didn't dare say a word other than what she had been instructed to.

She wondered what was in the letter – of course she did. She was only human. But her trust and faith in Karl was so great that she was prepared to do as he said and bide her time for when she could know more. Katja would have found it hard to put her feelings into words, but it just felt like the right thing to do.

From then on, every week was the same. At some point, when they were alone in the garden or the infirmary or Karl's room where Katja legitimately had to go to make his bed, change the sheets, fill up the water jugs, in between their intimate moments, Karl would pass her a letter which she would stash away in a safe place about her person and give to Laura at the Sunday service. Her job as postwoman gave Katja a new sense of purpose. She ventured on one other occasion to find out more about the letters' contents, but Karl repeated that he couldn't tell her – yet. And then he distracted her with a kiss so passionate that, if Katja had been in any further doubt about the missives being love letters, it would have been immediately dispelled.

Not only was Karl's lovemaking increasingly ardent and intense, he also seemed to be able to read Katja like a book. He could tell when she felt down, when the loneliness and monotony of her life got to her.

'You're so young,' he said to her one autumn day, as he twisted a lock of her hair around his finger. They were in his room, sharing a few precious moments of privacy before Katja's absence might be noticed by someone. Katja snuggled a little closer to him. 'You should be in the city,' Karl continued, 'going to the theatre and the ballet, hosting dinner parties and soirées, like the fine ladies did before the war.'

Katja burst out laughing. 'Don't be ridiculous,' she responded. 'I've never been a fine lady and never will be. As for "before the war" – it's as if that time never existed. It seems so long ago.'

Karl was silent. Puzzled, Katja shifted position and propped herself up on her elbow to observe his face more closely. He looked as if he was far away, back in an era before conflict tore all of their lives asunder. Or perhaps he was in the air, flying his fighter plane, knowing that at any moment he might be shot down.

'It will end,' he said, eventually. 'Not this year, but next. I'm sure of it.'

His words were so final that it was as if he had read the future.

A surge of hope burnt through Katja. The war, over. Hans, growing up in peacetime. It was almost unbearable to imagine such a prospect. And yet Karl made it seem real.

There was another long pause. And then, suddenly, the dark shadow lifted from Karl's eyes and he smiled. 'But who knows what is going to happen between now and then,' he went on, pulling her down on top of him. 'So we need to make the most of the present.'

As Katja's relationship with Karl intensified, with Katja increasing the amount of time she spent at the convalescent home, it was the one good thing on the horizon. Whatever Karl's predictions, the news from the front was getting worse and worse. At the beginning of the war, the reports had all been about great German military victories. Now they focused on the Red Army, describing in vivid detail the dreadful things Russian soldiers did to women, and to children.

Inevitably, this affected the mood in the convalescent home, but as autumn turned to winter and then to the approach of Christmas, everyone seemed to make a concerted effort to enjoy themselves and celebrate. A huge tree was delivered and decorated, standing proudly in the entrance hall, and the cooks spent hours on festive baking. The home was able to get hold of commodities and ingredients that had long been absent from the shelves of ordinary shops. Each week, alongside Karl's missives, Katja sneaked a few bits and bobs home with her: a little white sugar, a cinnamon stick and a nutmeg, some sweet chestnuts to make a stuffing.

As she was finishing work on the twenty-third of December, Karl beckoned Katja over. She was surprised as he rarely spoke to her in public anymore. He wasn't going to give her a letter here, was he, where everyone could see? But she needn't have worried. This time, it wasn't an envelope that Karl gave her but a box, wrapped in silver paper and tied with a red bow.

'It's something for your son,' Karl explained, smiling a little sheepishly. 'I made it. I hope he likes it.'

Katja's face flushed bright red from the heat of the roaring fire and her high emotion. 'Th-thank you,' she stuttered, so overcome she almost lost the power of speech.

'And here's one for Oma Gerta,' Karl continued, handing over another package. 'And finally – for you.'

Katja could hardly take it in. It was so generous of him, and so unexpected. 'Gosh,' she said, inadequately. 'I'm overwhelmed. It's so kind of you.'

The smile Karl bestowed upon her made her legs go weak. 'It's my pleasure,' he said.

When she left a short while later, Katja paused in the hallway to drink in the sight of the Christmas tree, how the candles that adorned its glossy branches glowed in the half-light of the midwinter's eve. The hand-blown glass angels and crystal baubles sparkled and shone as they twisted and turned in the pockets of warm air created by the flames, and from the kitchen the scent of gingerbread and cinnamon rolls and stollen wafted towards the front door.

With a lightness to her step, Katja headed for the station.

The next day, opening Karl's gifts, she felt overcome again. Hans had received a hand-carved wooden horse, Gerta a pair of gloves and Katja a bottle of scent. These last two items must have been hard to come by and expensive in the current times, but that was not what was important about them. Their significance lay in the thought that had gone into Karl's choosing. Spraying a smidgen of the perfume onto her wrists, Katja closed her eyes as she inhaled the delicious aroma. She felt as if she were floating on a cloud of love and adoration and it was far too soft and nice to ever want to get off.

On the twenty-sixth of December, she set off for the home once more. That night, there was to a be a ball and Katja had arranged to sleep over with one of the nurses in her room, as otherwise she'd have to return before the party had even got going. As it was, she was free to stay up late and dance till the small hours.

The evening was everything she had hoped it would be. Someone had turned a parachute into a canopy that billowed above the dining-hall-turned-ballroom. Candles in jam jars cast a soft, golden light while leaving the corners in deep and romantic obscurity. A succession of tall and handsome military men spun Katja around the room until finally it was the turn of Karl.

'May I have the pleasure?' he asked her, extending his arm for her to take.

Katja smiled demurely. 'Of course you may,' she replied.

Karl led her to the centre of the ballroom and held her close as they began to sway to the music, cheek touching cheek. He had been exercising every day to build up his strength and his body, so close to Katja's, was strong and muscular. In his arms, she felt those feelings of safety and security that only Karl could evoke in her, banishing the cold of that wartime winter. Karl's leg was so much improved that he moved with only the slightest dragging of his right foot and their intricate waltzes flowed, one into the other, like rivers running to the sea.

CHAPTER TEN

LONDON, MAY 1994

I felt almost winded when my mother finished telling me this
latest part of her story. To have spent all these years with no
inkling of this great love, this man who was certainly as important to her, if not more so, than her first husband, Horst. I maintained my hope – my belief – that my father had meant more
than either of them.

But there was a bigger mystery than this brewing.

'So this business with the church, and Laura, and the letters
– what *was* going on?' I asked, unable to contain my curiosity.

My mother shrugged. 'At first, I didn't know. Of course I
wondered, but I accepted what Karl asked me to do and I got on
with it. I hadn't particularly wanted to go to church, but the
more I went, the more it grew on me. Gradually, I began to like
it and even to look forward to Sunday mornings. There was
something so peaceful about that building, and the minister was
very eloquent.'

'And Laura was always there?' I asked.

My mother nodded. 'Yes, every week, week after week,

month after month. I took the letters from Karl and gave them to her.'

Springer, who was lying somewhat heavily on my feet, shifted in his sleep. I wriggled my toes, relieved that they were free to move again.

'You must have wondered who she was, didn't you?'

My question was not as innocent as it sounded. I wanted to find out at what point my mother had come to the realisation that I'd had almost as soon as Laura's name was mentioned. That she was a spy, maybe working for the Resistance. And that Karl was a double agent, passing information to her, secrets that he would know due to his senior position in the air force. Though the men at the home were convalescing, they would still have been in contact with the highest echelons of the Waffen-SS and therefore would have access to intelligence that could be useful to the other side.

But could it possibly be true? It sounded almost fantastical, and to find that my own mother had potentially been involved in intrigue and espionage was scarcely believable.

She ran her hand over her eyes. 'I'll be absolutely honest with you, Jo – if you mean did I know that I was getting involved in undercover work, then I really didn't. I was young and naive, in love with Karl and totally in his thrall. As long as Laura wasn't his mistress or whatnot, I didn't really care what was going on. Not yet, anyway. I trusted him implicitly, and I think that there was a part of me that told me it was better not to know. Safer.'

I nodded. '*Ask no questions and you'll hear no lies* kind of thing.'

She gave a short laugh. 'Exactly.'

'So – did you ever find out for sure? Who Laura was, what was in the letters?'

My mother sighed and pulled the bedcover further up her

chest until it was almost covering her mouth, as if she were trying to conceal herself.

'Yes and no,' she said. 'Some parts of what happened are so hard to remember now. But other bits are as clear as day. Something happened one day that made me realise what they were doing, Laura and Karl. And, of course, what I was doing.'

And with that, my mother told me what she saw happen to Laura and as she spoke, I realised why she might want to hide away from the horror of those memories.

CHAPTER ELEVEN

MEINDORF, 1945

It was a Friday and Katja was on her way back from the convalescent home. She'd done a morning shift, so it was early afternoon now, but instead of going straight from the station to Herr Wagner's house beneath the mountain, she needed to pop to the shops to buy some groceries. Everything was in short supply and essentials were often only available on the second, third or fourth visit, so it was necessary to shop every day. If she were still running Horst's store in Berlin, Katja couldn't imagine how she'd be coping. The worst thing was how angry some customers got when they couldn't get hold of what they wanted, accusing the shopkeepers of favouritism, keeping things back for their friends, or of profiteering, manufacturing the shortages so that they could charge more.

Katja shivered, partly from the cold and partly from apprehension. The news of the war was never good these days and everyone was anxious all the time. Now Christmas was over, there wasn't much to look forward to. Just a conflict that seemed to be heading inexorably in the wrong direction. Her hand closed over the latest letter in her pocket, which she must carefully guard until the time came to hand it over to Laura at church on Sunday.

Emerging into the town square which provided a short cut to the butcher's shop, at first Katja thought she must be mistaken. There was a woman on the street in front of her, only twenty or so paces away, and from behind, she looked just like Laura. Katja didn't know what to do. She had never seen Laura in the town, only ever in church, and she wasn't sure if she were supposed to know her or not. It probably wasn't Laura anyway; this woman was wearing a different coloured coat, drab black rather than her usual blue, though she did have a green headscarf, just as Laura always wore. That was nothing remarkable – it was so cold that everyone was covering their head with something.

As Katja hesitated, unsure what to do, a sudden noise from the opposite side of the square made her turn around. Trundling over the cobbles was a dark-coloured Mercedes-Benz. Katja watched in frozen horror as it pulled up alongside the woman and, before the vehicle had fully come to a halt, four men in trench coats, brandishing pistols, jumped out. In seconds, they had surrounded the woman and, as she turned to face the pack, Katja saw that it was indeed Laura. For a fleeting second, an expression of pure terror flitted across Laura's face before she recomposed herself. Watching the men close in on her, Katja slunk back into the shadow of a nearby house. Her heart was racing, her palms slick with sweat. She wanted to cry out to Laura – 'run!' – but to do so would be certain death to both of them.

At the same time as fear for Laura seared through Katja, so the letter burned a hole in her pocket. What if the men were coming for her, too? A deep, nauseating dread seized Katja, paralysing her. She wanted to help Laura, to wrest her away from the sinister, black-clad men, but she couldn't move. She wanted to flee, to get back to Herr Wagner's house and hide, like a wounded animal returning to its lair, but she was frozen to the spot.

Katja looked towards Laura again. Her head was held high as two of the men caught hold of her roughly by the arms and began bundling her into the vehicle. Her eyes locked with Katja's and, even from the distance of twenty metres that lay between them, Katja read the secret message they conveyed.

Do nothing, say nothing. Don't give yourself away. Tell only Karl.

Within moments, Laura was in the car and so were the men and off they sped, rattling across the cobbles in a cloud of diesel fumes, leaving behind a thousand unanswered questions and a feeling of utter trepidation such as Katja had never experienced before.

Finally regaining the power of movement, she stepped forward. On the ground lay a splash of green. Katja bent to pick it up. Laura's green headscarf. Katja clenched her hand around it, trying not to cry. From the folds of the fabric arose the subtle scent of Laura and the smell wrenched at Katja's heart. A few onlookers who Katja had not previously noticed began a slow handclap.

'*Verräterin,*' shouted one, in the direction of the departing car. Traitor.

And, '*Auf Nimmerwiedersehen*' from another. Good riddance.

More townsfolk, those passing through the square or drawn by the commotion from the surrounding streets, joined those already there, clapping and hurling insults. They hadn't even seen what happened, but they did it nonetheless, unthinkingly, unquestioningly. Katja wanted to go up to the applauders and slap their faces and tell them to stop. But of course she didn't. And then, suddenly, a voice beside her was saying her name and Katja almost collapsed with fear.

'You aren't clapping, Frau Schmidt?'

Struggling to maintain her composure, Katja slowly turned her head towards the speaker. Monika, her next-door neighbour. Meeting her gaze full on, Katja held it steady for a few moments.

'I don't know what happened exactly, and even if I did, it's none of my business,' she replied, refraining from adding, 'nor yours, either.'

As she walked away, she felt Monika's eyes boring into her back. It was almost as if she could see Karl's latest letter in her pocket. Katja shivered. In a daze, errands forgotten, she hurried back to the house beneath the mountain.

THAT EVENING, once Hans and Gerta were in bed and she had the kitchen, warmed by the giant *Kachelöfen*, to herself, Katja removed the letter from her coat pocket. She sat, contemplating it, turning it over and over in her hand. She should probably just return it to Karl. But having watched Laura's 'arrest', the fact of which she was still trying to process, fear ran through her veins. She needed to know exactly what she was doing, what she had so inadvertently become caught up in. She couldn't be one of the unthinking, unquestioning ones anymore, not like all those townsfolk in the square that day.

What she had witnessed today had effected a quiet revolution within her soul, and caused the scales to drop from her eyes. The German state, with Hitler at its helm, was without doubt absolutely wicked and evil and must be stopped. If these letters were meant for the Resistance, which Katja had to admit to herself she secretly knew they must be, they might be instrumental in achieving that goal.

The envelope's flap was hard to open without tearing it, but with the help of steam from the kettle, Katja managed it. The paper inside was wafer thin and flimsy. Katja unfolded it and studied it closely. On one side, it was covered in lists of figures, dates, times, calculations and on the other were a couple of small hand-drawn maps. Staring at them, Katja tried to make sense of what she saw, but failed. She had no idea what it all meant.

A wail from upstairs made her jump out of her skin. Hans had woken, and would likely wake Gerta as the bedrooms were side by side. Hastily stuffing the paper back into the envelope, she returned it to her pocket and rushed up to Hans to soothe him back to sleep.

Katja resolved not to look at the letter again. But all day on Saturday, she couldn't concentrate on anything else. All she could think about was the envelope and its contents. That night, Katja opened it once more. This time, as she stared at the page, it began to come clear. These were military figures and formations, backed up by the maps, plans of attack, dates and times they would take place.

So Karl must be a double agent, passing secrets to the enemy and, as she had been carrying the letters, Katja was now a spy or counter-insurgent – or just a plain old traitor, as Laura had been accused by the baying mob in the town square. A sudden, excruciating stabbing pain in her stomach made her curl up in a ball on the kitchen floor. She wasn't brave. Did she want to be a hero? Officials terrified her, especially those associated with the Nazi regime. She recollected how scared she'd been of the police officer in her shop, when she'd helped out the struggling mother with no ration book and no money. She'd got away with her defiance of the law then, but there was no guarantee she would again – and this was so very much more serious.

And then another burst of memories flooded her mind, disordered, random, visceral. The bombing in Berlin, the terror she and Gerta had experienced. The German man and his Czech wife, driven out of their home and banished in order for the repellent Monika from Cottbus and her revolting children to occupy it. The ever-increasing stories of disappearances, not just of individuals but whole neighbourhoods and communities, Jews and gypsies taken away in trains and never seen again. Hans' innocent newborn face, so trusting, so unaware of the horror he'd been born into.

Suddenly it all came clear. She would do whatever she could to secure a good future for Hans. It was a mother's job.

ON SUNDAY MORNING, Katja went to church as normal. She knew it was naive, but she harboured a faint hope that Laura would be there, familiar in her blue coat, though without her green headscarf. But of course she wasn't.

This week, a different minister was officiating. Instead of the usual calm, reasoned sermon, this man's was full of fire and brimstone, retribution and revenge. Katja listened, terror pinioning her to her seat. Did he know what she had done? What she was doing?

In a moment of quiet that followed the sermon, Katja heard someone speaking to her, a voice in her head. Or maybe it was God. *You're doing the right thing,* it said. *Stay strong.* As the words rang around her mind, she became acutely aware of the envelope's hard edges, pushing against her fingers, reminding her of its presence.

The organ struck up the first bars of the closing music, somehow leading Katja to fully confront Laura's fate. The beautiful young woman had been taken away by the Gestapo and would not be coming back. If Katja continued her work for Karl, she might very likely be next.

But how could she give up now?

CHAPTER TWELVE

As my mother finished speaking, a tight band of apprehension had tightened around my chest. Her story was full of foreboding; not knowing exactly how bad it was going to get made it worse. It wasn't just her sudden propulsion into the world of espionage, but also the constant jeopardy that hung over her, Hans and Gerta, the little cobbled-together family that had become her whole world.

Right now, what was going on with Karl and Laura was centre stage. But, at some point, the tale would presumably lead to the fate that had befallen my half-brother, little Hans, which I both wanted and did not want to hear. It could only be a tale of unbearable sorrow – and it already felt as if my mother's words, the memories she was imparting, were filling every corner of the room and, indeed, the whole house, and seeping out into the newly bright spring sunshine outside, the fragile warmth of which was in such sharp contrast to that frozen Sudetenland winter.

'I'm sorry,' I repeated once more. How many times had I

said that already? I'd lost count, but I didn't know what else to say; words seemed inadequate, useless.

In a rare gesture of intimacy, my mother reached out and pressed my hand between hers. Her palms were smooth and dry, barely warm at all.

'You're cold, Mum,' I cried. 'Shall I put the heating on?'

'Oh good gracious, no!' she protested, immediately. 'It's May! No one puts the heating on in May!'

Suppressing a smile, I tucked the covers around her more tightly. My mother had never been able to bear even the tiniest hint of extravagance; any expenditure that could possibly be deemed not strictly necessary was deeply frowned upon. Another legacy of living through the war. I leaned forward and gently tucked a stray strand of hair behind her ear.

'*Liebchen*, I'm tired again,' she murmured, shifting in the bed to get more comfortable, 'even though I've only been awake a few hours. I'm like one of those old biddies in the geriatric ward.'

'No, Mum, you're not in the least like that,' I laughed, the sudden burst of humour a relief after all the intensity. 'It's all right to be worn out after what you've been through. Rest, and enjoy it. You deserve it.' I collected up the tea things. 'Get some sleep, as much as you can. You'll feel better soon.' It felt strange addressing the well-worn phrase that I had said so often to my children to my mother.

'Just forty blinks will be enough,' she muttered, confusing her English again.

'As long as you need, Mum,' I responded. 'I'm going to pop over to the flat to check up on everything – the builders told me they'd be working today. I'll be back for lunch and then I'll take Springer out.'

My mother sighed. 'I'm sorry, Jo,' she murmured. 'I'm making so much extra work for you.'

'No!' I exclaimed, shaking my head vehemently. 'It's fine. No trouble at all.'

By the time I had reached the bedroom door, my mother was already asleep.

TAKING the car for speed's sake, and because I could park outside my mother's block on a Saturday, I drove to Camden Town, where I found the work making good progress. The old kitchen and shabby, outdated bathroom fittings were gone, and the new combi boiler already installed. The foreman had a few questions, so I spent some time with him, choosing tiles from amongst his samples and selecting a bathtub, toilet and basin from a catalogue; neutral white instead of the rather sickly shade of pink they were replacing.

Once the immediate decisions had been taken, I went through to the sitting room to appreciate again how much bigger it was without the fire surround. Plus, of course, most of the furniture was gone; I had put it into storage to protect it from the dust and dirt. My mother's prized sideboard had been too big for the unit, however, and it stood shrouded in dustsheets and littered with the workmen's coffee mugs, packets of sugar and teaspoons. Also upon it was the mail, neatly piled at one end, and on top of the heap a bag from Gamages department store. The shop had not existed for several decades and I gasped at the sight of it and the recollections it brought back, of trips to buy school shoes, see Father Christmas, grab some sale bargains. Picking the bag up, I peered curiously into it.

Inside was a black notebook, about A5 size, scuff-marked and with dog-eared corners. I pulled it out and leafed through it. The pages were wafer thin, reminding me of the Bible I had read from one Christmas, my first at primary school. I clearly recalled the opening words of the reading: 'And it came to pass in those days, that there went out a decree from Caesar Augustus...' How proud I had been, seeing my mum and dad watching me performing such a special task.

It was the last good memory, before the bullying began in earnest.

Each page of the notebook was covered with tiny handwriting, the words so densely packed together as to be almost illegible. I screwed up my eyes and stretched out my arms their full length, but still I couldn't make most of it out. Recently, I'd had to reluctantly concede that I'd reached an age when I needed reading glasses for small print. The final reckoning had occurred when I'd tried to visit a newly opened garden centre and had to turn back because I simply couldn't see the street names in the A–Z.

Reaching for my bag, I fumbled inside for a pair of specs but found none; I must have left them at home. Cursing, I flipped through to the end of the book. The last two pages held between them an envelope. It was addressed to my father, Lou Robby, at this address in Bayham Street – this I could make out, as the writing was large – and had a stamp that looked foreign, though both it and the postmark were so faded as to be illegible.

I turned the envelope over. There, on the flap, were the sender's details: Janez Novak, and an address in Slovenia. The envelope had been roughly torn open, obliterating the name of the town and, when I looked inside, it was empty. No note or card; nothing at all. But it had been kept inside this notebook, and presumably there was a reason for this. As I puzzled what that reason could be, the builders' foreman came through.

'Oh, you found that old lot then?' he asked, pointing to the Gamages bag. 'It was in the cupboard-thing in the kitchen, buried right at the back under a load of old jam jars.' He halted abruptly. 'I told the lads to throw those away – is that all right? Couldn't imagine you'd want to keep them. But the other stuff – I thought it might be something important.'

'You did exactly the right thing on both counts,' I reassured him. 'I should have emptied out that cupboard myself, but I clean forgot about it in the rush to get things ready for your guys to start. Thanks for saving this. It'll be...' I faltered, searching for the right word. 'Interesting,' I settled on. 'To find out what it is.'

'Right you are,' replied the foreman. 'We're going to be off soon – early finish on the weekend. Can you make sure you choose the kitchen asap – the workshop's got a two- to three-week order time even for the off-the-shelf designs, so we need to get onto it. I gave you the brochures, didn't I?'

'You did,' I assured him. 'And I will.' I got out my Filofax and clumsily made a spectacle-less note, sure that I'd forget otherwise. Satisfied with everything else that was going on, I put the notebook and envelope back into the carrier bag and set off for home.

The mood darkened considerably, however, when I entered the house. The phone was ringing and I didn't manage to get to it before the answering machine cut in.

'Hi, Jo, it's Ed,' wavered out over the airways. I was immediately filled with irritation. Why the need to announce himself in this way? Did he really think I didn't recognise his voice after twenty-five years of marriage? 'I'm going to pop round. We need to talk. I'll be there about three.'

Slowly, I raised my eyes to the clock. It was already gone one. I had just enough time to make lunch for Mum and me, then give faithful Springer the walk he was waiting so patiently for.

The meal over, I got outside as quickly as I could and climbed briskly to the top of Kite Hill, Springer racing about madly with the joy of being free. All trace of the spring sunshine of earlier in the week had gone, leaving a day that was cloudy and grey, intermittent rain half-heartedly breaking out. The distant horizon was smudged and bleary, as if being seen through just-woken eyes still heavy with sleep. Hazy in the mist, the familiar landmarks of the London skyline could just be made out – the Post Office Tower, St Paul's and Battersea Power Station. Three years ago, these well-known icons had been joined by Canary Wharf, on the top of which the helicopter warning light continually flashed.

Grateful to pause for breath at the top, I took a moment, as I always did at this place, to remember my father. His death during school exam season was part of the reason for my lamentable results – or at least that was the rationale I'd always placed upon it. The other part of my failure was due to the lack of confidence and self-esteem engendered by the relentless bullying.

My mother and I had scattered my father's ashes here, one of his favourite places, coming up early in the morning to avoid the joggers and walkers and kite-flyers, none of whom would probably have appreciated a face full of the contents of a funeral urn, but also just to be alone and say a last goodbye to a beloved husband and father. I still missed him, each and every day.

I sank down onto one of the benches, ignoring its rain-slicked surface, and put my head in my hands. My mother and father had had so many tough times to endure as they had endeavoured to build a life in London, but they had succeeded, and done it together. Ed and I had failed and I didn't know if it was my fault or his.

Eventually, conscious of the time, I checked my watch and saw that I needed to get a move on. Saying a silent farewell to my father, I got up and turned back towards home. Living so close to the Heath and my father's final resting place was vital to me; I could not imagine leaving. As I walked downhill I wished, as I always did, that he was still with us, had never left. But at least, on the Heath's high hill where the wild wind blew on days both fair and foul, his soul and his spirit were always close.

Though my intention had been to go straight home to give

me some breathing space before Ed's visit, Springer had other ideas, deftly and deliberately leading me to the first of the ponds where he always loved to swim.

'Oh dear,' I groaned as I saw how muddy the area was. There'd been so much rain recently. 'Do you really have to, Springer?'

Evidently, he did.

Springer's ablutions left me with no time to dig out the solicitor's letters and other correspondence I had wanted to find before facing up to Ed. When I got back to the house, my soon to be ex-husband was already waiting outside.

'You could have gone in,' I said mildly, as he turned to face me. I was secretly glad he hadn't, but at the same time perversely annoyed by it. If Ed was making some kind of point by standing on the doorstep like he no longer belonged here, it was hardly my fault. It had been his choice to move out.

'I didn't want to intrude,' Ed responded, primly.

Stepping past him, I unlocked the door. Once inside, I grabbed Springer's towel off the radiator and began to dry him.

'Jo?' Ed's voice, a little impatient now, broke across my vigorous rubbing. 'Can you sort the dog later? I haven't got much time and there's a lot we need to talk about.'

I paused for a moment to look up at him. 'Fire away,' I said, glibly. 'I'm all ears. And before you say anything, I can do two things at once; it's called being a woman.'

The exaggerated sigh with which Ed greeted this remark was designed to show how long-suffering he was and how exasperating I was.

'OK,' he responded, with a tone of resignation. 'Look, the thing is...' He paused, clearly uncomfortable about something. I saw no reason to help him out. 'Annabelle and I have moved in together,' he blurted out. 'In her flat.'

I pursed my lips while continuing to rub Springer, caressing his silky ears and head. I wasn't sure what the point was here.

Was Ed gloating? Boasting? Glorifying in the fact that it had taken him no time at all to move on and find another partner?

At which thought I experienced a sudden, lurching surge of nausea. Ed had always insisted that, though he'd known Annabelle for some time, their friendship had only become more than that after our separation. But could that really be true? It was all accelerating so fast, they were cohabiting so quickly. It hardly seemed credible that this was a relationship that was only three months old. Suspicion that Ed had been more than economical with the truth subsumed me and I had to swallow hard before responding.

'That's nice,' I managed to articulate, weakly, the opposite of what I actually felt.

'Yes, it is,' agreed Ed, somewhat complacently. 'But the thing is, her apartment is tiny and we need our own place.'

I nodded. Another realisation, almost as bad and vomit-inducing as the first, was slowly dawning.

'She's set her heart on a little cottage in Hampstead Garden Suburb – you know, one of those lovely ones near the Heath extension. Quiet road, original features. It's what she's always wanted.'

I fought back incipient tears. I couldn't care less about the Heath extension, or any nice cottage there, original features or none.

'But in order to buy, I need to realise my assets. That's this house, Jo.'

God, he really did think I was a simpleton, the way he was talking, the language he was using.

A gasping sob emitted involuntarily from my throat. My house was my everything, all my memories, my stability and security. I had poured my heart and soul into it, and the glorious garden which I would never be able to equal anywhere else. It was the still point in a world whose turning so often seemed incomprehensible, unmanageable. I could not lose it. I simply couldn't. Ed knew all of that but was choosing to ignore it to serve his own interests.

'We need to sell, Jo,' he concluded, unaffected by my silence, my paralysis. 'And quickly. The house must go on the market as soon as possible so that I can get my money out. OK?'

CHAPTER THIRTEEN

Despite my attempts to quell them, tears began to gather in my eyes as Ed's bombshell sank in. I wiped them away with a corner of Springer's towel, taking a perverse relish in Ed's flinch of distaste as he saw me do so. He didn't like my dog and he didn't like this house. It was becoming increasingly obvious that he didn't like me very much either. Perhaps he never had.

'I'll buy you out,' I muttered quietly. 'Just give me a bit of time.'

Ed raised his eyebrows. 'You can't afford to do that, Jo,' he said, with the elaborate patience you would show to someone you considered very dim indeed.

My blood boiled, but I felt too defeated to retaliate.

'This house is worth 160 K,' he continued. 'So unless you can give me 80 K in cash straight up it's a no-go. I doubt you'd be able to borrow more than forty or fifty on your salary. You're at least 30 K short, Jo, you have to accept it.' Ed finished speaking and groaned, rubbing his hand over his eyes as if that might wipe away my ridiculous suggestion. 'Do me a favour and don't make this any worse than it already is.'

Do me a favour! For God's sake, what was he on about? I'd

spent my married life doing him favours: the housework, the childcare, enabling him to have his magnificent career while I did a dead-end job at the same time as toiling away doing all of the so-called 'peripheral' stuff that was actually essential to the seamless functioning of life. His life, more specifically. What about my life?

And why was he repeating my name as if he hardly knew me, and saying 'K' rather than thousand, like he was some hotshot city broker? It was so – pretentious. But then that was Ed all over. He'd always been a show-off and, if truth be told, the house had never been nearly grand, pretty or posh enough for him. He could have decided to let me have it while he moved onto pastures new. But he wasn't big enough for that.

I saw him out and then went to the living room and stood there for a few moments, helpless, not knowing what to do with myself. On my desk in the corner lay the Gamages bag containing the notebook and the mysterious envelope. I went over to it, put my reading glasses on and studied the envelope again. Perhaps I should write to this Janez person, just for curiosity's sake, see why he had contacted my father.

Meanwhile, there was the notebook to read. The hard work involved in deciphering the handwriting would take my mind off the conversation with Ed, which still reverberated between my ears. I was going to have to dig deep and find reservoirs of strength within myself that I last had to use when fending off the bullies more than thirty years ago. But, I reflected, as the notebook's stiff cover creaked open, my mother had had to do that in the dreadful situation that had confronted her all those decades before. And if she could, then so could I.

Little did I know that I was about to find out how vast my father's qualities of resilience and survival had also been.

POLAND, 1945

'*Raus, raus! Raus, raus!*' The guard's harsh voice sliced through the bitter cold like a blade. 'Get out! Get out!'

Stumbling, tripping, scrabbling to gather possessions, the men roused themselves from their bunks and ran towards the door that had been flung open. Outside, the night was pitch black, the moon obscured, the lowering blanket of cloud intermittently letting loose flurries of snow to join the drifts that had already fallen. Men were gathered there, lined up in columns, heads down, shoulders huddled into whatever coats or warm clothing they had, waiting.

The word went round, rippling through the jumbled ranks of those standing, and those arriving: their orders were to march. But so many were they, crammed onto the track that led to the prison camp's exit, that there was barely space to move. The first in line had been mustered for twenty minutes already, with scores more falling in behind every moment, yet the gates were still closed, the road beyond that led to Sagan still empty.

There had been speculation for days. That the Nazis did not intend to leave their prisoners of war to be liberated by the rapidly advancing Red Army but were going to marshal them away, to the west, to heaven knew where, perhaps to keep them moving until they fell off the edge of the land and into the North Sea.

As the rumours grew louder and more detailed, the senior officers amongst the prisoners had been instructing the men to prepare for evacuation – to exercise, to eat all they could to build their strength, and, above all, to keep calm. Some had torn up floorboards or dismantled beds to make sleds to transport their few possessions – the most important of which were food, blankets and warm clothing. Others had fashioned backpacks out of anything they could lay their hands on: sheets, worn-out shirts, socks to tie the bundles together.

And now, after so much desperate anticipation, so much fear and apprehension, it had come to pass. The camp's ten thousand or more Allied POWs – British, American, Canadian, Australian – were on the move.

'*Raus, raus! Raus, raus!*'

The cry rose up, again and again, echoing all around the north section, as hut after hut was emptied of occupants. The shouts were devoid of panic or emotion, containing instead just the deadly efficiency, the calm precision, Lou and his fellow captives had come to know so well during their years of incarceration.

'You ready?' Lou asked, to no one in particular, just in general.

A few men grunted an affirmation. They were too busy for lengthy replies, checking and rechecking their packs.

Lou's was already prepared, rolled and unrolled a hundred times in the preceding days, everything stowed in special pockets he had constructed from spare bits of fabric and stitched with a small sewing kit he had somehow managed to keep hidden throughout his years in captivity.

Stomach clenching in a confusing mix of fear and elation, Lou shouldered the pack and left the hut, at the same time as busily cramming his face with the food that he couldn't carry with him. The *Kriegsbrot* – war bread – was thick and heavy, clogging the mouth and throat, and there was only so much that anyone could eat in one go.

Lou threw the crusts to the floor, along with two full loaves. At a couple of pounds each, they would weigh him down. They joined a multitude of discarded items – powdered milk, tins of fish, potatoes, turnips, carrots – that were crushed into the snow as more and more feet trampled over them.

In the freezing cold and biting wind, Lou was chilled to the bone within minutes of being outside. He clenched his fists, then raised them to his mouth and blew on them. It had little effect. But stoicism had got him this far and now was no time to lose it. He did what every captured airman did in times of trouble: thought of his family at home, of his long-lost crew, of his country and of an end to this interminable war.

'If we were brave enough, we'd make a run for it.' Stubbs' dour, harsh voice, which made everything he said sound confrontational, cut across the snowy silence.

It was an Allied prisoner-of-war's duty to try to free himself, and indeed this very camp had been the scene of some of the most extraordinary escape attempts of the war. Lou wondered briefly if, as Stubbs had suggested, now was the time to try again, in the chaos of this evacuation, whether the guards in this dying hour of the war would continue to play ball, to obey their masters, to count and recount their prisoners, to ruthlessly track down and shoot anyone who tried to get away. And then he looked at the two goons, Dummkopf (stupid head) and his wingman Hässlicherkopf (ugly head), striding up and down the ranks, eyes narrowed against the ever-thickening blizzard, and he knew. Knew they would follow their orders to the last.

'You can try it if you want to,' he replied, curtly. 'If you want a bullet in your brain, that is.'

Stubbs snorted, but whether his disparagement was for Lou or for the guards, Lou had no idea. He shuffled into position in the ranks. There was nothing for it but to fall into line, for now at any rate.

Finally, the column began to move. As they passed the rows of prison huts that had been home since 1943, Lou saw for the first time the sheer size of the encampment. Saw also the uniformed men dousing the wooden structures in petrol, methodically and systematically coating every surface. At the perimeter fence, they halted once more. Lou turned and observed the moment when the match was struck and thrown. With an almighty whoosh, the flames shot straight towards the snow-laden sky, an intense roar of fire and smoke and heat oblit-

erating the camp, eating up everything that was familiar, that
had been his and his companions' normality for so long.

Inside the camp, the prisoners had done all they could to
alleviate the boredom: publishing newspapers, putting on
theatrical performances, studying for degrees, organising foot-
ball teams and leagues. But, despite this, life had been
monotonous in the extreme, filled with hunger and the depression born of inactivity. Lou had lived that life not only here but,
prior to that, in Italy after being shot down over Sicily in 1941.
When the Italians had capitulated, he and his fellow prisoners
had simply walked out from behind the prison's confining walls;
the guards had left the doors wide open, though the barbed wire
fence still had to be breached. That done, Lou had enjoyed five
glorious days and nights of freedom before being given away.
The Germans, desperate to round up all the escapees, offered
1,200 lira to anyone who provided information leading to an
arrest and this had been enough to convince a farmer, who
found Lou sleeping in his field, to hand him over.

Back in the hands of the Nazis, he'd been quickly trans-
ported to Sagan and here he'd stayed. To see the camp swept
away in a crazed fireball aroused a mixture of emotions that
Lou, after so long spent suppressing all feelings in order to
survive, could not put a name to.

He could not mourn the camp's departure, was not in the
least bit sorry to see it devoured by the ferocious fire. But
neither could he welcome what lay ahead.

Up until now, the *kriegies* – short for the German word for
prisoner of war, *Kriegsgefangenen* – had waged a relentless,
daily war of attrition, where small victories such as the building
of a contraband radio set, or the harbouring of handmade tools,
were often the highlight of the week. These tiny acts of rebel-
lion – duping the goons, giving them insulting nicknames –
were all the men had to sustain them through months or years of
imprisonment.

Now they were released from their cages and, though liberation in the form of the Russians was nearby, they were being pushed inexorably away from it.

Through the heightening blizzard, the column was moving, a slow but relentless lava flow of men, their black forms soon cloaked with white as the snow fell and the drifts beneath their thumping feet hardened to packed ice. Trees, signposts, landmarks, all were wiped out by the storm. In the whiteout, there was nothing but the man in front and the men beside to navigate by. The temperature was twenty below zero and they were walking into the unknown, into what seemed certain to be an abyss of cold and desolation and hunger.

A man just ahead stumbled and fell. Lou raised his bowed head and tried to make out who it was, but the driving snow quickly coated his lashes and obscured his vision.

'Come on, Jonesey,' he heard a voice exhort. 'You can't give in now. Think of your Bella. And your ma...'

Dimly, Lou was aware of the man being hauled to his feet and the voice fading as his part of the column, moving faster, left them behind. He looked, as far as was possible, at the men on either side of him. He'd spent so long locked up with these guys, who'd become both friends and surrogate family, with all their concomitant faults and virtues. They needed to look out for each other, as the stranger had done for Jones. Sure as hell, no one else would. Already they'd passed men who had collapsed by the side of the road, unable to carry on. They would die there, where they lay, as the column marched by, on and on.

The further they travelled, the more they saw that it was not just soldiers and POWs who were on the move. Their numbers were swelled by civilians, displaced people, retreating soldiers, who joined them in ever-increasing numbers, desperate to outrun the rapacious Red Army; those who the *kriegies* prayed for as saviours, these people feared more than anything. Lou could hardly bear to see how they struggled. Most were in an even worse physical condition than he and his fellow prisoners, who had had some protection at least from international conventions and the Red Cross. Ordinary people had had no such support for a long time now. They slunk along in the shadows, young boys supporting lame old men, weeping mothers clasping wailing babies to their chests, pitifully small girls carrying packs bigger than themselves, grandmothers struggling to keep up.

A child who could not have been more than five years old held out its arms towards Lou as he passed, imploring eyes gazing out from a starvation-shrunken face. Fumbling in his pockets, Lou pulled out a tin of sardines and handed it to the child, whether boy or girl it was impossible to tell. He regretted the food thrown away in the haste of leaving; it seemed obscene to have wasted it amidst so much need and want.

A scuffle broke out, drawing his attention away from the desperate little one. As the column, moving steadily on, neared the site of the altercation, a single shot rang out. A body fell to the ground. The guard responsible for the shooting kicked the corpse to the side of the road with barely a glance and continued.

'Fucking bastards,' hissed Bride, a young lad who was Lou's closest friend.

Lou opened his mouth to reply. Bride should be careful. If he was heard, it could be him in a ditch. But he didn't have the energy to speak. He was too cold to talk, to smile, to breathe. The snow was coming down so thickly it suffocated, closing up nose and ears and airways. They were drowning in snow; in the cruel blanket it threw upon them.

Time was impossible to tell accurately, but after about another hour or so, the column ground to a halt.

'*Zehn Minuten Pause,*' someone heard the goons shout.

'Ten-minute break,' came the words, rippling down the lines. 'Ten minutes... ten...'

'We've got to eat something,' breathed Dobson, through teeth clenched tight with cold. 'Or we'll collapse.' Dobson had been shot down in the thousand-bomber raid over Cologne in '42. Lou knew that what he had seen from the air that night, a city on fire, blazing like the depths of Hell, would never leave him. Yet he was always the calmest, the most stoic of all of them.

No one dared to sit down for fear of freezing to the spot and never getting up again. Standing, they ripped chunks off loaves of bread and stuffed them into their mouths, along with morsels of cheese and spam.

'It's fucking frozen,' Stubbs said reproachfully, flicking his head towards the tinned meat. 'Shouldn't eat it frozen.'

Lou, who could anyway hardly find the impetus to chew, let the spam fall from his wedge of bread. He didn't know if it was bad to eat it like that. But just in case. Bride scoffed his down. Lou tried to smoke, but the snow extinguished the match and, in any case, he couldn't hold his hand steady enough to light the tip. Clumsily, he stuffed the cigarette back into the box and shoved it deep into his pocket for later.

Assuming there was a later.

'Let's hope those bloody Ruskies get to us soon,' muttered Bride as they set off again, mustered by the guards armed with pistols and submachine guns and blockheaded determination to do what they perceived as their duty. 'We can't keep going like this for too long.'

The snow had abated, the temperature fallen even lower. Looking ahead to the column of men that stretched as far as the horizon and back into the smoky haze from the burning pyres, Lou knew that Bride was right. Nothing they had been through so far was going to be as brutal as what lay ahead.

'It's a death march,' he murmured. The rest of the sentence he did not articulate. *If we survive this, it will be a miracle.*

CHAPTER FOURTEEN

By the time night fell again, Lou and the other prisoners had been marching for more than twelve hours. When he could think at all, which wasn't often, Lou thought that it seemed as if the guards themselves had no idea where they were going. Just onwards, ahead of the Russians – that seemed both motivation and destination.

The opportunity to escape was there at all times, but no one took it. To run away was to commit suicide. In this cold, amidst the hostility of a broken and battle-weary population, no mercy would be shown to a stray Allied soldier. Though some settlements they passed through were friendly, at others they were stoned and spat at. Perhaps, when the war was actually over, things would change. But for now, there was safety of a sort in numbers.

Eventually on that first day, they reached a village with a church and a school and village hall in which the guards decided that they would stay for the night. The building was far too small for the number trying to seek shelter from the snow, which had begun to fall again. There was no room to lie down and stretch out, barely room to sit. But the guards kept pushing them in, packing the men one on top of the other.

Lou was no longer hungry, nor thirsty, just desperately, desperately tired. But as he tried to shut his eyes, slumped against a wall with two men across his legs, he became aware of Bride groaning and moaning.

Reaching out towards his friend, his hand made contact with his skin. It was burning hot, furnace hot, and slicked with sweat. In the half-light, Lou saw Bride's eyes were glazed with fever, his lips cracked and bleeding from the cold and dehydration.

'Shit, mate,' Lou said, unable to hide his alarm. 'We need to get you water.'

Standing up was almost impossible, moving could not be done without trampling on hands, fingers, legs, feet, toes. Cries of protest greeted Lou's stumbling half-crawl, half-walk towards the door. In the absence of a water tap, the only thing to do was to fill bottles with snow and wait for it to melt. Given that the temperature inside was barely higher than that outside, and only different at all due to the sheer number of bodies piled together, that was not a great solution. But it was all Lou had.

Slipping through the heavy wooden door, Lou was struck first by the cold, then the freshness of the air after the foetid interior. And then, rounding the corner of the building, another odour hit his nostrils: that of the makeshift toilet area, already yellowed with urine and blackened with faeces. Desperately searching around for cleaner snow, he scooped it up with frozen fingers before creeping back inside.

Reaching Bride after another curse-laden clamber over supine men, Lou lifted his friend's head and prepared to drop a clump of snow onto his lips.

'Open your mouth, kid,' he said, for Bride was so young, only nineteen years old, and Lou, at thirty-one, had always felt like a father figure to him.

Bride's lips parted infinitesimally. Gently, Lou dabbed snow upon them. As he held his friend's head steady, he saw Bride's expression contort with agony.

'Toilet,' gasped Bride, 'quick!'

At the same moment, a terrible smell emanated from him and it was obvious it was too late to get him outside, even if there had been any chance of lugging him across the packed and slumbering men to the toilet area.

Lou gagged at the stench and then again as Bride turned his face to the side and puked, feebly and weakly.

'It's all right, mate,' he coaxed, wiping the vomit from Bride's mouth with the man's own floppy arm and resuming with the dripping of the snow-water. Lou was no medic, but he knew that Bride needed hydrating. Dysentery, once it had taken hold, was a quick and ruthless killer.

As the night passed, it became obvious that Bride was far from the only one who was suffering. Half the prisoners in that benighted place were clutching at stomachs and mouths and nether regions as disease took over.

By the time morning came, Bride was semi-conscious.

'We'll have to leave him,' Stubbs said, his voice more gravelly and hoarse than ever.

'No.' Lou's reply was curt, his tone unequivocal. 'We never leave one of our own. The SS has already said they'll shoot anyone left behind.'

'It was the fucking spam,' continued Stubbs, bitterly. 'I said not to eat it frozen, but nobody listened.'

'Story of your life,' snapped Lou. 'Now shut up and get out of the way if you're not going to help.'

As the hall emptied out to the shouts and commands of the guards, Lou put one of Bride's arms over his shoulders and Dobson, another from the same squadron, took the other. Between them, they hauled Bride to his feet and manoeuvred him outside and into line. Looking around him, Lou thanked his lucky stars that he had not attempted to take his boots off. Those who had done so found the leather had frozen solid and it was not possible to force their feet back into them. They had to walk barefoot.

The column set off, limping, staggering, hobbling, joining the endless, infinite queues of people already on the road. All day, through furious snow and biting winds, Lou and Dobson dragged Bride between them, refusing to accept what seemed to be his inevitable fate. Men who fell and could not get up were pistol-whipped to their feet by the guards or the SS troopers accompanying them. If that failed, they were abandoned in the snow, not even deemed worthy of wasting a bullet on.

'Just leave me,' whispered Bride, at various stages in the journey, 'just leave me to die. It's all right, I don't mind. Tell my mother I love her...'

'Shut up,' hissed Lou, with uncharacteristic anger, disguising panic and despair with wrath, 'you're not going to die. And we're not going to leave you.'

'I don't mind,' repeated Bride. 'I don't mind.'

'It's nearly the end,' hissed Lou through gritted teeth. 'The war is almost over. Just a little bit longer, kid, that's all you've got to do. Just hang on for a little bit longer.'

Stubbs remained silent throughout. But he had taken all three men's loads onto his handmade sled, which he pulled indefatigably, though with an air of suppressed indignation, all day long.

As they trudged, they saw more of the chaplain, Padre Stewart, than of Dummkopf and Hässlicherkopf.

'Keeping a low profile,' Dobson asserted. 'They're starting to waver, to hedge their bets. They want to be remembered as the good guys,' he snorted to Lou through clenched teeth as they dragged Bride between them, 'to be on the right side of history.' And then, gasping with breath, he concluded, 'Some chance.'

They passed corpses, lots of them – dead guards, civilians

and fellow POWs – and German soldiers heading in both directions, towards the front as reinforcements or back from the front, wounded and bandaged, riding on horse-drawn carts because all motor vehicles were reserved for the fighting.

As dusk deepened on the second day of their march, a surreal sight loomed towards them out of the fog: a boy, fourteen or fifteen, in the blue winter uniform of the Hitler youth, marching over the compacted ice, a huge hunting rifle from the last century slung across his shoulders. Lou, blinking in disbelief, caught a glimpse of the boy's expression as he passed. It was one of manic purpose, of reckless pursuit of a lost cause.

The Russians were only sixty miles behind them now, pushing towards the River Oder, ready to cross as soon as they got there. The boy was heading to a certain death. Lou closed his eyes and thought of the young kids back home, in Camden Town, children of neighbours, friends, cousins, desperate to be old enough to join up.

'No,' he muttered to himself beneath his frozen breath. 'No, you do not want this.'

The chaplain came past yet again. He said a prayer and Dobson joined in with a loud 'amen'.

'The guards tell me we'll be stopping at the next village.' Padre Stewart's voice was still strong and forceful, even though his pulpit was now a rugged, wind-torn highway and his flock a ragtag bunch of half-dead men.

No one responded.

Whatever, thought Lou, the weight of Bride seeming to have quadrupled throughout the day.

When they finally entered the village and followed the column to a farmyard, Lou thought he was hallucinating. A miraculous vision greeted their disbelieving eyes: barns and stables, through the open doors of which Lou could see thick piles of straw and hay, and outside them black-clad German women presiding over tables laden with bread and water, while huge cauldrons of soups and stews bubbled and boiled over crackling fires.

'This can't be real,' breathed Dobson. 'It's a mirage, a bloody mirage.'

Stubbs' eyes, too, were wide with wonder.

'Let's get Bride inside,' instructed Lou, 'and then we can sort out what we can trade.'

Money was worthless and the men had none anyway. But the women wanted the soap, chocolate and cigarettes from their Red Cross parcels, and other POWs were already making successful exchanges.

Stubbs, always commercially minded, organised their supplies and negotiated good prices: a slab of soap in exchange for a mug of stew each, two chocolate bars for bread and ersatz coffee, cigarettes for unlimited hot water.

Once he had eaten, Lou turned to Bride, stretched out and comatose upon the straw. With infinite care, he undressed him, cleaned him with soap, water and rags, and dressed him again in whatever dry clothes they could muster up between them. Then he propped Bride up, getting Dobson and Stubbs to support him, and shook him until he woke.

'You have to drink. As much as you can. To clean out the infection and get you hydrated. Drink and drink and drink.'

'Can't drink,' mumbled Bride. 'Lungs ache, limbs ache.'

His fever was as high as ever. His skin burnt to the touch. 'You have to drink,' Lou insisted. 'I'm going to make you.'

Lou feared that Bride had pneumonia as well as dysentery. But he couldn't even think about that. There was nothing he could do, no medicine he could give, for a chest infection. At least for tonight they were warm, they had hot food and water and even a toilet of a sort, a pit latrine in an outhouse. They had each other and they had the knowledge that this could not go on forever.

It was the twenty-ninth of January 1945 and, on the smuggled and hidden radios that existed amongst the POWs, they heard that Sagan had fallen to the Russians. They were surely just a few days from freedom. Weren't they?

CHAPTER FIFTEEN

Dazed by what I had read, I sat back in my chair, trying to take it all in. The narrative was so vivid, the picture of the men's ordeal in that snow-covered landscape so visceral, so real, I found myself surprised, when I looked outside, to see only the dull but benign grey of an English spring day.

Turning back to the notebook, I flicked through the pages. The words it conveyed were clearly telling a true story, but one I had never heard before. How could my education about the war have completely missed out this cataclysmic event? More importantly, how had I never known what my own father had endured?

I shuddered, feeling cold all of a sudden, as if I had absorbed the chill of that winter-white world. Beyond the window, clouds lowered and rain threatened. The wind stirred up some dried leaves on the terrace, whirling them round and round in a wild devil's dance. I thought of those men, my father among them, cast out, walking onwards to nowhere. People talked glibly about fates worse than death, but this really did sound like that.

Getting up, I rolled my shoulders to relieve the tension, Springer regarding me with a confused mixture of alarm and anticipation. Had his owner gone mad or did this mean a walk? I bent over to pat his head, which set his tail frenziedly wagging. I should take him out, however uninviting the weather. As if he could read my mind, the dog snuffled his damp nose hopefully against my hands.

'Good dog,' I murmured, sitting back down again. 'Soon. We'll go out soon.'

But, fifteen minutes later, I remained motionless at my desk, gazing through the glass into the garden with unseeing eyes. Just as there was so much in my mother's past that I was completely ignorant of, so it transpired that there also was in my father's. His presence imbued the tale; I could feel him in every word and phrase, every piece of dialogue, each action he took. The sense of being near him was so intense that I could almost feel his rough, broad hand take mine as he led me to school, to the shops, to the park. Those hands of his symbolised to me how he had always been there to catch me when I fell, literally and metaphorically.

My mother had been so protective of him, never wanting me to bother him, always fussing that he was tired after work, he needed to be left alone, to eat, to go the pub, not to be disturbed. It had confused me, this loving father who my mother seemed to want to keep at arm's length from me. This was one reason why I had never told him about the bullying either, even though I was sure I would get a more sympathetic hearing from him than from my mother. I'd listened too hard to her remonstrations about not pestering him, about letting him be.

But, I realised now, my mother's precautions were under-standable in the light of what my father had been through. And

I also saw, with a sharp flash of clarity, that my father had always actively worked to find ways around the obstacles that my mother put up, never drawing attention to them, just eluding them, subtly and without fuss. Some of my best childhood memories, the good ones that sat alongside the terrible, were of going to work with him, in the holidays or at weekends, when my mother, needing a break, had allowed it, though always with remonstrations to me not to get in the way, to be good, to keep quiet.

I would give her fervent assurances and my father would say, 'She'll be fine, love, don't worry, she's my helper,' and off we'd go, our steps quickening and our moods lightening as we neared the big front door of the apartment block. As soon as we were out, the cloud of expectation would disperse, blown away by the excitement of the adventure, and by the time I had climbed into the front seat of his van, I'd have forgotten all about my mother's caveats and warnings.

'She just worries,' my father would explain, both of us knowing to what and to whom he was referring. 'She knows the work is tiring and she wants to protect me. And she doesn't want me to lose my job.'

'But why would you lose your job?' I'd asked once, suppressing the panic that suddenly gnawed at my stomach. 'You're good at it, aren't you?'

My father had shrugged and patted my knee and said, 'Of course! I'm the very best. But there are rival newspapers, and, in your mother's case, once a worrier, always a worrier, I suppose.'

And there the subject had been left and I had stowed it away along with all of the other things about my mother that I didn't quite understand.

The van would trundle off to Fleet Street to collect the newspapers, me watching as my father and the packers loaded up the great, heavy bundles of the *Standard* that were far too weighty for me to lift. I'd sit up front, feeling the thrill of excitement as my father sped through his round, dropping papers off at newsagents and sales stands – Tottenham Court Road, Warren Street, Euston and, the name I liked the best, High Holborn. I remembered being surrounded by a cacophony of sound, the roar of the traffic competing with the constant cry of the newspaper vendors: '*Standard*! Get yer *Standard*!' with the rise and elongation of the 'ard'.

My father's pocket knife was another source of deep fascination. It was specially designed for the job and bought from Mundy's cutler's shop at Elephant & Castle, with a hook at one end to grab the string that bound the bundles together and a razor-sharp blade at the other to cut it. He used it so fast that the metal became a flash of light, lifting, snipping, dividing, distributing.

Each new edition – and there were six a day – that came off the printing presses had to be collected and delivered, with increasing speed as the height of the rush hour approached, when almost everyone entering the tube stations or waiting for a bus would buy a copy.

The hectic pace meant that my father barely stopped the van for long enough for his assistant, known as his boy, to throw the bundles at the sellers. Everything about the newspaper business, then as now, demanded speed, a constant rush of adrenaline, the wit and intelligence necessary to always be one step ahead of the competition. I could see, looking back on it now, that it was no wonder my father got tired – and that my mother had tried to shelter him from domestic concerns of any kind.

Did that make it right for her to put barriers between father and daughter? Probably not. But perhaps, given her own experiences of loss that she had divulged to me so recently, it was understandable. If this current voyage of discovery, learning about my parents' pasts, was about anything, it must be about laying those old shadowy resentments to one side, and seeking acceptance – of my mother, of my father, and most importantly, of myself.

I couldn't wait to find out more – from my father's diary, but first of all from my mother. What had happened after that first, terrifying, brush with the Gestapo? Over the next few days, she was able to tell me more.

CHAPTER SIXTEEN

MEINDORF, 1945

When she returned from church that fateful day of Laura's absence, Katja was greeted by Gerta exclaiming her belief in Hitler's *Wunderwaffen*, the secret weapon that rumour and speculation maintained he was about to unleash to finish off the Allies and ensure a glorious victory. Katja humoured her, agreeing that such a weapon definitely existed but clever Hitler was waiting for the right moment to launch it. Of course she didn't believe a word of it.

The day dragged on as she waited for Monday and her return to the convalescent home. What if it was all a trap? What if Karl had set her up, given her the letters just to expose her as a traitor, too?

But no, Katja could not believe that was the case. She knew Karl too well by now.

And then a terrible thought gripped her. What if Karl didn't know about Laura? In fact, the more she came to think about it, how could he possibly know? Oh God, was it down to Katja to tell him? She must find the words, and the courage.

As soon as she arrived at the home, she sought Karl out. Fortunately, he was alone in the dining room, reading the newspaper, looking calm and collected as usual. Katja bustled around him, gathering up the unused cutlery and crockery.

'How was your breakfast, Herr Hausmann?' she asked breezily. And then, more quietly and masked by her crashing of the cutlery, 'Laura was not at church. I saw her – taken.' The words rushed out of her, so quickly as to be almost incomprehensible.

Karl took a sip of his coffee, which must by now be cold. There was no trace of emotion in his face or his voice. Katja couldn't work out whether he already knew or not, or what he felt about it.

'There's an old man who sits on the bench by the train station,' Karl murmured, keeping his voice low. 'He wears a flat cap and always has his dog with him.'

There was such a complete absence of surprise in his voice that Katja immediately deduced that he had known. How, she had no idea.

She nodded as she loaded a heap of saucers onto a tray. Karl slipped another letter under one of the tray's edges.

'Take the letter you already have and this one. It must be done today – 5 p.m., when the dusk will cover you. Take the child – the old man will chat to him as you hand over the letters.'

Out of the corner of her eye, Katja saw another member of staff, a middle-aged woman called Helga, enter the room. Karl had his back to her and didn't know she was there.

'It's so lovely outside, Herr Hausmann,' enthused Katja, loud enough for Helga to hear. She gesticulated to the bright sunshine that masked the still brutal cold. 'If you would like a turn in the gardens later, I'll be happy to accompany you.'

Karl nodded, instantly taking the cue. 'That would be most pleasant,' he said. 'Thank you.'

Helga's appearance meant that Katja couldn't pick the letter up now. Instead, she pretended to go about her normal duties. She went to another table where the chairs had been left awry and tucked them neatly in, covertly watching as Helga walked over to Karl's table. The corner of the letter, sticking out from under the tray, seemed the size of an elephant. There was no way Helga wouldn't spot it. Cursing inwardly to herself, at that moment more angry than fearful, Katja stood motionless, no idea what to do.

Helga said something to Karl that Katja didn't catch and Karl smiled and laughed. Helga blushed, as if delighted by Karl's reaction. *Please God, she's so blinded by her obvious adoration that she doesn't look down at the tray*, thought Katja. But she wasn't going to be that lucky. In a flurry of righteous efficiency, Helga seized up the tray, exclaiming loudly that she was sorry Katja had left so much mess...

Jealousy seared through Katja as Helga practically genuflected in front of Karl. Everyone knew that Katja was Karl's favourite, had been almost since the day of his arrival, and lots of the other women who worked at the home wished that they were the chosen one, Katja was sure.

And then time seemed to stand still.

'What's this?' questioned Helga, wedging the tray against her ample bosom so that she could support its weight with one hand, leaving the other free to seize the letter. 'Does it need to go to the post? Let me take it for you.' Only then did she falter, as she peered long-sightedly at the envelope. 'But there's no address? Shall I write it for you, Herr Hausmann? I can fetch a pen...'

Katja's heart was in her mouth. She pretended to straighten tablecloths and pick up discarded napkins as she waited to see what Karl would do.

She need not have worried. Of course he was in complete control of the situation.

'Ah no, Frau Müller,' he said, with a smile of complicity. 'It's... well, it's rather private.' He winked at Helga, long and slow.

Katja, whose emotions were swinging wildly back and forth, almost let out a giggle at his audacity. The implication that it was a love letter – the very thing she had initially feared – was the perfect foil.

Helga dropped the letter back onto the table like it was on fire as her gaze swivelled wildly between Karl and Katja.

'Er, well, good day Herr Hausmann, I must be off... get this little lot to the kitchen for washing.' Helga brandished the tray before turning and fleeing as fast as her short little legs could carry her.

Katja had a desperate, hysterical desire to laugh, the relief of tension was so great. But Karl maintained his focus.

'Take it,' he hissed under his breath, lest Helga should return. 'Remember. If you are caught, deny everything. Plead ignorance. Say you were blinded by love.'

A stray knife Katja had collected up fell out of her hand and clattered to the ground with a noise as loud as an explosion. She stared at Karl's face, so handsome but in that moment impassive, as if nothing he was saying meant anything to him.

But I am blinded by love, she thought. *I don't have to lie because it's true.*

She fussed around with a pile of napkins, folding and refolding them. She wanted to say something to Karl, to tell him she knew what he was doing and supported it. But then he'd know she'd opened the letter, which she shouldn't have done.

'Katja,' said Karl, softly.

Immediately, her hands fell still, an unfolded napkin dangling from them.

'Thank you,' he continued. 'For what you are doing.' His tone was unusually solemn. Katja felt the weight of all the secrecy, and the risks, contained within his words. Karl reached out, put his hand to her face, tilted her chin towards him. 'You have earned my everlasting admiration, and my love.'

Katja's heart lurched and her stomach flip-flopped backwards and forwards. How long had she yearned for Karl to use that word. Love. She opened her mouth to respond, but then, with a clatter of crockery and torrent of mindless chatter, Helga was back and the moment had gone.

No matter how she tried, Katja didn't have another opportunity to be alone with Karl that day. In the afternoon, when her shift was over, she returned to Meindorf and collected Hans, as instructed, before setting off back to the station to find the bench. Hans had only begun to walk a couple of months previously and was still a little unsteady on his feet, stumbling forth on chubby, ungainly legs, arms flailing, a smile plastered across his face no matter how many times he fell. But even though it often took longer, Katja liked him to have some exercise everyday; when he was cooped up inside, he was always harder to settle at night. So she decided to let him walk, and leave extra time to get there.

Reaching the rendezvous point twenty minutes later, bang on schedule, Katja stood and stared at the bench. It was empty. There was absolutely no one there. She glanced awkwardly around, not sure what to do now, acutely aware of the letters – not one, but two – in her pocket, of the jeopardy that surrounded what she was doing. The air was thick with tension, as if her fear and trepidation were tangible, palpable. Hans was pulling at her grip, trying to break free, making Katja unable to think straight.

'Stop it, Hans,' she snapped. 'Stand still.'

Should she wait? Leave and come back later? Give up? So many questions that Katja did not know the answer to.

When the hand descended on her shoulder, heavy and

deadening, her heart lurched almost out of her chest and she screamed involuntarily. Paralysed by terror, Katja closed her eyes and concentrated on staying upright. Her arms were trembling uncontrollably and she tried to still them by clenching her fists, which had the result of making Hans cry as she was holding him so tightly.

Eventually, she managed to open her eyes. The sight that greeted her was the worst it could be. Three men, identically dressed in grey uniforms, faced her, glaring at her with stony cold stares. Their peaked caps bore the ubiquitous *Reichsadler*, or Imperial Eagle, and on their lower left sleeves were diamond patches with the insignia 'SD'. These men were not Gestapo officers but something potentially even worse – agents of the *Sicherheitsdienst*, the Nazi's security force.

In an instant, Katja's legs turned to jelly and collapsed beneath her.

As she fell, some survival instinct kicked in. She managed to turn the fall into a crouch. Kneeling next to Hans, one hand on the ground supporting her, she reached out to her son and rubbed her thumb across his face.

'Poor poppet, did you get dust in your eye. Here, let Mummy make it better.'

After a few moments, she had succeeded in transforming the stricken expression on her face to one of careful blankness.

She stood back up and smiled queasily at the officers. 'It's so windy today, you know,' she explained, her voice calm and even. 'The grit gets everywhere.'

She waited, her heart pounding against her ribs.

But almost as soon as she'd finished speaking, she knew she had failed. Her display of faux innocence hadn't convinced herself, so it was hardly likely that the officers would fall for it. Paralysed with fear, she waited for what would happen next. She was guilty, the letters proved it so. There was no way she would be able to get out of this one.

Another terrifying thought gripped her. If they took her away, what would happen to Hans?

One of the officers smiled at her, a steely smile that was completely absent of warmth. He said nothing. Katja's bowels slithered and slid and she had an urgent need for the toilet.

'*Mama, Katze!*' Hans' reedy voice broke the terrible silence.

Distracted, Katja's eyes followed where Hans was pointing. A skinny tabby cat slunk along in the shadow of the station building, prowling for prey. Katja was unable to suppress the shudder that ran through her. The hunter and the hunted. How apt.

She looked back at the smiling officer who had stepped forward from the other two. As she watched, he reached down to his side. Katja's breath caught in her throat. His gun. He was reaching for his gun.

'*Miauen, miauen,*' shouted Hans, once more shattering the tension.

Unable to utter a word, Katja gazed helplessly at the child. She couldn't look at the gun. *This man is going to shoot me here in front of my son*, she thought.

She couldn't think what to do, couldn't form a plan.

There was no plan.

The officer's hand was stretching out now. Any moment, when the trigger was pulled and the bullet released, she was going to feel an explosion of cold, hard metal in her head... and that would be it.

The hand reached further.

But not to her. To Hans. And not with a gun.

Instead, the officer dropped a sweet into Hans' open palm. Katja watched in amazement as Hans popped the piece of candy straight into his mouth and began sucking it, a broad grin on his face.

The officer clicked his heels and then turned, gesturing to the others to follow him. Everything seemed to be happening in slow motion. The time it took for the men, striding in step with each other, to reach the corner of the square and disappear out of view, was something between forever and eternity.

And then, suddenly, they had gone.

'Mama, Mama,' Hans cried, tugging at her hand and reaching out, wanting more sweets.

Katja was hyperventilating, dizzy and light-headed, struggling to take in oxygen. Ignoring Hans' pleas, she sank down onto the bench, letting her head drop between her knees until gradually the panic subsided. Why had Karl told her to take Hans? Had he known that the boy's disarming charm and childish innocence would win over hardened and brutal SD personnel? But Karl surely hadn't known that the old man would not be there but the security forces would. He had not intended her to get caught, Katja was sure about that. Beyond that, though, she really didn't understand any of it.

Eventually, when she had begun to shiver violently from the deepening chill, Katja managed to muster the strength to tackle the walk home. As she rounded the corner and came in sight of the house, something caught her eye. It was Monika, hanging out laundry on the line, though it was hardly good drying weather.

Katja hurried on, not wanting to get into a conversation. She'd seen a lot more of Monika recently. Ever since Laura's disappearance, in fact. The woman always seemed to be around, popping up wherever Katja went, in the town, on the track to the mountain, in the garden. It was almost as if she was watching Katja. At this thought, Katja's heart leapt into her throat and she tripped on the stony path.

Perhaps Monika was doing precisely that. Watching her. Monitoring her movements. Oh God, could she really be a spy? Katja had dismissed that idea when it had first come to her, but now she was not so sure. And even if not a spy, she could be informing on Katja to her husband, to any of the many police and security officers the Nazi state had spawned.

Katja was so anxious, she could not eat that evening. She and Hans had had a lucky escape – but how long would it be before their luck ran out?

The letters were an accusation, burning a hole in her pocket. As soon as Hans and Gerta had gone to bed and Katja was left alone in the kitchen, she acted.

Snatching the envelopes out of her pocket, she ripped them open, her eyes rapidly scanning the contents. Forcing herself to calm down, to concentrate, she studied each letter in detail, reading each word and number, repeating them under her breath, then covering each small section and reciting it back, seeing if she could remember correctly.

She took one of Hans' crayons and copied out the maps onto scraps of paper, again and again, until she was sure she knew them by heart. She had to keep reminding herself that nobody could see her in here, with the window shuttered and the door locked. No one could look through the walls, not even Monika.

It was late at night by the time she was finally sure that she had memorised everything. Then, taking a deep breath, Katja ripped the letters and her practice papers into tiny pieces, opened the door of the *Kachelöfen* and threw them inside. Grabbing the poker, she smashed the flakes into the glowing heart of the fire, where they quickly flared up and then turned to ash. A huge sense of relief washed over her when the flames had eaten up the letters' last vestiges. She'd tell Karl what she'd done, explain that keeping the letters indefinitely with no one to pass them on to felt foolishly risky. Assure him she could rewrite everything if need be. She was sure he'd understand.

Wearily, Katja hauled herself up from the hearth and went to the sink, where she washed her hands, again and again, trying to rub away the stain of the letters' ink, scrubbing at them until the skin was raw and bleeding, as if only this way would she cleanse them of the stain of treachery. Whatever Katja thought, or Karl, the Allies were Germany's enemy. And collaboration with them made Katja a traitor, in her own country's eyes.

That night, Katja hardly slept. In her wakefulness, she waited for the knock on the door that did not come. But just because it hadn't happened yet didn't mean it never would. From now on, Katja would have to be forever on her guard.

CHAPTER SEVENTEEN

LONDON, JUNE 1994

At the culmination of this latest instalment of her story, I looked at my mother, lying in the bed, so small and frail. Though the operation had taken a physical toll on her, I could still see and sense the indomitable spirit that had enabled her to embrace the task Karl Hausmann had given her, despite the danger, despite her fear.

Now, though, she needed to rest. And I had work to do. Alongside my quest to understand the war years, the other mission I had to fulfil was saving my house. This could not be ignored, however compelling my parents' stories.

I'd already decided to increase my hours at work to full time, and to speak to the bank about how much I could borrow, rather than just taking Ed's word for it. And if I couldn't afford to buy him out straightaway, I'd offer to pay him the extra in instalments over a period of time. It had to be worth a try. No more ostrich-Jo – taking inspiration from my mother, from now on I would be Jo with my head held high and my eyes wide open.

With that thought making the blood pulse in my veins, I seized Springer's lead, ready to set off for the Heath. A cold blast of air, together with the familiar figure of my best friend Sue, greeted me as I opened the front door.

'Sue!' I called out. 'I didn't know you were coming.'

Sue stepped forward and we hugged. 'I should have called before I left,' she said, 'but I didn't want the phone ringing to disturb Katja.' She held out a cake tin. 'I brought this for the two of you. It's nothing fancy, just a Victoria sponge, but good invalid food.'

'Well, you should know what's best for patients,' I smiled, delightedly. 'How many do you think you treated in your career?'

Sue had joined the nursing profession fresh from school and worked for three and a half decades, thus earning her the right to retirement at fifty-five – a fact about which I was openly envious. But, on the other hand, I knew that I'd be a useless nurse. I was far too squeamish, hating the sight of blood, so I couldn't really complain.

'Thousands, my friend, thousands,' Sue responded.

I took the proffered tin and stowed it in a corner of the porch. 'The hound and I are just off on a walk. I'll leave it here until I get back. Thank you so much.'

'No problem. It's my pleasure,' rejoined Sue. 'But – well, my gift does come with strings attached.'

I rolled my eyes exaggeratedly. 'Oh right. And those are?'

'Can I swap it for some of your tomato plants?' Sue asked. 'I'm determined to crack this green-fingered thing, or at least to give it one more chance before I finally give in. At least these days I can't say I don't have time to water them – and I might be more successful with outdoor plants than I am with indoor ones.'

I laughed. Sue's ability to care for people was not matched

by a similar skill with the natural world; her capacity to kill houseplants stone dead was legendary.

'Of course you can,' I said, at the same time as shushing Springer, who had begun to whine in his desperation to get going.

'I'd come with you to the Heath, but I can't be too long,' Sue explained, as she followed me along the side path to the greenhouse. 'I've got my piano lesson in twenty minutes, I'm going to have to fly home.'

Already carefully selecting the seedlings, I shook my head. 'You're exhausting me with all your activities. I thought retirement was a time to slow down!'

'Good grief, no!' Sue cried in horror. 'I'm packing in all the things I haven't had time to do during thirty-five years of motherhood and working full time.'

Sue didn't mention the other reasons she had for living her life on six cylinders. She had no need to, as I knew them all – knew about her abusive, aggressive husband who she'd left when his violent behaviour started to spill over to the children as well as to her. Knew about her battle with breast cancer, from which she had only recently emerged after being given the five-year all-clear.

'I admire you,' I responded, as I gently pressed potting compost around the base of a stem. 'And you deserve to do exactly what you want when you want for a change.' I could not prevent the heavy sigh that followed this statement.

'What's up?' asked Sue. 'You seem a bit down. Has something happened?'

I trickled some water over the pots I'd prepared so far. 'Nothing's wrong. Well, who am I kidding? Everything's wrong, actually.'

As I relayed Ed's demands to Sue, I observed how her face fell.

'The thing is,' I explained, 'I'm not even sure that going full time will be enough to allow me to live somewhere even halfway decent.'

'Oh!' Sue's habitual cheerful smile had been replaced by a sorrowful frown. 'That's such a shame. I'm sure the worst won't come to the worst with the house. You'll find a way to stay, I'm convinced of it. But I was hoping – well, I thought that maybe, once you were freed from the shackles that bound you to Ed, you'd be able to give up work and become a full-time gardener.'

A tender shoot snapped in my fingers. 'Blast!' I threw the damaged seedling to the ground. 'Oh, Sue. Don't even mention it. That's been my secret dream for so long, but it's well and truly dead in the water now. So let's forget it or I'll become maudlin and you know I'm no fun when I'm like that.' I uttered a somewhat forced laugh.

Sue's brow was creased with worry on my behalf. 'Maybe now's not the right time,' she began, haltingly, 'but, as you know, I'm always singing your horticultural praises and trying to drum up clients for you.'

This was true. Sue was about the most well-connected person I'd ever met – it often seemed that she knew literally everyone in north London. She'd certainly nursed half of them. I'd redesigned gardens for several of her friends and acquaintances, hardly charging anything but doing it for the experience.

'And,' Sue continued, 'I have this friend, Melissa, from the cancer survivors group – she's got a massive garden in Muswell Hill that backs onto the park and she wants to give it a complete overhaul. She'd love you to do it – but on one condition only.'

I hadn't been expecting this and it was so sweet of Sue to be thinking of me, as always. But I couldn't take on another no-fee project right now. I had too much going on, with Katja's recuperation, the house sale, Emma's wedding, going full time... I was about to say as much when Sue reached her conclusion.

'The condition is – ta-da! She insists on paying the full market rate. And I'll let you into a secret. She and her husband are filthy rich, with money to burn. So, on no account are you going to turn them down, and on no account are you going to undercharge or put in an invoice for anything less than a top Chelsea garden designer would!'

At this I had to laugh. 'Oh Sue,' I chuckled, 'I know you have my best interests at heart, but I'm no full-on garden designer, let alone a Chelsea one.'

Sue glared at me with faux annoyance. 'Jo,' she said, drawing out my name as far as one syllable could possibly go, 'you need to talk yourself up, not down, for once. I've said you'll do it and I've named your price. Only because I knew you wouldn't.'

Sue then told me what she'd quoted on my behalf and I nearly keeled over on top of the seedlings.

'What! I can't possibly—'

'Stop.' Sue cut me off in my prime. 'No such word as "can't", Jo.' And with that, the conversation was over and I knew I was defeated. And secretly, I was thrilled. Sue was no fool, and though she herself was hopeless with plants, she would never tell me I was good if it weren't true.

I smiled a smile of resignation mingled with gratitude. 'Thank you.' I picked up the tray I'd prepared and thrust it into her hands. 'Now – here are a dozen of the healthiest tomato specimens on the planet. Even you might find these hard to kill off.' I grinned at my best friend and felt in that moment so lucky to have her.

'Thanks, Jo,' she responded. She turned to go, but then halted and turned back round to face me. 'Melissa is just the start. Don't give up on your dreams,' she urged, softly. 'Promise me you'll never, ever do that.'

I shook my head and squeezed past her to open the door and let us both out of the greenhouse, where the warmth, usually so welcome, felt suddenly stifling. Locking up behind us gave me a few moments to compose myself. I didn't want Sue to see me so emotional and, anyway, I felt I had no right to be. Lots of people had it far worse than me and I just needed to knuckle down and get on with it. She had given me a wonderful opportunity and I would make the most of it.

We chatted about this and that as I walked Sue round to the front of the house. 'Keep your chin up,' she urged, as she hugged me goodbye. 'It'll be OK. We'll make it OK.' She set off towards the gate and, as she unlatched it, called back to me, 'And don't forget about the life drawing! The classes start on Thursday.'

I raised my fist in mock threat as Sue left. The bloody life drawing. She'd insisted I sign up with her, however reluctantly, and she was right, I had almost forgotten about it, probably because it was the last thing I wanted to do.

As she disappeared from sight, I bent down and, with a sharp tug, pulled out a weed that was daring to show its head in my herbaceous border. Sue was so infectious in her enthusiasm for taking on new challenges and I knew it was good for me to be shaken out of my comfort zone of isolation and retrospection. The Chelsea gardener nonsense was one thing – but life drawing was going from the sublime to the ridiculous. I didn't have an artistic bone in my body; I'd be hopeless at it.

I'd almost resolved to phone her and tell her I wasn't going to go after all, when I checked myself. Sue never let lack of innate talent put her off anything. She'd never played a note on a musical instrument in her life but was already now on Grade 4 piano. I would take a leaf out of her book and swathe myself in some of her can-do attitude.

That decided, I put life improvement skills out of my mind and looked around for Springer, eventually spotting him curled up beneath the medlar tree.

'Come, boy!' I called. 'Let's go.'

Normally, I spent my walks absorbing the ever-changing scenery of the Heath, noting which trees were coming into leaf, which wildflowers blooming beneath hedgerows and shrubs, but today my mind was elsewhere. With my father on that terrible march, and with my mother who had unwittingly found herself an accomplice to espionage. God, it was true when old people said that the young don't know they're born. Whatever any of my generation had been through, it was nothing compared to our parents.

By the time I headed for home, the sun was beginning to set and a gust of chill wind made me draw my jacket more tightly around me. I thought of my father and mother, struggling to stay alive in the frozen wastes of a country ravaged by war.

CHAPTER EIGHTEEN

POLAND, 1945

The sky was still dark, the sun not yet risen, the sinking moon and stars obscured. But not, this time, by snow clouds. By planes. German planes. Hundreds of them: fighters, bombers, transport aircraft, all shapes and sizes, but all with one thing in common. They were flying west.

'They're evacuating the airfields,' pronounced Lou. 'It can't be long now.'

But his words fell into silence. The rumour mill was in full swing and word was spreading that the POWs were being taken to Berlin, to be scattered over the city so that Allied HQ would know that bombing would bring certain death to thousands of brothers in arms. As the men limped across a frozen continent, the war was also limping to a close, but no one underestimated the passion and determination of the Nazis to fight to the bitter end.

On the thirty-first of January, Dobson brought news from one of the POW's covert radios. The Germans had announced that the march westwards had been undertaken at the POWs' own request. That the *kriegies* themselves had insisted on not sticking around to wait for the Russians. Therefore, if they died, it was their own fault, their own fear of the Soviets that had caused their deaths. It was propaganda of the highest order, but the men had no way to defend themselves, to counter the lies with the truth.

A clatter of iron wheels on cobbles disturbed the pensive, tense mood. A dozen horse-drawn wagons had pulled up outside the church they'd slept in that night – not that anyone had managed more than a couple of hours' kip – and Red Cross parcels were being tossed down, distributed by the guards, one between four men. Stubbs leapt up to lay claim to that owed to him, Lou, Bride and Dobson.

Even Bride smiled weakly when Stubbs returned triumphant from the melee, brandishing the parcel as if it were the holy grail. He had survived another night, his fever had abated somewhat and, as the light broke through the dull grey clouds shrouding the horizon, Lou thought he was looking a bit better. He couldn't work out how that could be when the care he had received was so rudimentary, but he wasn't going to argue.

Stubbs ripped open the box and they immediately ate the heaviest foodstuffs, saving the cigarettes, soap and chocolate for bartering, dividing them up between them for carrying. And then they were being called to fall into line, and somehow they managed to get Bride up and lug him with them, Stubbs taking Dobson's place while Dobson pulled the sled.

'Just a little longer,' urged Lou, as the march began anew. 'Not too far.'

Bride still stank, despite Lou's attempts to clean him. He'd soiled himself again in the night and they'd had nothing to clean him with, no fresh clothes to put on him. Lou felt his own bowels slipping and sliding. He clenched and held on, but suddenly it was urgent. Hurling Bride's arm around Dobson's shoulders, he fled to the verge, tore down his trousers and felt his insides fall out. He ran his hand across his forehead and it was hot, and clammy.

'Shit,' he thought, literally. 'You cannot be ill,' he snarled out loud at himself. 'You just cannot.'

But as the day's march continued, his toilet stops became more and more frequent, his stamina depleting with each outpouring of his bowels. He did not know how he could keep going, only that he must, that he had not endured over four years of captivity just to keel over in the moments before the release that seemed imminent.

He began to hallucinate, to see monsters and ghouls appearing and disappearing from the pines and linden trees that intermittently lined the road, to mistake the snow for sunshine and to feel the scald of the ice as sunburn.

'I'll have a tan to go home with,' he mumbled, as the cold grazed his skin, and then he laughed at the thought of turning up at the old tenement building in Bayham Street, Camden Town, brown and sleek from his time on the continent.

In his waking dreams, he recalled something that had happened in the brief days of freedom after he and his fellow captives had been let out of the Italian prison camp. Once through the open doors, they'd broken holes in the barbed wire fencing and escaped into the warmth of an idyllic autumnal morning. Lou had walked by night and hid by day, and in the afternoon of the second day, starving and thirsty, he'd been discovered in a shepherd's hut by a girl looking for an escaped goat.

Communicating as best they could given the limitations on their linguistic abilities, the girl, whose name was Eva, had told him that there were Germans everywhere, looking for the escapees, determined to find them. This had made sense. An airman was the most valuable prisoner of all; only if he was firmly behind bars could he be guaranteed to wreak no more havoc on his enemy.

Eva had brought him food and water, leading her goats to and from their pasture on a variety of different tracks to avoid arousing suspicion by always taking the same route. In war, time compresses and expands in unlikely and unexpected ways. Relationships can be forged in fractions of seconds and friendships turn to more in the blink of an eye. Because of this, and because he was a twenty-seven-year old man who'd been deprived of human comfort for two years already, and because she was so beautiful, with sun-kissed skin and shining hair, and so kind, and smelt of rosemary and eucalyptus and green olive soap, and because her hands were so gentle as they carefully and delicately cleaned and dressed the wounds he'd received from the barbed wire, they had made love, not just once but many times.

Lou had meticulously archived this memory, preserving everything about it in multiple layers, stacking all of the colours and scents and emotions into separate compartments and then cross-referencing them, doing whatever he could to make sure that he never, ever forgot a single precious moment of it.

He had recalled it while he was being psychologically tortured by the SS patrol who picked him up after he'd been betrayed and held him in a requisitioned baronial castle, refusing him food and taunting him by eating huge meals in front of him. The Germans had desperately tried to get him to reveal everything about his mission, the rest of the squadron's mission, the British and Allied armies' mission – but Lou never gave them anything. Nothing except his name, number and rank. Perhaps this sounded more virtuous, more courageous, than it really was. The fact was that he couldn't tell them anything else because he didn't know anything; he'd been locked up and out of action for years already.

In the end, realising this, his offended and disappointed

tormentors had sent him disgustedly to the camp in Poland to fester the rest of the war away. And every now and again, when things were particularly bad, when he felt especially low or dispirited or demoralised, he'd get his memories of Eva out of their special repository and let them drift across his mind's eye, filtered by the sepia tint of nostalgia and longing. With Eva, the bitter cold of the Silesian winter was banished, the harsh treatment of the guards overcome, the deprivation made bearable.

The men marched on.

They reached a small industrial town and were housed in an old factory, where, again, it was possible to trade with the local women. Now Dobson and Stubbs were taking care of both Lou and Bride. In his delirium, Lou managed to feel pleased that Stubbs had not been right about the dysentery being caused by eating frozen spam. It didn't matter, of course. But it meant Stubbs couldn't say 'I told you so' as Lou hadn't touched it.

Hours, weeks and days merged into one. At some point, they were moved on again.

As they marched, more rumours spread. The SS and the Gestapo did not believe in the Geneva Convention. The POWs were to be executed. As if to greet this news, the skies were once more heavy with planes. A massive all-out attack on the Western Front, with the entire Allied air force supporting ground troops, would surely bring this war to its climax. A stray fighter flew low over their column, strafing them with small arms fire.

'They don't know who we are!' Stubbs' voice was a squeal of fear and anguish. 'They think we're Germans!'

Lou, for whom every step was a superhuman effort, could not even be bothered to look up.

At the railway station, they were loaded into filthy cattle trucks strewn with dung and mud. So many men were piled into each carriage that there was room to neither sit nor lie.

Once the doors were shut and locked, there were only the faintest glimmers of light, the smallest chinks through which air could filter. Someone organised boxes and empty food tins for use as toilets – a good idea but useless as it was impossible for anyone in the middle of the carriage to get to them.

It was freezing cold. Nearly all had diarrhoea, many were vomiting; shit and puke and blood covered everything. There was no water, and the men's lips, throats and tongues were dry and swollen, their muscles cramping as dehydration set in. Lou, feverish, guts twisted and wrenched in pain, knew that this was hell and that there was no end to it, there never would be an end, and not even thoughts of Eva could save him now.

The cattle cars lurched on, their motion slow and jerking, picking up speed one minute just to judder to a halt the next. Sometimes they remained inexplicably stationary for hours. At one point, the doors were opened and prisoners spewed out of the carriage, dazed by the twin onslaughts of fresh air and bright light, determined to find water. Dummkopf turned and cocked his rifle, aiming it at the men, all of whom were unarmed and defenceless.

'Use that gun and don't expect to be saved when the time comes,' challenged Dobson, his voice steady and even. Lou, in his delirium, marvelled at Dobson's unwavering insouciance, his constant calm unflappability. 'We'll tear you limb from limb the minute we get a chance,' he continued. 'You should be thinking of your future now – if you believe you've still got one.'

A flicker of something passed across Dummkopf's face. Lou could hardly read the look. Was it apology? No. Lou realised what it was.

Shame.

Shame makes us see ourselves how others see us, to look in a mirror and contemplate what stares back. The guards were finally facing up to their own reflections – and realising there was a problem with what they saw.

Dobson and Stubbs filled their bottles with water and brought them back to Lou and Bride. The doors were closed and the train lurched on.

In the distance, they heard the bombs falling, and beneath them the ground shuddered. The noise grew louder and louder. So it was true. They were heading for Berlin, and Berlin was being pulverised.

Hitler's last dance would waltz them all to their deaths and Lou didn't have the energy to care.

CHAPTER NINETEEN

Shame.

There it was again, in my father's story as well as my mother's.

When it came to war, fear was inevitable. Anger, likewise. Sadness, loss, misery and countless other emotions doubtless all reared their ugly heads. But here was the evidence that feelings of shame pervaded, providing the backdrop for all others. The *kriegies'* shame stemmed from the humiliations and depredations they had suffered. The shame of so many Germans came from their willing support of an evil, deranged leader and a regime that was rotten to its core. This shame was easy to understand.

The root of Katja's shame was a mystery still to be uncovered.

I pondered on this as I prepared a Moroccan-style tagine with lamb, chickpeas and couscous – an exotic new grain that was the latest culinary trend. The recipe in the Sunday supplement I'd saved from the weekend promised the flavour of North Africa. I just hoped it would taste good enough to rid my mouth of the bitter tang of rejection.

I'd plucked up the courage and spoken to the bank and, of course, Ed had been right. The very most I could borrow as a sole mortgagee was fifty thousand pounds. Now I had to not only deal with that fact, but also with how I was going to broach it to Ed. I could still try my original plan of paying him the rest in instalments, but would he accept that?

Who was I trying to kid? He almost certainly wouldn't.

The only scant consolation I had was my belief that it might take a while to sell the house. I loved it, of course, but the furniture, most of which we'd inherited from the previous owner, was deeply unfashionable G-plan. At the time, newly married and expecting a baby, we had been delighted to be spared the cost of furnishing every room from scratch. But these days, people wanted en-suite bathrooms and Poggenpohl kitchens, and every room co-ordinated with trendy furniture from Habitat. That's what all the property pages in the Sunday supplements would have you believe, anyway.

I jumped as the shrill, strident ringing of the telephone rent the silence. Not Ed, I thought wearily, calling to drop another bombshell. I put down the kitchen knife and hurriedly wiped onion juice from my hands, then went to the hall to answer the phone. Thankfully, it was not Ed but Emma, a far more welcome caller.

'Hello, darling!' I greeted my daughter with genuine enthusiasm, though with an underlying hope that she wasn't about to embark on one of her long diatribes about whatever wedding supplier had let her down or in some way fallen short of her expectations. It wasn't that I didn't want to listen, I absolutely did. Just not while an experimental Moroccan tagine was bubbling on the stove.

'Hi, Mum,' came Emma's voice from the other end of the line. 'What are you doing?' And then, without waiting for an answer, 'I'm coming round to check up on you both – you and Grandma. I'll bring wine. I've got a couple of things I need to do for the wedding first, so I'll see you in an hour or so.'

'OK,' I replied. 'That'll be lovely. See you—'

But Emma, in a hurry as ever, had already cut the call.

Taking the lid off the casserole dish, I poked dubiously at its contents. It looked all right. It smelt good. But now I didn't just have my mother's scepticism about 'foreign food' to deal with; I also hoped that Emma would eat it. She was desperately trying to lose weight before the wedding, something of which I heartily disapproved. In my opinion, Emma was perfectly proportioned, and Giles clearly thought so too or presumably he wouldn't be marrying her. But every one of the wedding magazines that Emma eagerly bought and pored over had some kind of article about pre-wedding diets, weight-loss regimes or body-toning programmes.

I sighed as I got the plates out of the cupboard and put them on the worktop ready for later on. They were just out there, weren't they, these expectations for women, for how we must look, how much space we must take up, how we should behave, and marriage only served to magnify them.

All my ideals, the hopes and dreams that, however ludicrous they had been, had at least existed, had been unceremoniously and precipitously dumped on the pyre of motherhood and drudgery. Who was it who said that the pram in the hallway was the enemy of good art or creativity or something? I couldn't remember and though I'd love it to be a pearl of wisdom from Virginia Woolf, along with the importance of having a room of one's own, I had a sneaking suspicion that it had actually come from a man.

Thinking about this now, though, it all seemed so trivial and unimportant, especially viewed in the light of what I was learning about wartime suffering.

I went to my mother's room, to tell her that Emma was coming and we'd wait for supper until she arrived. Wanting, as ever, to know more, I asked her, 'What happened next, Mum? When did it all start to really fall apart?'

CHAPTER TWENTY

MEINDORF, 1945

The day after the failed delivery of the letters and the petrifying encounter with the SD, Hans came down with a fever. Laying her hand on his burning forehead, and listening to his pitiful cries, Katja wondered if this was her punishment for her betrayal. Perhaps God knew, and God was German, and was judging her.

Whatever the case, she couldn't leave her son to go to work. Not today, and probably not for the next two or three. In all the time they'd been in Sudetenland, they had not had need of a doctor and now that they did require one, Katja didn't know where to find one. She asked Herr Wagner, who gave her the address of his physician.

Running to the house, lungs on fire, Katja hoped and prayed that Dr Weller would be persuaded to come to Hans' aid.

Her frantic knocks on the door were eventually answered by a sour-faced woman – whether housekeeper or wife, Katja didn't bother to enquire.

'I need the doctor to come to my son,' Katja gasped, fighting to draw breath.

The woman shrugged. 'Do you have money?'

Katja could hardly believe it. Luckily she did, but was this how practitioners of medicine worked now? Pay first, treatment after?

'Yes,' she replied, trying not to let her anger show. She needed this woman to help her and send the doctor.

The woman sniffed and looked Katja disparagingly up and down. 'He'll come in the morning,' she said, and slammed the door in Katja's face.

Disconsolately, Katja turned on her heel and ran back to Hans' side. There was no medicine to buy in the pharmacy, nothing that she could get hold of herself to ease his fever or make him more comfortable. The night was almost unendurable, long and riven with worry. When dawn broke, Katja almost cried with relief.

Thankfully, the doctor arrived as promised. He gave Katja a dark brown bottle containing a liquid he said would help.

'Two spoons, twice a day,' the doctor instructed. He cast a final, appraising gaze over Hans' little form lying in his bed, sweating and whimpering. 'He's young and healthy. He'll pull through.'

Almost faint with relief at these words, Katja showed the doctor out and collapsed in a chair by the oven. It was a few moments before she had recovered enough to go back upstairs and administer the first dose of the medicine.

By some miracle, the doctor's cure seemed to work, but it was still an entire week before Hans was well enough for Katja to feel she could put him into Gerta's care for the day. Her love for her son overrode all other considerations, and yet she was sorely missing Karl and desperate to see him.

At Stahlbach, she jumped eagerly off the little train as soon as it drew to a halt and bounded off in the direction of the home.

Traversing the snow-rutted road, leaping from ridge to ridge to avoid the slushy parts, she pushed her recent trauma to one side and for a moment allowed herself to dwell in the past, in that magical Christmas that had just passed, in the love she and Karl shared.

She was almost at the convalescent home now, its edifice imposing and somehow regal. But there was something different about it today, she noticed, a strange quietness, a lack of activity, shutters closed tight over windows when normally they would be flung open to let in the light.

Quickening her pace, she reached the front door. It was firmly shut. Nothing unusual there; in January, the frigid wind and icy cold had to be kept out. The men convalescing within, including Karl, were the cream of the German air force; they must be protected and nursed back to health at all costs.

Katja lifted the brass knocker and rapped it against the oak door in short, insistent bursts. Through the thickness of the wood, she could hear the sound echoing down the wide hall-way. No one came.

She tried again. Still nothing.

Mystified, desperately trying to suppress a surge of panic, Katja stepped into the flowerbed beneath the window of the day room, impatiently pushing past frozen stems of fuchsias and peonies. Placing her hands on the windowsill, she tried to pull herself up to see between the slats of the shutter, but could make nothing out. Irritated now, as well as increasingly fearful, she stepped back onto the path, shaking out the cold from her fingertips. What if they'd all come down with an infection, measles or the flu? Such things could quickly lay low people already weakened by injury and exhaustion. Katja's own parents had died of influenza, after all. She knew all too well the toll that disease could exact.

Then, *Don't be silly*, she chided herself, *you're letting your imagination run away with you.* A whole hospital of men could not be wiped out in one fell swoop.

Determinedly, her heart thumping in her chest, Katja marched round the side of the building towards the back door. In the kitchen, she was sure, the cook and her assistants would be busy and bustling as usual.

But this door, when she got there, was just as firmly secured as the one at the front and there was no sign of anyone.

Helpless and distraught, Katja made her way back to the driveway. She stood, in the snow, her freezing feet burning with cold, her mind incapable of forming any coherent plan. Go into town and fetch a doctor? Find a passer-by and beat the door down? She had to do *something*.

For a moment, she stayed motionless in indecision, then determined to make her way back to the main road and hope that a plan came to her. She had just taken the first step when a voice from nowhere stopped her in her tracks.

'They've gone.'

Katja, heart thumping, looked this way and that. At first, she saw no one. And then, out of the shadows of the thick rhododendron bushes that lined the driveway, a female form emerged. Katja vaguely recognised her as a neighbour who brought homemade cakes and fresh flowers for the officers from time to time.

'Gone?' Katja heard her own voice asking the question. It sounded unfamiliar, high-pitched and wavering. 'But... gone where?'

It was impossible. Unbelievable. Karl was almost better but not fully recovered and many of the men were still deeply unwell. They were in no condition to be moved.

The neighbour shrugged. 'Back to the front, or to their aerodromes, of course. Someone's got to win this war for the Fatherland.'

Panic rose up inside Katja again as her breath came in short, fast gasps. The men could not be in active service. Karl could not be. She had already lost one husband to this god-awful, never-ending conflict. To lose another – even if not a husband – was unthinkable.

Struggling to get a grip on herself, Katja moved closer to the neighbour, noticing for the first time the greedy curiosity in her pinched, grey face. It occurred to her that this woman was glad to see Katja's distress. In this war, people in dire straits often rejoiced that others were even worse off. Katja did not want to indulge her nosiness, but she had to ask.

'When did they leave? What day, what time?'

'I don't know exactly,' the woman snapped back. 'Why so many questions? What is it to you?' And then, clearly wanting to find out exactly what it was to Katja, relented and told her, 'The day before yesterday. Wednesday, was it? They packed up and left, every last one of them.'

Katja's head reeled. She had been here only last Friday, cleaning up the breakfast things in Karl's company, then reading to one poor man who had been blinded in an explosion, and then she and Karl had taken a walk around the frozen garden, stopping amidst a small grove of snow-laden trees to kiss and cuddle, wishing they had a private space to go to rather than having to snatch furtive moments wherever possible.

Why had he not said that they were leaving? He must have known. He must have. And if he really hadn't had prior knowledge, then surely once the plan had gone into motion, he could have got a message to her somehow. Did he know about the old man, his absence, the SD approaching Katja? How could he? He'd never have asked her to take such a risk if he'd known, surely he wouldn't.

The thoughts spilled over, overwhelming her. She tried to pull herself together by focusing on the memory of Karl's handsome face, the high cheekbones, the thick, new-grown hair that she so longed to plunge her fingers into. He wasn't fit enough to fly an aircraft yet. But if they told him to, he'd have to. If he refused, he'd be shot.

Suddenly she wondered if he'd managed to escape, to go on the run. He could not want to take part in further bombing raids if he'd been passing secrets to the Allies. Maybe he'd crash his own plane, kamikaze style. He was brave enough to do so, Katja was sure of that.

'You're sweet on one of the officers, aren't you,' asked the woman, interrupting Katja's thoughts, her curiosity turning to prurience. 'I can tell.'

Katja, eyes brimming with tears, looked down at the snow, so white and pure, while she tried to blink the moisture away.

'Of course not,' she responded coldly, once she'd composed herself. 'Just that I've been coming here for a long time. I'm fond of all the men, as anyone would be. All I ever wanted was to help them – and I would have liked to say goodbye.'

'You're German?' the woman suddenly demanded, Katja's relationship status quickly forgotten. Her face was more pinched, her lips more tightly puckered than ever, like she was sucking on a sour lemon. She said the word 'German' as if it tasted bad. 'From Germany, not Sudetenland?'

Katja nodded.

'Hmm,' snorted the woman. 'As I thought.' And with that she turned and left, leaving Katja alone in front of the huge, empty, forlorn building.

Eventually, forced to action by the bitter cold, Katja stumbled back to the station to take the branch line from Stahlbach to Meindorf. Her feet were so numb with cold that walking was difficult. They had arrived in the Sudetenland in wintertime, herself, baby Hans and Gerta, but in 1943 their boots had been in good condition. Now Katja's were so full of holes, they could no longer be mended and she could not possibly buy a new pair. She still had money, but that was irrelevant. All the leather went for soldiers' boots, all the factories produced goods and garments to support the military. And now there were not even enough materials for the basics and fighting men were marching bootless and without greatcoats to withstand the harsh winter weather. Katja, like so many other Germans, had to put up with leaky shoes.

The little train puffed its way along the valley to Meindorf. Feeling sick and disorientated with cold and disappointment, combined with the terror that her part in passing on the letters might still be uncovered, Katja climbed down onto the platform with none of the alacrity and vigour of her outward journey.

Setting off for home, she was reminded of their arrival here, how serene and beguiling this new place had seemed. Then, as now, the air had been suffused with the scent of burning pinewood, wisps of smoke curling from every chimney pot. So different from Berlin, where they had left behind the smell of dust and rubble and destruction.

Even now, five years into a war that seemed without end, the town still retained its magical quality, the whimsical embodiment of a perfect picture-book world of fable and make-believe. But, with the unannounced evacuation of the convalescent home, the disappearance of Laura, the non-existent old man, the brushes with the Gestapo and the SD – all of a sudden, the real world seemed a whole lot closer. It sent shivers down Katja's spine and chilled her to the bone.

Back at the house, Gerta would in all likelihood still be prattling on in defence of the Führer and the Reich. But Gerta was a silly old thing sometimes, naive and gullible, despite being in her sixties, trusting totally in Germany's overweening power. If Katja ever had believed in this, she most certainly didn't anymore. Her experiences, her involvement with Karl's activities, had turned her against everything Hitler and his regime stood for. The best thing that could happen now was for the other side to win and it all to be over. She knew, though, without a shadow of doubt, that it was going to be nowhere near that easy.

Taking a deep breath, Katja opened the front door.

'Hello, Gerta,' she said, trying to sound normal, as if nothing had happened. At least she'd had the sense not to mention anything about Karl to Gerta. Instead, she braced herself for the torrent of chat that would greet her as soon as the floodgates were opened. If Gerta had not had anyone to talk to for an hour or so, once she started up, she could not be stopped.

'Hello, my dear,' answered Gerta. 'How was your morning? Back early, aren't you? Hans was a little fractious but soon calmed down, though he's awake now and hungry, I think. I put something on for dinner, I don't know if it'll be any good...'

Katja drifted off. Hans was sitting beside the *Kachelöfen*, playing with some blocks. As soon as he saw his mother, he held his chubby little arms up towards her, babbling the familiar word, 'Mama, Mama.' With a rush of love, Katja seized him up and gathered him to her. Settling herself down into a chair to nurse him, she sucked in her breath at the sudden stab of pain as he latched on. She had found nursing comforting once she'd mastered it, relishing the closeness, the nurturing feeling it gave her. But these days she had hardly any milk. It was time to wean him off the breast; he was old enough now.

Smiling down at her son, she saw her smile reflected in his dark pupils. They were as unfathomable as her love for him. Katja thought of Karl, too, and how much she loved him. Biting her lip, she bowed her head to hide the tears that, all of a sudden, began to cascade down her cheeks. She loved him. She missed him already. And she would probably never see him again.

CHAPTER TWENTY-ONE

In my little house, now under so much jeopardy, time seemed to have stilled and stopped, holding within it all my mother's pain and disappointment. To all intents and purposes, Karl Hausmann was nothing to me, yet still I felt so sad, on my mother's behalf, that he had disappeared.

'Did you ever hear from Karl again?' I asked, though I already knew the answer.

With sorrowful eyes, my mother shook her head. 'No. I believe he was sent straight back out to fly and was shot down. I heard on the news that his squadron lost twelve out of fourteen planes in one night. The chances are that his was one of them, but there was no way for me to find out for sure, no way to contact him, not even an address to write to. And I think I would have been too scared to get in touch, even if I'd been able to. Once he'd disappeared, I was petrified that someone would find out that I'd been helping him in his undercover work. I wasn't sorry that I'd done it. Not at all. Just of what would become of Hans if it were found out... That Monika spooked me; I was convinced she was an informant. I kept my head down and hoped that our secret was lost with Karl.' She paused and emitted a long, shuddering sigh. 'I mourned for him more than I had for Horst, in all honesty, but—'

My mother stopped abruptly, leaving the 'but' hanging in mid-air, along with the dust motes that danced in a shaft of sunlight from the window.

'But what?' I prompted, gently. My mother was being uncharacteristically forthcoming, but I knew I needed to temper my eagerness to hear more – to hear everything. Her moods could be unpredictable and she might quickly revert to disclosing nothing.

'But later... well, later, once I'd met your father, I realised that neither Karl nor Horst were a patch on him. Lou was the best of men. I couldn't have been luckier. Or happier.'

She had said or intimated as much before, but somehow, today, her words sounded a little hollow. It wasn't that I doubted the deep love between her and my father, so what was I questioning? Perhaps I was still curious about Karl, about what his true feelings had been for my mother and what had motivated him to pass secrets to the enemy – and to involve her in doing it, too.

'There was one particular day,' my mother went on, before I had a chance to fully unpick my reaction to what she had said, 'when I suddenly understood that the tide was turning. That the Germans in the Sudetenland would not have the upper hand for much longer, that the day of reckoning was approaching. If we had but known it, that day marked the beginning of the end.' She sighed, and her lips quivered. 'I was frightened. But, as it turned out, not frightened enough. I had no idea what was to come.'

A deep melancholy had descended, as thick and stifling as fog on a winter's morning. I reached out and took my mother's hand, passing her a tissue, which she used to dab at her moist eyes. My heart went out to her young self, so green and impressionable, alone with a child trying to make sense of an increasingly senseless world. She had done her bit of being a hero, and now she was just a woman struggling to survive.

Silence again, and the clock ticking.

'It was the first time I was forced to confront what might happen to us,' my mother concluded. 'Whether we had been right to leave Berlin. And that thought was terrifying.'

CHAPTER TWENTY-TWO

MEINDORF, 1945

It was bitterly cold, those early months of 1945. In Herr Wagner's house, the *Kachelöfen* spewed out heat that at times barely seemed to touch the sides. The wind howled down from the mountains, and in the forest, the branches of the pine trees were bowed low to the ground with their weight of snow. The radio news programmes disgorged ever more lurid tales of the Red Army's violence, their lack of the most basic standards of human decency, the disgusting vengeance they wreaked on German women.

One thing seemed clear. The Russians would come. But when they got here, who knew what hell they would unleash.

A kind of paralysis fell upon Katja. She carried on as she always had, tending to her son's needs, changing him, boiling nappies over the stove, wringing out the water with hands that were sore and red-raw, hanging them on the line in the fierce cold. But she did everything without feeling, on autopilot.

Without the trips to the convalescent home, without Karl to buoy her up and lift her spirits, the afternoon hours when the chores were done hung heavy on her shoulders. Taking advantage of Gerta's continued willingness to mind Hans, she began going out on long hikes, venturing ever further up the hill and into the forest. When they had first arrived, Herr Wagner had warned her of straying too far from the path. There were wolves and bears, he said. But these stories no longer frightened Katja as they had done, and tales of *Rotkäppchen*, Little Red Riding Hood, haunted her no more. Wild animals were the least terrifying beings prowling the land in these increasingly tense, fraught times.

Climbing and climbing, she discovered hidden glades and snow-bound meadows buried in the forest's depths. Scrambling over stiles and fences slippery with hoar frost, she would chase the afternoon shadows as they rose over the mountaintops. Once, she came across a hidden village, just half a dozen houses huddled around a shingle-roofed church. Every now and again, it was a lonely farmhouse she encountered, where a dog might run out, barking, and the lowing of cattle echoed in the emptiness.

One day she met a team of woodcutters at their work, loading mighty trunks of pine onto a sledge, to which was harnessed a pair of enormous carthorses with shaggy manes and giant, feathered hooves. The workmen seemed delighted, and unsurprised, to see Katja, greeting her jovially and calling out for her to stop and chat.

'Where have you come from?' the tallest asked. He spoke in German but Katja could tell that his first language was Czech.

Katja faltered for a moment. Should she answer Meindorf, or Berlin? Increasingly, she did not know where she belonged, where she ought to be. Germany had taken this land from its people. Surely the time would come when they wanted it back?

Unsure, she gestured towards the valley. 'From down there,' she replied. 'The town.'

The woodcutter nodded, happy with such a vague response.

On closer observation, Katja saw how young he and his companions were, fourteen or fifteen, no more. All the men – their fathers, uncles, brothers – were away fighting, or already dead, leaving children to do the work at home.

A silence fell. Katja couldn't think of anything to say but, at the same time, did not want to leave. These were the first people she'd spoken more than a word to in weeks, other than Gerta, Hans and Herr Wagner. It was obvious they weren't Gestapo or SD, they couldn't possibly know what she had done. Yet still she found herself looking over her shoulder, checking there were no approaching jackbooted, uniformed men bearing down on her.

One of the youths swung a canvas backpack down from the driving seat and pulled out a bottle of schnapps, plus a stack of small glasses.

'You'll join us?' he suggested. He had a cheeky smile beneath his tousled hair; no slicked-back Hitler youth haircut here.

Katja eyed the bottle. She hardly ever drank. Despite the sun that shone bright in the sky, it was bitterly cold. Something warming was very appealing. She took the glass the youth handed to her and watched as he distributed the rest to the others in the team.

Breaking the silence and making her jump, a rook cawed loudly from its perch in a nearby tree, a cry full of mourning that jarred against the brightness of the day.

'*Eins, zwei, drei,*' the woodcutter called, and then lifted the glass to his lips and drained it in one.

The others, including Katja, followed suit, the fiery liquid burning down her throat. Exhaling a great cloud of vapour into the frosty air, she grasped the side of the cart for support as her head spun. She giggled briefly, quickly covering her mouth with her sleeve to suppress the sound. She didn't want to look stupid – she was much older than these boys and they didn't seem to be at all affected by the alcohol.

'Thank you,' she murmured. 'That'll warm me up for my walk home.'

The boys laughed and the cheeky one looked as if was about to say something, but before he could, a cry rang out from the track ahead. A man came over the brow of the hill, marching purposely towards them, swinging an axe. He was old, at least seventy Katja reckoned, but burly and fit as an ox. He wore animal-skin trousers with the fur to the inside and as he approached, he swung the axe up into the air and called out a sharp instruction in Czech.

Immediately, the lads jumped to it, stowing the rucksack back on the cart and scrambling to turn the patient horses around before setting off up the hill.

A dog appeared, huge and shaggy, catching the old man up and then racing ahead of him.

'*Tschüss!*' cheeky-smile called over his shoulder to Katja.

'*Tschüss*,' she shouted back, waving. '*Auf Wiedersehen.*'

An angry growl emitted from the old man's mouth, matched by a snarl from the dog.

'Be off with you,' he jeered, speaking German now. 'Back to where you came from.'

The words hung momentarily in the air before evaporating as if they had never been. By now, the sunbeams had paled and were dulled by gathering clouds. Katja shivered, her skin erupting in goose bumps. The boys had been full of warmth and fun, but the image that remained with Katja was the lingering look of hatred the old man bestowed upon her after he'd heard her speak. His eyes burnt into her back as she descended the track towards Meindorf and Herr Wagner's house, stumbling awkwardly on the stony ground in her haste to get away, a feeling of foreboding settling deep within her.

Gerta was waiting for her, full of stories of Hans' burbles, his games and antics, his many cutenesses. Katja felt bad for leaving her for so long. However much Gerta got on her nerves on occasion, the elderly lady had shown her nothing but kindness and support. They had needed each other in Berlin and they needed each other now.

Whatever the future held, it didn't bode well for any of them.

CHAPTER TWENTY-THREE

As winter progressed towards spring, town after town fell to the Red Army.

Beneath its normally tranquil, uneventful facade, terror fizzled and festered in the little town of Meindorf. But no one did anything. It was as if the whole population was in a state of paralysis. Life continued as it always had, except for the shortages, the scarcity of basic goods, the increasing instances of stockpiling of whatever paltry necessities were available. Everyone was on edge, maintaining a veneer of normalcy while underneath preparing for the very opposite.

In the house on the edge of the forest, Katja and Gerta continued the everyday routine of meals, washing, feeding, changing and bathing the little one. Katja no longer worried so much about the Gestapo coming for her because there was a new fear now. Instead, at every moment, she wondered when the Russians would arrive. And what they would do when they got there.

Gerta, meanwhile, listened avidly to every piece of propaganda promulgated by Goebbels and seemed to believe all of it,

much to Katja's frustration. On the other hand, Katja understood Gerta's need to believe in something.

'The Führer will come good!' Gerta enthused one day as
Katja stirred a boiling pan of nappies and Hans clambered
clumsily up and down the bench beside the *Kachelöfen*. Katja
watched him indulgently, full of pride. He was a lovely, healthy
boy, and so handsome already with his shock of white-blond
hair. Passers-by on the street would comment on how she was
raising a good strong son for the *Vaterland*. Katja would agree
while crossing her fingers behind her back and silently vowing
that her child would never be sacrificed to a heinous war.

Hans, now heading across the tiled floor to where a toy train
lay, tripped and took a tumble.

'Oop-la,' Katja called, 'upsy-daisy.'

Hans emitted a curtailed whine of pain but quickly stopped
and pulled himself upright again on one of the wooden kitchen
chairs.

'The Führer has a plan,' Gerta gurgled on, 'a plan that only
he knows but that will overcome the British and the Americans
– and the Russians! Those devils, those heathen ignoramus-
es... all will be eradicated! Of course it has to be kept secret for
the element of surprise, you know, it must...'

Katja, once again, had all but switched off. Gerta's chatter
was the soundtrack to her life, the backdrop of everything that
happened in Sudetenland.

'Those Russian beasts!' Gerta exclaimed, before proceeding
to repeat every terrible thing she'd ever heard about the Soviet
army.

A cry from upstairs, agonised and fearful, silenced Gerta
immediately. The two women looked at each other. The noise
had come from Trudi, the maid who came to clean and cook for
Herr Wagner a few times a week.

Another scream, muffled this time, accompanied by Herr

Wagner's stern voice. 'What's the matter, Trudi? What happened?'

Katja heard Trudi flying down the stairs and into the small sitting room where Herr Wagner read and wrote letters every morning. She was screaming hysterically and sobbing loudly.

Pulling the kitchen door open, Katja leaned out, Gerta right behind her peering over her shoulder. Herr Wagner was there, standing awkwardly on the sitting-room threshold, clearly uncomfortable with Trudi's outpouring of emotion.

'Russians,' she managed to gasp, pointing weakly in the direction of the track leading to the house. 'Out there.' Her voice fell to the faintest whisper. 'They're coming this way.'

Katja's stomach turned over in a wave of nausea. She knew only too well what Soviet soldiers did to women. Everyone did. The newspapers had been telling them for months. Rape. Murder. Either one or both were inevitable. Or kidnap... There were stories of women taken into Soviet army units as trophies to be horrifically used over and over again.

'Hide in the attic!' Herr Wagner's command was clear and definite. 'Get up there now.'

Trudi was up the stairs before the echo of his voice had receded, but Katja stood, incapable of movement. She could not hide with Hans. She could not leave him behind.

'Frau Schmidt,' said Herr Wagner, his tone gentle and patient now. 'Leave the boy with us. We will say he is our grandchild and the parents are not in. I promise we will look after him.'

Gerta, sniffing and snuffling, grey hair coming loose from its habitual bun and sticking up at angles around her face, nodded. 'He's right, *liebchen*. We'll protect him. But you – you need protection yourself. An old lady like me... I'm not who they're looking for. But you—'

A knock at the front door froze Katja's blood in her veins. She looked wildly around her, at Gerta and Herr Wagner, at

Hans, still oblivious, shuffling and toddling around the kitchen.

'All right. I'll go.' If she died, if she were murdered by a Russian soldier, Hans would be orphaned before he was even two years old. Better that she hid now, took no chances. With that thought, she turned and fled, taking the stairs two at a time and then on up the ladder to the attic. Trudi was waiting at the top, her panic-stricken face gazing down at Katja. With wild movements, she gesticulated to Katja to hurry up. Katja sped up the ladder and helped Trudi pull it up behind her, dropping the access hatch into place just as she heard the front door opening and the sound of heavy rubber-soled boots on the stone flags.

Desperately clutching onto one another, Katja and Trudi stowed themselves on top of the water tank, the only space available. A gable of the roof came down almost to the top of the tank, meaning that someone looking in would not immediately see them. That was what Katja calculated anyway. But she didn't know for sure. Trembling with cold and fear, squeezing her mouth tight shut to prevent her teeth from chattering, she gripped Trudi's hand and prayed.

They heard the soldiers climbing the stairs, and then the bedroom doors being flung open, banging against the walls behind. The boots tramped on, through each and every room. Katja imagined them finding her clothes, knowing that a young woman lived here. A whimper of fear that she was unable to suppress emitted from her mouth. Trudi dug her in her ribs with a sharp elbow. Her eyes were fierce and judgemental. *Don't give us away*, they said. *Don't give me away*.

Katja understood her anger. She gritted her teeth and pressed her face flat down on the tank, her nose squidged against cold metal. The discomfort momentarily took her mind off the terror. But her heart was thumping so hard against her chest, she was sure they'd be able to hear the echo in the rooms beneath.

Many minutes passed. Or perhaps it was just seconds. Katja lost all track of time. She strained her ears to hear what was happening but could not catch the sound of voices. Of course, the soldiers hadn't come for a conversation, had they? And anyway, they most probably didn't speak German and Gerta and Herr Wagner certainly didn't speak Russian.

Katja wondered what Hans was doing. Playing quietly in a corner, she hoped, not drawing attention to himself. They wouldn't take a little boy, would they? Surely they wouldn't. The thought of Hans, vulnerable, wondering where his mama was, calling out for her, broke Katja's heart. It was all she could do to stay there in the attic, pressed against the water tank, when all she wanted to do was scramble down the ladder and go to Hans.

Eventually, after what seemed like an age, the sound of the boots receded, accompanied by the harsh Russian voices, gradually fading.

'Stay here,' hissed Trudi, only just audible, as if Katja was stupid enough to try to get up and leave.

Mutely, she nodded her agreement.

In the end, they were there for another half an hour or so before Herr Wagner's voice alerted them to the all-clear. Cautiously, they slid off the water tank, limbs stiff and uncooperative, and crawled to the loft opening. Lifting it, Katja had the sudden feeling that it was a trap. That the Russian soldiers had Herr Wagner at gunpoint and had forced him to reveal their whereabouts. But the removal of the hatch revealed only Herr Wagner's familiar, dignified face, with no one else around.

'You can come out now,' he said, softly. 'They've gone.'

Awkwardly, the two women descended. Gerta was waiting in the kitchen, a protesting Hans clamped so tightly against her ample bosom he could hardly move.

'Oh my God, oh thank God.' Tears streamed down Katja's

cheeks as she reached out for Hans and he in turn stretched out little arms towards her. Kneeling beside Gerta's chair she caressed his hair and kissed his forehead and nose, every now and again wiping away her tears so as not to wet him too much.

Looking around the kitchen, she saw that all the cupboard doors stood open and the shelves were empty, the contents pulled out haphazardly and strewn across the floor, the larder ransacked of butter, sugar and their last remaining block of chocolate.

'What did they want?' she asked, faintly.

Herr Wagner shrugged. 'They want it all. They want Germany finished and everything we own to be theirs.'

Katja noticed that the watch that he always wore was gone from his wrist, but she didn't mention it. They had not taken Hans. Nothing else, in all honesty, mattered.

THE NEXT DAY, she saw Herr Wagner walking purposefully across the garden pushing a wheelbarrow. He stopped beneath a tall linden tree and stood for a moment, straightening his aged shoulders while he caught his breath. His expression was one of sadness and anger and, worst of all, resignation. This old man, who had seen a previous war come and go, recognised all too well the signs of defeat.

Katja followed him outside.

'What are you doing?' she asked.

He had taken a spade off the barrow and was digging a hole beneath the tree, throwing the snow to one side before reaching the soil beneath.

'I'm burying my family heirlooms, the silver, everything precious,' he replied, his breath coming in deep gasps with the exertion of breaking and lifting the frozen earth. 'If I don't, the next time they come, they'll steal it, for sure.'

'Will they definitely come again?' Katja asked the question even though she was sure she knew the answer.

Herr Wagner stood up straight, hands rested on the spade handle, eyes narrowed against the low shafts of feeble sunshine.

'Oh yes,' he replied, 'for sure they'll come. For sure.'

CHAPTER TWENTY-FOUR

LONDON, JUNE 1994

The doorbell sounded, making both me and my mother jump, jolting us out of our contemplation of Herr Wagner's dire prophecy. The noise was quickly followed by the rattle of Emma's key in the lock and my daughter erupted into the house in her usual shower of noise.

'Hi, Mum!' she called down the hallway, expecting me to be in the kitchen, and then, 'Hi, Grandma!' through the partially open bedroom door.

I leapt to my feet and went to meet her.

'Oh, there you are!' Emma exclaimed, wielding the promised bottle of wine. Once in the kitchen, she planted a kiss on my cheek and then proceeded to scrabble around in the drawer for a corkscrew. 'You all right?' she asked, pouring the wine into glasses. 'Will Grandma want one, do you think?'

I shook my head. 'I shouldn't think so. She's got water already. You go on in and I'll follow with the tray.'

Emma burst into the spare bedroom and over to the bed,

enveloping Katja in a voluminous hug, strands of her honey-brown hair covering them both.

'Grandma! How are you?' she boomed. 'I hope you're being good and following doctor's orders.'

I smiled to myself. My mother would be furious if I spoke to her like that, as if she were three years old or an idiot. But her love of her grandchildren meant they could get away with anything.

'Emma, my dear, how lovely to see you!' my mother was saying, with not a hint of annoyance, exactly as I had predicted. 'And of course – I've been very good, as your mother will vouch for.'

Emma laughed. 'Don't worry, I believe you. But you need to look after yourself. You gave us all a bit of a scare when the doctors sprang this one on us.'

'Well, they didn't exactly "spring" it, Emma,' I interjected. 'Grandma had known about its inevitability for months – she just didn't tell us.'

'Doctors! What do they know?' my mother rejoined. 'And I'm as fit as a fiddle, Emma, and don't you forget it. Nobody needs to treat me like a bucket case.'

'A what?' Emma laughed her infectious, earthy laugh as she tried to interpret the idiom.

'I think you mean "basket case",' I suggested, chuckling also. 'And no one is going to treat you like that any time soon, you really don't need to worry.'

'Still...' my mother sniffed reprovingly. 'I'm still all here, you know.' She accompanied this statement with an emphatic jabbing of her forefinger against her head. 'Let nobody forget that.'

'Nobody does, Mum,' I assured her, handing around the plates of tagine. 'Now we should all stop talking and start eating. You need to keep your strength up.' I turned to Emma and viewed her with narrowed eyes. 'And so do you,' I said firmly, just in case she was thinking of refusing her food.

'No worries on that score, Mum,' she responded. 'I'm starving.'

The atmosphere in the house had completely changed with Emma's arrival; she was quite literally a breath of fresh air, bringing with her a revivifying waft of the cool evening breeze along with her habitual cheeriness. It hit me how much I still missed her, three years after she'd officially moved out, and how much worse that might get once she was married. Because Giles wouldn't want her popping around to her mum's for a casual meal once or twice a week, would he? He'd want his wife with him, sharing the news from their days at the same time as sharing their supper.

At least my mother was tucking in, with not a murmur about the outlandish couscous, and no sign of the lacklustre appetite she'd had when she first came out of hospital. Being with Emma was good for her, and I felt a wave of relief. I hadn't realised, or perhaps had been in denial about, the level of responsibility I felt in nursing my mother back to health. Seedlings and plants I was confident about keeping healthy. Elderly parents were another matter completely.

Once the food was eaten, Emma and I left my mother to rest while we cleared up. Everybody these days seemed to have a dishwasher, but my kitchen was far too old-fashioned for that and there wasn't room for one anyway. I washed and Emma dried, in between riffling through the piles of post and paperwork that littered the kitchen counter, searching for mail; she'd still not changed her address for lots of her correspondence.

'What's this?'

I looked up. I'd forgotten that I'd put my father's diary down in here when I'd come in to start cooking and now Emma had it in her hand and was scrutinising it closely.

'Man, this writing is hard to read!' she exclaimed. She held the book up to her eyes. 'What is it anyway?'

I smiled faintly. 'It's something of your grandfather's, so it seems. Something he wrote about the end of the war.'

'Wonderful!' exclaimed Emma. 'More history. It's like you've become a one-woman local historical society, overnight. Highgate branch.'

I raised my eyebrows. 'I think they're already well served with historians, both amateur and professional,' I responded, drily.

Emma laughed. 'I guess. But, nevertheless, you should type this up and send it to the memorial project along with Grandma's story. If it's interesting,' she added.

'Or you could!' I joked. Emma's enthusiasm was sometimes a tad tiring. 'I'm glad you're so quick to assign such a time-consuming task to me.'

Emma encircled my waist with her arms. 'Come on, Mum,' she cajoled teasingly. 'You know you need things to keep you busy, now we're all grown up and...' she halted, then continued, 'and moved out and stuff.'

My heart twisted inside my chest. I knew what Emma had been about to say, but had stopped just in time. She had been going to add 'now you're single again'. Which was only the truth, but, as all of us know, the truth sometimes hurts. Badly.

I bit my lip. 'You're right,' I agreed, decisively. 'I absolutely do. But you know – these stories – they're so personal.' The intimacy of my father's revelations about Eva leapt to the forefront of my mind, their fervid passion in the midst of battle. Just as I'd wondered if my father knew about Karl, did my mother know about my father's past love? 'Should such things be shared, without the person knowing?' I asked Emma.

'Of course they should! It's the fact that they're personal that makes them compelling; people love that stuff,' Emma enthused, emphatically. She flipped through the pages of the diary and the envelope fell out and fluttered to the floor. Picking it up, she studied it inquisitively. 'Who's Janez?' she asked.

I shrugged. 'No idea.'

Emma clicked her tongue against her teeth impatiently. 'Well, we have to find out, don't we? Ask Grandma what Grandad was up to, and who this guy is.' Her eyes blazed with curiosity. 'I want to know all this stuff, and I want my future children to know it, too. They already can't hear it from their great-grandfather and... well, you never know what's going to happen, do you? I don't intend to have kids for ages yet, so they might not get to hear it first-hand from Grandma Katja, either.'

It was hard not to smile at Emma's words, despite their bluntness. I could always rely on my daughter to call a spade a spade. And she was right; of course my mother would not live forever, and although in no immediate danger, who knew what was round the corner for someone in their seventies. Much as I didn't like to dwell on my mother's inevitable demise, at the same time I was glad that Emma was not in as much of a rush to have children as she was to get married. It was wise to wait awhile and embark on parenthood with maturity and wisdom. If I had done that, how different might my life have been? But as soon as this thought came into my head, I shook it as if to get rid of it. I regretted nothing about the birth of my two children and, as a family, we had had many good times over the years. Ed might be driving me mad now, but he had always been a good father – not like Sue's awful ex-spouse.

'It's not just that I'm worried Dad might mind,' I tried to explain to Emma. 'The thing is that I haven't told your grandmother that the builders even found the book, let alone that I've been reading it.'

'Ooohh naughty Mummy,' gasped Emma with mock horror. Then, more seriously, 'She won't be bothered, will she?'

I pulled a face that said, 'no idea'.

'I don't think that's something you need to worry about,'

encouraged Emma. 'And to prove it, we're going to talk to Grandma about it now.'

Before I had a chance to protest, Emma had marched off to Mum's bedroom. Flinging down my rubber gloves and the dish-cloth, I hurried after her.

'Grandma,' Emma was saying as I entered. 'The workmen found this book in the flat – it seems to be something Grandad wrote. But there's an envelope with it, with a name on it. Do you know who this person is?'

My mother lay amongst the pillows, staring out uncompre-hendingly as Emma waved both diary and envelope in front of her widened eyes. I wished momentarily that Emma had tried a more softly-softly approach – but that wasn't her style and never had been.

Anxiously, I bustled forward. 'Don't worry, Mum, it's nothing urgent,' I intervened, soothingly. 'We – Emma and I – were just curious. The story in the diary – it's interesting. Heart-wrenching, really. A bit like...' I dried up, not sure whether to mention her own half-told tale in front of Emma. 'Like all these wartime experiences. We can hardly believe what people went through, and survived. It's very humbling. And the envelope – intriguing.'

I took the diary from Emma and handed it to my mother. As she grasped hold of it, I saw something in her face that I couldn't name.

'It's Lou's... well, I suppose it's a journal of sorts. It's some-thing he started to write, oh, many years ago. He had the idea that he might turn it into a novel eventually, about the Long March,' she said, as she leafed through the pages. 'He wanted to fictionalise it, make it about all of the men, not just him. I'd forgotten all about it. I can't remember why he never did anything with it.'

'It's quite gripping,' I responded, a huge sense of relief coursing through me that my mother wasn't upset. 'Though the writing is hard to make out.'

'And what's this?' my mother pointed at the envelope which Emma still clutched.

'That's what we need to ask you, Grandma,' answered Emma. 'There's nothing inside, just a name on the back.' She glanced up at her grandmother, and then back down. 'Janez Novak. Do you know who he is?'

I was watching my mother as Emma spoke. I expected a flash of recognition, a slow dawning of realisation. Instead, there was nothing. Just a blank look.

'It sounds Eastern European?' mused Emma, questioningly. 'Perhaps,' she added, unsure of her prediction.

Slowly, my mother's brow unfurrowed as a memory fought its way to the surface.

'It's coming back to me,' she muttered, struggling to recall the facts. 'He was a friend of Lou's, I believe. Someone he met in the camp. The Italian one, not the German.'

I regarded her. There was something wooden in her tone, stilted. Had this Janez really been a friend? Perhaps something not quite so benign? But then, she smiled and pushed herself forward on her elbows.

'I've got it now,' she continued, a note of triumph in her voice. 'I was worried for a moment then that my mind was failing me. But it's all come flooding back. He was the one who organised the reunions – they had them every five years for the first twenty years or so after the war ended. Then, the meetings tailed off. I suppose people died...'

I nodded. So it was as I had thought; Janez was someone who knew my father from his years spent in captivity. I bent forward and tucked in a loose end of my mother's bedsheet, then moved her glass of water so it was within easy reach of the bed. I could tell that she was tired.

'Thanks for the inside info, Gran-Gran.' Emma leaned forward and kissed her grandmother's cheek. 'I've got to be off now,' she chirruped, cheerfully. 'But I'll come round again soon and see how you're getting on.'

My mother smiled faintly. 'That will be lovely,' she said. 'Take care, my dear. See you soon.'

The bang of the door as Emma let herself out reverberated around the house. I sat down on the side of my mother's bed.

'I hope it's OK, Mum, that I read Dad's diary. Some of it. I hope you don't mind.'

She was silent for a moment, staring at the ceiling with sightless eyes, her thoughts clearly elsewhere.

'I don't mind,' she said, eventually. 'It's good that you find out more about your father. He wrote it all down, thinking to get it published. He was angry, for a while, that so few people knew about this dreadful end to the war. But I don't know – he got distracted, never did anything with it. What's the phrase? Life got in the way.'

I traced a pulled thread in the white counterpane with my fingertip. 'That's what so often happens, isn't it? Well, I'm going to carry on reading, if you're OK with that, and maybe – what do you think – we could put forward both of your stories to the museum project?'

'I suppose so. I can't think who would be interested – but if you wish to. Whatever you think is best.' Her eyelids were flickering shut even as she spoke.

Kissing her goodnight, I got up and left the room, shutting the door softly behind me.

Despite the wine I'd shared with Emma, I poured myself a finger of brandy and sat down heavily on my favourite armchair. It was a huge wingback, an antique that was part of what we'd inherited from the previous owner, but which I'd had expensively recovered in luscious blue velvet a few years ago. I ran my hands up and down the fabric, with and against the pile. If I had to move – which seemed inevitable with the news from the bank – I probably wouldn't be able to take it with me as I doubted wherever I went to would be roomy enough. I was spoilt here, and that was the truth of it. A single woman did not need a three-bedroom house.

Glancing at the clock, I saw that it was getting late. I could give Evan a quick call; it would be early morning in New Zealand. The expense and the time difference meant I spoke to him much less than I would like. At the same time, I was aware how busy he was, how wrapped up in his own life and affairs – as well he might be at twenty years of age, I told myself robustly, as the phone rang and rang. No answer being forthcoming, I left a brief message on the answerphone and hung up.

Over the next days, as I went through the motions at work, I repeatedly found myself pondering the story of my father and Eva. I thought of their love affair, so vital and necessary, conducted during the turmoil of wartime, of imprisonment and escape, heightened emotions taut as piano wire and feelings raw as fresh wounds. I wondered if it had been like that for my mother and father, when they met in Berlin. The easy way to find out would be to just ask Mum, but somehow I knew I wouldn't. I preferred to wait as their respective stories unfolded, and find out the truth that way.

CHAPTER TWENTY-FIVE

GERMANY, 1945

Morning had broken, like the first morning in hell.

Carnage lay all around them. The cattle trucks had ground to a halt in a siding somewhere, and the men, half-living, half-dead, were scattered across the rat-ridden platforms. There were civilians, too, Lou now saw, the old and the young, mostly women.

It was bitterly cold. Icicles hung from the roofs of the carriages and puddles were crackle-glazed with layers of frozen ice. Breath hung in the air and extremities shrank back against the shock of exposure.

The POWs stood on the sidings, waiting for orders. No one had the strength to resist, nor to question. Lou saw that a crowd had gathered around one of the trucks, and amidst the commotion, shrill, brittle voices rang out into the still air. Eventually, the cluster of people moved aside, clearing the way as if expecting someone to come. Lou saw a woman, blonde-haired, waxen-faced, lying on the metal floor. At first, he thought she was resting on a red blanket. And then he saw that it was blood, frozen solid.

She had suffered some injury, from a haemorrhage, an assault, a bomb, a miscarriage, who knew? There were so many things that could kill you. Had she died of the blood loss or the cold? Did it even matter which? Her life was gone. A German life, but a life all the same. Men arrived with a stretcher and the crowd closed in behind them, once more hiding the woman from view.

Guards Lou had not seen before strode down the platform, bayonets attached to their guns.

'I think I've been to sleep for thirty years and woken up in the wrong war,' commented Dobson, wryly. 'Bayonets and hand-to-hand combat. Is that the best they can come up with? Fuckers.'

Lou, still feverish, nodded. 'Guess so.'

The men marched again.

Now the rain started pouring, and poured and poured all day, freezing rain that pummelled faces, hands and limbs and got into every crevice of the men's inadequate clothing. They reached a prison camp at Weisenwalde and waited hours, standing in the rain, to enter. Once inside, there were four times as many men assigned to each hut as it was intended for.

'You'll be all right,' said Dobson to Lou, as they struggled to find a place to lie down. 'We'll see you right. It can't be long now.'

'Thank you.' The words meant nothing. Lou had long since given up looking into the future. Not only did he not care if he lived or died, but he also no longer knew which state he was actually in. Perhaps he had died, and this was hell.

And yet, niggling at the back of his impassivity was a tiny germ of something, not quite hope but not total surrender, either. A nagging, persistent voice that said, over and over again, *The whole war, for this? It cannot be, it simply cannot be.*

Lou slept.

When he woke again, he felt better. Or, at least, not worse. Though he was soaked in sweat, the fever had abated somewhat. Dobson and Stubbs, together with the now-recovered Bride, had ersatz coffee ready for him. It was disgusting, but Lou didn't care. It was hot, burning down his throat and into his stomach. It even managed to stay there for half an hour or so, rather than coming straight out again like everything else he'd ingested recently.

But though Lou was recovering, over the next few days, all the horror and fear and tension and anxiety of the previous five years seemed to erupt out of the captive men, like a volcano millennia in the making vomiting forth its broiling, suffocating, lethal innards in a matter of hours. Discipline fell apart, and the men turned in on themselves. It was as if, now the end of imprisonment was in sight, imprisonment became unbearable, insufferable, enraging. With so many thousands crammed into spaces built for hundreds, it was bound to lead to trouble. Fights were frequent, arguments and disagreements constant. Guarding food and cigarettes became a full-time job. Nothing was too big or too small to be pilfered, and the tiniest morsels were capable of evoking a brawl.

Lou, still afflicted by intermittent, agonising bouts of diarrhoea, withdrew into himself. His days were permeated with fear of a kind he had never known before – not while navigating his fighter plane across enemy territory, not while ejecting from a furnace of burning metal, not while being interrogated by the SS.

Meanwhile, more and more men piled into the camp. Some had come even further than Lou and the others, trudging all the way from the furthest reaches of Poland, and were now nothing more than walking skeletons, teetering on the brink of life or death. Food rations were less than they had ever been, and the scale of the conflict and the chaos, in those grim, dying days of the Third Reich, meant that charity parcels were not getting through, so there was next to nothing to supplement the men's diets.

February came and went in a fug of boredom, sickness, pain and desperation. The war, which as 1944 became 1945 had seemed so certain to end in a matter of days, was now well into its sixth year. As the month turned to March, some small relief came in a surprise delivery of Red Cross parcels containing meat, jam, chocolate, tinned fish and peanut butter.

Lou crammed his mouth with the sweetness of the strawberry jam and watched the planes scream past overhead. Nobody bothered to save food anymore, to squirrel it away for a rainy day. That worst-case scenario had already arrived and there was no point in keeping hold of stuff for a time in the future when you'd probably be dead.

'Did you hear what the Berliners were saying last Christmas?' said Lou, as he scraped his finger around the inside of the jam pot, savouring every last morsel of flavour. 'Be practical; give a coffin.' Black humour was the only type anyone had left.

Bride and Dobson laughed, while Stubbs maintained a stony indifference.

One night, taking his turn to lie in a bunk rather than on the floor, Lou focused all his attention on the small piece of night sky that he could see through the smeared and dirty window. An eerie orange glow illuminated everything. Berlin was burning and the gunpowder and cordite and fire spread gas and fumes and smoke into a sky consumed by flames.

'Have you ever tried to count the stars?' he asked Dobson.

Stubbs snorted disparagingly in the background.

'No,' replied Dobson, briefly. 'Never had the time, nor the inclination.' Then he laughed, bitterly and ironically. 'Which is pretty much nonsense, given I've been banged up with you lot for the past God knows how long. I've not had anything else useful to do.'

'We'll be out soon,' replied Lou, relaying the same tired refrain, his voice utterly lacking conviction.

'My uncle's a stargazer,' piped up Bride from the bunk below. 'He lives in the Borders and has a telescope in his attic so that he can look into space. He made it himself. The telescope, that is, not space.' He laughed, stopping when no one joined in. 'The skies are so clear there. It must be wonderful in the blackout, no artificial light at all.' He paused and Lou heard him shifting to try to get comfortable. There were two men to every bunk, so this wasn't easy. 'I wonder if he's still got it, if it's still there,' Bride concluded, and there was a yearning and a wistfulness in his tone that nearly made Lou cry.

None of them knew what would still be waiting for them at home. If they even ever got there again.

CHAPTER TWENTY-SIX

LONDON, JUNE 1994

Rain had hammered down on my glass conservatory roof in London that whole afternoon, just as it had in Germany all those years ago. Now it had suddenly stopped. I lifted my head from the diary, dazed and discombobulated, noticing the quiet that filled the air now the relentless drumming had ceased. I felt that I could smell the blood and sweat that my father had described, and the acrid stench of burning; I needed fresh air, the stimulation of a brisk walk to blow myself out of the past and into the present.

'Walk?' I said to Springer, who leapt eagerly up.

I headed into the hallway and picked up the phone. 'Walk?' I said to Sue across the airwaves.

'Usual place?' Sue responded.

'See you there.'

Putting my head round the bedroom door to say a quick goodbye to my mother, I pulled on my wellies. Grabbing Springer's lead, we set off.

A fresh wind was blowing, tearing at the blossom on the

hawthorn bushes and tossing it up into the heavens, from where it slowly descended in a delicate scattering of white.

'So, what's new?' asked Sue, as we strode uphill. 'You seem preoccupied.'

I concentrated on the stony path beneath my feet for a moment before replying. 'You know I started teasing out of my mother her wartime experiences. And now I've also found something my dad wrote. It's strange – finding out all sorts of really fundamental stuff I didn't know but feel I should have done. I'm not sure how they kept it so dead and buried for so long. These days, you'd have years of therapy if you'd been through all that and you'd use it to justify any and every piece of bad or odd behaviour you ever committed. But for that generation – it was shoved under the carpet and left there.'

Sue nodded. 'I'm sure Katja's finding it cathartic to talk about it all now.'

'Yes, maybe,' I agreed. 'And now I've started, I want to uncover everything I can.' I told Sue about the mysterious empty envelope with the name Janez Novak.

'Well, it's obvious, isn't it?' she declared. 'You need to write to him, this Janez, see if he can fill in any gaps. I would, if I were you.'

I laughed. 'That's because you're incorrigibly nosy,' I teased. 'But, actually, Emma suggested the same thing.'

We reached the reservoir. I leaned against the iron railings while Springer gallivanted around chasing a feather that tossed and turned on the wind. My eyes searched the bank; one of the Heath conservationists had told me that kingfishers nested here. I'd long hoped to see one but had never yet done so. Sue came to stand beside me. The water was green and utterly still, the life-saving ring that floated in the centre stained emerald with algae. Notices warned against diving and I shuddered at the thought. Nothing looked less inviting than leaping in.

I turned to Sue. 'It's not just my parents' stories that are preoccupying me,' I blurted out. 'It's also that I can't borrow enough money to keep the house. I'm going to have to leave. Not just my home – but all this.' I swept out my arm to indicate the reservoir and the whole heath beyond it, the ancient trees and lakes and grasslands and woods that I loved so much.

Sue patted my shoulder. 'Oh dear,' she said, 'that's really rough.' There was a pause and then she added, 'Whatever happens, you'll still have the kids and Springer. And me, your best friend.' She nudged me in the ribs with her elbow. 'Lucky you!'

Though she was covering it up by being light-hearted, I could see how bad she felt on my behalf and I felt awful. Sue had lived in fear of her life throughout her breast cancer experience; I should be grateful that I had my health, and much more besides. It was difficult to think of exactly what else I had to feel positive about right at that moment, but I knew there were things.

'Come on,' I said. 'I should be getting back.'

We parted by the tennis courts, where enthusiastic sportspeople were thrashing balls energetically back and forth across the nets.

'Write that letter!' Sue called, as she receded along the path towards the lido and her home in Gospel Oak.

'All right,' I rejoined, in mock indignation. 'I'll think about it. But I'm not promising anything.'

But already, I was composing in my head what I would write to Janez. I didn't know who he was or what he might be able to add to my parents' stories, but I had a sudden premonition that he was important, that he would have something vital to contribute to the memory project.

What exactly it would be, I had no idea.

CHAPTER TWENTY-SEVEN

All Germans are ordered to assemble at the train station tomorrow at dawn by order of decree. Any refusers will be punished.

The notice was short, simple and utterly clear. It was over. The war, if not yet quite altogether lost, was in its death throes. The massed might of the Red Army was on its way – and the Czechs were already taking matters into their own hands. Some people – braver than Katja and Gerta, or more foolhardy and reckless, Katja wasn't sure – had left Sudetenland already, running ahead of the Russians through the frozen wastes of a continent gripped by the hideous cold.

She and Gerta had stayed, not by choice but rather by lack of ability to make a choice. For a moment, after the death of Roosevelt on the twelfth of April, the news had reported that 'victory will be ours'. But that had been short-lived. Three days later, the radio announcer spoke of sustained and relentless attacks against the German lines along the Oder River. And now this notice made the situation clear: Germans go home.

Reprisals had already begun: windows smashed, log piles doused in petrol and set alight, shopkeepers refusing to serve anyone who could not speak Czech. Meindorf, with its fairy-tale enchantment and ethereal elegance, had morphed into something from the worst of the Brothers' Grimm imaginings, a place of fear and loathing and constant watching of one's back. The advent of spring had brought not only unseasonable warmth but also dire fear.

Stuffing the loaf of bread she had bought into her bag, Katja turned back to Herr Wagner's house. The sound of boots on cobbles, threateningly, terrifyingly rhythmic, echoed out from a side street. A new local police force had been formed by the Czech population, those few old men and young boys who remained in town digging out uniforms from pre-1938, forming an impromptu law enforcement agency that had no laws to follow – other than hatred of Germans. Katja shrank into the shadows of a nearby building, clutching her bag to her chest as if she needed to protect the loaf rather than herself.

Before, it had been men in Nazi garb who had symbolised terror. Now, it was anyone. Literally anyone could be an antago-nist, a vigilante possessed by the need for revenge. The Czechs were rising up against the many insults and indignities of occu-pation and anyone tainted with the sin of being German could find themselves targeted.

The men passed by. Katja remained still for a moment, allowing her heartbeat to return to a more normal pace. Her armpits were sticky with sweat, her palms clammy. Plucking up her courage, she tiptoed into the open street and then walked, as fast as she could, back home. The words of the notice ran through her mind and icy fear suffused her veins. She tripped and nearly fell. Righting herself just in time, she clenched her fists into tight balls and ploughed on. She had Hans and Gerta to think of.

In the house by the forest, everything was as normal. Nappies flapped in the wind on the washing line and, from indoors, Katja could hear Hans's high-pitched chattering. She smiled to herself despite everything. Hans had thrived in Sudetenland, growing up strong and healthy with the good, fresh food and the clear country air.

But that was over now. The smile turned to a grimace. They had to go.

She broke the news to Gerta as soon as she got inside. Katja felt a surge of pre-emptive annoyance rise up within her as she saw the elderly woman draw breath as if to respond. She loved Gerta but couldn't bear how impressionable she was. If Gerta mentioned the *Wunderwaffen*, Katja would not be responsible for what she would do to her. Hitler had no such weapon, that much was clear. There was nobody and nothing to help them now. But Gerta, open-mouthed in shock, was speechless.

From the cupboard in the bedroom, Katja pulled forth the two rucksacks they had arrived with. At that time, in 1943, it had been possible to have a trunk sent on behind. It was there, at the end of the bed, now used in summer to store the heavy winter bedding. They could not take it. All they would have was what they could carry.

Reaching up to gather the few paltry garments she possessed, a stab of pain hit Katja in the belly. Mentally, she shoved it away. She could not deal with this now; illness could not be contemplated. She longed for Karl, for his comforting, authoritative presence, though generally she tried not to think of him too much. What was the point? She was sure that he had already joined Horst, dying what the newspapers called a *Heldentod* – a hero's death. On the battlefield or in the hospital, hero or not, what did it matter? Those millions of men were just dead.

And what was it all for? It had been obvious for a long time that this war was unjustified. If she had thought any differently, once she had known what the letters were she would have refused to be involved. Now she had a double burden of worry – that the Czechs hated her for being German, and that the Germans might still arrest her for her betrayal.

Her legs trembling, Katja sank onto the bed and put her head in her hands. As if she didn't have enough to concern her, she also had to think about what would greet them when they got back to Berlin. There had been continual bouts of bombing since they had left. Would their building still be standing? What would they do if it wasn't?

'Katja!' Gerta's voice roused her, making her jump up and busily begin sorting piles of belongings. 'Katja, Hans has been sick. I think he has a fever. We should not go anywhere tomorrow.'

It took all of Katja's willpower to stop herself from snapping. 'Gerta,' she explained, as calmly as she could, 'this is not an option we're being given here. It is an instruction. We have to obey it. If we don't – well, I'm not sticking around to find out what might happen then.'

Gerta stared at her, eyes wide, mouth open, as if having difficult processing what Katja was saying.

'So,' continued Katja, 'let's put Hans in his cot – I'm sure a good night's sleep will set him right. And you and I need to work out what to take. We need to be out of this house by five o'clock tomorrow morning.'

'Where... where...' Gerta's voice wavered and cracked. The poor woman was clearly terrified. 'Where are they sending us?'

A surge of pity ran through Katja. Gerta was getting on in years and understandably struggled with such shock and uncertainty. 'Well,' she replied, carefully choosing her words so as not to further fluster Gerta, 'given that the assembly point is the station, I assume they've arranged trains to Berlin. So we'll be back in Charlottenburg by teatime, don't you worry.' She smiled at Gerta, hoping she'd said enough to prevent her from descending into full-on hysteria. 'Come on, chin up,' she added, encouragingly. 'It won't be that bad.'

'Won't it?' questioned Gerta, tearfully.

'No, of course it won't.' Katja had a sudden jolt of memory, of Gerta announcing the plan to go to the Sudetenland on that fateful morning after the bombs had rained down above their heads. Gerta had looked after Katja then and now Katja must return the favour. 'Now let's get packing. Come on. It won't take long if we do it together.'

THAT EVENING, Hans was fractious and hard to settle into bed. In addition to being unwell, Katja knew he must be picking up on the tense, fraught atmosphere in the house. When she'd finally got him to sleep, she and Gerta said their goodbyes to Herr Wagner, sharing a glass of schnapps with him as they half-heartedly toasted a bleak future. The elderly man, though German himself, had decided to stay. His family had been in the Sudetenland for many generations. He had nowhere else to go and said he was too old for a long journey. He would remain here, in the house of his ancestors, and face whatever fate had in store for him.

Not sure whether to admire his bravery or condemn his foolishness, Katja bade him farewell. The only certainty at that moment was that they would never see each other again.

At the train station, its walls stained black with the soot of decades, a restless crowd was assembling. Hans had seemed much better when he had woken that morning but now, unsettled and unhappy about being in the pram, began to wail and Katja tried in vain to shush him. The waiting room smelled of urine and coal dust, mixed with the nervous perspiration of the dozens of people gathered there. It seemed a totally different place to the one Katja had used to pass through so joyously on her way to the convalescent home at Stahlbach. Now, the memories she had of this place were more about her attempt to find the man with the dog and the terror of the *Sicherheitsdienst*. In a vain attempt to stop Hans from crying, Katja rocked the pram as she would have done when he was a baby, at the same time as glancing anxiously around her. Everybody her gaze fell upon looked as ordinary and bewildered as she and Gerta.

And then she caught sight of Monika and her unruly children. She was dressed to the nines in what was obviously every piece of good clothing she had left, but the children were dishevelled, their hair unbrushed, cardigans wrongly buttoned and shoes unpolished. They were pestering their mother for food, but Monika had none to give.

Hah! thought Katja. Not even an officer's wife from Cottbus could rely on the special favours bestowed upon the highest echelons anymore. They were all in the same boat. Monika had always made Katja feel lacking as a mother somehow, with her constant preaching of how there was no greater calling in life than to be devoted to one's family. Now her kids were as untidy and hungry as everyone else's.

Serves her right.

But at the same time as thinking this, Katja thought about the letters, about Laura, about how she was so sure that Monika had been watching her. Fear unfurled in her stomach and settled there, a dead weight. Did Monika know what Katja had done? At this time when everything was falling apart, would she still be able to use it against Katja? Katja didn't know, but she was sure of one thing – she needed to stay as far away from this potentially dangerous woman as possible.

Pointing to the end of the platform furthest from Monika, Katja indicated to Gerta that they should move there. As they pushed through the throng to find a space, Katja heard a few people greet each other with muted 'Heil Hitlers', but most people were silent, expectant. Thankfully, Hans too had quietened. For the amount of folk gathered here, the lack of noise was eerie, uncanny. No one knew what was coming.

The ticket officer was just the same as always, though, in his shabby old uniform. He sold his tickets with his usual impassivity, as if it were just another day, despite the war being all but lost and the Russians all around. Those waiting to be expelled did not need to purchase a ticket.

Katja helped Gerta to put down her rucksack and plonked her own beside it. Everything they hadn't been able to fit inside was stuffed under or slung across Hans' pram. A big sign instructed them to wait; a train was coming at 6.30 a.m. that all should board.

'But where is it going?' cried one woman, her wail sounding especially loud amidst the general quiet. Her elderly husband kept trying to undress himself and she had to constantly wrestle him back into his clothes.

'Loopy,' mouthed Gerta, sticking her finger to the side of her head and turning it to and fro to indicate his dementia.

Katja, frowning at Gerta's lack of subtlety, pulled herself up to her full height and pushed her shoulders back, trying to remain calm and aloof. It pained her slightly that, like Monika, she had elected to wear her best – in her case, her only good – clothing, her fur jacket, with a smart green hat and gloves. It was far too hot for such attire and Gerta thought she was mad.

'You're not going to a fancy restaurant,' she'd snorted, as they'd set out from Herr Wagner's house for the last time. 'What do you want to dress yourself up like that for?' The pressure and anxiety made both of them snappy and irritable.

'I want to look respectable, not desperate,' Katja had retorted. Filled with so much anxiety, they were both being short-tempered with each other. 'We're much more likely to be treated well if we look like fine, upstanding citizens than if we resemble a couple of hobos.'

This answer had silenced Gerta, as Katja had hoped it would. Now, finger-brushing her wind-blown hair as they waited, she could only hope this journey was going to be short and sweet.

Eventually, at seven forty-five, a train rumbled into the station. It had only three carriages.

A muted murmur ran through the crowd. Was this their train? It couldn't be?

It was.

'There are too many of us,' protested a woman's voice. 'How can we all fit on?'

Katja looked around. It was the woman with the crazy husband. As Katja's gaze fell upon her distraught face, a man in an ill-fitting and old-fashioned uniform, who seemed to have appeared from nowhere, stepped forward and pistol-whipped her to the side of the head. With a cry of agony, the woman's hand flew to the wound, where red blood seeped out between her fingers.

More violence, thought Katja, with an overwhelming sense of weary acceptance. It seemed inevitable.

'Get on,' commanded another young man. The power vacuum left by the departing Nazis had clearly been quickly filled.

Mutely, they clambered aboard. A mother indicated to her young son to help Katja with the pram. Thank God Monika was boarding a different carriage.

The train was absolutely packed, barely space to stand let alone to sit, noses pressed against shoulders, jostling elbows struggling for position. Hans began to wail and Katja's heart sank; memories of the nights in the basement in Charlottenburg flooded back. Discomfort merged with defensiveness to put her on edge. She tried as best she could to soothe her son, stroking his head, clammy now from the heat rather than a fever, and murmuring lullabies, at the same time as thinking that if anyone told her to make the baby quiet, she'd tell them what she thought of them, no holds barred.

But nobody did. Everyone stood and swayed in a stunned silence, seemingly unable to process what was happening.

The railway was a branch line, Meindorf the last stop at the end of the valley. They couldn't be kept on this train for too long – they'd have to change at the terminus a few stops on from Stahlbach. The torture of this journey would be limited; there would be a bigger train, with room for all, for the next leg. Katja told herself this as she tried to be stoic.

The train jolted into Stahlbach station and ground to a halt.

'Surely they're not going to try to shove any more on, are they?' someone commented.

A murmur of antagonism rippled through the packed carriage. It was unbearably hot with so many bodies packed together and Katja could feel the sweat gathering in the small of her back and trickling down her legs.

They stood for many long minutes. And then the carriage doors were wrenched open and a cry of '*Raus*' rang through the train.

'Why do we have to get out?' Gerta's tone was alarmed, disbelieving. 'We're nowhere near Berlin.'

Katja forced down the panic that was rising within her. 'Perhaps there's another train coming,' she answered, without much conviction. She wrenched the handle of the pram. 'Come on. Help me get this down.'

On the platform, Katja struggled to dismiss the visions of Karl that rose in her mind. He could not help her now.

Hans' hand reached out to Katja from the laden pram, star-shaped, imploring. 'Mama, mama,' he said. 'Mama.'

He was thirsty, Katja could tell. But he'd have to wait until she could pause for a moment and get out the water bottle.

'In a minute,' she whispered.

A guard was pointing to the exit gates. 'Go. That way.'

'But there's no train there,' wailed Gerta.

The guard shrugged. 'No one said there was.' He clicked his fingers. 'Come on, hurry up. Get out and never come back.'

A sea of people rippled along the platform, a seething mass of the old and the young, and the female, all confused and disorientated, not knowing what to do.

'Where do we go?' pleaded Gerta. 'How do we get home?'

The guard barely looked at her. 'I don't know. Walk. The border's that direction.'

'Walk?' Gerta's expostulation turned heads all around them.

'Come on,' commanded Katja. She needed to take control of this situation before it took control of her. She had to be the strong one, for Hans. For Gerta. For herself. 'There's no point arguing,' she continued. She was fearful of what might happen to them if Gerta protested too much. 'Let's go.'

CHAPTER TWENTY-EIGHT

LONDON, JUNE 1994

'So what did you do?' My words came out as a whisper, as if there were shady policemen and shadowy guards listening beyond my mother's bedroom door. Perhaps it was the knowledge I would soon lose my own home that made me feel so viscerally my mother's trepidation at her situation, cast out into a hostile world, scared and fearful for the future. I thought of how conscious I was of appearing unbreakable to Emma, of not showing her my fear, nor my distress at being cast aside by my husband, of how I still tried not to cry in front of her, just as I had when she and her brother were little. I remembered my own desperate need for my mother to be strong, not to be ill, not to be sad, how scared I had been during those times in my younger years when she had seemed to be absent emotionally even while she was there physically.

Now, finally, I was beginning to understand. My mother had put everything into that terrible situation in which she had found herself and she had simply not been able to sustain the same levels of strength, all of the time. The moment of clarity sent a shudder down my spine and goosebumps rose on my arms. I shivered as my mother resumed her story.

'We did the only thing we could,' she said, raising her hands in a gesture of acceptance. 'We walked.'

'Walked where?'

'To Berlin, of course. How else were we going to get there?'

I shut my eyes and did a mental calculation. I didn't know a lot about the Sudetenland, but I guessed it was probably about 200 to 250 miles to Berlin, and that was as the crow flies. It was hard to imagine taking on an odyssey like that, on foot, together with an elderly woman and an infant.

'But – that's some walk, Mum.' Springer, hearing his favourite word, jumped up, tail wagging, ears pricking. I batted him affectionately away. 'Not now, Springer,' I muttered. 'Long by anyone's standards.'

My mother nodded, slowly, and sighed as if she was still experiencing the exhaustion and fear of that moment when she had descended from the train and understood the magnitude of the challenge ahead.

'In the end,' she continued, 'we realised we were lucky. The wildcat expulsion happened early for us. Many Germans – both newcomers and those who had been there for generations – stayed put, like Herr Wagner, I suppose. But life got progressively worse and worse for them. By midsummer, they were forced to wear white armbands marked with an "N" for *Nemec* – the Czech word for German.'

'Gosh.' I sat back in my chair and conjured up a mental image of what my mother was describing. It was payback, of a sort, against the people who had made the Jews wear yellow stars. But surely a good example of how two wrongs don't make a right.

'We weren't all Nazis!' she exclaimed, as if reading my mind. 'Myself, I was never one. Horst was not a party member. But we were all cast in the same light, tarred by the same brush.'

Her voice faded, the passion gone. 'I suppose it was inevitable that ordinary people should reap what their ruler had sown,' she concluded, sadly.

'History seems to tell us this is the way the world works,' I mused. Just look around right now, at the genocide raging in Rwanda even as we were sitting here talking about a different Holocaust. There it was a terrible slaughter that seemed to have arisen from age-old resentments, just like those against the European Jews, and about which the rest of the world appeared powerless to act.

'The reprisals didn't end there,' my mother continued. 'On one occasion that year, German women and children were dragged from a train, forced to dig a mass grave, then shot in the back of the neck and buried in it.' She paused, examining the backs of her ageing hands. 'After the annexation in 1938, the Germans did so many things to cause resentment – they were given the right to go straight to the front of the queue in shops, had access to better food and housing – like in the dreadful Monika's case – and given the best seats in theatres and cinemas. Even park benches had notices on them saying "Nur für Deutsche". You can understand how the people who weren't German must have felt.'

I considered this. Without doubt, my mother was right. But could the murder of innocents ever be justified?

'How did you feel?' I asked.

She gave a derisive snort. 'I'm not sure I had the right to feel anything. I had gone to the Sudetenland in the spirit of self-preservation. I didn't offer the people there anything, other than at the beginning I had money. By the time we left, money was worthless; there was nothing to buy. We were a burden, and an unwelcome one at that. No wonder they wanted rid of us.'

There it was again. The shame. The acknowledgement that retribution was owed – an eye for an eye, a tooth for a tooth.

I squeezed my mother's hand. 'Tell me about the walk.'

CHAPTER TWENTY-NINE

SUDETENLAND, 1945

Within an hour, the mass of refugees disgorged from the station had dispersed. Some were trying to reach Frankfurt or Munich, others Bonn or Hamburg. Katja and Gerta, heading for Berlin, found themselves walking with the elderly couple – the woman and her deranged husband – plus the mother and boy of about eight who had helped them onto the train, and two young girls – one eighteen years old, beautiful and terrified, named Alice, and the other, Maria, in her twenties, plump and plain. Katja had no idea what they had been doing in the Sudetenland and didn't bother to ask. What did it matter? She was just grateful that Monika seemed to have melted into the crowd. Hopefully, she would never see the woman again.

Looking around at the motley crew she now seemed to be leading, Katja had to suppress an ironic laugh. *We'll never make it to Berlin*, she thought. *We must be crazy. All as insane as him, the madman.*

His name was Friedrich, and his wife was Frieda. The cut

from the pistol blow the policeman had given Frieda had stopped bleeding now, a congealed layer of blackened blood having formed over the broken skin. It was obvious the couple were very close; their dependence on each other would have been beautiful if it wasn't so sad. Frieda had tied a piece of string around Friedrich's wrist so that she could lead him like a dog, but he kept worrying at it, trying to undo it and take it off. He jabbered and blabbered continually.

He'll drive us all mad, thought Katja, and then immediately hated herself for being so unkind and judgemental. It was not his fault he was senile. And his wife was so patient and loving towards him. *We could all learn a lesson from her*, Katja reflected, and vowed to be more understanding. This was going to be a hard enough journey. They all needed to be kind.

At first, the country roads were quiet. Wild flowers grew on the verges: oxeye daisies, cow parsley, speedwell. There were few pedestrians and even fewer vehicles. But as they approached the main road that led towards the German border, the traffic increased. They stopped for lunch at a roadside tavern, but all that was available was bread and beetroot soup, and not enough of it for anyone.

By the time evening came, tempers were fraying. Friedrich had wet himself and Frieda wanted to stop to get him changed. But Katja thought they should press on.

'We're not safe here, in the Sudetenland,' she declared. She wasn't sure how she'd ended up being in charge, but it was clear someone needed to assert their authority and make decisions, or they'd never get anywhere. 'We need to reach Germany proper as soon as we can. Then, it will be better.' As soon as the words were out, she knew how weightless they were, how unfounded. Nothing was going to be better any time soon.

An intense roar rose up, shaking the earth, thundering down from the now distant mountains. Katja looked up. A formation of American bombers was approaching, a hundred of them or more, propellers whirling, throbbing engines booming. Sunshine glinted off metal so that they resembled a shoal of silver fish darting through the blue sky.

Hans began to howl and Katja tore her fascinated, horrified gaze away and leaned over the pram to comfort him.

There were so many of them, so many planes, so many bombs to drop. What could possibly be left of Berlin when – *if* – she, Gerta, Hans and the others did eventually get there? But at the same time, where else could they go?

They walked on. As they progressed, they were joined by countless other groups like themselves, all moving westwards, following the sun as it sank in the sky ahead. There were hundreds of people, carrying bags and packs, babies and boxes, pushing prams and flimsy pushchairs. The lucky ones had carts that were piled high with possessions; others, bent almost double, stumbled under the weight of huge sacks slung across their shoulders. Every now and again, a bicycle wove through the masses, but the majority plodded on in foot.

'We should stop soon,' pleaded the plump girl, Maria.

Frieda nodded. 'Please,' she begged.

Katja turned to look at them both. It must be exhausting for Frieda, dragging Friedrich along behind her like a reluctant sack of potatoes. But they needed to get as far as they could, to keep moving for as long as there was daylight to see by.

'Let's keep going for a bit,' she suggested. 'The next town we get to, we'll find somewhere to sleep. It's only five kilometres.' She'd seen the distance on a signpost they'd passed. It wasn't too far. They could make it.

They limped on. Katja could tell that Gerta was feeling her age in every step, but there was nothing she could do to help. Weariness silenced even Friedrich. As dusk began to fall, Katja surveyed her companions. What a sorry bunch they were. If this journey depended on survival of the fittest, she feared for them all.

When they reached the town, a hastily hand-drawn sign on a piece of cardboard torn from the side of a box read 'Flüchtlinge' and an arrow pointed towards a schoolhouse that had been opened up for sleeping accommodation. So this was what they were now. No longer people, individuals with histories and personalities, but refugees reduced to one single word: Flüchtlinge.

The school was already full to bursting, but in one of the classrooms, Katja managed to find a space for herself, Gerta and Hans. She laid out the couple of knitted blankets they'd brought with them, and rolled up her fur jacket as a pillow. It would have to do; thank goodness the nights were warmer now. Earlier in the year, they would likely have frozen to death. Indeed, that had purportedly been the fate of many who had left before them.

Now, if ever, was the time to be grateful for small mercies. But as Katja tried to sleep, her fear for the future threatened to overwhelm her. Holding Hans tight, she breathed in the comforting, familiar smell of him, and prayed that they would get through this ordeal.

In the morning, Katja and the other mother, Lilli, went out in search of food. They managed to get a loaf at the bakery, but there was nothing to go with it. The grocer's store was empty, the shelves bare. Katja thought of Horst's shop in Berlin, the stock that had still been there when she had left, tins of fish and beans, boxes of biscuits. Her mouth salivated at the thought. It would all be gone now, looted or destroyed by the bombs, that was for sure.

They shared the loaf amongst them, all nine of them. It was barely enough for a couple of mouthfuls each.

'Let's get going,' instructed Katja. 'The sooner we get to Berlin, the sooner...' Her words trailed off. The sooner what?

The sooner they were killed in an air raid? By Russian soldiers?

Planes flew over constantly, day and night, not just bombers but aircraft of all types, shapes and sizes. By now, everyone ignored them. If they did start dropping their ordnance, there was nowhere to run to, no shelter available for the *Flüchtlinge*. If their number was up, so be it.

As they trudged on, Katja saw that the planes had, indeed, dropped something – but not bombs. On the ground all around them lay cardboard rolls a few centimetres wide, that had split open to reveal leaflets printed on pink paper.

Lilli's son, Ernst, picked one up and unfurled it. Over his shoulder, Katja saw what it proclaimed in thick black block capitals.

THE WAR IS ALMOST OVER.
HITLER'S DAYS ARE NUMBERED.
STAY IN YOUR HOMES AND OFF THE ROADS
AND NO HARM WILL COME TO YOU.

Katja saw tears gather in Ernst's pale blue eyes.

'*Mutti*,' he sobbed. 'It says we need to stay at home. But how can we when it is so far?'

Lilli grabbed the leaflet from him and tore it into pieces which she threw on the ground behind her. 'Take no notice,' she snapped, 'it's nonsense.' And then, seeing Ernst's deep distress, more gently, 'It'll be all right. Don't worry.'

Over the next few days of walking, they came across many similar leaflets. They also encountered ever greater numbers of *Flüchtlinge*. An endless column of refugees was heading west. It was the greatest migration in human history, millions on the move, seeking sanctuary, hoping for a future.

Looking around her, Katja could hardly take in the sea of humanity that surrounded them, people ten deep on the narrow country road. Women, tired and downtrodden, clutched the hands of children whose expressions were grumpy, exhausted or simply uncomprehending. Some groups seemed to have a household of possessions in bags and trolleys and sacks and suit-cases, while others carried little more than a knapsack and a check blanket folded over their arm.

Where were they all going? Katja wondered. Some would be heading home, like Katja and Gerta, but so many others were leaving their homes behind, in Prussia or Silesia or Pomerania. Wherever they ended up, these poor benighted folk would be homeless; they would have to begin again. The very notion exhausted Katja.

As they plodded on, following roads and tracks and paths through field, forest and meadow, the crowd ebbed and flowed, some leaving, some joining, but always moving, following the setting sun.

Passing through a beautiful valley, a startled deer stood staring as if transfixed by a sight never seen before. It caught Katja's eye for a brief moment before fleeing, bounding nimbly over tussocks of spring grass and disappearing into a distant clump of trees. Even though so fleeting, Katja had recognised the doe's expression. She had young in that wood, her fawn or fawns, and she must protect them.

Katja looked at Hans, slumped forward in the pram. He was too big for it, certainly to spend all day in it. But, at eighteen months old, he was far too young to walk alongside the adults. And anyway, he needed to preserve energy. There was not enough food for a growing infant as it was; if he started exercis-ing, he'd just need more. She bitterly regretted her decision earlier in the year to wean him. If only she had milk for him now, he would have nutrition, and it would be clean, when they were surrounded by so much filth. She needed to get him to Berlin as soon as possible.

But it was getting harder and harder to make progress every

day. Not just how crowded the roads were, but how weak from hunger they were all becoming. Katja had shared out everything she and Gerta had carried with them – the tins of beans and tomatoes, the black bread, the rice. She had nothing left. Everyone else was in the same position. They passed farmers tending their fields, milking cows and collecting eggs, and market gardeners harvesting early greens and new potatoes. But they could rarely be persuaded to give or sell any to the *Flüchtlinge*. The group survived on what they could barter or steal, and it was never enough.

To make matters even worse, on the sixth day of walking, one of the pram wheels started to work loose. Every hundred yards or so, Katja had to stop and kick it back on, relying on the weight of its cargo and gravity to keep it in place. But each time they hit a stone or rock or a bump in the road – which was often – it would shift again and have to be rectified. Lilli would tut and Frieda fret as they paused, and Katja got more and more irritated, with the pram, with her companions and with herself. She hated being so helpless.

All round, patience wore thin. Lilli's audible sigh at yet another interruption made Katja see red. She was doing her best, she needed the pram. She couldn't carry Hans all the way to Berlin. Things were difficult enough as it was; the least the group could do was support each other. Her temper flaring, she shouted, 'You don't have to stay with us, you know. You can find another group to walk with, or walk alone – do whatever you like! It's not my choice to have you tagging along, relying on me to make all the decisions.'

As soon as the words were out, Katja regretted them. In reality, she was happy to help these strangers and sure that sticking together was better than going it alone. But she was so tired and worn out already, and so hungry, it made her snap and lash out. She must try to control herself. After all, they still had a long journey ahead.

An awkward silence descended as they trudged on. Even Friedrich sensed the discomfort, but instead of becoming quieter, he began flailing around on his piece of string so Frieda could hardly hold him. Everyone stared at each other as if seeing them for the first time, realising how mismatched they were. Ernst shifted closer to his mother, and Maria and Alice gravitated together, as if mutely proclaiming where their allegiances fell.

Limping along, Katja observed their little group. She hadn't sought out a leadership role, but as it had fallen to her to be in charge, she had to do her best. Often, that was just finding out which way to walk. Katja was continually asking, of locals or other refugees, *Is this the road to Berlin?* She could only hope she was getting the right answers.

A little later, the pram wheel hit a pothole and fell almost completely off. Hans, jerked awake, regarded her imploringly for a few long moments before beginning to cry. Katja's heart sank and her will nearly failed her. Surely it would be easier to just sit down here on the verge and give up? But then she looked at Hans again and rallied. Of course she couldn't do that. For her son, if for no one else, she had to keep going.

Lilli bent down to help her wrestle the wheel back on and this small gesture was a sign of reconciliation. Katja was about to thank her when she was interrupted by angry shouting from behind.

'Get a move on, *Arschloch!*' someone shouted, followed by jeers and cries of agreement and encouragement.

Katja felt her shoulders droop and the last remnants of her anger melt away. It was a hostile world all around them and that made it more imperative than ever that they stood by each other.

'Come on,' she said, wearily. 'We're going to get trampled standing here. We're all on our last legs. Perhaps tonight we'll find a decent meal somewhere.'

But as they trudged onwards, that possibility became more and more unlikely. At every village and hamlet and small town they passed through, they were met by hostile stares and dismissive gestures. It was clear that they were in an area where *Flüchtlinge* were not welcome and Katja began to be scared about what would happen if they tried to stay here. At one point, they came across a field hospital, where wounded men with bandaged heads and limbs loomed out of the darkness like mummies from ancient Egypt. The stench of death and rotting wounds hung heavy in the air and, despite their exhaustion, their group sped up in silent desire to get away as fast as possible.

Katja fell into position walking alongside another woman of around Gerta's age.

'The Ivans are at the Oder. But it's all right.' The woman looked suspiciously over her shoulder, and then to the left and right, dark eyes darting to and fro like a crazed metronome. 'The Russians sustained heavy losses. And Hitler still has the *Wunderwaffen* and the Werewolves. We will still win; the Fatherland will always win.'

Katja didn't know whether to laugh or cry. The Werewolves the woman mentioned were nothing more than young boys, hiding in the woods, determined to get themselves killed by any means possible in the name of their country. As for the idea of the miracle weapon that Gerta had once believed in so fervently – it was total rubbish, everyone knew. But some people preferred to carry on deluding themselves rather than face the truth.

Looking around at the faltering, shuffling, hobbling bunch of refugees as she thought this, Katja had a sudden flash of insight. Delusion might well be preferable to reality. Perhaps she should try it.

She didn't say anything, though, either in agreement or disagreement. It might be deemed unpatriotic and you never knew who anyone was, what connections they had, what trouble they could cause. Always at the back of Katja's mind lay the knowledge that she had been a traitor, carrying the letters for Karl, passing on information. Even now, with the war so nearly over, she could still be caught and arrested at any moment. Under torture, she'd buckle, she knew she would. At first, she'd done what Karl had asked out of love and belief in him, but once she'd realised what was going on, it had all been for Hans, for his future. Though she was proud of her actions, the knowledge that it could come to be her downfall was ever-present, like a throbbing sore beneath the skin.

As if to confirm her fears, at the next crossroads stood a gallows.

'What's that?' asked Ernst, pointing. Lilli ignored him. '*Mutti*,' he pestered, 'what is it? Is it for hanging?' His voice grew more excited as he realised the wooden structure's purpose. Still, Lilli took no notice.

Katja stroked Hans' blond head. 'My poor baby,' she muttered under her breath, 'what a world you have been born into.' Thank goodness he wasn't old enough to ask such questions yet.

Ernst broke away and ran to the gallows, standing underneath and looking up at the stained and tangled noose that hung there. All the adults knew what it was for – Wehrmacht deserters, spies or those who had committed treason against the Führer or the *Vaterland*.

Katja suppressed a shudder at the thought that this number included her, for the letters she had carried. The fear that her crime would be found out rose again, threatening to suffocate her.

Lilli called Ernst back. When he returned to her side, she shook him roughly by the elbow. 'Don't ever do that again,' she hissed. 'You stay here, right by me.' She glanced fearfully upwards and gesticulated around them. 'There are bad people out there. Don't ever forget it.'

Whimpering, Ernst fell into position.

Katja's heart broke for the boy, as it did for her own child. This world of violence was not right for any of them.

That night, weary beyond imagining after the miles they had covered, the only shelter they could find was in an abandoned barn. It was cold and damp and stank of cow dung, but it was a roof over their heads on a night that was already dank, fitful blasts of rain propelled into their faces by a squally wind.

They had almost no food, just some new potatoes Maria and Alice had stolen from a field, nipping in behind a farmer departing for his lunch and burrowing with bare hands deep into the soil to unearth those tubers he had left behind. They got water from a still-working pump, built a small fire and set the half a dozen potatoes boiling.

'Has anyone got anything else?' asked Katja. 'Any tins of fish or dried beans or anything?'

Everyone said they had not. But there was something about Lilli's demeanour that made Katja doubt her.

'Lilli?' she demanded. 'Are you sure? Are you hoarding stuff for yourself? Because if you are, you should know that you are behaving very badly. We've all shared with you.'

Defiantly, Lilli shook her head.

The rapprochement between the two of them of earlier evaporated in an instant. Katja jumped up, determined to find out for herself. She reached out for Lilli's rucksack and, as she did so, Lilli grasped her arm. Her grip was surprisingly strong.

'Don't you dare go through my things,' she shouted. 'You have no right!'

'Oh yes I do,' countered Katja, her voice steely with resolution. 'Get off me,' Fiercely, she shook herself free, seized the rucksack with both hands and shook the contents out.

Clothes, a hairbrush, some trinkets and pieces of jewellery

fell to the ground. But, also, three tins of sardines, a bag of black beans and a jar of home-bottled sauerkraut. Plus, the holy grail, a bar of chocolate.

The items lay there, on the floor of the stinking barn, an accusation. Katja had known that Lilli was lying. But finding the proof turned her anger to a raging fury. The worst part of it was that they were travelling with someone who lied, who could not be trusted. And in this world of pain, trust was everything.

CHAPTER THIRTY

Lilli was weeping.

'It's my food,' she cried, 'in case I need it. In case Ernst needs it. He's a growing boy, don't you understand?'

It was impossible to feel sorry for her when they were all hungry and struggling. Katja seethed. All this anger, it wasn't good. But how could she prevent it? She was doing her best to protect her fellow refugees, these people she barely knew, to make them all pull together on this perilous journey, and that took energy that she should really be preserving for herself, Hans and Gerta. A little gratitude from Lilli would go a long way, but instead everything Lilli did was self-serving.

'Oh, we understand all right,' Katja spat. 'We have shared everything with you, all that we have. Isn't that right, everyone?' She looked around at the group, all of whom nodded silently. Friedrich had dropped off, his head on Frieda's shoulder, mouth open and dribbling. 'But we've been walking for nearly a week and, all this time, you've selfishly kept food for yourself. How can you be so heartless? I don't think we want to be walking with someone like you,' she went on, unable to stop herself. 'You don't deserve our company.'

'Please,' begged Lilli, fear in her eyes, 'I'm sorry. I-I-I didn't think; we're all confused. I didn't do it on purpose, I just forgot I had that stuff. Please let me stay with you.'

Without responding to Lilli's obvious lie, Katja leaned over and picked up two of the cans of sardines. Swiftly, with a strength born of fury, she opened them and mixed them into the pan of potatoes, making sure she got out every last drop of oil from each tin, then stirring it all around. Everyone had their own bowl or plate and Katja divided out the mash, filling a spoonful at a time and flattening it with a knife to be sure that each measure was identical. Each adult had four spoonfuls, Hans three and five for Ernst. A tiny amount remained.

'Breakfast,' said Katja, definitively, slamming the lid down on the pan.

But Friedrich had other ideas. He'd woken up, slurped down his food and was clearly still ravenous. Lunging forward, he tried to grab the pan. With lightning speed, Alice snatched it away from him. But he was already in motion and he could not stop his forward propulsion. Always unstable, he teetered for a moment and fell, landing face and hands down in the fire.

The scream he unleashed was one of pure agony.

As one, Alice, Maria and Katja pulled him off, but he was burning, his hair, his shirt, his skin. The nauseating, acrid stench of frying flesh filled the air. Wildly, Katja slapped her palms against the flames, while Alice snatched up Katja's fur coat and covered Friedrich's body with it, pressing him to the ground and lying almost on top of him to smother the fire. His screams, like those of an agonised and trapped animal, rent the foetid air at the same time as Frieda began to howl and wail like a banshee.

Despite his mental impairment, Friedrich was strong and he quickly threw Alice off. Katja's jacket was ruined, the fur blackened and charred. It hardly mattered. Far, far worse was the state Friedrich was in. Clumps of skin dripped from his face, shoulders and hands. His eyelashes and eyebrows were burnt, and one of his eyes was red, bloodshot and half closed. He looked terrible. The shock hit Friedrich in a rush and he lay, whimpering and panting, occasionally shivering.

There was no doctor, and the hospital they had passed was over half a day's walk back the way they had come. They could not return there.

Swallowing down her horror, Katja grabbed two nappies from the pram handle where they had spent the day drying. With her kitchen knife, she cut and ripped the nappies into strips and she and Gerta wrapped them around Friedrich's head, his eye and his hands. His shoulders she did not know what to do with, so had to leave them uncovered.

Alice and Maria sat watching in stunned disbelief. Lilli had taken Ernst outside, away from the hideous sight. As Katja dressed the wounds, Frieda crept close to her husband and took one of his damaged hands in hers. Katja's own burnt hands were agony. She could feel the blisters forming and they seared as if still on fire. But her injuries were nothing compared to Friedrich's.

In her heart, Katja knew that what they were doing was just a salve to their need to do *something*. What Friedrich really needed was a proper doctor, pain relief, sterilised bandages. None of this did they have. They had nothing to offer him but a hand to hold, as Frieda was doing. The situation was desperate and Katja would have done anything to make it better. The helplessness she was feeling was the worst of all.

Eventually, they all slept, after a fashion. Katja couldn't wait for morning to come so that they could get out of that stinking barn where the smell of burnt skin and singed hair lingered. As soon as dawn had broken, the little group packed up their paltry possessions in an uncomfortable silence. They gave the last of the food to the children. And then they set off again, Friedrich dragging behind even more than ever. Frieda had tied his hands loosely together to stop him tearing at Katja's makeshift bandages, so instead he continually shook his head to and fro as if that might dispel the pain he was obviously feeling. It was so pitiful that Katja could hardly bear to look at him.

Her own seared hands were sore on the pram handle and the wheel was even looser. Now it was step, kick, step, kick, step, kick.

Alice must have noticed Katja repeatedly shaking out her hands, licking her palms for some relief from the blisters. 'Let me push,' she urged, gently taking her place behind the pram. 'Give those hands a rest.'

Gratefully, Katja accepted – though she hated having to watch Alice struggle with the broken wheel. They had started the walk as a mismatched, ragtag group but now they were even more wretched.

Around midday, they arrived in a larger town than normal. Here, some shops were open and there was a friendliness in the air that they hadn't experienced for a while. They found a place to wait in a small square and Alice and Maria went to see what they could buy. Katja, restless from worry about Friedrich and the pain of her hands, could not sit still. Instead, leaving Gerta in charge of Hans, she wandered off around the square searching for water. In the central courtyards of most apartment blocks, there would be a tap that they could fill their bottles from. As she hunted, Katja admired the window boxes that bloomed with fiery red, yellow and orange tulips. Such prettiness, the cultivation of beauty, was almost unimaginable in these times.

Reaching the entrance to a block that had no gate to bar entry, Katja looked inside. There was indeed a tap, in the far corner. But of far more interest was what lay in the middle of the courtyard.

Carts.

A whole phalanx of medium-sized wooden handcarts with

long handles stood in a row, tethered to a central rail. But at the end Katja saw one that was loose. Something clicked in her head. She had to have that cart.

Venturing out of the shadows and into the sun, Katja tried to look bold and as if she had every right to be there.

Something moved to her left. She jumped, held her breath, paused. But it was just a cat, slinking across the paving slabs.

She got to the carts. Reached out and laid her hand on the wooden handle of the one that wasn't secured. It was a beautiful cart. Sturdy and roomy, plenty of space for Hans and the plethora of items stashed in and on and under the broken pram. They could probably get one of the rucksacks on there, too, maybe both. It was like a dream come true.

Katja pulled the cart towards her.

And then she saw her. A wizened old witch of a woman sitting in the shade beside a planter containing a dead camellia bush, eyes narrowed, scowling.

Damnation. Katja swallowed down her disappointment, and her fear. Stealing was a crime, and criminals were not treated well at the best of times. And this was the worst of times. An image of the gallows flashed before her eyes. She looked up from under her eyelashes. The old lady was sitting completely still, watching. Katja caught her gaze. She plucked up all her courage.

'We've got a long way to go to Berlin and I have a young child and an old lady to take with me. Would you shut your eyes, just for a minute?'

There was a long pause. The expression on the woman's face had altered, but Katja could not read it. It was impassive, emotionless.

And then the old woman spoke. 'Yes, go on,' she said. 'Take it. I haven't seen anything.'

Without waiting another moment, Katja tightened her grip around the handle, ignoring the squeal of resentment from her blistered palms. Twisting around, she jerked the cart over the ridge of the paving slabs and ran.

She was still running when she arrived back where the others were waiting.

'Did you get water?' asked Gerta. 'Hans is thirsty.' She didn't even comment on the cart. The omission caused a surge of irrational fury within Katja.

Catching her breath, forcing herself to remain calm, she shook her head. 'No. No water. Just this cart.'

'Oh yes,' answered Gerta, as if she'd only just seen Katja's bounty. 'That's superb. Well done. It will be a huge help. But what shall we do for water?'

Katja handed their bottles to her. Gerta was right. They all needed to drink. 'Over there,' she said, pointing to the apartment block she had just left. 'There's a tap in the corner. I can't return in case they want the cart back. You go.'

Gerta fetched the water and then Alice and Maria returned. They had struck lucky, and had bread, ham, cheese and apples. It was a feast, and there was enough for everyone. But Friedrich was unable to eat, his mouth too swollen from the burns. Hans, thank goodness, ate heartily but Katja had to force her food down her throat. A child in her home village had been badly burnt once – the little girl had thrown sawdust on the fire and then, thinking she'd smothered the flames, peered into the oven to see. At that moment, the flames had reignited. Two weeks later, the girl died. The burns never even began to heal. Instead, they became infected and sepsis took over her body.

Friedrich was in a bad way, that Katja knew. But she was just as worried, if not more so, about Frieda. The old woman looked half crazed with worry, and she'd started saying things that made no sense, mumbling on about the past, about their son, who had died on the Eastern Front, about their wedding, a dog they'd once had called Roger. It was as if she, too, were losing her mind.

A clattering sound drew their attention.

Trucks and army vehicles spouting noxious fumes, many listing to one side with tyres gone, running on bare wheels, were passing through. Gerta pushed Hans' pram further back from the road, away from the dust and noise, while Katja and the others stood and stared. On the back of the last vehicle sat a soldier in a mud-caked uniform, Schmeisser submachine gun by his side, his hand resting upon it. Katja fixed her eyes on him. He looked so old, far too old to be in the army, sixty or seventy. Then she realised that he was not old at all, just absolutely exhausted.

The truck drew away. Behind it came wooden wagons, drawn by people, not by horses. There were almost no dray animals left alive these days.

When the convoy had passed through, the little group waited in silence for the dust to settle, the sobering truth descending on them like the hazy motes caught by the watery sunlight. This was a once great army most definitely in retreat. And there was an inevitable consequence of that.

The Russians must be just behind.

The thought was terrifying. Head bowed, Katja turned away. She could not dwell on their perilous situation. She must transfer Hans and their possessions into the cart as quickly as possible so that they could keep going.

Raising her eyes, a dreadful sight greeted her. The pram was gone.

With a blood-curdling scream, Katja raced towards where it had been. A couple of nappies had fallen off the handle and she seized them up and threw them to one side. She couldn't care less about any of her things. Hans had been sleeping in the pram. And now it was gone.

Katja's howl echoed around the buildings, bouncing off walls, only dying when caught by the waving branches of the poplar trees.

'Hans! Hans is gone.'

As one, the group spilt up, all searching in different places. For a moment, Katja couldn't breathe, was paralysed with terror. When she regained the power of movement, she began running randomly here and there, screaming Hans' name over and over. She had allowed herself to be distracted by the army convoy and now she was being punished. If she had lost her son, how could she ever forgive herself? How would she begin to live another day without him, the only thing she had that mattered anymore?

CHAPTER THIRTY-ONE

LONDON, JUNE 1994

A terrible silence filled the room. My mind reeled with the horror of Hans going missing amidst that crowd, so many people on the move, tens of millions across the whole country and continent. The thought crossed my mind that this was when my mother had lost Hans for good. I had always thought he must have died, but maybe that was not the case. Maybe she just never found him again, amongst the melee, the hordes of destitute refugees. If this were the case, it was too horrendous to contemplate.

I looked at my mother, whose eyes were now closed, her breath shallow and rhythmic. She seemed to have nodded off, presumably exhausted by these emotional memories. I didn't know whether to laugh or cry. It seemed ridiculous that she could sleep when her account had reached such a moment of jeopardy. On the other hand, did I want to know the worst? Was I ready to hear my brother's fate?

I sat for a few moments, lost in thought. And then suddenly leapt out of my chair. Emma's wedding dress fitting! I'd almost forgotten about it. Rushing to the door, I grabbed my bag and my cycle helmet, raced to the garage to retrieve my bike and hared off at full pelt, pedalling like a maniac.

It was only when I was halfway down Kentish Town Road that I remembered Emma's plea for me to be suitably dressed. Glancing down at myself, I was pleased to see that the jeans I was wearing were perfectly respectable and my trainers passably clean. My hands, however, were a case of 'could do better', the nails a little less scrubbed than was ideal. I'd have to keep them hidden, avoid any wild gesticulations – and definitely no touching of the dress fabric whatsoever.

In the bijou little wedding dress shop in a tiny alleyway off Upper Street, the fitting was just about to start as I arrived. I felt somewhat intimidated entering its sanctified interior; it was so perfect, immaculate, managing somehow to be both cosy and sophisticated, which, as anyone knows who's tried it in their own home, is a very hard act to pull off.

Refusing the glass of champagne I was offered – how much, exactly, was this dress costing? – I stood in front of the changing area in a state of heightened anticipation. The shop's proprietor theatrically flung back the curtain and there was my daughter, my precious Emma, attired in a dress of ivory and gold that brilliantly complemented her fair colouring. I heard a gasp of wonder and realised, to my surprise, that it was me. The dress was beautiful. My daughter was beautiful.

Emma stepped forward and the layers of shot silk that enveloped her rippled in the light like flowing water, and the tiny pearls around the sweetheart neckline shimmered and glistened enchantingly.

'It's so lovely,' I breathed, stunned by Emma's transformation from ordinary mortal to fairy-tale princess. 'I mean, you always look gorgeous, but you've made the perfect choice here – it suits you so well.'

Tears welled in my eyes, which I hurriedly brushed away. It

wasn't like me to get overemotional – but your only daughter getting married was a milestone moment for any mother. Had it been for my mother when I had wed?

I thought back to the occasion. It had been a whirlwind event, undertaken at speed because of the pregnancy. Those were the days when the only respectable options for an expectant woman were to get married or to give the baby up for adoption. As the second of these was clearly out of the question, only the first remained. I couldn't recall my mother being anything other than practical. But now that I was finally getting to know her better, I wondered what had lain beneath her matter-of-fact demeanour.

My hippy friends, on the other hand, had made their opinions more than clear. They couldn't believe I was conforming, that I was tying myself down, and to an architect of all things, the kind of bourgeois occupation they despised. In many ways, I agreed. I'd probably known from the outset that Ed and I were not really compatible, but I didn't want to admit it to myself. Pregnant and bewildered, I craved normality, the sensible, straightforward life that Ed seemed to offer after so much turbulence. And he, for his part, seemed attracted to my bohemian side, perhaps because it was so opposite to his own background and personality. I seemed to be everything he had never dared to be.

Sadly, this had now transpired to be everything he didn't want to be.

We'd barely had a bean to rub together all those years ago, so there had been no fancy wedding dress fittings for me. At our shotgun wedding, I wore a borrowed dress that just about hid my incipient bump and Ed was attired in a slick navy suit I'd found for him in a charity shop. My mother had given me away as my father was no longer alive. I remembered walking up the aisle of St Pancras Old Church and missing my dad so badly that I could feel his hand in mine, skin rough and calloused from gripping the string that bound the newspaper bundles, a work-horse of a hand, a hand that was always steady, reliable, capable.

I missed him now, too. I wished he were here, to talk to about everything, the way I was with my mother. As well as the long march during that terrible winter, I wanted to know about Eva, and Janez, to be able to ask him questions.

'Mum!' Emma's voice broke across my reverie. 'I was saying, what do you think about the train? Do you like it? I'm not sure about it.'

Focusing my eyes and my attention on my daughter, I regarded the waterfall of exquisite lace that fell from the shoulders of the simple, elegant dress. It was designed so it could be taken off once the ceremony was over for ease of movement and, of course, dancing at the reception.

'I think it's beautiful,' I replied. 'It really makes the whole outfit.'

'Oh, good.' Emma looked relieved, but continued to twirl to one side and the other, examining her reflection. Her husband-to-be, Giles, was the youngest of four siblings and already had several nieces and nephews who were going to be flower girls and page boys, so there was no shortage of cute youngsters to hold the train when she walked up the aisle.

'So we just need a little more of a tuck in at the waist here,' the dressmaker was saying through a mouthful of pins, 'and a tiny adjustment to the buttons at the back and I think we'll be there.' She pulled the pins out of her mouth, put them into the pincushion attached to her wrist and flipped her tape measure back around her neck. 'So, please don't do what so many of the brides do and lose half a stone or we'll have to take it in all over again!'

Emma shook her head ruefully. 'No danger of that, I can promise you. I've been trying and trying, but I'm rubbish at diets. I just can't keep one up for more than about four hours.'

It was hard to be sure whether it was me or the dressmaker who was more relieved by this news.

Once we'd left, Emma kissed my cheek joyfully and then grabbed my hand. 'I didn't say anything in there but...' she indicated towards my fingers.

'My nails! I know, I'm sorry,' I laughed, guiltily. 'But I didn't come in wellies and I wasn't late, so two out of three...' Pulling my hand out of Emma's grasp, I unlocked my bicycle. 'And I made sure not to touch anything.'

Emma smiled. 'It's fine. But look – I'm too excited to go home. Let's have a drink somewhere, shall we? Mother and daughter time.'

I nodded. 'Lovely.' It would be lovely, but I couldn't help thinking about all the mother and daughter time I was having with my own mother. How painful it often was, but how necessary. As if neither of us could truly understand each other until the whole story was out there, revealed after so long under wraps.

After Emma and I had had our drink, we hugged for a long time outside the bar.

'You looked amazing,' I said again, my face scrunched against her shoulder. 'Utterly gorgeous.'

'Thanks, Mum,' Emma replied. 'I don't know what I'd do without your support. And I'm so pleased you love the dress.'

I watched as she glided off up the street, the elegance and glamour of the wedding outfit still surrounding her like an invisible aura. *She's so beautiful,* I thought, again. *So young and full of promise, her whole life ahead of her. Her star is rising, shining brightly, as mine dwindles and fades.*

It was a sobering thought, but as I released my bike from its tethering to a lamp post and wheeled it to the road, I reminded myself that, whatever the date on my birth certificate, I felt thirty-five, not pushing fifty. I was not ready yet to be put out to grass, to give up on life and love the way I knew I had been resigning myself to since Ed's announcement.

What would Sue say? I pondered as I cycled home.

Forget stars, they're for the movies, be a meteor! or some equally ridiculous but fundamentally profound piece of advice.

Stowing my bike in the garage and going inside to make tea, that's what I resolved to do.

Be more meteor. What could be simpler?

CHAPTER THIRTY-TWO

'And how was the dress?' asked my mother, when I returned from my outing.

I smiled, picturing Emma in my mind's eye, how resplendent she had looked. 'Wonderful,' I sighed. 'So perfect. You'll be so proud of her, on the day.'

'I'm always proud of her,' she countered, making my smile even broader. Of course she was.

We chatted some more about the dress fabric, the veil, the boutique itself, my mother expressing every bit of the horror I expected her to when I told her about being offered champagne.

'Alcohol!' she exclaimed. 'While you're shopping! I never heard the like.'

I laughed. 'I guess it was a fairly specialised type of shopping,' I remonstrated. 'Not your everyday-off-to-Sainsbury's sort. It certainly would be a bit odd to be necking a bottle of vodka as you navigate the aisles with your trolley.'

My mother sniffed. 'I suppose so.'

A silence fell. I knew that I had to ask about Hans, but I didn't really want to. I'd lay down my life for my own children. I had once lost sight of Evan for a few minutes in a crowded shopping centre and thought that, if anything happened to him, I would die. The short time I had spent frantically looking for him seemed the longest of my life. I could not even begin to imagine the panic that must have gripped my mum when she realised her precious boy had disappeared, so far from home and amidst so much turmoil. So it was with a heavy heart and a lump in my throat that I said to her, 'What happened next? Did you find Hans?'

GERMANY, 1945

Katja stood, paralysed, frozen to the ground. Her first frenzied searching, her fevered dashing hither and thither, had not led to Hans. He was nowhere to be seen. Gerta was sobbing and Lilli was standing with an arm clamped around Ernst's shoulders, vaguely looking around her as if to demonstrate that she was doing something. Maria and Alice had disappeared from sight, pushing through the throng still milling around by the road, desperately calling Hans' name. Katja didn't know where Frieda and Friedrich were, but she couldn't worry about them now.

Think, she told herself, *think, for God's sake.*

She saw a teenage boy, tall and lanky. He might have a big voice. She ran up to him, poured out an incoherent explanation that her son was missing, that he must be found. Begged the boy to shout his name for her, as loud as he could, over and over again.

Embarrassed, the boy's first efforts were pathetic, his voice puny and barely audible above the chatter of the crowd.

'Louder!' screamed Katja. 'Much louder!' It was only a few minutes since she had noticed Hans was missing. It was still possible that the little boy would hear his name, if it was loud enough.

The boy shouted again, and this time a few heads turned towards him. Thank goodness there were so few men around, or she'd have people running to her from all directions. Hans was a very common name. But no matter how the boy shouted, Hans did not appear.

Distractedly, Katja thanked the boy. She tried to work out what might have happened. The pram had gone, presumably with Hans in it. But perhaps Hans had managed to climb out, or even been thrown out. After all, a wheeled mode of transportation was highly sought after amongst the refugees, but a baby possibly less so. Who needed another mouth to feed?

Bolstered by the hope that Hans might be sitting by the roadside somewhere, Katja ran on. With its broken wheel, the pram could only move painfully slowly. Whoever had taken it could not have got far. But what direction they would have gone in was anybody's guess. People were heading to all corners of the country; the thieves could have gone any which way.

Shaking with fear, Katja pushed her way through the mingling hordes. The passing by of the military brigade seemed to have discombobulated everyone. But, at that moment, Katja didn't care about the advancing Ivans. She just cared about Hans. He was so young and vulnerable and, unable to express himself in words, he would be terrified when he realised he'd been parted from his mother and Gerta.

A bunch of ten or so women blocked Katja's path. 'Excuse me,' she shouted, '*Verzeihung, Bitte*, let me pass.'

The women stared at her as one, but did not budge.

'Move!' screamed Katja. 'I've lost my baby, I need to find him. Get out of my bloody way.'

'Rude!' retaliated one of the women. 'Where are your manners?'

'If you've lost your child, that's your fault,' said another. 'You should have taken better care of him.'

Katja paused, tearing her hair with her hands, half-blinded

by her tears. 'Don't you have a heart?' she questioned. 'You should be ashamed of yourself.'

This was what war and fear and deprivation had done. Made people cruel, hostile. What kind of woman didn't help another in her hour of need? There were some good people left, of course. But, in general, that kind of pity and empathy was for another era.

Neither of the women who'd spoken answered. But they almost imperceptibly shifted their position, letting Katja past. She raced on, intermittently grabbing people as she went and asking them, imploringly, 'Have you seen a pram with a broken wheel, or a baby boy with white-blond hair? Answers to the name of Hans... Have you seen him, please?'

But nobody had.

Eventually, dizzy with shock and fear, Katja's light-headedness forced her to slow down. On a dusty patch of grass beside the road at the edge of the town was a tree with huge, gaunt roots. She sank down into a nook between two of them, put her head in her hands and wept. Without Hans, there was no future. If he was gone, she could not go on.

Then another shot of adrenaline kicked in. She could not give up on him, not to her dying day. She would carry on searching, to the end of the world and back if necessary, but she would find her son.

Standing up, she paused for a moment to let the stars of hunger and exhaustion that danced behind her eyes settle down and then she pressed on. She'd only gone a few hundred metres or so before she saw it.

The pram, her pram, overturned in a ditch, its hood ripped, their belongings strewn everywhere, the broken wheel lying a short distance away. With a speed Katja had not known she possessed, she got to the site in seconds. Leaning forward, she seized the pram and lifted it, hoping to find Hans still inside, perhaps a little bruised from the fall, hungry and frightened, but otherwise all right.

But the pram was empty. Hans was not there.

CHAPTER THIRTY-THREE

GERMANY, 1945

Broken, Katja stumbled away from the abandoned pram. No wonder whoever had stolen it had dumped it, stupid, wrecked thing.

Somehow, she began to make her way back to the town centre where she had last seen the others. Gerta would be out of her mind with worry. How would Katja break the news to her that Hans was gone? At that thought, her knees went weak and she nearly collapsed to the ground.

She heard the voice calling long before she realised what it was saying. Her name, over and over again, faint at first but gradually getting louder. She couldn't think who it was; it didn't sound like Gerta or anybody from their small group.

Eventually, she couldn't ignore it any longer. Turning, for a moment Katja was immobile, riven to the spot. And then she was part-running, part-staggering, pushing the ever-present tide of refugees to the side, forcing them to let her through.

'Hans!' she screamed, 'Hans!'

Finally getting to the little boy, her little boy, she fell to the floor and flung her arms around him, hugging him tighter than she'd ever held him before, her breath coming in great, uneven sloughs, her head spinning, her heart beating out of control. She could hardly believe she'd found him.

It was many minutes before Katja managed to clamber to her feet, picking up Hans and sitting him on her hip. Only then did she turn to face the person whose hand Hans had been holding when she had seen him.

The woman regarded her with an unfathomable expression. Katja stared back. Was it a dream? But no, it was definitely her. The mother who'd taken Hans under her wing, who'd clearly been helping the tot to find his own mum, was Monika.

'M-M...' Katja found she couldn't form the name. The unbearable relief of finding Hans was suddenly tinged by the hunch she'd always had about Monika, the belief that Monika suspected her of something. Apart from anything else, it was an extraordinary coincidence to have come across her again after all the days of walking. Had Monika been following her and her hapless band? To what end?

But Monika did not seem interested in Katja at all. 'I didn't expect to see you again,' Monika said. 'But when I saw your little boy, alone by the roadside, I recognised him immediately. I'm glad you've found each other. A mother needs her children.'

Katja wondered where Monika's were. And then suddenly it became clear to her. She and the rest of the group had arrived in Cottbus, Monika's home town. Her brood were probably already in a cosy home somewhere, with their grandparents minding them while Monika was out. Perhaps she'd been trying to buy food when she'd stumbled across Hans, who'd obviously been cast aside by the pram-stealers. Katja wished her luck with finding any provisions; there was almost nothing available anywhere.

But, right now, all that mattered was that she had Hans. She reached out her free hand to Monika. It seemed she had misjudged the woman all along. 'Thank you,' she said. 'Thank you so much.'

Monika barely touched Katja's outstretched fingers. 'You're welcome,' she replied. 'I'm glad I could help. And to see that you and your son are well.' She hesitated. 'But I must go. Good luck and Godspeed back to Berlin.'

And with that she was gone.

Squeezing her son to her, Katja lumbered back along the road until she found Gerta, Frieda, Friedrich, Lilli and Ernst. Maria and Alice were still searching for Hans, but eventually they too returned, and were overjoyed to see the little boy, covering him with kisses. To Katja's great relief, Hans seemed unperturbed by his ordeal and was relishing the attention.

Equilibrium restored, they pushed on. Monika might have completed her journey, but they had miles still to go.

Unfortunately, though the reappearance of Hans was a mini-miracle, the group was far from all right. Friedrich, who'd been walking more and more slowly, was becoming extremely unwell. Fever raged. Katja had tried to keep his wounds clean, but it was impossible. There was no disinfectant, no fresh dressings, and to compound the problem, the old man was so confused and afraid that he would not let anyone get near him, not even Frieda, who herself seemed to have deteriorated both mentally and physically since the accident happened.

On their ninth day on the road, it was clear that his situation was becoming desperate but there was simply nothing that could be done. Far from diminishing, the number of refugees seemed to be swelling every day, meaning scarce resources had to go even further. Everyone was in a state of distress or destitution, thin and weak with hunger, clothes filthy and hanging in rags. Some still had heaps of possessions, bags and boxes and suitcases piled on carts similar to Katja's. But others had next to nothing, having discarded all they owned for easier movement, or lost it, or had it stolen. Women's careworn faces stared bleakly out from heads swathed in scarves, and everybody looked old, even those who had babies strapped to their chests in makeshift slings.

That evening, Katja and her band stopped in a village which had opened its school hall and in which they managed to find a small spot to accommodate them all. Not long after they arrived, Friedrich fell into semi-consciousness. It meant that Katja could at least attempt to uncover the wounds and splash some water on them.

Cautiously, taking care not to disturb him, Katja knelt down beside him and gently removed the makeshift nappy dressing. Gagging, she stared in horrified fascination at the stinking, putrid, bloody mess, simultaneously repulsed and unable to drag her gaze away. Then she carefully laid the cloth back around his head and refastened the safety pin.

Leaving Frieda with her husband and Hans safe with Gerta, she went outside, desperate for fresh air. This village they were in now was friendlier than some, so she did not fear jeers and taunts by being in the open alone.

The church lay on the outskirts of the settlement and the hall opened up onto water meadows that led down to a fast-flowing river. Katja walked down to the water's edge and stood watching the torrent as it roared past, racing towards the sea. The riverbed was gravel and the water crystal clear and Katja could see fronds of weed frantically waving to and fro in the current as if signalling for help.

Eventually, it started to get chilly. Katja's stomach was rumbling loudly and she felt sick and faint with hunger. These days, this sensation was with her all the time. It had started to feel normal.

Inside the school hall, there was little hope of assuaging the craving for food. They had a cabbage, some turnips and potatoes. It was better than nothing. They were all getting thinner and thinner, stick-like bodies hidden by clothes that were now shapeless and baggy, worn to holes in places. Their skeletal frames made it harder and harder to sleep at night; bones pressing on hard floors and allowing little possibility of rest and respite.

In the morning, after another night of fitful sleep, the little group gathered up their few belongings and prepared for another day's walking. As they were about to leave, Katja noticed that Frieda and Friedrich were not there. Their small bundle stood, neatly packed as always, on the parquet flooring, but there was no sign of the old couple.

'We can't wait for them,' said Lilli, urgently. 'they're holding us up enough as it is. We should never have let them join us.'

Katja flashed her a look of utter disdain. The woman's innate self-interest was really getting to her. But maybe it wasn't innate. Maybe it had been awoken by the terrible situation they all found themselves in. Perhaps Lilli, in her desperation and fear for herself and her son, her only living relative, couldn't help it.

'No,' she intoned, firmly. 'We'll spend five minutes looking for them. They can't have gone far and a short delay won't make any difference in the long run.'

Lilli muttered something about wasting time under her breath.

'Come on, Lilli,' Katja exhorted her, trying to make her tone as conciliatory as possible. 'Let's just have one last quick look and then – well, then we'll get going. We can't just leave them behind now we've come so far together.'

With a long-suffering sigh, Lilli nodded and stomped off in the direction of the toilet. Alice and Maria wandered around ineffectually, while Ernst sat guarding his and Lilli's paltry possessions.

Katja handed Hans to Gerta while she joined the search.

'I'll look outside,' she said. 'You wait here.'

In the school yard, the milling morass of *Flüchtlinge* was

starting to move. At least outdoors the terrible stench of them all was somewhat dissipated. Katja pushed her way through the crowd and out to the banks of the river where she had stood the night before. It had rained in the night and the water seemed to be rushing even faster now, breaking into small eddies and whirlpools where rocks protruded to the surface. In a spot just to her right, there were muddy slip marks and the reeds that grew in profusion were trampled down. Katja gazed intently downriver, rubbing her eyes as if to clear them.

Far in the distance, she was sure she could see something on the surface of the water, a bulk of dark clothing, moving rapidly downstream. She blinked, looked again, but it had rounded a bend and was out of sight.

Head bowed, she turned back.

The group was waiting, shifting from foot to foot, impatient.

'You didn't find them, did you?' asked Lilli.

'No.'

Lilli's pouty moue indicated her satisfaction at being proved right, but she didn't criticise Katja's decision. Instead, 'Sorry,' she murmured. 'I'm sorry they're gone.'

Tears flooded Katja's eyes at Lilli's conciliatory gesture. Perhaps the woman wasn't so bad after all.

'Let's go,' she said, working hard to keep her voice steady and to stop the crying.

There was nothing in Frieda and Friedrich's bundle worth keeping, so they left it there, forlorn and abandoned as the empty room.

Walking, Katja felt bile rise in her throat and she stepped aside to vomit into the hedgerow, though hardly anything came up as her stomach was so empty. The retching tore at her stomach muscles and left her shaky and trembling.

Mustering every ounce of strength and resilience she could find, she eventually managed to stand up straight, push her shoulders back, take hold of the cart and push it as fast as possible to catch the others up. As she trudged, flashbacks to the previous evening plagued her. She could not erase from her mind's eye what she had seen beneath Friedrich's bandages. In the unhealed wounds of his burns, maggots, plump and sinuous, had crawled and feasted upon his flesh, even though he was not yet dead, just decaying day by day, rotting while still alive.

Katja swallowed down hard. She would never be able to unsee that appalling sight. It would be with her forever, seared into her consciousness. It would never go.

She was pretty sure what fate had befallen Frieda and Friedrich, and her sorrow for the pair was incalculable. The old woman, knowing it was hopeless, had taken her husband of fifty years to the river, pushed him in and then jumped in behind him.

She had chosen suicide over a living hell. And Katja found she could not blame her.

CHAPTER THIRTY-FOUR

LONDON, JUNE 1994

'Oh Mum!' I was shocked to the core of my being by what I had heard. The relief of finding Hans, immediately countered by the horror of what had happened to Friedrich and his wife. It was quite literally unbelievable – and yet it was true.

I recalled again the days of my childhood when my mother had seemed to retreat into herself. I would catch her, standing at the window looking out at the passing traffic, but clearly not seeing it. In my childish way, I had assumed she was bored – of me, of life, I didn't know, or simply unhappy. I would counter it by demanding her attention, thinking I could shake out of her the sorrow I had no way of comprehending.

Now I thought I knew what she had been seeing. Hans' empty pram. Friedrich, being eaten alive. At the latter image, my stomach turned, just as my mother's had all those years ago. Throwing the window open, I leaned out, feeling the soft breeze against my cheek.

'I had no idea...' I said, eventually. 'All these years and I didn't know what you had had to go through.' My words

sounded feeble to my ears, but they were the best I had. 'You
and all the *Flüchtlinge* – and those poor people, Frieda and
Friedrich...' My voice tailed off as I contemplated the old
couple's desperate fate. 'Thank God you found Hans. But the
whole thing – I don't know why we have never heard of all this
before, what went on...'

My mother sighed. 'The vast majority of us were women.
Almost the only men were the very old or the very young. And
women's stories are never given the most importance, are they?'

It was an unlikely remark from my mother, who was generally supremely unfeminist. But I recognised what she was
saying as a matter of fact, not a political statement.

'No, they're not, you're absolutely right.' It was becoming
increasingly clear to me why she had never had much patience
with anybody's peacetime tales of woe – neighbours moaning
about something the council should have done but didn't,
friends complaining about a perceived slight or a work problem.
They must all have seemed so inconsequential, so trivial and
self-indulgent, to someone who had been through so much.

Those English acquaintances of my mother's would not
have had any idea what she had experienced, would have
known nothing about the epic migration across the continent
of Europe. Most of them probably simply saw her as the
enemy, if not herself responsible for the war, certainly tarred
with the same brush as those who were. For the first time in
my life, the bullying I had endured retreated into some sort of
perspective.

'Even after I got Hans back, I still often wondered what we
were doing, why we were walking at all,' my mother continued.
'What was the point? But then the will to survive takes over and
you do whatever you have to in order to keep going. Though,'
she pondered, her voice quavering, 'that wasn't enough for
Frieda.'

'I guess it was different for you,' I responded. 'You had Hans to live for and you were much younger than Frieda and Friedrich.'

She gave an ironic laugh. 'I suppose I was, though being nearly thirty didn't always feel young, in those days. People had their families sooner than they do now. These days, I'd be travelling the world like you did or forging some brilliant career like Emma, or studying like Evan! Not battling every day just to stay alive, to find food for one more meal, to endure one more day. I had to do it, not just for me and my child, but for everyone in our group. I don't know how it happened, but they all relied on me. At the time, it was overwhelming for me and on occasion made me cross and irritable. I was terrified of letting them all down, and that kind of responsibility in such an uncertain, terrifying situation is a huge burden. But, in the end, I just had to do it.'

'Because you're so strong, Mum,' I told her, 'and they knew it.'

Outside, the breeze was strong and the branches of the wisteria that grew up the house wall tapped on the window. I went back to sit by my mother's side.

'As we walked,' my mother went on, 'we were not just struggling to survive but also to understand ourselves anew as a nation. How had this happened, when we had been told for so long that Germany was invincible? How insane such a belief seems now, looking back. That any country should think it has the right to overpower its neighbours and former friends. Back then, as if to constantly remind ourselves of how far we had fallen, in every town we passed through, next to the Town Hall and the pole flying the swastika flag, there would be an oak tree, just a few feet tall in many cases.'

'Why?' I asked. 'Were they a symbol of something?'

'Oh yes,' she responded. 'These were the *Tausendjährige Eiche* – representations of the destiny of the Third Reich, which was to last a thousand years.'

'I see.' I thought for a moment. 'Are they still there?'

My mother frowned and shook her head. 'I don't know. Maybe, maybe not. I would think they would have been pulled out by their roots, but you never know.' She sighed. 'What a joke. A sick, sad joke.'

I squeezed my mother's hands. I had probably never touched her as much as I was now, while she gradually regained her health in my little house by the Heath. 'So what happened next. After Frieda and Friedrich – after they left you.'

'Their death,' answered Katja, speaking slowly, her forehead furrowed as if she were trying to sort out a tsunami of memories, 'came at a significant moment. It was late April and we were in a community hall in some place or other. Someone had a radio and turned it on, tuned to the BBC. Usually, the censors jammed the broadcast, but that night it was loud and clear. I remember exactly how it began – with an ominous drumbeat that chilled us to the bone, repeated four times.

'The announcer told us that the British and Americans were across the River Rhine, and that American troops had met with Soviet battalions on the Elbe. Finally, we heard that the Russians had crossed the Oder. The breaching of those three great rivers symbolised the final destruction of Nazi Germany.

'The next day, as we walked, we saw piles of steel helmets and discarded uniforms. Soldiers fleeing from the front lines were ridding themselves of anything that connected them to the army. At one point, we had to clamber over a tank, a *Königstiger*, slung uselessly on its side across the road, an emblem of failure.

'We still had to get to Berlin. We had no idea what would greet us when we got there. But we walked knowingly towards it. There was nothing else we could do. I suppose, even when everything was so dreadful, I harboured a little slither of hope in my heart that, once we got to home, things would be better.'

CHAPTER THIRTY-FIVE

GERMANY, 1945

All around, chaos raged.

The refugees were joined by army personnel, convoy after convoy of dead-eyed soldiers staring straight ahead, or at the ground, knowing their mission was over, and that they had failed. A stink of rancid burning fuel and scorched rubber hung thick and heavy all around. The air rang with the sound of steel-rimmed wagon wheels hammering over cobblestones, screeching brakes and the straining engines of the few still road-worthy motor vehicles. What was missing was the sound of human voices. Everyone was too drained to speak. By this time, Katja and her gang had been walking for two weeks and were nearing Berlin, just twenty or thirty miles away. But as their physical condition deteriorated, they were covering less and less distance every day.

A stream of carts rattled frantically by, sparks striking from the horses' hooves, whips wielded by frenzied drivers, yelling at the animals to go faster. Driven to exhaustion, one of the horses collapsed, taking the cart over with it, spewing soldiers and miscellaneous equipment all around.

People rushed forward, into the melee, Katja thought to rescue the men and save the horse. But instead they pulled forth knives and began to hack into the poor beast's living corpse, slicing off cuts of meat. The blood that spurted forth was a rich, deep, ruby red, thick and viscous. The horse gave one last desperate scream of agony and died, eyes rolling backwards in its head and frothy sputum erupting from its nostrils.

Oh God, thought Katja. *Dear God. Poor thing. Poor all of us.*

Ernst was sobbing and Hans, taking his cue both from the older boy and from the mayhem all around him, began to wail plaintively too. Katja leaned forward over the cart to pat and soothe him, whispering in his ear, 'It's all right, it's fine, it's all going to be all right,' all while her inner voice told her, *I don't know if it will be, I'm not sure. More than likely it will be far from all right.*

To add to the nightmare was the prospect of the Red Army soldiers, who had broken through the German lines in many places and were running rampant. It was all Katja could do not to continually look over her shoulder in case a Russian was right behind her, about to seize her and do the terrible things the news accused these men of. But alongside this fear, and often overriding it, was Katja's terrible hunger. Because their nutrition was so inadequate, the little group was finding it harder and harder to walk all day and needed to take longer and longer midday breaks. The weather was hot and they were plagued by insects, big, blue-black flies that landed on sweat-slicked skin and settled there, rubbing repellent legs together while rotating their beady eyes.

One day, about the twelfth or thirteenth day on the road, they'd lost count by now, they managed to buy some sausage from a roadside vendor and to forage some carrots and greens from an unguarded market garden. Of course, everyone else did the same and Katja felt bad for the owner who would return at some point to find his crops stripped bare. But she didn't feel bad enough not to take the food. Hunger overrode all other emotions.

They stopped at a crossroads in the shade of a magnificent linden tree. An old stone trough had no tap but contained a few inches of water. Katja went to inspect it, dubiously eyeing the film of scum and dead insects that covered the surface. A stray dog bounded up, propped its front paws onto the stone edge and began lapping at the grubby liquid. Katja shook her water bottle. It was still about half full. The dog, thirst sated, ran off. Katja decided to wait until they had access to fresh, running water to refill. She walked away, back to Gerta, Hans and the cart. Lilli was nowhere to be seen and as Katja looked around, trying to locate her, she saw Ernst at the trough, dipping his cup into it.

'No!' she shouted. She ran towards him to stop him drinking the dirty water, but she was so debilitated, her legs would scarcely move at speed. Crying out, she tried to attract Ernst's attention instead, but either he didn't hear or he did and took no notice.

Katja reached the boy just as he was refilling his cup. Snatching it out of his hand, she threw the water away. It sparkled in the sunshine as it arced into the bushes.

Ernst stared at Katja, looking confused.

'It's not good to drink,' she told him.

Immediately, Ernst's face fell and his top lip quivered. He was a nervous boy, not helped by Lilli's constant fussing.

'But it's all right,' Katja reassured him. 'I'm sure it'll be fine. Just better not to drink any more. We'll find a tap soon.'

Taking Ernst by the hand, she led him back to the others.

That night, they could not find anywhere to stay. Every-where they went, they found locked doors and no one willing to accommodate the *Flüchtlinge*. They tried to settle down in a covered market but were moved on by unfriendly locals wielding antagonistic fists and making aggressive gestures. Eventually, in a field of overgrown sedge grass, they found an empty chicken shed, its former inhabitants presumably eaten, stolen, or both. By this point, they'd been joined by another small group of wanderers. It had begun to drizzle so they all piled inside and huddled up, awkwardly trying to find space to lie down and sleep.

Hans had already dropped off in the cart and Katja managed to move him onto a makeshift bed of blankets and clothing. He looked so peaceful in his slumber. For a brief moment, Katja allowed herself to transcend their circumstances and imagine herself sitting beside her son's bed, settling him down for the night in a specially decorated nursery in a clean and cosy home, singing him a lullaby and kissing him goodnight with no fear of what the night would bring.

It was all far from reality. And this night brought the Red Army.

At first, the sounds of voices and heavy footfall reverberated around Katja's dreams until suddenly she woke and lay, in the stuffy, filthy chicken house, eyes wide with fear, clutching her dirty woollen blanket to her chest like a frightened child.

There were people outside – men – stumbling across the ragged field. They barked words in a foreign language interspersed with raucous laughter. As they got nearer, torchlight raked the shed, beams piercing the many places where planks were missing in the flimsy walls. Katja watched in terror as the shadows that loomed against the dark night sky grew closer and closer.

With a cacophony of sound, the door of the shed that they had tried to jam shut was thrust open. Figures appeared in the opening, jostling for position.

'*Wo ist Frau, wo ist Frau?*' The voices were hard and insistent, though slurred with alcohol.

The shed's terrified inhabitants froze. There was barely room to move as it was, but still half a dozen Russian soldiers blundered in, pulling the wired door off its hinges and throwing it to the ground outside. Katja smelt the drink on their breath and bodies and saw it in their uncoordinated movements and clumsy stumblings. The men began to move amongst the huddled bodies, shining torches in faces, taking hold of chins in rough hands and wrenching downturned faces towards them for inspection.

They're picking us out like they would an animal at the market, thought Katja, and then revised that opinion. They were not even taking the care that might be given to that task. This was more like choosing a vegetable, selecting a choice cabbage from the basket of second-rate ones.

The flickering light dazzled over face after face. Maria, no longer plump from the lack of food and constant exercise, seemed plainer than ever. The dancing light skipped over her, moved on and alighted on Alice's terrified, beautiful visage.

And stopped.

An overpowering stench flooded the cramped barn, rising above the alcohol and body odour of the Russian soldiers. For a moment, Katja couldn't identify it. And then she realised. It was the primal, base stink of fear.

With a harsh wrench on the arm, Alice was pulled up. She did not give in easily, yelling and screaming, hammering her fists against the chest of the soldier who had hold of her, but he just twisted her arm into a lock and marched her out of the barn. Katja, powerless to help, was struggling to modulate her breathing, each gasp coming in a great, shuddering wheeze. She clutched Hans to her chest – to protect him or herself, she wasn't sure. Unbelievably, he was still asleep and looked angelic lying in her arms with his shock of white-blond hair tousled over his forehead. Maybe they would take pity on her as a young mother, and leave her be.

Another couple of women were scrutinised and passed over. Lilli, her once pretty countenance now haggard and drawn, barely merited a second glance. Surreptitiously, Katja pulled her hair over her face, trying to make herself look as ugly and unkempt and unattractive as possible. It seemed ridiculous – but it also seemed to work. The soldiers ignored her.

Suddenly, on some command which no one understood, the Russians made as one for the door. Those left in the shed heard them retreating into the dark of the night, dragging their still shrieking prey with them.

The night that followed was sleepless and hideous, plagued by the flies that the shed was full of, and spiders, and the nightmarish contemplation of what Alice was being subjected to. Maria was inconsolable, weeping silently into a pile of straw.

As dawn broke, the refugees began their preparations to move in silence. No one dared voice their deepest concerns. At 7 a.m., as Katja and her group were about to set off, Alice returned.

CHAPTER THIRTY-SIX

Alice didn't arrive walking, but on hands and knees, crawling through the dew-laden sedge grass. At first, it was a relief. They had thought they would never see her again. But then it became clear that she could not walk, was too weak to stand upright. Her once angelic blue eyes were empty pits, devoid of any emotion, and her skin was bruised and blotchy. Her clothes had been ripped away, leaving arms and legs bare, revealing flesh covered in cuts and scratches. Dried blood caked her thighs, bearing terrible testament to her suffering.

Maria rushed over to her, taking water, and a small cup of acorn coffee she'd begged from another refugee. Alice raised herself up onto her knees, drank them both and then promptly threw up. Katja knelt down beside her to wipe her mouth, while the others looked on in fascinated horror.

'I can't walk,' Alice murmured, seeming unable to raise her voice above a whisper. 'I can't do it. You go on without me. Leave me here.' Collapsing back onto the sedge grass, she curled into a foetal ball and began emitting feeble, yelping groans of pain.

Katja and Lilli caught each other's eyes. They couldn't stay with her. They needed to keep moving, to get to Berlin before the Red Army completely surrounded them.

'You'll be all right,' said Katja, faintly. 'Just a few days' rest and you'll be fine.' She kissed the girl's forehead.

Poor, poor angel. What had she done to deserve this appalling treatment? This was not Alice's war, nor any woman's. It was a war waged by men, and yet the women and the children were suffering unbearably. All the petty angers Katja had felt during the walk dissipated to be replaced by one great big one. Her anger against Hitler and all his accomplices.

This is your fault, she hissed inside her head. *All your fault.*

With a dead heart, Katja laid her hands on the cart's handle. There was nothing she could do for Alice. She must be resolute, for Hans. Keep going. Never falter.

'*Auf Wiedersehen*, Alice. Good luck.'

They walked back towards the road, Katja and Gerta with Hans in the cart, Lilli and Ernst following. When they got to the field gate, they turned back. Maria had stayed behind and was helping Alice towards the shed.

Pray God those men don't come back again tonight, thought Katja.

As they set off once more, she reckoned they would be in Berlin in a day or so; they were very close now.

She felt constantly queasy and light-headed, her stomach distended from malnutrition; she gave everything she could to Hans. Even so, he had lost the energy to burble and babble as he usually did. Whatever Katja gave him, it was never enough. Every hour, this killed Katja inside. As a mother, the most basic thing you had to do was feed your child and she couldn't. Sometimes she would fantasise about everything she'd buy for Hans, once she could. Big, juicy sausages. Fluffy potatoes, mashed with pints of milk and pounds of butter. Rye bread spread thick with cheese. Great big chocolate cakes with oodles of cream. And apples. Fresh, red apples that crunched when bitten into.

Katja forced herself to stop with these thoughts when she realised she was salivating so much she was dribbling.

The night's rain had passed and it was getting hot again. As the day wore on, the sun screamed out of a blue sky devoid of cloud. There was precious little water and now they were thirsty as well as hungry. Katja rationed what they had to a couple of sips every hour. Hans alone had all he wanted.

Ernst had started to look pale and grey and had to continually stop to go to the toilet by the side of the road, behind a hedge or a tree if he could get there in time, a couple of times right out in the open, to his utmost humiliation. By the time the sun began to set, Lilli was beside herself with worry.

'He's shitting all the time,' she confided in a hushed, anxious tone, surprising Katja with her use of the vernacular. 'And nothing but blood comes out.'

Katja shook her head. She had so little medical knowledge. She didn't know what it meant. But it didn't sound good.

They reached a small village, where, with relief, they found that the hall was open for refugees to spend the night.

By daybreak, Ernst was in a very bad way. Katja regarded him. He looked terrible, feverish. His face and lips were tinged with blue and his breathing came in shallow, small, rasping gasps.

'He needs a doctor,' she said to Lilli, carefully modulating her voice to remove any hint of the panic she felt. 'Quite quickly. Now.'

Lilli's face clouded over with doubt and fear. 'But where? How?'

Katja rubbed her hand across her forehead. 'I don't know – there must be a doctor here somewhere, or a nurse – someone who'll know what's going on. You have to find them.'

Lilli began to cry. 'He's going to die, isn't he?'

'I don't know, Lilli.' Katja could only tell the truth. She had no idea, but she feared the worst. 'But he needs treatment.'

'Stay with him while I find someone, will you,' begged Lilli.

Memories of all the times Lilli had urged onward progress at any cost flashed through Katja's mind, how speedily she had voted for leaving Frieda and Friedrich behind. How things had changed, now the shoe was on the other foot. But, at the same time, Katja understood. Lilli was selfish, that was without doubt – but who could chastise her desperation to save her son? Katja had an awful feeling that Ernst was ill because of the bad water – that she had not got there in time to stop him drinking.

She helped Lilli to settle Ernst down in a springy patch of grass beneath some trees and they tried to make him comfortable.

'I'll go and find a doctor,' Katja said. 'You shouldn't leave him.'

Leaving Hans in Gerta's arms, with a thumping heart Katja searched through the village, knocking on doors, shouting through open windows. '*Arzt!* Doctor! Please, we need a doctor!'

Eventually, an elderly man responded to her cries, opening his door and eyeing her suspiciously. Katja had brushed her hair, the opposite strategy to that used for the Russians, and worn her cleanest blouse.

'Are you a doctor?' she questioned him desperately. 'Please can you help. We've got a sick child, a little boy. He's got diar-rhoea and he's vomiting a lot. He doesn't look well at all.'

The man pursed his lips. 'I'm a doctor, yes,' he replied.

Katja regarded him expectantly, waiting for him to say something else, to ask where he was needed. But he said nothing.

'So can you come?' she implored. 'Please. He's just a child and we don't know what's wrong with him or what to do.'

The doctor appeared to consider Katja's request. Finally, with a long-suffering sigh, he responded. 'All right. But I can't be long. It'll be dinner time soon.'

Katja felt that, if she caught sight of the doctor's dinner, she'd throw it in his face. Surely he couldn't be more concerned with his stomach than with an ill child? What about the Hippocratic oath or whatever doctors had to sign? But then she forced herself to calm down. He was coming. That was all that mattered.

By the time they got back, Ernst was lying still and silent, his lips slightly parted, the blue tinge to his skin more pronounced than ever. Lilli sat beside him, holding his hand, sobbing silently.

The doctor examined him carefully. 'He's not going to make it.' His words were short and to the point, and he stepped back as he spoke, fearful of infection or just because there was nothing more he could do, Katja wasn't sure. 'Cholera,' he explained. 'There's a lot of it about. He will have picked it up from some dirty water somewhere. When it takes hold, it can kill within hours.' He turned as if to leave, like he couldn't get away quick enough. 'I don't have anything to treat him with, I'm afraid. The sulfa drugs I had are all gone. I'm sorry.'

Lilli went mad, rolling on the ground, screaming, tearing her hair, weeping.

The doctor paused. 'If you want to get to Berlin, I would get a move on,' he advised Katja. 'You don't have much time.'

'Much time until what?' Katja could feel her skin blanched pale with the horror of it all, what was happening to Ernst, the doctor's cautionary words. She had the strongest urge to run away, to seize Hans and get as far from Ernst and his sickness as possible. She hated herself for it. Who was selfish now?

The doctor shrugged. 'It's not going to be long now,' he said, cryptically. Katja didn't know if he meant the end of the war or the end of Ernst. 'Take care of the little one,' he added, as he walked away. 'Wash his hands well, and only drink clean water.'

Katja felt rage surge within her. Oh yes, that was so easy for him to say, who wasn't walking anywhere, who had the luxury of his own house, running water, a bathroom, and dinner waiting. But still. He was right. She couldn't take the risk of Hans getting infected.

They left Lilli with her dying son and walked on, three where once they had been nine. She had known the walk would be difficult from the very beginning, but it hadn't occurred to her that they wouldn't make it. In addition to this awful outcome for those who she had befriended in such dreadful circumstances, Katja was weighed down by her knowledge of the truth. She was to blame for Ernst's illness; she had not managed to prevent him from drinking the water in the trough. The boy's inevitable death was her fault.

CHAPTER THIRTY-SEVEN

LONDON, JUNE 1994

'I still feel guilty.' My mother's face was contorted with the anguish of her memories. 'Ashamed.'

I seized her hands in mine. 'No! You did your best. You tried to stop Ernst from drinking the water. You were looking after everyone, you couldn't have your eyes everywhere all the time. It's a terrible thing that happened, a tragedy. But it wasn't your fault.'

But even as I said the words, I understood. I would feel guilty, too. I wondered if this was it, the real source of the shame I had identified in my mother right at the beginning of all this, but I wasn't sure. I still felt that there was more, things as yet unsaid that needed to be aired.

From outside, the sunshine beckoned. My mother was stronger now than she had been, able to walk short distances. I led her into the garden, where the roses were poised to burst into bloom and the herbaceous border was ramping up to its summer flourishing. We sat on a bench to admire it all. Though it was beautiful, the joyousness of such vigour and blossoming seemed almost too much to bear in the light of my mother's experiences.

She spoke again. 'The guilt was partly for Ernst's death,' she whispered, as if scared that the birds and insects, for there was no one else around, would hear and judge her harshly for past actions, 'and partly for leaving Lilli. For leaving Alice. For not being able to help Friedrich. Oh, Johanna, it was awful.'

I put my arm around her as my eyes cast about, searching for the right thing to say. A few hundred feet away, I could see the garage roof. The swifts were back, nesting under the eaves as they did every year, a pair on the wing right now, wheeling through the clear sky, making their peculiar high-pitched, single-note calls. Every spring, I awaited their arrival with eager anticipation. They were the sign that winter had been banished and summer was here and their familiar presence kept me company during long hours of work in the garden. If the swifts were here, I always thought, then everything would be all right.

But this year, it might not be. I would have to move out of my home at some point, when it was sold. And the more I delved into my mother's past and found out about the guilt and shame she still carried with her, the more despairing I was that I could help her deal with the burden she bore.

'We carried on walking,' she continued, lost in the past, 'just walking and walking. One foot in front of the other.' Her tone of voice implied that this was a failure of some sort.

'You had to, Mum,' I remonstrated. This was, without doubt, true. But still. The banal brutality of it all was shocking.

'I feel so terrible, Jo. Of that and so much else. I should have done more. Starting with the letters I burnt. I should have found someone to pass them onto, to give the information to. If I had – perhaps the war would have ended sooner.'

'No!' I shook my head vigorously as if that could shake out

my mother's bad feelings. 'No, Mum. You tried your best, I know you did.'

Whatever I said, though, I wasn't sure that she would believe me. She was so stuck in self-blame and self-recrimination.

'You did what you had to, Mum. To protect Hans. No one could have done more,' I insisted.

'Did I?'

'Yes. Of course you did.' A fly was buzzing around my head and I batted at it angrily. I wished I could bat away my mother's heartache in the same way.

'Sometimes poor Alice comes to me in my dreams, screaming for help.'

'Mum,' I said, tentatively, 'those Red Army soldiers had guns and knives and ten times the strength of you. How could you possibly stand up to them?'

'You see now why I don't like doctors.' She pursed her lips and wrinkled her nose as if something smelt bad. 'These here, the NHS, well, they're all right,' she went on, somewhat grudgingly. 'But then, in that war – no.' She shook her head violently to and fro. 'Those ones were no good. It was ironic, really,' my mother resumed, her eyes dark with reminiscence. 'If Maria had still been fat as a little goose, they would probably have favoured her over Alice. The Russians – they liked the plump ones by all accounts. By that time in the war, the only women with any extra flesh on them were the wives and mistresses of senior Nazis because only they had adequate food. I can't feel sorry for those women. But for Alice...'

'Mum,' I interjected, 'you have to move on from that. There's no point dwelling on the past.'

'But here you are, encouraging me to!' she exclaimed in retaliation.

I sank back, my spine hitting the hard wooden bench struts, feeling defeated. She was right. I had elicited this digging up of harrowing memories that had been buried for so long. If there were repercussions – I was the one to blame. And yet – I couldn't stop now. There was still so much to find out. And though my mother might protest, I felt that underneath the bombast and bluster, she was finding the process cathartic. To finally air such terrible memories, to let them breathe, to expose them to the sunlight – that had to be good and beneficial, didn't it?

'So you were nearly at Berlin,' I said, encouragingly.

'It was the last days of the war, though we had no idea that it would be finished in less than a week. In some ways, it felt as if it had already been over for months. I remember Gerta saying, "things will get worse before they get better" and dismissing it as an old woman's pessimism, born of exhaustion and the terrible way that her beloved Führer had let her down. All those years believing, for nothing, all that faith in his invincibility, blown to the four winds... At least I hadn't fallen into that trap.'

The sun went behind a cloud and a cool breeze blew. I nipped inside to fetch a blanket to put over my mother's knees.

'The next night,' she recalled, smoothing out the plaid fabric with rhythmic movements, 'the first time it was just the three of us together, we met a farmer. We came across him on his way back from his fields and he invited us in for dinner. Proper food, cooked in an oven! I can almost taste it now, I remember it so clearly. *Schweinebraten*, red cabbage, dumplings. It was delicious. And the prospect of sleeping in a bed! It felt too good to be true.' She halted and gave a short, dismissive snort. 'And, of course, I soon discovered that it was. Gerta took Hans to the outside bathroom to clean him up and the farmer asked me to marry him. Just like that! I think he thought I'd agree and climb straight into the bed right there and then.'

I couldn't help but laugh. Amidst all the mayhem, the farmer still wants a wife. 'What on earth did you do?' I asked.

My mother grinned mischievously and the atmosphere

mellowed perceptively. 'I said it sounded like a marvellous idea, but I needed to visit the bathroom. As soon as I got outside, I grabbed Gerta and Hans, ran back to the porch where we'd left the cart and fled. We slept under a hedge that night. I did have a few moments of regret, thinking of a mattress and sheets and a pillow, but at least we'd had the meal.'

'Oh, Mum!' I would have understood, I thought, if she'd acquiesced with the farmer's wishes. 'What you had to go through. I'm so sorry. It seems like a lucky escape, though.'

'Yes, it was,' she agreed. 'Though I remember being annoyed when I realised I'd left my hairbrush in the bathroom. I'd managed to look after it all that way and then it was gone. What a silly thing to be worried about, and yet it seemed to really matter.'

Her journey was a tale of the trivial alongside the bizarre alongside the macabre alongside the horrific. How to make sense of any of it?

The wind stirred the rose branches so that they rattled against the pergola and set the wisteria tapping on the windows. My mother shivered despite the blanket.

'OK, Mum,' I said, 'I think we should stop there for now.'

She nodded. 'I wouldn't mind a little lie-down,' she agreed.

Once I had settled my mother back in her room, I headed for the kitchen with a heavy heart. Littered all over the table was paperwork related to the divorce: solicitors' letters, bank statements, mortgage assessments. I regarded it all with a sinking sensation of despair. Trying to put my calamity into perspective alongside Katja's experiences didn't really help. Of course my situation wasn't so bad, nowhere near as horrendous as hers, but it was still bad.

To take my mind off my troubles, I decided I'd tackle a bit more of my father's almost illegible scrawl. It was a while since I'd last opened his little diary. But first, there was something I needed to do.

At my desk, I took a sheet of Basildon Bond writing paper from the drawer, together with my good fountain pen. I had been mulling over the wording I would use ever since Sue and I had discussed writing to Janez. She'd continued to nag me about it so I'd decided to stop procrastinating and get on with actually writing the damn thing. The name of the Slovenian town was ripped, with half missing, but I'd worked out what it must be by painstakingly studying each page of the European driving map that was always kept in the car – a legacy of the order Ed had always attempted to impose upon our lives in face of my rather more haphazard nature.

Though I had been planning it for ages, I still deliberated over how to address this person I'd never met. Dear Janez? Dear Mr Novak? Dear Janez Novak? In the end, I settled for the one that sounded friendliest.

Dear Janez, I wrote.

I hope this letter finds you well. I am writing to you on behalf of my late father, Mr Lou Robby, of Camden Town, London. Recently, I found some documents relating to my father's war years and amongst them was an envelope with your address on it. As we are preparing for the fiftieth anniversary of VE Day next year, I have been doing some research into my parents' wartime experiences. I wanted to get in touch with you as my mother tells me that you used to organise reunions of those who had been in the prison camp in Italy, and I thought you might be able to provide information about a period in my father's life of which we know so little.

Please do get in touch if you can. I look forward to hearing from you.

Yours sincerely,

Jo Sawyer

I added my address, and my phone number.

As I put the lid back on the fountain pen, the phone rang. For a fleeting, bizarre moment, I wondered if it was him. But of course not. My mind, spending so long in the past, was playing tricks on me.

In the hallway, the ringing was loud. I grabbed up the receiver, hoping that its clamour would not have disturbed Mum.

'Hello.'

'Jo.' It was Ed. 'It's me, Ed.' There he was again, introducing himself to me like a prat.

Twisting the cable anxiously around my fingers, I answered brusquely. 'Yes, I know.'

There was a brief pause. My stomach began to ache in anticipation. Ed could only be calling for one reason.

'We've had an offer on the house.'

Though I had been expecting it, his words still made my head spin. When had this happened? How?

'The agent phoned me earlier,' Ed was saying, answering my unasked questions.

'Look, Ed, I can get fifty thousand pounds,' I blurted out. 'Would you accept that and I'll pay you the next thirty in instalments, as quickly as I can. Please.' I hated myself for that final begging plea, but I was desperate. There was no point in hiding from Ed what he already knew.

There was a long silence. I held my breath. Was he at least considering it?

'No, Jo, I'm sorry, I can't.' His voice sounded distant, as if his mouth was too far from the receiver. He was talking to Annabelle, I realised. He spoke again, louder this time. 'As I told you before, I need all the money now to buy the Hampstead Garden Suburb property, otherwise we'll lose it.'

He was nothing if not stubborn and single-minded. Why had I expected anything different? He'd always been like this.

'I've said yes to the offer, by the way,' he added.

By the way? Good grief, where did this man get off?

But almost as soon as I'd had that thought, my anger turned to despair. It was over. My dream of staying in my beloved home was finished. I was going to have to leave.

CHAPTER THIRTY-EIGHT

GERMANY, 1945

'You are to prepare to march again.' Hässlicherkopf had not improved, in looks or temperament, during the journey.

'Where are we going?' demanded a voice from the back of the cabin.

'To Berlin.'

So it was true. The rumours had come to pass. They were, finally, to be taken to Berlin as hostages.

'The city is a fortress and will be defended to the last man,' barked Hässlicherkopf . 'So get ready.'

Lou felt a flash of anger more profound than he had ever experienced before. There were thousands of men packed into this compound, *kriegies* far outnumbered the guards and, even though unarmed, the hatred in each and every POW's soul surely meant that they could overpower the Germans if they wished to. What were they doing, following orders like dumb sheep? What had happened to the duty to escape, to serve the Allied cause?

But Hässlicherkopf had moved on and none of the men

showed any inclination to challenge him. Lou slumped down
onto the nearest bunk and let his head sink into his despairing
hands. It was hopeless. He didn't know what he was thinking. If
they rose up, they would be gunned down like so many sitting
ducks. They might have the upper hand in terms of numbers.
But they had not a single weapon between them.

Wearily, Lou picked up his old homemade pack. It was torn
and tattered, hand-sewn pockets flapping loose, full of holes
through which the watery light thinly filtered. There was little
to stow away these days, hardly any food and not many trading
goods either. He slammed a slab of soap angrily down onto the
fabric. He was aware of his temper, frayed to the limits like the
backpack, hardly strong enough anymore to bear the burden it
was required to carry.

Despite Hässlicherkopf 's exhortations of urgency, for two
days, nothing happened. Nerves, brittle as spun sugar and taut
as bows, frequently snapped. Arguments erupted regularly, and
it seemed that everyone was suffering low mood or depression,
if not a full-on breakdown.

Finally, the order came. They were on the move again,
marching back to the train station, loaded one by one into the
cars. But, this time, there were no threats backed up by bayonets, no petty brutalities, no pushing and shoving. It was clear
that each and every guard was anxious about his future, hoping
that a relaxation of cruelty now might encourage some mitiga-
tion in treatment later.

Lou, Bride, Stubbs and Dobson waited in line as one
carriage after another filled up before the doors were slammed
and it slid off up the tracks. Lou cast wary eyes towards the
heavens. There were still planes, up above the clouds. He knew
that the pilots and gunners and navigators on both sides were
trained and highly organised, just like he had been, though he
had not sat in a plane for over four years. Each individual knew

exactly what was expected of them. Their missions were clear, their targets well mapped out.

Just as he was thinking this, a Soviet plane descended to a few hundred feet above them and began strafing the station and the train tracks. Bullets bounced on metal, ricocheting off the steel girders and stone ballast.

'Shit!' Stubbs' face was ashen, his breathing short and sharp. A shard of flying wood had grazed his hand and he clutched it to him, staring at the welling bubble of blood forming on his knuckles.

And then a roar like the end of the world sent every man still on the platform flying to the ground.

'Get down!' screamed Lou. 'Get down!'

A triangle of bombers flying in formation swooped low. A terrible, grating screech signalled that they had dropped their bombs. Lou hardly had the time to register the sound before the ground was lurching and shuddering, sods and clods and chunks of tarmac flung into the air, concrete and steel cracking and splitting. And then the screams, the howls of agony and fear from petrified, broken men.

Lou raised his head a few inches and then slammed it down again as another blast hit. It was ten minutes or more before he dared to move again. The bombers' engines had receded into the distance and all Lou could hear were the sobs and cries of the injured and dying and then, cutting across it all, the guards shouting panic-stricken instructions to the few field ambulances that had begun to arrive. He staggered to his feet, looking warily around, brushing himself down, more as a way of finding out whether all his limbs were still there than in any attempt to clean himself.

'Lou!' a wavering voice called his name. It was Bride, also tentatively standing up. Stubbs and Dobson were nearby, and a hundred or more others, milling around or standing motionless, dazed and confused. The station was partially destroyed, chunks of concrete dislodged, great fissures across the platforms, the rails a tangled mess of metal. From an overhead cable hung shreds of clothing. How on earth had it got there? Lou surveyed the apocalyptic scene in stunned disbelief.

The station and the railway destroyed, the men were ordered back to camp.

'No,' groaned Lou, not even knowing why. At least going to Berlin had been action, of a sort, something happening, perhaps the chance, at some point, to escape, to join an Allied platoon, to actually fight and do something useful, rather than lying idle in a prison camp.

The men were filtering down off the platform and getting into line. Soon, only Lou and Bride and the last few stragglers were left.

'*Schnell!*' shrieked a guard.

Lou started as if he'd been asleep, or in a daydream, and reluctantly moved towards the column. Bride tripped, paused to tie the laces of his tatty boots.

The stray plane was overhead before they'd even noticed. A whistling noise, metal upon metal, the roar of aircraft engines on the ascent. Another hit to the stationary train.

'*Schwein!*' came a cry from somewhere.

The plane circled, came round again, lower this time. Lou could see its underbelly, the hatches from where the bombs would fall, and then the machine gun, poised for action. He fancied he made eye contact with the gunner in the seconds before the bullets flew, targeting the station, making the point clear. Get out.

Lou wheeled round, poised to run, and then halted. Where was Bride? His eyes swept the platform, raking over the piles of molten metal, the shattered pieces of destroyed carriages, the bodies. The disembodied limbs.

And then he saw him.

Bride was lying on the ground, arms and legs spread out like he'd been apprehended during a macabre game of snow angels. He was completely motionless, his head resting in a pool of vermillion red blood.

Bile rose in Lou's throat, and he gagged. His mind would not take in what his eyes were telling him. No, no, it couldn't be. The whole scene wavered and wobbled in front of him. As if in slow motion, he forced himself towards the body, each step taking the most monumental effort. As he approached his friend's supine form, his limbs stiffened with tension from the apprehension of knowing what had happened but refusing to believe it.

'No, please no,' he breathed, falling to his knees, grabbing Bride's wrist. He felt for a pulse. Nothing.

The pool of blood was still, shimmering in the sunlight that filtered from behind the clouds, its viscous surface sinisterly vivid. Lou's mind flitted back to the dead woman in that other train station, in what now seemed like another life, a parallel universe, and the blanket of blood that had enveloped her, just as Bride was now similarly covered.

'No!' He fell upon Bride's body, hugging him as he squeezed back tears, fighting off the fury and the anguish.

Bride could not be dead, not now, right at the very end, in the last few days or hours. And by friendly fire! But this was war. All targets were legitimate if that's what it took to stop Hitler's reign of evil. Even this young man with his whole life ahead of him, who had never wanted anything but to do his duty and get back home to his mother and sisters.

Lou did not know how long he stayed there, bent over Bride's body like someone in prayer. Eventually, he felt a gentle pressure on his shoulder, and then a tug at his elbow.

'Come on, mate.' It was Dobson, voice gentle but insistent. 'We've got to get out of here. They're giving Potsdam the full monty. It's not safe in the open.'

Lou nodded and tried to get up, but as he did so, his legs

gave way beneath him. Dobson was there, catching him on one side, while Stubbs took the other. Suddenly, it was too much. Now, the suppressed tears flowed, springing from Lou's sore and smoke-filled eyes, and he no longer cared who saw his weakness. If he couldn't cry for Bride, who he'd loved like a brother and a son and a best friend all in one, who could he cry for?

The next day, they buried Bride's body in the overflowing camp cemetery, and a few days after that, the German guards slipped away in the dead of night. For the *kriegies*, the war was over and the liberation had begun.

And no one could possibly imagine how bad it was going to be.

CHAPTER THIRTY-NINE

LONDON, JUNE 1994

My father's story was still echoing in my ears when I got to Camden Town that evening. Sue was already there, sitting on a bench by the statue of Richard Cobden, waiting. I felt decidedly odd, as if I myself had suffered an unexpected bereavement. During the time I'd spent reading my father's story, I'd got to know Bride as a friend and companion. And now he was gone.

Sue stood up to greet me. A pigeon flew low, right past my face, making me recoil in disgust. I hated pigeons, vermin that they were. The bird, unrepentant despite the glare I fixed upon it, took up a perch on Cobden's head. The statue, that commemorated the man who campaigned for the repeal of the Corn Laws, was made of Sicilian marble and had been paid for principally by Napoleon III. It must once have been a thing of gravitas if not beauty. But now it was dirty and smeared with droppings, functioning chiefly as an avian toilet stop.

'Come on,' I said to Sue. 'We should get going.' I wanted to get away from the bird and its malevolent gaze.

'What's up?' enquired Sue. 'Not having second thoughts?'

I shook my head. 'No, far from it,' I replied. Though I'd once dreaded it, I'd since come round to the idea of this class. It would be a welcome distraction from the sadness of my father's story, and my mother's, and my own selfish, but nevertheless deep, sorrow about losing my house. 'I'm really looking forward to giving it a go,' I assured Sue. 'I just hope I don't get the giggles when the model appears!' I added as an afterthought.

'We're middle-aged women!' she responded, laughing. 'I'm sure we can stare at willies and balls without so much as cracking a smile.'

'I'm glad you're so certain.' My laugh was genuine now, Sue having worked her magic already. I felt better just from being in her company. 'Because I'm not convinced that I am,' I concluded.

We stopped at the pedestrian crossing and waited for the lights to change. By the time we had crossed the road, our merriment had dissipated and Sue had fallen uncharacteristically quiet. It hit me that it was just possible that I wasn't the only one facing difficulties. I had been so wrapped up in myself and the gradual unravelling of my parents' stories that I had neglected my best friend, failed to register what was going on in her life.

'What's up?' I asked. 'You don't seem yourself, either.'

'Oh Jo,' sighed Sue. 'I've been trying to find a way to tell you, but however I do it, it's not going to make it any easier. So I guess I should just get on with it.'

My immediate thought was that Sue's breast cancer had returned. My heart lurched in my chest, fearing the worst. 'What? What is it, Sue?' Anxiety made me abrupt, brusque even.

Sue shook her head and smiled weakly. 'Don't worry, it's not my health. In fact, that's never been better. No...' Sue paused for a moment, as if searching for the right words.

'Jonathon and his wife have decided to make their move to South Africa permanent. And they've asked me to join them for six months of the year.' Sue grabbed my arm and halted abruptly in the middle of the pavement, other pedestrians parting in waves on either side, tutting in irritation as they did so. 'It wasn't easy, Jo, but I've said yes. No more British winters for me, the endless grey, the rain, the cold. From now on, I'm going to be a swallow – I'll do summer in the UK and then summer in South Africa.'

'Gosh,' I gulped. 'That's...' I faltered, not knowing what to say. It was the last thing I had expected, something I could never have imagined. Tears sprang into my eyes and I fought to stem them. 'Sorry,' I muttered, wiping my fingers over my cheeks. 'I'm being silly. Take no notice. Soppy old idiot...'

'No, it's me who should be sorry,' Sue was apologising. 'I shouldn't have sprung it on you like this. And I'm not being totally honest when I say it's my choice. The reality is that they could really do with my help with their children while they're getting their company established – I couldn't say no. And you know – it's a beautiful place, amazing climate, only two-hours' time difference, outdoor lifestyle... It'll be a new experience, stop me from stagnating.' She laughed self-deprecatingly, and brushed her hands down her body as if sloughing off the first mouldy bits of stagnation, preventing them from taking hold.

'Oh Sue,' I snuffled, dabbing at my nose with a tissue. 'I'm so happy for you. It will be marvellous. I'm sorry for being so emotional. I think it's just...' I broke off, unable to carry on. When I had composed myself, I gave it another try. 'I'm being totally selfish and only thinking about how much I'm going to miss you. And of course I'm jealous! Think of all that lovely wine and fruit and food...'

Relieved, Sue gave me a quick hug. 'You must come and stay!'

'That would be great,' I agreed, putting on as jovial a tone as

I could muster. 'But we should get a move on. A naked man awaits!'

We both chuckled but, underneath, my emotions were in turmoil. It was bad enough losing Sue for six months of the year – what if she decided to make her move permanent and all year round? Plus, everything Sue was saying about the attractions of South Africa – apart from the two-hour time difference – applied to New Zealand too, where Evan was currently living. It was always at the back of my mind that he might choose to stay there, make his life there, on the other side of the world, somewhere as far away as it was possible to be and so expensive to reach that trips would be feasible only once in a blue moon. Of course I wanted him to live his life as he wished to – I'd never want to hold him back. But that didn't make it any easier to face the idea of hardly ever seeing him again.

'I forgot to tell you,' Sue was saying as we approached the huge wooden doors of the Working Men's College, forcing me to concentrate. 'Jonathon is organising a hot-air balloon safari over the Kruger National Park as a belated birthday present for my sixtieth for when I get there! I'd always been terrified at the thought before. But now – well, you've only got the one life, haven't you?'

Sue's brush with death when she'd had breast cancer had changed her, made her more daring, more inclined to take risks. Made her more meteor. I wished I could have said I was doing as well as her, but it wouldn't have been true.

'That sounds totally amazing,' I said, my voice full of barely hidden envy. 'Lucky you.'

We'd reached the venue.

'Why exactly are we doing this again?' asked Sue, as we entered through the old Victorian doors. 'Are we actually insane or just behaving like we are?'

I laughed. 'Now you've changed your tune! You were the one encouraging me, saying it would be easy.'

'Umm,' snorted Sue. 'That might have been brash bravado that I'm going to regret.'

'Maybe,' I responded. 'But I think we're doing it because we've all only got the one life, to take the words out of your own mouth.' *And to be more meteor*, I added silently to myself.

'Touché,' laughed Sue. 'Right, we're inside, but where now?'

The building seemed to be full of purposeful-looking people, heading off to various rooms, where they were clearly going to indulge in mind-improving pursuits, such as learning a new language or computer programming or something equally worthy. In fact, I remembered, my mother had completed a book-keeping course here back in the 1970s when she wanted a job to occupy herself during the long days when I was at school and my father at work. Not to mention that, of course, we needed the money.

Sue's elbow nudged sharply into my side. 'Over there,' she muttered covertly, pointing discreetly at a queue of people casually holding sketch pads and pencils as if they knew what to do with them. 'Damn, they all look really serious and earnest. And *good*. Perhaps we should have gone for flower arranging?'

'Don't be daft,' I retaliated, with a confidence I didn't feel. '*We* look serious, earnest and good – and we are. Come on, once more into the breach, dear friend. We've got this.'

We filed into the large, high-ceilinged room with the rest of the class. It was overly warm, but I supposed it had to be if someone was going to be lying around naked for an hour. A young woman glided in, an angelic smile on her face. She introduced herself as Philippa, the course tutor, and launched into an explanation of how the sessions would run, what would be covered and what we would have achieved by the end of it. It doesn't matter about the results, Philippa kept insisting, it's about your journey, your development.

Our subject was a male who couldn't be more than twenty, I reckoned, muscular and dark-skinned. I worked hard to capture the light and the shadows, the dip of a collarbone, the curve of a cheek. Remarkably, the urge to laugh soon dissipated amidst the concentration required to follow Philippa's instructions. As I worked, my mood lifted and I began to actually enjoy myself.

At the end of the session, Philippa came round for a final look at what we had produced. As she stepped towards my easel, I watched as she tilted her head to the right and then the left, assessing my work from all angles.

'Well,' she began, 'it's, um, interesting. The style is...' she paused, searching for words. 'It has a naivety that is reminiscent of Picasso in his blue period,' she concluded, triumphantly.

A warm rush of pleasure surged through me at the praise. She liked it! Then I looked back at my work and reality hit home. What on earth was Philippa on about? It was absolutely dreadful, resembling nothing more than a random collection of oddly shaped, bulbous balloons.

I turned to the tutor with a look of amazement. She had her hand over her mouth trying to suppress her laughter. Beside her, Sue was bent double with silent mirth. For a split second, I felt an intense burst of annoyance. How dare they ridicule my work! I almost told them to shut up. And then I saw the funny side and I, too, began to laugh.

We laughed and laughed, oblivious to the other participants filing out of the room, peering curiously over to see what the hilarity was all about.

'Oh dear,' I gasped eventually, when I had regained the power of speech. 'Picasso... hahaha... Blue period... Oh dear oh dear.'

Philippa, once she had managed to stop laughing, looked mortified. 'Mrs Sawyer, I'm so, so sorry. It's absolutely unforgivable of me to be so judgemental of a member's work. Please do accept my apology. I don't know what came over me.'

'I do!' piped up Sue. 'You saw a picture that you'd only be kind about if a two-year-old had drawn it!'

That set all three of us off again into more gales of laughter.

Finally, I began to gather up my stuff. 'Come on, Sue,' I said. 'Poor Philippa must be wanting to get home.' I glanced over at Sue's easel. 'Where's yours, anyway?'

I went to stand in front of it, knowing it would be better than mine.

'You absolute beast!' I sighed as I studied it. 'It's so good. Where have you been hiding that talent?'

Sue shrugged modestly. 'Don't get excited, it's not that wonderful.'

'It is in comparison to mine,' I rejoined. 'Compared to mine, it's a masterpiece.'

'Practice makes perfect,' interjected Philippa, encouragingly. 'Everyone can improve.'

'Thank you so much for your optimism,' I laughed. 'I'm not sure that I believe it, but thank you anyway.'

We were still being assailed by random fits of giggling by the time we got to the pub. Some people from the course had said they were going for a drink afterwards and had invited us to go with them. I was pleased with myself for agreeing. My tendency to be antisocial stemmed from the legacy of the bullying, which had also left me with the conviction that strangers would find me boring, the belief that I lacked the wit and interesting conversation that would make me a good companion. With Sue as my wing woman, though, I was able to be more courageous. And I needed a drink after a class like that.

After a pleasant hour in the pub, it was time for me to be getting back to Mum.

'Now – I suppose I can't tempt you to join me on my water-skiing course at the Harp Reservoir, can I?' asked Sue, as we stood at the stop waiting for our respective buses.

I rolled my eyes heavenwards.

'Waterskiing? Why? Aren't life drawing and hot-air ballooning enough for you?' I shook my head in mock despair. 'I don't think so. Apart from anything else, I'm not sure it would go too well with my contact lenses. I'll leave that one to you. Being more meteor has its limits.'

'Meteor?' questioned Sue, looking bewildered. But at that moment her bus drew up and she clambered aboard, mouthing 'What are you on about?' through the window.

I smiled and waved cheerfully, mouthing back, 'I'll explain another time.'

When my own bus arrived, I spent the journey wondering what it was about waterskiing that appealed to Sue. Something to do with life in Cape Town with Jonathon, I assumed, with a sinking feeling that accompanied the reminder that my friend would soon be spending half the year a long way away. I thought of those characters from so long ago, Bride and Ernst, who had had their lives torn away from them before they'd even been lived, Frieda and Friedrich who had been denied the opportunity to enjoy a peaceful old age but instead been plunged into horror and trauma.

Sue was right. We've all only got the one life. Meteor or not, it should be lived to the full. I owed it to myself to make sure I did just that.

CHAPTER FORTY

Static machine guns looked down from the blank-eyed orifices of empty watch towers. Despite their promises to fight to the last man, the German guards had not dared to wait and face the Red Army's desire for revenge. The POWs collected up their discarded weapons, guns, pistols, daggers, and divided them up amongst the highest-ranking prisoners.

When, a few days later, the Russian tanks rolled in, the troops exhorted the *kriegies* to join them in the assault on Berlin.

No one obliged.

The tanks rolled out, onwards, ready for victory.

'Perhaps we should have gone,' mused Dobson. 'It might have been better than waiting here like a lot of lame ducks. To fight for Berlin – that would be worth something, wouldn't it?'

Lou snorted ironically. He looked at them, the sorry bunch that they were. They were all still very underweight, still suffering the after-effects of the long march. 'I think we'd just slow them down,' he said, wearily. 'Leave it to the Ivans, roaring for revenge. They still have the stomach for the fight.'

In the camp, anarchy reigned. Civilians lived amongst the POWs, women and children, drawn to the camp in the hope of food and company, or the sham promise of safety it seemed to offer. The men were on territory liberated by the Russians, and the Russians wanted to be in charge of what happened to them now. One day, American jeeps came to begin transferring the POWs to freedom, but the Soviets put a stop to it. They would decide who left, and when.

Tired of the delay, men slipped away under cover of darkness, slinking into the shadows, heading for American lines. All anyone wanted was to get home. Lou thought about joining the fugitives, constantly weighing up the pros and cons of breaking free and leaving, or of staying put and, by obeying the rules, perhaps getting back to England quicker. He was paralysed by indecision and so did nothing.

When, as they waited for news of the repatriation that they knew would happen soon, but hardly soon enough, they heard on the radio that Europe was celebrating VE Day, it was hard not to lose all hope. Lou knew his spirit was breaking, knew also that he couldn't let it. There were no parties, no joyous dancing or festivities. He had nits in his hair, lice on his body and dread in his heart. There was little to rejoice in.

The only thing to alleviate the misery was the arrival of a Red Cross delivery; enough for each man to receive his own parcel. It was manna from heaven.

A few days later, however, the mood dipped again when newspapers arrived in the camp containing the first pictures of Belsen. So atrocious were the images that a fresh wave of anger and fury swept through the camp. *The bastards, the pigs, the motherfuckers.* Every nationality had its expletives and none were spared. The few German guards who had hung around were shot on sight, without mercy.

'They got what they deserved.' Stubbs, as usual, was unequivocal, and sure as always that he occupied the moral high ground.

'Two wrongs don't make a right,' answered Lou, wearily. He felt drained, deadbeat. He didn't want to argue with Stubbs, but sometimes the man's self-righteousness was insufferable.

'Oh, Prince of Peace now, are we?' retorted Stubbs, sarcastically.

'Shut it, Stubbs.' Lou dropped the pretence of forbearance, politeness. 'But while you're on about the Bible, haven't you ever heard that the meek shall inherit the earth? That won't be you then, will it?'

'My Bible says an eye for an eye and tooth for a tooth. Hitler laid siege to Leningrad, killed 800,000 civilians. And you saw those pictures in the paper – piles of emaciated corpses, the living dead with skeletal faces, the gas chambers. Seems only fair and honourable to exact justice.' Stubbs was adamant and Lou knew better than to continue the argument.

They were outside, smoking cigarettes that had arrived in the Red Cross handout, taking advantage of the mild late-spring evening. Normally, they didn't spend too long near the camp's periphery as it was constantly surrounded by hordes of starving women and children who begged for food and made it impossible to enjoy a peaceful smoke. But today the weather had been too good, and the atmosphere amongst the cabins too dismal, to remain inside.

Ken Bales, a new acquaintance, joined the little group.

'I feel so helpless,' he said.

'Yes,' agreed Lou. 'We all do.'

Surveying the civilian crowd, Bales rubbed his hand across his eyes. 'Lots of men sleep with them, you know, in return for food and soap and stuff.'

'Yes, I know.' The sight of them just made Lou desperately sad.

It was getting dark and Lou began to think about going back to the cabin to bed. To wait, again, for news of freedom.

He stood up and stretched, dropped his cigarette butt to the floor and ground it out with his heel.

'Mr, sir, officer.' He heard the words being called through the still air, suddenly noticing how quiet it was, no planes in the sky, no tanks and trucks on the road, no patrolling guards shouting orders.

He looked around. There, at the broken-down, patchy fence, fingers clutching the wire, eyes fixed upon him, was a woman. She was skinny and deathly pale, bedraggled as all those who hung on the camp gates were. But there was something different about this woman. Despite how thin and unwashed she was, she was beautiful. Like everyone else, she had probably lost everything. But as Lou regarded her, he saw that she had not lost that most precious quality.

She had not lost her dignity.

The woman, standing tall with her shoulders back, was clutching something to her chest. Lou stepped nearer and saw that it was a tiny baby. The infant was pale, porcelain-skinned like its mother, minute hands flung out in distress. The young mother began to cry, perhaps unknowingly, a trickle of tears running unchecked down her cheeks. But her head was still held high. Fixing all her attention on Lou, her expression changed. She freed one hand from its hold on the baby and pushed her hair back from her face. Her dark blue eyes flashed in the dimming light.

'Please,' she said, in faltering English, 'food?' And then in German, 'We are starving and I have to feed the baby. Anything, if you have it.'

Before Lou could answer, Stubbs leapt in.

'Shove off,' he snarled. 'We don't give to Germans.'

The other POWs who had been around them melted away, not wanting to get involved, to get drawn into this unfolding drama. Lou saw Ken Bales, always wary of conflict, deter-minedly heading in another direction.

He looked back at the woman. It was quite possible that, without any food, she might die, and her child with her. This was Lou's chance to save someone amidst all the death and destruction.

'Wait a minute,' he said.

He went to the cabin, seized up his pack and pulled out the Red Cross package. There were tins of fish, Bovril, corned beef, Klim powdered milk, Maple Leaf butter, Marmite, chocolate and soap. There were several cartons of Player's cigarettes which she could trade if she didn't smoke. He took the whole box outside.

Stubbs, fed up with glowering to no effect, was sitting on a tree stump lighting up. When he saw Lou approaching, he glared at him scornfully. 'Here he is, the new bleeding Messiah.'

Lou smiled sorrowfully in Stubbs' direction. 'I just want to help, if I can,' he said, simply. 'If it were your mother, or sister, or daughter, wouldn't you do the same?'

For a moment, Stubbs looked contrite.

Seizing his advantage, Lou carried on. 'They're people, Stubbs. They didn't cause any of this. Surely it's better to be kind than to be consumed by hatred?'

Stubbs took a long draw on his cigarette. Then he dropped his head into his free hand and sat like that for a while, staring at the ground. When he raised his head again, his expression was completely different.

'You're probably right,' he said. He gesticulated towards the woman, still waiting, gazing imploringly at Lou. 'Give her your food today and if she's still there in the morning, she can have mine, too.'

Lou could scarcely believe it.

He looked at the woman. Her eyes met his. In very slow, halting, mispronounced English, she spoke. 'I pay,' she said, indicating with her gaze towards her breasts and then further down, to her loins.

Wordlessly, Lou shook his head. He moved closer to the woman, close enough to see the mud on her skin and blood-stains on her clothes. The baby was really new, only hours old. He held out the box. 'Take it. It's not much but *vielleicht hilft es.*' Maybe it will help.

The woman almost snatched it from him. She called behind her and an older woman came stumbling over, took the box and retreated to the shelter of some trees. The beautiful brunette stood waiting.

'You want *Geschlechtsverkehr?* Sex? *Kommen Sie, bitte.*' She took a step towards him.

In a bizarre thought process, Lou wondered what she planned to do with the infant if he said yes. He could hardly bear her abject offering up of herself to him. And yet, still her chin jutted defiantly forward and the sharp brightness of her eyes was undimmed.

'No,' he said. 'No, I don't want anything from you.'

The woman didn't seem to understand. She stood, waiting.

Suddenly, Lou got it. In this degraded country, in the last desolate days of war, nothing was for free. She simply didn't believe him. Lou felt himself blush deep red. Embarrassment suffused him. They were all part of this, he thought, nobody totally innocent.

Lou felt a desperate need to erase all the sin and suffering this war had caused. There was a hedgerow nearby, the last remains of a field boundary that must have existed before the camp was built, scorched leaves, ragged branches, bushes of stunted growth. Yet within it, something was still struggling to survive. A briar scrambled between tortured limbs of hawthorn, reaching for the light, for the sky. Lou went to it and plucked a flower, a pale pink dog rose. He took it to the woman and, as she watched in amazement, tucked it into the folds of her newborn's grimy blanket. Its tiny arms, wrists blue-veined and delicate as china, flailed wildly as it began to cry.

'Shush,' whispered Lou, reaching out a finger to the infant, who wrapped its own around his. 'Quiet now. Here's a flower for you, to wish you a good future.'

The mother's gaze regarded him still, eyes guarded now, fearful. She tightened her grip on her baby. Lou could see what she was thinking. Why was this soldier being nice to her? If he didn't want sex, what did he want?

Lou knew, however much he felt drawn to help her further, that there was nothing else he could do. He had to let her go, and hope she made it to some kind of sanctuary.

'Goodbye. And good luck.' Scrabbling in his pocket, he pulled out a scrap of paper, scribbled something on it and handed it to the woman.

In a split second, she was gone.

Lou stood motionless, gazing after her, for a few long moments. Then he walked back to the cabin. It was crowded and stuffy and Lou couldn't bear to be there with all the other men. Instead, he went to sit outside and smoke yet another cigarette.

He thought of Eva, all those years ago, in another time, another era. Had he exploited her? But that hadn't been the same, not at all. That had been two people finding each other in the twilight, fighting the alienation all around them. He thought of the dead woman in the railway carriage, frozen in her own blood. The three women's faces mingled together and he fought to separate them, to give each the gift of her own individuality.

That night, as he went to sleep, Lou prayed that the food he had given was enough to save the proud brunette and her pale, delicate child.

CHAPTER FORTY-ONE

LONDON, JUNE 1994

I shut the diary and laid it on my desk. It was the weekend after the life-drawing class, and work had been particularly busy. I was still getting used to being in the office full time – it was certainly taking its toll. It was hard not to wonder why I was bothering, when all my efforts were still not going to be enough to save my house. But I'd committed to the hours and I had to stick to them, for the time being at least, and as I kept reminding myself, I could put the extra money away for the next rainy day – there was bound to be one, sooner or later.

In addition, I was working in the evenings and at weekends on Melissa's garden. In the midst of all the upheaval of dealing with Ed and the emotion of hearing my parents' stories for the first time, Melissa had approved my designs. She'd actually been delighted with them, which was great but all the work this involved left me even less time to read or to chat with my mother. Fortunately, a couple of her friends from her OAPs club had taken to coming round every other day or so to keep her company while I was out, which was a godsend.

I should go to her now and check up on her, but I needed a moment to digest the latest instalment of what I had read.

This is the way a war ends, I mused, as my father's words ricocheted around my mind. Not with a bang but with anarchy and disorder, shattered lives bleeding misery in all directions, mayhem and lawlessness taking hold, a dog-eat-dog world of fighting for survival.

It wasn't something I was aware of having contemplated before, but if I had, I would have assumed that once a war was over, everyone tidied up the guns and the tanks and collected in the uniforms and that was that. The victors said 'jolly well done, everyone' to each other and the vanquished crawled away into a corner somewhere to lick their wounds. I recalled, in the Cabinet War Rooms that I had visited once, a pile of carefully hoarded sugar lumps still hidden in a drawer, the sheets of paper for top-secret missives still secured in the typewriters, as if everyone, on the last tolling of the VE Day bell, had simply got up and left, moving seamlessly on to the business of peacetime.

But, of course, this couldn't really be how a conflict of such epic proportions reached its conclusion. Sworn enemies didn't make it up overnight.

I wondered who the poor woman with the baby was, whether they had survived. My father had done the right thing and it heartened me to know that, after all he'd been through, seen, experienced, he had retained his humanity to the very end. But that couldn't be said about everybody. So had the woman and her child found sanctuary and security outside of the camp gates?

Pondering this, I fetched my mother a jacket so that we could have a walk around the garden. I had been to the flat again the day before and it was progressing nicely. Installation of the new kitchen was nearly complete and I hoped all the work would be concluded soon, enabling Mum to move back after Emma's wedding. It wasn't that I wanted her to leave, but I knew she was itching to go home to her own space. But, of course, for that to happen, she would have to be fit and well enough to manage on her own. So it was important for me to make sure she actively engaged with her rehabilitation, even though it sometimes made her tired and cranky.

Fortunately, the weather was glorious, the sun dappling through fully leafed branches. In the flowerbeds, aquilegias flourished and on the rose bushes, blooms proliferated.

'OK, Mum, twice round the lawn and then we can sit down,' I said, encouragingly.

'Hmph,' she exhaled, sceptically. 'I can do this on my own, you know. You've got other things to do....'

'Nice try, Mum, but you're not going to get shot of me that easily,' I responded. 'I'll be poking my nose in and interfering until I know you're completely back to your normal self. Judging by your grumpiness right now, it seems like you're getting there.'

'Ha!' she exclaimed, indignantly.

I pulled a sheepish face. I'd surprised myself by making such a statement, however tongue-in-cheek. The time I'd spent with my mother, talking to her about her past, seemed to be fundamentally changing our relationship, breaking down barriers and enabling an easy companionship between us that had never existed before.

'I've nearly finished Dad's notebook,' I told her. 'He seemed to end up somewhere outside Berlin. So when did you reach the city?'

There was a long pause.

I looked at my mother. A shadow had descended over her face. Perhaps I had upset her, after all. I cursed myself; there I was congratulating myself about our newfound intimacy and it seemed I was still capable of inadvertently getting it wrong.

But then she answered and she didn't sound cross, just

bewildered somehow, lost in the past. 'I don't remember the exact date,' she said, flatly. 'It's all so faint now, after all this time, fainter and fainter with every day that passes.'

'Let's enjoy the sunshine for a minute,' I suggested. 'Perhaps that will help you to remember.'

We completed our two rounds of the lawn in a companionable silence. A swing seat stood by the pond and I guided my mother there and indicated to her to sit down. Almost as soon as she'd done so, my mother resumed the story, as if there'd been no hiatus at all.

'I think we walked for more than two weeks, three at least...' she said. 'All along the route, we'd had to ask the way. But we also knew we were getting nearer as more and more of the places we passed through were bombed to smithereens, reduced to towering mountains of rubble. The dust hung so thick in the air, you could taste it; it blocked our noses and stung our eyes. And the smell! The stench of death, of bodies still lying buried beneath the debris. Can you imagine it, Jo? It was terrible, so very terrible.'

My mother stopped, overcome by emotion. She didn't often get weepy, but I saw how she was squeezing her eyes tight shut, holding back the tears.

'We were nearly there, nearly at Berlin, when...' Her voice trailed off once more. Her hands were clenched into fists and her whole body was shaking.

'Mum? What's the matter?' I felt a pang of guilt. I hated to see my mother distressed but didn't want her to stop. Perhaps it was selfish, but I needed to know everything. I needed to get to the end of the story.

She took a deep breath. 'It's nothing, Jo,' she said eventually. 'Just sometimes remembering is hard. We were so tired and hungry, starving by then, always scared out of our wits. We stopped for a few days on the outskirts of Berlin, too terrified of what we would find in the city to continue. Only when we heard the news that Germany had surrendered did we resume our journey. We had got hold of some food and we decided we had to carry on. We knew we were almost there, almost home, when we saw the train, the S-Bahn, running on its raised tracks. We couldn't believe it hadn't been destroyed – or that we'd actually made it.'

My mother paused and the ecstatic song of a blackbird filled the silence, while mayflies darted across the surface of the pond.

'But you still had to get to your house?' I questioned. Getting through a city into which the armies of the most powerful countries in the world were descending en masse seemed hazardous to say the least.

'Eventually we made it to Charlottenburg,' she reminisced. 'I could barely identify it as the place I'd left less than two years before. Huge parts of it were completely obliterated, buildings ripped open at the seams or just gone, erased from the earth. It had been given the nickname *Klamottenberg* – heap of rubbish – because that was pretty much all that was left. Everywhere we looked, women and children were living in basements and cellars, air-raid shelters and makeshift tent houses, amidst the ruins. There were as many rats as people, sneaking around, noses snuffling. Revolting things. The devastation was beyond belief. It broke what was left of my heart to see it.'

CHAPTER FORTY-TWO

GERMANY, 1945

Katja knew it was her street. A pockmarked sign of twisted metal still proclaimed that it was so. But it was unrecognisable. Four whole blocks, two-thirds of the houses, had been completely annihilated.

She and Gerta picked their way through the rubble like phantoms arrived from another world, tracking an uneven course with the cart, weaving backwards and forwards around potholes and rubbish heaps, their eyes unable to take in the utter devastation that surrounded them. Amidst the piles of bricks, tiles and stone lay traces of people's lives: fragments of patterned china, shattered glass from a ceiling chandelier, damaged books with torn leather covers and ripped pages.

A photograph caught Katja's eye and she bent to pick it up. It depicted a family group, carefully arranged by the photographer: a pretty mother, two smiling children and a father looking stern and paternal for the camera. Where were these people now? thought Katja, as she studied their faces. What had happened to them? If this was their house, and they were still alive, they had lost everything.

Not knowing what to do with the picture, she tucked it gently into a nook in the rubble pile, hoping it wouldn't blow away and be lost forever. The family might come back and find it, perhaps. Katja hoped so.

Trance-like, she and Gerta moved on. All familiar landmarks were gone: the bus shelters, the post boxes, the signposts. There were no cars on the roads where once there had been many. One lamp post still stood, incongruously tall and straight. On its side a metal board painted with a swastika hung crookedly from a single remaining nail.

And then Katja saw it.

Their building, miraculously still standing. She couldn't believe it. In her pocket, she had the keys, that somehow she'd managed to keep hold of throughout the journey. Her stomach in knots, she rubbed the smooth, cold metal between her fingers. But as soon as she reached the entrance, she realised that the first key was not needed. The front door had been kicked in and lay on its side, a mass of splintered wood and detached hinges. Inside, they found that families had taken up residence everywhere – in the cellar, on the stairwells and the landings.

Gerta lifted Hans out of the cart for him to climb the stairs himself. She and Katja took one end of the cart each and made their way to the first floor where Katja's flat lay. The reinforced door Horst had had fitted before he left for the front still stood firm, though dents bore testament to attempts to kick it in. Katja fitted the second key in the lock and the door swung slowly open.

Their arrival disturbed the thick dust that had settled on every surface, setting motes dancing in the sunlight. There was no glass left in any of the windows; several, including the kitchen, had blown before Katja had even left for the Sudetenland.

Hans, fascinated by this new place, toddled further in, but Katja and Gerta stood transfixed, paralysed by relief. And then Katja became aware of movement on the staircase, of the unwelcome attention they were attracting, and she quickly bundled themselves and the cart inside, slamming and bolting the door behind them.

'Oh my God,' cried Katja then, as if it had only just hit her where she was, sinking to the floor. 'My God, we're home. Oh thank God, thank God.'

She stayed on her knees for long minutes, unable to get up, suddenly feeling every tortuous mile of their walk, overwhelmed by absolute exhaustion. They had left with such joy in their hearts that they were escaping the bombing, never imagining the circumstances in which they would have to make their way back. The flat had not seemed like a home when Katja, Gerta and Hans had left, but a prison, or, more accurately, a building waiting to become a morgue whenever a bomb would destroy it. But now, after their walk that had seemed interminable, this small and simple dwelling felt like the best place in the world to be. It felt safe.

Gerta was just standing, staring, seeming unable to make sense of where she was. Hans chattered away, wandering from room to room, eager to explore this new environment. Katja roused herself. She needed to sort things out, find fuel, search for wood, fetch water as the taps were dry. There was no point in checking the shop. She had seen when they came in that it had been broken into and looted, just as she had expected it would be. There would be nothing left inside, she knew. But who could blame desperate people for taking desperate measures? Think of everything they had pilfered and filched as they walked. Morals and standards quickly fall by the wayside in such terrible times.

Hans came toddling back to Katja and handed her something.

'*Schau, Mutti,*' he said. Look, Mummy.

She glanced down absentmindedly at what Hans had given her. It was a shard of glass, its shattered edges thin and diamond sharp.

'Hans!' she cried.

The little boy, only a moment ago so proud of his discovery, immediately burst into tears at the volume and note of alarm in his mother's voice, his angelic face crumpling and reddening as he howled.

Katja grabbed his hands, but there was no blood. It was another miracle. He had not cut himself. While she had been thinking they were in a safe place, this piece of glass that Hans had found could have sliced through an artery. Her heart pounding, Katja tried to calm herself. She took hold of Hans and led him through to the bedroom. There was her bed, all made up, candlewick bedspread pulled over sheets and blankets. It was unbelievable. The swinging from potential tragedy to incredible good fortune numbed her senses and she wondered if perhaps it wasn't actually happening, if they had in fact died en route and this was a dream, a fantasy.

Gerta's presence beside her brought her back to reality.

'We should go and check your place out,' said Katja, 'see what kind of a state it's in.' She turned back to survey the bedroom. 'But first I need to sweep up this broken glass.' She pointed to where a picture frame had fallen to the floor and smashed.

Once the mess was cleared up, they ventured out into the stairwell again, locking the door carefully behind them. On the top floor, where Gerta's flat was, a woman had created a home in the crawl space beneath the roof. She huddled there, surrounded by three or four filthy children. Her hair was sparse and lank and every inch of her body, even the palms of her hands, were covered in a violent red rash.

Appalled, Katja could bear neither to look nor not to look. It was Gerta who gently pulled her away. At Gerta's apartment, the door swung on its hinges and, once inside, it was clear that it was being squatted by several people. Belongings were strewn in every room and the entire place stank of sweat and faeces and urine and despair.

Dumbfounded, Gerta stared, slack-jawed and defeated.

'You can't stay here,' Katja pronounced, decisively. 'There's no way you'd be able to get these people to leave and even if you could, where would they go?'

In a city with over a million homeless, it was hardly surprising that any building still standing had been overrun. Katja mentally thanked Horst for having the prescience to fit the new door.

Gerta shook her head, in slow motion, like a wind-up doll or a puppet.

Katja put her arm around her and pulled her close. 'It's all right,' she reassured Gerta. 'We're a family now, aren't we? You'll stay with me and Hans, where you belong.'

Gerta nodded sorrowfully, and did not protest when Katja led her back downstairs.

Later, Katja left Hans with Gerta and went out into the city to look for food. The streets were both busy and eerily silent. Women picked their way through the carnage without the energy or will to speak. She saw a *Hausfrau* hurrying somewhere and ran to catch up with her. Anyone moving with that much speed must have some inside knowledge of a shop with something to sell. But when Katja approached the woman to ask her, she just resolutely lowered her head and continued marching, telling Katja nothing. Helplessly, Katja followed from a distance. Eventually, they reached a baker's shop where a long queue stretched from the door. Not knowing what else to do, Katja joined it. She felt inside her underwear where she'd tucked some money along with her food coupons.

But in the end, neither were needed. Long before Katja

reached the front of the queue, the bread had sold out. The proprietor came to the door and waved all those waiting away.

'Come back in two days' time,' he said. 'We might have something then.'

Katja was weak with hunger. Her stomach growled and gurgled and ached.

'Please,' she called out, spurred on by desperate need, 'I have chil— I have a child. He needs to eat. Don't you have anything at all?'

The baker disappeared back inside his shop.

Katja stood, motionless, rooted to the spot as if unable to drag herself from it. The other women in the queue melted away, shopping bags empty. Katja wondered where they were going and what they would put on their dinner tables that evening. Perhaps they had supplies at home, unlike her who'd been away for so long. Or perhaps they were doing what so many Berliners were forced to do and eating dogs or cats or rats, weeds and grass.

Katja shuddered. She glanced around her. If a cat slunk past just then, would she catch it and kill it? Before she'd had a chance to answer her own question, the baker was beside her.

'Take this,' he hissed, surreptitiously checking all around before handing over a brown paper bag. 'Now be off with you. Get yourself inside before...' His voice tailed off as he retreated to the safety of his shop.

'Before what?' called Katja.

The baker paused. 'The city is full of Russians,' he whispered. 'Get back, stay inside. Good luck.'

Dumbstruck, Katja looked down at the bag in her hand. She wanted to open it, discover what was inside, cram her mouth full of it, whatever it was. Mouldy bread, stale cake, she didn't care. She'd eat anything.

But, of course, she had to share with Gerta and Hans; they

must eat before her. And she needed to keep out of sight of the Russians. She fled for home as fast as her enfeebled legs would carry her.

CHAPTER FORTY-THREE

GERMANY, 1945

The next day, a huge clamour from outside roused Katja from the deepest slumber she had experienced since leaving Sudetenland. At the window, she looked out onto what remained of the street below.

An entire Russian battalion seemed to have set up camp outside her apartment block, complete with campfires and sturdy Cossack ponies, long forelocks and shaggy manes blowing in the wind. As she watched, she saw one soldier emerging from what had once been her beautiful shop, adjusting his trousers as he went, and then waving to another disappearing inside. A wave of revulsion flooded through her veins. They were using her grocery store as a public toilet.

For a moment, she thought of storming down there and demanding that they stop, have some manners and human decency. And then she began to laugh, quietly and ironically to herself. What was she thinking? The Russians were the victors, they owned the city now, and by all accounts they were systematically working their way through it, terrorising all who came into view. She remembered the terrible things they had done to Alice, and felt sick.

And then her attention was drawn again to the men outside and the smells emanating from their fires. In the makeshift field kitchen they had set up in the street, bacon sizzled in huge frying pans, cooked with plenty of butter. From only one floor up, Katja could see the loaves lined up ready for the men's breakfasts, and the jars of pickles to accompany their meal. Saliva gathered in her mouth and hunger gnawed at her stomach. Last night's meagre fare of stale buns and bread seemed a long time ago. And where would food for today come from? She had no idea.

And, the thought hit her with the force of a body blow, how would she be able to go in search of anything edible now? There were Russians right outside her door, they'd be there day and night, with their collection of stolen bicycles that they didn't know how to ride and their forearms sporting a dozen wristwatches each. She remembered the soldiers who'd taken Herr Wagner's precious timepiece, and how he had buried his silver beneath the linden tree. That seemed a million years ago now, a memory from another life, another world.

She withdrew from the window and went to the kitchen, scooping Hans out of bed on the way. She and he were sharing her double bed while Gerta slept on the sofa. The flat only had one bedroom. Katja and Horst had never got round to discussing how they were all going to fit in when the baby came. Katja had hoped she'd be able to work a bit less and perhaps move somewhere a little further away from the shop so that work wasn't always there, right beneath them, demanding that any spare moment be spent tidying and stacking shelves or checking invoices or dusting and cleaning. She had hoped, when she was a mother, to spend time with her baby, doting on it, nurturing him or her.

Well, she thought defensively, as she picked through the

remaining scraps of bread to find the choicest bits for Hans, she had doted and nurtured, whatever the circumstances. And, once they'd got to Sudetenland, she had given Hans a happy life. It was only now that daily horror had become normality.

In the back of the kitchen cupboard, she'd found a few jars of preserves, most of which were so old and mouldy that their original incarnation was impossible to even guess at. But the oil that covered them was pretty much untainted, in Katja's opinion anyway, and she had siphoned it off with a sieve. She thought of the Russians' bacon breakfast and salivated anew. Pouring a tiny smidgen of oil into a frying pan, she put it onto the oven. She'd found a canister of paraffin, so, for now, they could cook without lighting the *Kachelöfen,* for which there was the smallest amount of pellets still stashed in the wood basket.

She fried the bread crusts and tried to imagine serving them up along with lashings of butter and hot, fresh coffee not made from acorns, and pancakes not made from birch bark flour. She failed.

Gerta came into the kitchen and joined Hans at the table, where he solemnly handed her his cutlery one by one and she handed them back to him and so on until the bread was fried and ready. Katja sat down beside her son. Gerta looked done in, utterly despondent.

She's lost everything, thought Katja, as she chewed each mouthful a hundred times to make it last longer. *At least I've still got the flat and Hans. She's got nothing, apart from us, her surrogate daughter and grandchild.*

A massive clamour from the direction of the door made them both jump out of their skins. The hammering paused momentarily, then restarted, louder than before. It was accompanied by shouts in Russian and German, unintelligible through Horst's thick door but undoubtedly aggressive, giving no sign of going away.

'You should open it,' said Gerta, staring at her plate from which she had scooped up every last crumb.

Fear almost made Katja retort, 'Why me? Why not you?' but she stopped herself in time. Of course she should do it. She was younger, fitter, more agile. Not that any of those things gave her an advantage over soldiers of the Red Army; if anything, they were decidedly disadvantageous.

'Perhaps they'll think there's no one here,' ventured Katja.

'They won't,' responded Gerta, immediately. 'Listen to them! They'll kick the door in or blow it up or shoot the lock off. Then we'll have nothing to protect us. Better to stop them before they have completely destroyed it.'

'Maybe they just want to... chat?' Katja knew her suggestion was ridiculous.

Setting her shoulders straight and holding her head up high, she went to the door, refusing to be cowed.

'I'm coming,' she shouted.

As soon as she'd pulled the door open, half a dozen Russian soldiers spilled through it. They marched inside, turning things upside down as they had at Herr Wagner's all those months ago. They checked Gerta and Katja's arms for watches, pocketed the carriage clock that stood on a shelf in the sitting room, then tickled Hans under the chin and gave him a bag of black toffee.

Katja looked on, bemused at the incongruities in their behaviour, changing from careless theft to kindness in a matter of seconds. It was as bewildering as it was frightening.

Having hunted through every cupboard in the place, the Russians approached Katja.

'Schnapps,' they demanded. 'Vodka.'

Katja shook her head. 'We don't have any,' she replied, 'nothing at all. Sorry.' It was surely the most misplaced apology ever, but she couldn't think of what else to say. Now please go away? Leave us alone? She snorted derisively to herself. As if they'd take any notice of anything she said or did.

In the corner, Gerta was pale with fear. Katja longed to comfort her but didn't dare go over to her. Hans, sitting on the floor, was having the time of his life, laughing delightedly as he stuffed toffee into his mouth, his face covered in smudges of sticky brown sugar. It had been a long time since he'd had anything sweet. *He'll make himself sick*, reflected Katja, but didn't have the heart to stop him. Let him take pleasure where he could. There was little enough of it about.

The Russians were still clattering about, huge boots shaking the wooden floors. Their smell filled the air, strong and raw and pungent, stale alcohol, stale cigarettes, stale sweat. Katja too was sweating, could feel it in her armpits, the sticky, odorous perspiration of suppressed fear. She was desperately thirsty but couldn't fetch a drink of water from the standpipe in the street in case it drew renewed interest in her from the Russians.

Eventually, the soldiers left, laughing and shouting, their footsteps and their voices echoing down the hallway. As soon as they had disappeared, Katja rushed to the door and slammed it shut, fastening the lock and then leaning on it, resting her forehead against the cool wood of the door jamb.

After a few moments, she retreated back to the kitchen, where she and Gerta threw their arms around each other and sank down onto the wooden chairs.

Eventually, Gerta roused herself. 'I'll go and hunt for food,' she announced.

Gratitude flooded Katja's whole being. To not have that responsibility herself for one day filled her with relief.

Gerta left. Hans, who'd been rushing around madly on a sugar rush, sank onto a cushion on the floor and fell asleep. Katja took him to bed, got in beside him, and they both slumbered for a while. All Katja wanted to do at the moment was sleep and sleep and sleep. However many hours she got, it was never enough.

When Gerta returned a long while later, she'd been almost

entirely unsuccessful. All she had was a bunch of wilting nettles and dandelion leaves that she'd gathered from a small patch of waste ground. Sadly, she laid them onto the kitchen table and turned her back on her paltry offering.

For dinner, Katja cooked the leaves in some water and mashed in some of the oil from the mouldy jars. Gerta refused to eat.

'You have it,' she said. 'I can go without. You are a mother and Hans a child. You need it more than me.'

Katja shook her head. She took a little more of the food for Hans and then pushed the dish back towards Gerta. 'You must have something,' she insisted. 'Even just a little. Please.'

Reluctantly, Gerta picked up a fork and joined Hans and Katja in the meal, which took all of two minutes to devour.

There was no electricity and they had no candles, so as soon as dusk started to fall, they went to bed. *Thank God we have a bed*, thought Katja, *thank God we have a roof. We are the lucky ones.*

Just as she'd had that thought, a loud noise caused her to sit bolt upright again, ears acutely listening. The noise came again, the same as that morning. The soldiers were back, hammering at the door, clamouring to be let in.

Gerta appeared at the bedroom door, deathly pale and shaking. The Russians coming at night could surely only mean one thing.

'I'll go this time,' said Gerta. 'They might not know you're here. They won't want an old woman like me. They might go away.'

Katja shook her head. She couldn't let Gerta put herself in such danger. She'd go herself.

Shaking with fear, she opened the door. Five soldiers burst in. In her panic and fright, Katja could not tell if they were the same or different to those who had visited that morning. They all looked the same, these Russian peasant fighters, broad and squat, brown-haired, brown-eyed, brown-souled. Because that's how Katja saw them. They were not bad or evil, no more than anyone else. Their searing quest for revenge was understandable. Hitler and the Nazi Party had unleashed horror upon the world, upon their compatriots, their towns and their cities, and now all Germans had to pay the price. That was the way of the world.

The men stank of alcohol. They must have found some from somewhere, if not from her. For a second, Katja was back in the chicken shed with Alice, knowing what was to come.

'Sex,' the men were shouting, 'we have sex.'

It was not a question, nor a suggestion. It was an order.

Two of them alighted upon Gerta, grabbing her arm and forcing her to the sitting room. Before she could see what they were doing, the other three had taken hold of Katja and dragged her into the bedroom. She tried to close her mind to what was going on, to drift away to some other world.

She couldn't.

It went on for hours, or maybe it was no time at all, over in a matter of minutes. Katja couldn't judge how long and the Red Army had already taken her clock so she had no way to check.

It wouldn't have been so bad, if it hadn't been for Hans.

As the men had bundled her into the room, Katja had been dimly aware of the little boy scrambling down from the bed and scuttling into the corner, crying and wailing. While the attack continued, Hans' cries diminished to pitiful whimpers. His desperate calls for *mama* faded away to indistinct sounds with no meaning.

Katja wanted to strangle the men, fetch a kitchen knife and castrate them, stab the blade into their hearts and watch their life blood drain away. She didn't want to do this to save herself, but to save her son, terrified, watching.

The soldiers fell into drunken comas all around the apartment, in the bedroom, the living room and the hallway. Katja took Hans and, stepping over their prone bodies, she staggered to the kitchen. She made Hans a makeshift bed with some blankets on the floor and then, leaning over the sink, she retched. Nothing came out; her stomach was completely empty.

She wanted to get out of the apartment, to take Hans and flee to the forest or the lakes, to hide out there in some hole or cave and never come out. But she was too weak to even think about walking to the next neighbourhood, let alone to the outskirts of the city. She lay on the floor beside her son and tried to sleep.

At about 6 a.m., the men woke up. They stood up and walked out without taking the slightest bit of notice of Katja, now hovering anxiously in the kitchen doorway, or of Gerta, whose supine form still lay on the sofa. When the men had left, Katja went over to her and touched her gently on the shoulder. At first, the elderly lady did not move, but eventually she groaned and shifted onto her back, then tried to sit up. She looked utterly crushed, as if she'd been run over by a tank.

'What happened?' she asked, desperation cloaking her face in a deathly pallor. 'What did they do to us? Why did they do it?' Tears poured from her eyes and she let them fall, along with snot from her nose.

'Come on,' said Katja, softly. 'Clean yourself up.'

There was no point in talking about what had happened.

'I'll get the tin tub out later. We'll fetch enough water to have a proper wash. For now, splash your face at least and you'll feel better.'

In truth, Katja wasn't sure she was brave enough, or had the energy, to lug enough water from the street pump to wash in. But it felt better to be doing something.

Once Gerta had followed Katja's instruction, Katja rubbed water on her own face. She brushed her hair with her fingers and straightened the collar of her worn, torn and ill-fitting blouse.

She went out of the flat and up to the Russian soldiers who, having enjoyed their breakfast, were lolling around in their encampment.

'Please give me some food,' she stated, keeping her tone as neutral as possible. 'You have got what you wanted. Now let me have what I need.'

At first, the men stared at her, flabbergasted. Then one stood up, went to their crates of supplies and pulled out a loaf of black bread, a can of meat and then, as an afterthought, a bundle of white candles. He handed the booty over with a broad smile. 'Take,' he said, gruffly, and then turned to say something to his colleagues in Russian.

'Thank you,' replied Katja, stiffly. She went back inside the apartment building and got all the way back inside her home before the tears sprang from her eyes.

That day, they feasted on the Russian food. Only Hans was not satisfied, tugging on Katja's arm and begging for toffee. He'd got a taste for the sweet treat and bread was a poor alternative.

'No, *liebchen*,' she said to him, with a feeble smile and a shake of her head, 'no more toffee. Another day.'

After that, various men came on various nights and Katja let them in, if they had food. If they didn't, she sent them back to get some.

Sex for food. But at least it kept them all alive.

CHAPTER FORTY-FOUR

Shame. Shame piled on shame. Friedrich, Alice, Ernst, and now selling herself for a hunk of black bread. It was almost beyond comprehension what my mother had had to endure.

'What else could I do? We had to live. If this was the only way, then so be it.' Her voice was calm but plaintive. 'You think things can't get any worse and then they do.'

My stomach turned again, as it had during the telling of the story, and I felt breathless. I couldn't think of anything to say so said nothing.

My mother seemed to interpret my silence as censure or disapproval.

'I hated myself,' she whispered. 'But I had no choice. I did what any mother would do to save her fam— to save her child.'

I nodded. 'Of course you did, Mum. No one's judging you.' I thought for a moment, not wanting to ask, knowing I had to. 'Did Dad know?'

She emitted a derisive snort of laughter. 'We never spoke of it. But he knew. Everyone knew what happened to the women of Berlin in 1945.'

We had been outside for far longer than I had intended. The greenhouse was full of plants that I needed to pot on for Melissa's garden. But this was more important.

'It didn't last long,' she continued. 'Not long at all, in the scheme of things.'

I wasn't sure if this was a pitiful, or necessary, attempt to alleviate the horror of it all, to make light of something appalling.

'But – it was rape, Mum. Brutal, horrendous rape.' I shuddered. Rape had always been, and presumably always would be, a weapon of war, used to demean and subdue women and girls, to exact revenge, to take power from people who were, in most cases, utterly powerless anyway.

My mother pulled her jacket closer around her shoulders. 'I must tell you something, Jo. It wasn't always rape. After a couple of weeks, one man came, a senior officer from somewhere in the Ural Mountains. He used to talk about his homeland; he made it sound romantic, enormous, enchanted. He liked me and things got much better after that. He kept the others away, the lower ranks, and he was pleasant and educated. He brought us everything we needed and presents for the... for Hans – sweets, a hand-carved spinning top, a skipping rope. He made those things for my son. Those Russian soldiers were so peculiar. Capable of utter brutality and heartrending kindness. Once Yuri came, things weren't so bad.'

My mother shivered, from cold or from the memory of Yuri and the other men, I didn't know.

'Now, I would like to go in,' she said. 'And, Jo, if you don't mind, I don't want to speak of this again. I told you because I promised to you – and to myself – that I would be honest, that I would tell the whole truth and nothing but the truth. If this is to be a historical document, it's essential that it's accurate. Otherwise, we leave behind us a false narrative of the past. But now I want the subject closed.'

Though I burned with questions, I couldn't press her when she had made her feelings known so clearly, especially after what she had just revealed to me. Whatever she said, however pragmatically she spoke about giving the Russian soldiers what they wanted in order to get what she wanted – in my eyes I could only see that rape was rape. But perhaps it was easier for her not to see it that way, perhaps that viewpoint was how she had lived with it all these years, and it was not my place to dispute that.

'This question isn't about you, Mum,' I ventured, as I escorted her to the house. 'So I'm not breaking the rule. But the woman in the attic – what was wrong with her? You said she had lost her hair and had a terrible rash.'

Katja drew in her breath as if she had a sudden pain. 'I think she had syphilis. Many did, or gonorrhoea. I think she died. Maybe not just because of that but malnutrition, too... any manner of things could have killed her.'

I did not even want to think about what would have happened to the woman's children, orphaned and alone.

In the sitting room, I settled my mother down in front of the television – she was a huge fan of *Countdown* – and made tea for us both.

'By July, they were carving Berlin into zones. We were very lucky – Charlottenburg became part of the British zone. Once it was all sorted – that was the end of the Russians, then.' She picked up her mug of tea and nursed it in her liver-spotted hands. 'I just wish Hans and... That Hans hadn't had to see it. That's all I wish.'

The tea I was sipping scalded my throat. The moment I had dreaded and longed for in equal part had come. The elephant in the room that we had all tiptoed around for so many years, never daring to disturb it, had raised its metaphorical trunk and bellowed, loud and clear.

'Mum,' I began, then hesitated, edged a little further forward in my chair. 'I know how hard this is. But – what happened to my brother. What happened to Hans?'

CHAPTER FORTY-FIVE

GERMANY, 1945

As the Russians began to leave Charlottenburg, a new assailant swept through the city. Diphtheria was an evil avenger that took advantage of a population too weak and starved and enervated to fight it off. There was not a household, nor a family, in Berlin that didn't have members succumb to the disease.

Hans fell ill.

Katja searched and searched for a doctor to come to the apartment, as she had done for Ernst, but there were none to be found. Eventually, Gerta persuaded her that there was nothing to be done but to take him to hospital. They wrapped him in a blanket and Katja set off through pitch-black streets to the Charité hospital. It was a long way carrying a child, but she had heard on the grapevine that it was one of the few still functioning. As she stumbled through the wreckage of her once proud and beautiful city, Katja thought how her little boy, who was not even two years old yet, had already seen more pain and suffering than anyone should witness in a lifetime.

When she reached the Charité, she was horrified to see how much of it had been destroyed. And yet the doors were open and when she entered, almost collapsing with exhaustion and the weight of her son, a nurse appeared to greet them, a white-garbed phantom of the night.

In no time at all, Hans had been found a cot and a doctor been called.

'You can go now,' said the nurse, with a kindly smile.

'Oh no,' countered Katja. 'No, I'll stay, until the morning at least. Or until he's seen the doctor.'

The nurse shook her head. 'We have nowhere for you even to sit while you wait. You can see how many sick people there are in here.'

Katja argued for a little longer, but the woman wouldn't budge. Eventually, realising her protests were futile, she resigned herself to leaving, too brain-addled with fatigue and worry to know what else to do. She would go home for a few hours, try to sleep, and be back at first light.

As she limped down the long, white corridor, her footsteps echoing in the emptiness, she looked back at Hans. He was standing in the cot, leaning against the bars, reaching out his skinny arms imploringly towards her. She just made out his cries of '*Mutti*' getting fainter as she drew away.

Tears streaming down her drawn and hollow cheeks, Katja had no memory of getting home, just that the next morning she jerked awake at the crack of dawn and, before she'd even thought about what she was doing, jumped out of bed, grabbed her threadbare shawl against the early-morning chill and left the flat. Her only thoughts as she navigated her way through the annihilated city streets were of Hans, her beloved son, the one thing that brought her joy, her reason for living.

She arrived at the hospital to find Hans' cot empty. She stood, open-mouthed, staring. He must have been taken for treatment somewhere, or to a doctor's office, or perhaps to where they ate meals. Frantically, she looked all around her, her eyes searching every corner of the ward, snapping in different directions, not knowing which way to check first.

A nurse appeared, a different one from the night before. She had a uniform and a cap and an unnaturally beatific smile upon her face. Perhaps she was an angel. Or the devil. It was hard to tell.

The nurse glided to Hans' cot, where she began to change the sheets.

'Wh-where is he? Where is my boy, Hans?' Katja's voice wavered so much, she wasn't sure if her words were audible.

The nurse snapped a sheet over the mattress.

'He's dead, Frau Schmidt. He passed in the night. His body has been disposed of.' She glanced up from her chore. 'You can continue to use his ration coupons until the end of the week.'

LONDON, JUNE 1994

Once she had recounted what had happened to Hans at the hospital, once more my mother wanted to be alone.

Reluctantly, I left her. I felt I should be able to do something, say something to assuage the grief my mother still carried with her, though she had hidden it so well over so many years. But I couldn't think of anything.

Listlessly, I tried to set my mind to some chores. Cupboards needed emptying, drawers clearing, wardrobes sorting. There was so much I should throw away or organise in preparation for moving. It was pointless, though, as I couldn't concentrate. I found myself staring into space for long minutes, Springer watching me with a perplexed expression on his kind, familiar face.

No wonder the subject of Hans' death had always been brushed away if ever it dared to raise its ugly, unwelcome head. No wonder that my childish questions about my half-brother had gone unanswered, my inquisitiveness been left to languish, and that I had learnt not to go there, to leave well alone. The memories had been too raw, too tender and sore, to be shown the light of day.

I contemplated now, as I had in the past, if Hans' death was why Katja and my father had had me so soon after meeting. An attempt to make up for the loss of the little boy? But as soon as I thought this, I realised how crass I was being. More likely, my birth had been a result of the complete lack of any kind of contraception at that time, in Berlin.

With so many thoughts tumbling and jumbling through my mind, I couldn't concentrate on anything. A deep silence had descended on the little house by the Heath, a silence so deafening, I found it unbearable. Ed's record player, along with his treasured vinyl collection, still languished in the sitting room. Selecting a disc, I put it on and sank down into my armchair as Mozart's Requiem filled the air.

At least I knew now. It hardly gave me much comfort but at least, after all these years, I knew exactly how my mother had lost Hans.

Eventually, the record finished playing. Rousing myself, I phoned Melissa to see if it was convenient for me to go round. She answered that it was, so I set off, first filling the 2CV with boxes of plants; perennials and shrubs, plus Alpines for the rockery I had created. Once there, I set about dotting the pots in various spaces, moving them around like a giant jigsaw puzzle until I was happy with how they looked.

Digging, mulching, watering and surveying fully occupied my time until it got dark. Melissa came out with a cup of tea for us both, absolutely delighted with how it looked.

'If you want more work, I've got lots of friends who need garden help!' she exclaimed. 'I'll recommend you.'

I thanked her profusely. I didn't tell her how little time I had, not wanting to put her off from spreading the word to her friends. If there was any interest, I'd just have to find the time to fit it all in, meteor style. It wouldn't be easy, but following one's passion rarely is.

As I left, I felt hopeful about my future for the first time in ages. There was life beyond Ed and my failed marriage, perhaps even life beyond having to move house, though that was hard to convince myself of. In any case, nothing I had ever suffered was as bad as my mother had experienced. And the increasing closeness of our relationship in part made up for no longer having a husband's love.

When I got back home, I decided to ignore the divorce paperwork that, far from diminishing seemed only to be growing, like some hideous fungus that spreads invisibly over every living thing. The latest was that I had to provide details of everything from my monthly income to my expenditure on haircuts, clothes, beauty treatments. None of which amounted to much; I was shockingly low-maintenance.

'Ed, we have a joint account,' I'd reminded him during our most recent meeting. 'You know what I earn – and what I spend. If you think I've got money squirrelled away somewhere – think again.'

'It's not about me not trusting you,' he had said, patiently, as if I needed to be spoken to very carefully to be sure of understanding. 'It's just what needs to be done.'

Someone Sue knew – truly, she knew *everyone* – a lawyer friend of hers, was handling my side of the proceedings. I just wanted it all to go away. What on earth I would do without Sue's contacts and acquaintances when she was no longer a full-time resident of the British Isles, I had no idea.

Wearily, I swept all the letters and bank statements together into a big pile. Pulling the phone cord to its full length, I went into the sitting room, settling myself into the armchair with a glass of wine. As soon as it was a decent time in the morning in New Zealand, I dialled Evan's number. Hang the expense; in the light of what had happened to Hans, I wanted to speak to my own son. Evan was so far away and of course I worried about him sometimes, as any mother would. But I'd never had serious cause for concern about his health or well-being. The worst illness he'd ever had was the rather ominously named hand, foot and mouth disease, which though accompanied by a high fever and some alarming rashes, ulcers and blisters, had duly cleared up after the normal seven days. I had never struggled to feed him or find shelter or medical care for him. He had never had to look on as I was set upon by huge, terrifying men in uniforms. I had never had to leave him, sobbing, in a hospital cot, not knowing that I would never see him, alive or dead, again.

Did my mother even get to hold a funeral for her first-born? I had forgotten to ask, but I assumed that if the body had already been 'disposed of' – what a horrendous phrase that was – it was unlikely.

Within a few rings, Evan answered and, after the time delay on the line, I heard his voice, familiar even with the slight New Zealand twang he'd acquired.

'Hello, Evan here.'

'Evan! It's Mum.' I paused, suddenly unsure what to say. I couldn't tell him what I'd been finding out over the phone. 'Are you OK? Everything going well?'

Another pause and then, 'All fine, great. Um, why are you phoning?' There was a tinge of worry in his voice. 'Are you all right?'

'I'm fine,' I answered, truthfully. 'I just wanted to hear your voice,' I continued, simply. 'To tell you I love you.'

'Thanks, Mum. It's good to hear you too,' Evan laughed. 'Er – anything else?'

'No. Just that.' I smiled at Evan's obvious bafflement.

We chatted for a few minutes about this and that, and then

Evan apologised and said he had a meeting to get to. 'It's an early start, Mum – bit of a drive to get there.'

'I hope it goes well.' I pictured my son, in his jeep, driving through sunlit vineyards on the other side of the world.

'Bye then,' Evan said.

'Bye, love. I'll see you at the wedding.'

The phone beeped as I ended the call, dropping the grey handset into the cradle. Evan would be in Europe soon, on a flying visit taking in a few days in London for his sister's nuptials and then a tour of France and Italy with his New Zealand girlfriend who had never been to either country. The relationship seemed to be serious and I could feel myself losing my son to the Antipodean lifestyle he had taken to so wholeheartedly, exactly as my worst fears had predicted. He loved the outdoor life, surfing, skiing, climbing, hiking and trekking, the emptiness and space after growing up in the hectic, crowded London borough of Camden. I was more sure than ever that he would settle in New Zealand and stay there for good, on the other side of the world, far away from me.

If he did that, I must give him my blessing. He would still be my son, still alive and healthy, still available any time at the end of the phone. Not like little Hans, who my mother had lost for ever.

I checked the time. It wasn't too late to call Emma.

'I just wanted to tell you that I love you,' I said to my daughter, who I'd interrupted watching an episode of *Frasier* that she'd videotaped.

'Thanks, Mum,' replied Emma, sounding at once somewhat distracted and pleasantly surprised. 'I love you, too. I would have come round more, to help with Grandma – but the wedding – I've been so busy.'

'It's fine.' Her words had set my mind running through a mental list of everything that I needed to do before the wedding day. It had to be perfect. Emma deserved nothing less.

'Bye then,' said Emma, 'speak soon.'

'Bye. Love you.'

I didn't feel ready for bed quite yet. Instead, I picked up the black notebook; I was not far from the end now. I felt trepidation at finding out how it all finished. Of course, I knew that my father had survived – but at what cost?

CHAPTER FORTY-SIX

GERMANY, 1945

Finally, it came to an end.

There were false starts, plenty of them. Convoys of American trucks loading up POWs, only for all to be forced to disembark by Russian soldiers who wanted to be in charge of repatriation. Several times, Lou and his fellow airmen watched the American vehicles drive off empty, leaving them even more deflated and depressed.

Lou was overwhelmed by a tremendous desire for solitude. He should be happy, because even if they'd been thwarted yesterday, and today, and would be again tomorrow, they'd be on their way at some point soon. But all he felt was a deep dread. The experiences of the last five years played through his mind incessantly, jumping and jumbling, capture and incarceration, release and freedom, Eva, recapture, another prison camp, the years there that all melded into one blob of boredom and frustration and impatience and resignation. There seemed to be no rest from it, no respite from his own head, nowhere to find any peace.

Finally, a few weeks after the war's official end, the Russians loaded the *kriegies* into trucks and took them to the banks of the mighty River Elbe.

With mixed feelings, Lou crossed the rickety pontoon bridge. As his feet touched the ground on the other side, he paused, raised his face to the sky and took a deep breath. This was the fresh air of freedom. He didn't know what he expected. An epiphany, maybe, a sudden onrush of exhilaration or elation, an uplifting of the spirits. Instead, there was nothing. He felt nothing. Just numb and tired and desperate to get home. Though that, longed for over so many years, now seemed also fearful.

London, with all the bombing, would have changed. The people he had left behind there would have changed. Above all, he had changed. Whatever he found when he got back, one thing was certain: nothing would ever be the same again.

After being together for so long and going through so much, in those final hours Lou became separated from all of his prison camp mates. With a disparate bunch of strangers, he was flown to Brussels, and then to an airfield in the south of England, from where he travelled by train to a rehabilitation centre for POWs. Lou stayed twenty-four hours before checking himself out. There was nothing wrong with him that these people could fix. He had already started to formulate a plan for the only thing that was going to make him feel better.

He took a train to London.

In Bayham Street, Camden Town, an old dog called Ruby lay on a doorstep. At about four o'clock, she pricked her ears up, lifted her gnarled old head and then struggled awkwardly to her feet. Lumbering along the uneven paving stones, suddenly she forced her old bones into a run. By the time she reached the corner, she was at full pelt.

In the doorway of the laundromat, two women stood, enjoying the sunshine.

'That's Una Robby's dog, isn't it?' said one to the other.

Her companion nodded. 'Or her son Lou's more like.'

A silence descended as both women thought of what they knew of Lou, how long he had been away, imprisoned. How Una, at the VE Day celebrations, had been too full of sadness to take part in the dancing, drinking and carousing. Her son had been imprisoned for four and a half years, and she had heard nothing from him during the last six months. She had begun to despair of him ever returning.

At the street corner, Lou stopped, his eyes widening in amazement.

'Ruby!' he called, his voice breaking with emotion. 'Ruby old girl! You've come to meet me, have you? I should have known you'd be here, waiting.' He bent down to the dog's rough head, hair coarse with age, and rubbed her nose and her ears as she frantically wagged her tail and attempted to jump up, her ancient limbs not quite making it, but the sentiment behind it clear to see.

Lou stood up, laughing. The sky seemed brighter, the clouds of the morning had cleared and the sun shone. It was summer in England, and he was home.

He waved cheerily to Elsie at the laundromat and her customer Betty. Dumbfounded, they waved back.

'Well, there's a thing,' remarked Elsie, as the two of them retreated back inside to get on with the important business of washing clothes, bedsheets, towels. 'Una'll be that surprised. I'm sure she didn't know he was coming. She never mentioned it if she did.'

Betty pursed her lips. 'I reckon she would have said if she'd known, you know what a chatterbox she is.' Her face broke into a broad smile. 'Oh, she's going to be made up, she'll be the cat that got the cream. Her Lou back, after all these years.'

When he reached the flat, Lou realised he didn't have keys. The thought seemed ridiculous. After years of imprisonment, the idea of being able to come and go at his own free will was incredible. He rang the doorbell and leaned against the door jamb while he waited for an answer. A wave of exhaustion swept over him. Perhaps he should have stayed at the rehabilitation centre for a week or so, taken the time to do nothing, just eat and sleep. But no. He was glad he'd left. He'd spent enough of his life cooped up.

The sound of footsteps on the stairs filtered through the front door. If it was his mother, she had got slower during his years of absence. The war and time had taken its toll on everyone. He heard the sound of the key in the lock on the inside and the door swung open. He moved into the centre of the doorstep, smiling. His mother took one look at him and fainted, right there on the threshold.

By the time she'd recovered and Lou had got her upstairs and into the flat, he was beginning to think he should have sent warning of his impending arrival. Una was hyperventilating, speaking in riddles, unable to form a coherent sentence.

'It's you, is it you? Oh, where's Dad, I need to tell, Ruby knew it, saw her running, street, Dad... where, how?'

Laughing kindly, Lou tried to calm his mother down. When she finally got a grip of herself, she made tea. Lou let her do it; the kitchen was his mother's domain and making tea the most important activity that took place in it. The tray with pot and milk jug and sugar bowl and teacups and saucers placed on the coffee table, Una sat back, folded her hands in her lap and looked at her son.

'So,' she said, 'you better tell me what you've been up to since you've been gone.'

Later that evening, Lou used the excuse of needing to stretch his legs to leave the flat for a few hours. He hated the way he felt. He loved his mum and dad, but their questions, so trivial and anodyne, annoyed him – what did they give you to eat? What did you do all day? He didn't know why they were asking as he'd told them all that stuff in his letters, but then, of course, he understood why they were asking. How else to fill the chasm of nearly half a decade?

At the Queen Vic, a couple of old boys who worked in the local Post Office sorting facility were propping up the bar. They looked exactly as they had the night before he'd left, just older and thinner from the years and the rationing. But not as thin as the German civilians, all those refugees passing by the camp, old men like skeletons, malnourished children with huge eyes, women worn to skin and bone.

'You back at last? Let you out, did they? What have you been doing all this time?'

Lou smiled and emitted a self-deprecating exhalation of breath. 'Not much, mate. Not much at all.'

When he got back to the flat, his mother was sitting up waiting for him.

'I know this must be really difficult for you, son,' she said. 'We none of us know what to say. We can't even imagine what you've been through.'

They sat looking at each other as the dusky light of a summer's evening sifted through the old and draughty windows. Ruby had lain down at Lou's feet and he stroked her side, contemplatively. She'd been following him everywhere, never letting him out of her sight. She'd even been to the pub with him, but she was tired now. It was more exercise than her thirteen-year-old body was used to. She snored and Lou and Una smiled.

'What are you thinking?' asked Una.

'I'm thinking I missed the whole bloody war,' he said. 'All of it. I missed the lot.'

He went to the bedroom in which his mother had kept a bed always made up for him, in readiness for his return. That night, he made his decision.

Only a few weeks later, he was gone.

CHAPTER FORTY-SEVEN

LONDON, JUNE 1994

In my mother's flat in Bayham Street, the exact same one that my father had returned to and then left again so precipitously, everything was nearly ready for her return. I wandered around it, making mental notes of what needed to be bought, how the furniture would be best arranged when I brought it back from storage.

But what was really occupying my mind was my father. How strange it must have been to step back into normality after all he had been through, an Alice through the looking glass moment. All those men, those soldiers and sailors and pilots, must have had to make a monumental effort to adjust.

But I couldn't dwell on this now. With everything that was going on, I'd lost track of time passing and it was only a week until Emma's wedding. My mother was feeling much stronger, so I'd decided that it was now or never. We would have to brave a trip to Brent Cross and hope that John Lewis would provide us with everything we needed to kit out the grandmother-of-the-bride in something suitable.

My mother did not immediately take to the idea.

'Can't you get something for me?' she protested. 'You know I loathe clothes shopping.'

'Not more than I do,' I muttered under my breath. And then louder, 'Well, I suppose I could. But it would be much better if you were there to choose and you'll need to try things on. It's so hard to gauge sizes otherwise.'

She pulled a face that said she wasn't convinced.

'Come on, Mum,' I coaxed, 'you want to look good for your only granddaughter's wedding day, don't you? We'll take it really easy, park right outside the store. Evan's asked me to get him a tie as he doesn't possess one, so you can help me with that, too.'

At the mention of her adored grandson, my mother broke into a smile. 'All right,' she agreed, 'I suppose it won't be too bad. I need to put on a good show for Emma, as you say, and as for that boy of yours – what does he wear for work in New Zealand, then?'

I laughed. 'A, he's a student, and B, I'm not sure that winemaking is the kind of job that requires business dress.'

In the trusty old 2CV, we rattled our way up the A41.

'Your father was a sucker for a nice outfit,' my mother mused, as the houses, allotments and traffic signs flashed by. 'He really suited a suit.' She chuckled at her own pun before resuming. 'He looked so handsome in the uniform. Blue it was, with a short jacket and a tie, very smart.'

'What uniform was that, Mum?' I asked. There were fragments of this story that had been mentioned over the years, but I wanted to hear it all again, wanted every detail.

'The Control Commission for Berlin. He couldn't settle to civilian life in London. In fact, he didn't really give it a try. He signed up straightaway, as soon as he was demobbed, and he was back in Germany by July, right after the whole thing was set up.'

I looked in the wing mirror to see if it was safe to overtake the bus in front of me. 'I just read that in his book. I hadn't realised before how little time he spent back here before leaving again.'

She nodded. 'Oh yes. He was never one to wait around, my Lou. Well, apart from the years waiting around as a prisoner of war, I suppose. He felt he'd been useless for so long that he wanted to be useful for a while.' She followed my eyes as I checked before turning right. 'It was the only thing he could think of to do.'

'Poor Dad,' I replied. 'It must have been so hard to suddenly be back in London after such a terrible few years. But he made a good life, didn't he, with you and me, afterwards? It wasn't all bad.' Perhaps I felt the need for this reassurance.

'Oh yes,' my mother concurred, 'not bad at all.'

'And what were his responsibilities, in Berlin?' We were in the car park now and I searched for a parking space as I listened.

'Well, the Commission was responsible for policing the city,' my mother explained, 'dividing it and the rest of the country into the four zones of occupation and re-establishing the country's old borders. It was very important work. Your... Lou worked in the administration. There was a lot to do.'

'I'm sure there was,' I affirmed. It was unimaginable, how a whole new country could be carved out of such a disaster, or two countries, as it turned out. I found a space and manoeuvred into it, then turned to my mother. 'You ready for this?'

She grimaced. 'As ready as I'll ever be.'

I smiled. With my mother's wartime history, it was hardly surprising she had never developed the shopping habit. For so many years, both during the war and after, there'd been nothing to buy. Even decades later, when the family's financial situation had stabilised and the shops in London were full to bursting with gorgeous, desirable clothing, she could rarely be induced to spend a penny on herself. I had offered to buy the wedding outfit for her to counter her reluctance for self-indulgence, but she had flatly refused.

'Come on then, out we get,' I exhorted, helping my mother out of the car and towards the doors that led directly into John Lewis. Once inside, I steered her firmly towards women's clothing. On the other side of that floor, I knew from long experience, lay the nursery and children's shoe department. I didn't know why I was so conscious of wanting to keep her away from that section. Did I really think that, even after all these years, the sight of all those prams and babygros would be too painful a reminder of her lost son? Or was it myself that I was protecting, me who, having finally found out exactly what fate had befallen the brother I had never known, did not want to contemplate it further?

Pushing my thoughts from my mind, I concentrated on the task in hand. Spread out before us was a plethora of glorious summer outfits, arrayed on rails, mannequins and feature walls. It was bewildering, far too much choice than could ever be necessary. After half an hour of aimless wandering, with me pulling things from rails and my mother immediately dismissing them – too bright, too dull, too long, too short – I began to feel frustrated.

'Mum, honestly, you've got to try *something*. You sit down here,' I indicated towards one of the benches in the shoe section. 'I'm going to fetch five outfits and you are going to try each and every one of them on, even if you don't think you like them. OK?'

She pursed her lips in disapproval. 'If you say so.'

I marched off, suppressing a growl of annoyance. This was my mother, stubborn as ever. The last thing I wanted was an argument. And, of course, I wanted her to find an outfit she'd like and be comfortable in. But at some point we needed to make a decision.

Searching among the racks, I piled jackets, shirts, skirts over my arm, not really taking much notice of which brand's concession I was in, just choosing things that caught my eye. And then I saw it. A beautiful belted midi-length shirt dress in a soft, muted dark green crepe. Hastily snatching it off the rail as if ten other shoppers were about to grab it, I clutched the dress proprietorially to my chest.

I was sure this was the one. Searching for the label to check the price, I gulped slightly. The dress was Jaeger and the cost reflected that. There was no denying it was expensive, but on the other hand, you couldn't put a price on looking good for your grandchild's wedding, could you? This is how I would convince my mother.

In the end, winning her over wasn't as hard as I had envisaged. I think she recognised from my aura of determination that this was the endgame now. Resistance was futile.

'Yes, I like it,' she admitted grudgingly as I showed her the dress. I held it up alongside another one, just to make the contrast between the two clearer. The green one was so obviously superior that my plan worked. 'I don't need to see anything else,' she said. 'Let's just take this and go.'

'You're trying it on first,' I insisted. 'I'm not coming back because the size is wrong.'

Once this task had been done, and it had been confirmed that the green dress was, indeed, perfect in every way, we found Evan's tie and then gratefully exited the store. Fluffed up with satisfaction, I carried the bag to the car and laid it carefully on the back seat. My mother hadn't even flinched at the price, barely seeming to notice it.

On the way home, the time suddenly seemed right to ask the next burning question.

'So Dad went to Berlin to work for the Control Commission,' I said, 'and what happened next? How did you and he meet?'

'What happened?' my mother frowned. 'Well, I got a job on the buses. That's what happened.'

CHAPTER FORTY-EIGHT

GERMANY, 1945

Katja could barely rouse herself from the grief of Hans' death. It was as if all the sorrow and pain and hardship and loss of the war years had accumulated in the passing of her precious little boy. Katja couldn't help but think that she and Gerta made a pathetic twosome these days, two women grubbing in the dirt to stay alive, which in itself seemed pointless now there was no Hans to look after. Gerta was stalwart, though, doing everything she could to raise Katja's spirits. They had been close for so long, thrust together by circumstance, but now Katja began to rely on Gerta in the same way that Gerta had relied on her during their walk. Gerta gave her emotional support and she also saw to Katja's physical needs, getting her to eat and drink and, now that the Russians had gone and it was safe to venture outside, making sure she had some fresh air every day.

'It's good for you,' she would say, 'to feel the sunshine on your face.'

After the first week or so, going out became a necessity. The arrival of the British hadn't alleviated the food situation and it was each person for themselves in the quest for enough to eat.

If she and Gerta weren't to join Hans in the grave, Katja had to pull herself together and join the thousands cramming onto the trains every day, heading for the countryside to forage for anything edible – mushrooms, berries, leaves – and for fuel. Gerta knew the roots of a certain plant that burned well and they sought these out, filling bags and bundles, then joining all the other thousands of women heading back home before night-fall. So many people packed themselves aboard that some had to hang from the roof, and the trains became known as the 'hamster express' because of how crowded they were.

On days when Gerta went on the forays and Katja stayed in the city, she joined the *Trümmerfrauen* – the rubble women. Using buckets and pails, they formed human chains to clear the debris that littered every street and alleyway and green space, salvaging anything that could be reused for rebuilding the city.

The Brandenburg Gate became the main focus for the black market and the barter system. It was here that women prostituted themselves for food or for the city's chief currency, cigarettes, which had far more value than the almost worthless Reichsmark. Katja knew the place, how the system worked. But, after what she had been through with the Russians, she would not partake. She would rather starve.

On many days, that's exactly what it felt that she and Gerta were doing. But then, one day, Katja saw a job advertised. The administration was running buses for British personnel and their wives, as well as for Berliners, and they needed conduc-tors, people who knew the British zone and could help the passengers, telling them what stop to get off at, directing them to their accommodation or to the shops. It was a chance to earn money, to improve their situation. And Katja hoped that having something to do might help her cope, and give her a purpose other than grieving for her son.

'How good is your English?' they asked her at the interview.

'Oh, well...' replied Katja, non-committally. She didn't speak more than a word or two of the language. 'I can...'

Katja had intended to say that she could learn, but the woman seemed to think she had been reporting some proficiency and did not investigate further.

'Start on Monday,' said the interviewer, already sifting through applications, looking for the next candidate's details. 'Report to the bus station at 7 a.m.'

CHAPTER FORTY-NINE

'So I got the job,' my mother said, 'and I loved it. It was so good to have a reason to leave the flat in the mornings. I expected things to continue that way forever, I suppose. I certainly didn't envisage what happened next.'

I eased into the traffic on the dual carriageway, listening intently.

'One day, only a week or two after I started, I met Lou. Our eyes met across the seat backs and that was that.'

'Love at first sight,' I filled in. How romantic, how marvellous, after all that pain.

There was a tiny hesitation and then my mother said, 'Yes, precisely that.' She gave a short, amazed laugh. 'It was crazy. He spoke a little German – what he'd picked up in the prison camp. I was studying as hard as I could to learn English – they gave us a book, you see, to teach ourselves words and phrases. We could communicate with each other – but only just. But it didn't matter. I knew from the start that he was someone special.'

Halted by traffic lights, I leaned across and patted my mother's hand. 'He was. I know you still miss him.'

'Yes, I do,' she sighed. 'Every day. But I was lucky to have had him for the time I did. He was a wonderful man, there's never been a man like him. I consider myself fortunate.'

I pondered this as I negotiated the traffic in Hampstead. It was hard to imagine enduring what my mother had and still feeling grateful. But everything was relative, I supposed.

'Can we go to the flat?' she asked, out of the blue. 'As we're in the car anyway. I'd like to see how it's coming along.'

'Of course!' I hadn't suggested it as I had thought that the shopping expedition would have worn my mother out, but the fact that she had requested it unprompted was great – a really positive sign that she was feeling much better, getting her energy back after the gruelling operation and recovery. Much as I loved taking care of her, we both needed our own space.

In Bayham Street, I parked up as close as I could get to the apartment block. I helped my mother up the stairs with some trepidation. The work was all but finished, just some plumbing and tiling to be done, and a final lick of paint. But my mother was notoriously exacting and hard to please and it had been quite a weight on my shoulders to get it just right.

Inside the flat, my mother prowled around, touching things, sniffing, running her finger along shelves and worktops and inspecting the dusty residue that fell over everything.

'We'll get a cleaner in, Mum,' I said, trying hard not to sound impatient. 'There's always dust after building work.' I hoped my mother wasn't going to criticise after all the effort I'd put in.

She paused, came to the centre of the sitting room and took a good look around. 'It's marvellous. More than I ever expected. Thank you.'

I breathed a mighty sigh of relief and then was immediately pained by a stab of guilt. I shouldn't have thought the worst of my mother. It was just her way to be cautious. She rarely enthused about anything. But, of course, that was understandable. What did anything much matter, when you had been through so much and it had culminated in your child dying in such tragic circumstances?

My mother sank down onto the sofa which had been delivered back from storage and was now covered in a dust sheet as the final touching up of the paintwork was done. 'I hardly recognise it as the flat that we lived in when we came to London.'

'Well, I guess that's a good thing,' I joked, 'after spending all this money on it!' I sat down next to her. 'When was it again that you – we – came to England?'

'Oh,' she exhaled, 'in 1949, it was, a few years after you were born. Things were very difficult. Lou and I couldn't get married until I had the official notice that Horst was dead, and that took a long time to come through. All the administration was in chaos, records lost, offices bombed to smithereens. It was impossible to get a passport, travel documents, anything really.' She fiddled with a piece of plaster that had fallen onto the chair covering. 'And Lou had signed up for a four-year term, so he had to serve it out in full. But the situation in Berlin, far from improving, got worse and worse. The tension with the Soviets was increasing all the time. We were so lucky – the British were nothing but good to us. But for those in the Russian zone – all the horrors of the past returned. The knock on the door in the night. The fear of who was listening. Well, we all know now how it was for those in the East. The Gestapo were terrible, the Stasi just as bad.'

I shuddered. To live in the knowledge that, at any time, anyone might betray you – your employer, your friend, even your own spouse – how was such a life possible?

'When the blockade started, it was a terrible time in the city,' my mother recalled. 'We had been through so much, so many were still living in desperate conditions. It was another setback to endure. Those pilots were so brave, flying in and out over and over again. I recall so clearly the noise of the aircraft, the Dakotas and the Hastings, coming over all the time. The aim was to provide 1,700 calories a day for Berliners! It doesn't sound like much, does it, but it was more than many of us had had for a long time.' She chuckled to herself, though why an impoverished diet was amusing, I couldn't fathom. 'One of the pilots started a fashion of using parachutes to drop candy to the children lining the fences alongside the runways. I took you there, sometimes, when I wasn't working. If we were lucky, we would find some of the sweets and chocolates. It was the best thing you'd ever known!'

'I don't remember any of it,' I countered, shaking my head regretfully. 'Nothing at all about living in Berlin. I suppose I was only three.'

A strange shadow crossed my mother's face, as if a long-forgotten memory had suddenly been reawakened.

'Are you all right, Mum?' I asked, alarmed.

For a moment, she did not reply. When she did, it was to change the subject completely. 'Come on,' she said, standing up and brushing her hands against her jacket to rid them of dust, 'we've been here long enough now. I'm very happy with everything and I will definitely be moving back in the minute we've got Emma married. The very next day, if possible.' She held up her hand to quell my interjection, my protests that this would only happen if she was quite, quite well. 'It's what we agreed – and I really want to be home with my own things around me. Coming here has reminded me how much I miss the old place. And I'm getting better so quickly. So very quickly. I will be fine.'

She said the words with such finality of tone that I knew better than to argue. The main thing was that, if she thought she was ready, then I must trust that. In any case, much better for her to be at home in plenty of time than to be turfed out when my house sale went through. I was pleased that everything was progressing at the most glacial pace, the buyers in a complicated chain. But, nevertheless, the process would be completed at some point.

'I'd like to hear about my birth,' I said, as I pulled out of the parking space. Like so much, this was something my mother and I had never discussed before. 'Where was I born? In hospital or at home? I guess the hospitals were back up and running properly by then, not like when—' My voice cut off abruptly. Best not to mention Hans again.

My mother didn't answer. I glanced across at her and saw the same dark cloud of earlier shrouding her face. I cursed myself for not being more sensitive. It was all too easy to blunder into a mention of Hans when, to me, he was a shadow figure, insubstantial and unreal. But for my mother, of course, things were different.

'At least we had running water again by then,' she said. 'That was something.' She looked out of the window. 'The first time I saw Camden Town,' she went on, totally changing the subject, 'I thought what a dull, grey, dreary place it was, full of undesirables and miscreants. Now...' She paused as we approached the famous markets, where the streets thronged and throbbed with people as always. Leaning against the canal bridge was a group of black-clad punks, complete with multi-coloured Mohicans, safety-pinned lips, ears and noses, chains draped from clothing and limbs. 'Pay a punk to get drunk' read a notice one of them was carrying, as tourists handed over cash to have photographs taken with the group. 'Well, I'm not sure it's much better now,' she sniffed disapprovingly, peering out of the window as we passed.

'Oh Mum, those guys add a bit of local colour,' I teased. 'Bring it on, I say. Wouldn't it be awful if everyone was exactly the same?'

As soon as I'd said the words, I realised that this had been my mother's early experience: boys attired in the brown hats, shirts and swastika armbands of the Hitler Youth; girls in the blue skirts, white blouses and black neckerchiefs of the *Bund Deutscher Mädel*. My mother always maintained she'd never been a member of the latter group, but I wasn't entirely sure about the veracity of that. Apart from anything else, I'd read that membership was compulsory. And even if it were true that she had managed to keep out of it, it was a sure bet that she wouldn't have strayed too far from the strict rules of conformity society in Germany at the time had required. The reality was that she probably would not have looked much different to anyone else, BDM member or not.

'So what about the airlift?' I asked. 'And coming to England for the first time?'

It was only later that it occurred to me that my mother had completely avoided answering the question about my own birth.

CHAPTER FIFTY

GERMANY, 1949

Lou's time in the Control Commission was coming to an end. After four years of relentless hard work, he finally felt that he had expiated his guilt at having done nothing to help win the war by busting a gut to win the peace.

The airlift had been a huge success. The Soviets had had to give in, conceding that the West was not going to break. Another conflict had been avoided – for now, at least – and the citizens of Berlin were safe. Though the blockade was officially over, the supply planes were still flying, filling warehouses and factories with surplus stock so that, should such a thing happen again, the city would have a buffer to ensure survival.

Travel for civilians, however, was still severely restricted, and documents for German citizens to enter the UK limited and hard to come by. Fortunately, Lou's time in the RAF meant he had friends in all the right places.

It was August 1949 and, today, his plan was to come to fruition. He had arranged to take some leave and he, Katja and their small child were going to fly to England.

Katja's eyes filled with tears as she clambered up the steps into the plane. She was heartbroken at leaving Gerta behind, but the old lady would not have wanted to come, even if it had been possible to arrange it. Katja had transferred the lease of the apartment into Gerta's name – hers had long since been given to another family – and left her all the furniture, crockery and pans, such as it was.

'There's nothing for you here,' Gerta had said, sadly, as they made their farewells. 'Your future is in London, with that wonderful man of yours. And your little one, of course. Go with my blessing, but keep in touch.'

Lou was waiting outside in a Control Commission car with a driver, so Katja had to hurry. She almost fell over the kerb, her eyes flooded with salty tears. They had very little luggage. Even four years after the war had ended, they still owned few possessions. Katja didn't mind. It was better to travel light, everything packed up so you could transport it with your own two hands. That's how they'd left the Sudetenland, and that was how she was leaving Germany.

The Dakota was loud and juddery, the entire journey accompanied by clanking joints and rattling metal.

'Is it supposed to sound like this?' asked Katja, petrified. The flimsy seat belts holding her and little Hansi into their seats didn't seem to promise much protection.

Lou just laughed. He was sitting opposite them, across the narrow body of the aircraft, alongside various other military and Control Commission personnel. A couple had smiled kindly at Hansi, but other than that, they had ignored their unusual passengers completely.

Hansi, also frightened, began to scream and didn't let up until they'd crossed the North Sea and were over England, when she suddenly fell asleep. Katja looked out of the window at the scenery unfolding below, the patchwork of fields, interspersed with woods and villages, cut through by gentle rivers and streams. She couldn't believe how low they flew, so low it felt that she could reach out her hand and touch the toy town land beneath. It was all exactly as she had imagined England would look. It gave her confidence, somehow, for the new experience that lay ahead.

The plane came down to land. There was a harsh rumble as the aircraft's wheels descended, an immense roar as they met the tarmac and a shuddering screech as the pilot applied the brakes. Katja's heart was in her mouth and Hansi began to howl again.

Lou leaned across and squeezed Katja's knee. His eyes met hers and he smiled. Katja knew he wished he was flying the plane himself, proudly carrying her and the child to his homeland, taking care of them, making sure they were safe.

'We're here, my love,' he shouted above the noise of the rumbling engines as they trundled to the aerodrome. 'We've arrived. Everything's going to be all right now.'

In the corrugated-iron hut that served as a terminal, Katja tried to make herself small to avoid attracting the attention of the pilots, crew, dispatchers and other miscellaneous and unidentifiable personnel. She had something she needed to say to Hansi. She looked down at her little girl, with her pale skin, red hair and cornflower blue eyes. Her frailty brought out a fierce protectiveness in Katja and she grabbed her by the shoulders with a sudden roughness. This mattered, it really, really mattered, and she needed Hansi to understand that.

'We're safe now,' she whispered, urgently and firmly. Hansi stared, wide-eyed, uncomprehending. 'We're going to live here forever, with Dad. It's all going to be all right.'

Hansi nodded mutely.

Katja relaxed her grip a little. 'But there are a few things you need to remember. Firstly, we have to speak English now. All the time. *Verstehst du?* Do you understand?'

Hansi nodded again.

Katja bit her lip and shut her eyes tightly for a moment, before reopening them, ready to carry on.

'The other thing is,' she continued, glancing nervously around her, as if afraid that secret eyes were watching, secret ears listening, 'you're not Hansi anymore.'

An alarm sounded, or perhaps it was a bell to mark another aircraft's arrival or a change of shift, Katja didn't know. But bells and alarms and sirens would terrify her for the rest of her life.

When the sound had receded and nothing, it appeared, had happened, she turned to her daughter again, making sure she was fully concentrating. 'You don't use your nickname now. This is a German name, not right for England. From now on, you use your proper name, Johanna. Johanna with a "J" like Daddy says it, not a "Y". Don't forget it.'

Hansi gave one final, silent, nod.

Lou reappeared, emerging from the cubbyhole where he had been dealing with some paperwork. Katja hoped that the amount of time he had taken didn't augur badly for her entry to the country. It all seemed most haphazard. She crossed her fingers and prayed. As she did so, Lou waved across to her and strode in their direction, jangling a set of vehicle keys to indicate that they had wheels and were good to go.

Hansi stood, eyes wide and staring, dazed with tiredness after the long journey and the waiting. 'Johanna,' she repeated, muttering the unfamiliar sound with tentative lips. 'My name is Johanna.'

CHAPTER FIFTY-ONE

LONDON, JULY 1994

My father and my mother's stories had come to an end, culminating in that remarkable journey in a Dakota. It was only as extraordinary as the rest of what I'd learned, and yet it was the bit that I'd been personally involved in. Now I'd heard about it, I thought that perhaps I did recall that shuddering plane journey, the smell of aviation fuel, the cold metal buckle that strapped me into my seat, the cacophony of noise that greeted us in the makeshift terminal building. But the nickname Hansi, that had been ditched in favour of my real name Johanna, I had no recollection of at all.

Just as much of a mystery was the letter that lay on the table in front of me. A couple of weeks had passed since I'd written to Janez and here was his reply. The stamp and postmark from Slovenia, plus the sender's address on the back flap just as in the original, left no doubt as to who the letter was from. But what was inside, I had no idea. Curiosity mingled with dread as I fingered the envelope nervously, imagining what its contents might be. It was thick and plump, seeming to contain more than just a sheet of paper. I longed to find out, but I simply couldn't open the letter today; this was the one day of the year when I didn't have time.

It was Emma's wedding day.

'Mum!' Emma's voice came from upstairs, plaintive and distressed, as if in confirmation of the fact that all my attention needed to be on her at this moment. 'MUM! I've laddered the bloody stockings... I need help!'

Giving the letter a last, lingering look, I tucked it behind the mug tree before heading to Emma's aid, silently congratulating myself on having the forethought to make sure I had spares of everything, from stockings to lipstick. We'd already both had our hair done and Emma had done her own make-up. At least all those hours she'd spent as a teenager, shut in her bedroom with her friends experimenting endlessly with foundation, eyeshadow and blusher, had come into their own, I thought wryly. How many arguments I'd had with my daughter in those days, trying to get her to go outside, get some fresh air, take the dog for a walk, whatever, and how resistant Emma had been to taking up any of my suggestions.

Upstairs, I went to my bedroom and fetched the bag containing the supplies. As I turned back towards Emma's room, the door opened and Emma stood on the threshold, backlit by the glorious summer sunshine that was pouring through her south-facing window.

I gasped. Even though I'd seen the dress before in the shop, once more the vision of my daughter took my breath away.

'Oh, sweetheart,' I murmured, overcome, 'you look incredible. So beautiful. Stunning.'

Emma smiled. 'Thanks, Mum.' And then, holding out her hand for the bag in my hand, 'If you give me the stockings and help me do the buttons up, I'm done!'

As I helped Emma, I heard a knock on the front door followed by the sound of a key turning.

'Hello!' A voice echoed up the stairs. It was Evan.

I rushed back downstairs to greet him, his girlfriend Josey, and Ed. Due to lack of space in my house, Evan and Josey were staying with Ed and Annabelle, in the flat's spare bedroom. I wished they could have been with me, but I just didn't have room for everyone.

Ed and I were conducting an uneasy truce for the duration of the nuptials. I was determined that nothing should mar Emma's big day. We'd managed an amicable dinner all together at a lovely Italian restaurant on the edge of Parliament Hill Fields the night before, during which Ed had somehow managed not to mention the house sale once.

As we stood in the hallway chatting, my mother emerged from the downstairs bedroom and everyone complimented everyone else on outfits, hairdos, jewellery.

'How are we getting on?' asked Ed. He looked nervous, jangling a set of keys from hand to hand. 'We should—'

'Where's Annabelle?' I asked, interrupting him. It had suddenly occurred to me who was missing.

'She's gone on ahead to the church,' answered Ed. 'She didn't want to... well, she felt that it should just be the family in the wedding cars. Emma's,' he added, gesturing over his shoulder to the cul-de-sac outside, 'is here, by the way.'

The white Rolls-Royce, resplendent with ribbons and bows, gleamed under the summer sun.

'I'll get her,' I said.

When Emma descended the stairs, beaming with anticipation, even Evan was momentarily speechless. As brother and sister, their normal form of interaction was relentless teasing and banter. But not today.

'Wow, sis, you've brushed up real good,' Evan said. The words were genuine, though he couldn't resist egging up the New Zealand accent to avoid an excess of sincerity.

At the church, the pews were already packed with guests.

Sue was there, almost jumping up and down with excitement. As I passed her on the way to take up my place in the front row, Sue surreptitiously felt for my hand and squeezed it.

'Well done, love,' she said. 'It's going to be a super day. Now you just relax and enjoy yourself.'

And I did.

Hours later, the wedding ceremony over, the reception finished and the last dance tune played, I joined the throng of family and friends to wave goodbye to Emma and Giles. The taxi was taking them to a hotel near Heathrow and in the morning they were to fly off to Sri Lanka for their honeymoon.

As the car faded into the distance, I took my mother's arm in mine. 'I can't believe you've lasted the whole evening, Mum!' I said. I really was truly astonished. But my mother had the strength and staying power of an ox. I supposed that was the gift a tough life bestowed on you.

'Always keep something in reserve,' she murmured, still waving, though the car had disappeared out of sight now. 'How else do you think my generation survived?'

I kissed her cheek. 'You're all amazing,' I concurred, quietly.

We turned to go back inside. Though it was nearly July, the evening had turned chilly.

'Did you and Dad have a honeymoon, when you finally did get married?' I asked.

'We went to Brighton,' she replied. 'It was supposed to be a day trip but we missed the last train home so we had to book ourselves into a hotel. It was the only night alone together we had for the first ten years of our marriage. I'm sure everyone thought we'd missed the train on purpose, but it honestly was an accident. We couldn't afford hotels like that, just willy-nilly, not like you young people nowadays.'

I laughed. 'I'm not sure staying in a hotel for your wedding night would be classed as "willy-nilly",' I protested. 'But it does seem like a rather lucky mishap...'

She grinned cheekily. 'As I say, I'm sure some thought so.'

'Mum!' I burst into a gale of laughter. 'You did do it on purpose, didn't you?'

She winked and then rolled her eyes skywards. I couldn't believe what a good mood she was in, had been for a few days now. It was a sure sign that she was feeling physically better and I knew that she was not only delighted and excited about Emma's marriage but also about the prospect of moving back home and having her own space again.

But there was something more than that. It was as if she had shed a burden, somehow, as if all the revelations about the past had lightened a heavy and troublesome load that she'd carried on her shoulders for almost half a century.

'We lived with Lou's parents until they died, remember,' she said. 'We didn't have a bedroom until his grandparents passed, had to sleep on the floor in the sitting room. Imagine a young couple doing that now! And you had a bed that Lou made from an old pallet that we stored behind the sofa in the daytime. I bought you a decent mattress, though. I put my foot down on that. You needed to be comfortable.'

At some point in my childhood, my father had achieved his dream of buying a car, a second-hand Rover, that he spent hours every Sunday tinkering with, washing and polishing, measuring the oil and fixing the fan belt and all the other numerous things that seemed to go wrong with it on a monthly, if not weekly, basis. Along with his work van, the car was at the centre of the happiest memories of my childhood. Bank Holiday weekends or holidays, school closed and the whole family – my father, my mother, my grandparents and I – would pile into the car and off we'd go, to Camber Sands or Butlin's at Minehead, to Lyme or Bognor Regis. One long weekend we even got as far as Polzeath in Cornwall and I still remembered the golden sand beach, waves dotted with surfers, the constant calling of the seabirds and the taste of the Cornish clotted cream ices we'd savoured while looking out to sea.

My father, with his ready smile and happy-go-lucky attitude, never minded how many times he had to stop for someone to use the loo or to vomit – I had been terribly carsick as a child – and whenever we got lost, which was frequently, he turned it into an adventure. We went to ancient roadside inns, beamed ceilings so low even I sometimes had to duck, beaches lined with smugglers' caves and towns of half-timbered houses that exuded the romance of the past.

'Thanks, Mum,' I said, referring in part to the mattress comment and in part to everything else I'd been thinking about. 'I'll always be glad for what you and Dad did for me.'

I looked around me at the now empty function room. The day had been a hot one and everything was a little limp, the frothy peony flower heads drooping slightly. *They look like I feel*, I thought.

'Time to go home,' I said. 'I'm done in, even if you're not.'

Back at the house, a wave of contented exhaustion surged over me. Emma was married and the day had been marvellous. I could relax, throw away the lists and memos stuck all over the fridge, and focus on all the other things that demanded my attention.

One of which was the letter behind the mug tree. I regarded it as I made a cup of tea for myself and my mother, then took it out from its hiding place and went up to bed. I would read it before I went to sleep.

CHAPTER FIFTY-TWO

In the event, I hardly slept a wink that night.

After opening the letter, reading it, examining the other contents of the envelope, I could not possibly rest. Eventually, I got up, drew back the curtains, and stood at the window for a long while, staring at the white moonlight that gleamed beyond the glass. I could hardly believe what had been revealed to me – or how long it had taken to come to light.

I knew something now that scarcely seemed possible. And yet it was true.

The story I knew was that, once upon a time, I had had a half-brother called Hans. He had died before I had even been born. Now, at the age of forty-eight, I had found out that I had another one. A different half-brother, born during the war, the product of the brief liaison between my father and Eva, the Italian woman who was actually Slovenian and who, after Lou's betrayal, went to her home country to join the Partisans and fight the enemy.

The name of my new-found brother was Janez Novak.

In his reply to my letter, Janez wrote that he had always wanted to trace his RAF pilot father. He had asked his mother if he could, and she had always replied that she did not know where he was or how to contact him. It was only after Janez turned eighteen that she came clean. She did have Lou's address. If Janez wanted to contact his father, he was free to do so.

Once finally in possession of the thing he had wanted for so long, it had taken Janez many months to pluck up the courage to write. He had sent his letter but received no reply. He had no idea whether Lou had received the missive but did not want contact with Janez, or whether the address was long out of date and had never got anywhere near Lou. Either way, he lost heart. He gave up his search, got on with his life, tried to forget the RAF pilot for good.

Janez went on to say that, even though he was sad to hear that Lou was no longer alive, he was so pleased to hear from me, a member of his long-lost English family. It was a dream come true. He hoped that we could communicate further.

At some point in the small hours just before dawn, I lay back down on my bed and attempted to sleep, but slumber continued to evade me. All I could think was that on the same day that Ed had given Emma away to her new husband, I myself had gained a brother.

I needed to talk to my mother about everything Janez had told me. But first, I wanted to tell Sue. It must all be straight in my own head before I broached it with my mother.

I had just reached out for the phone handset when it began to ring. Starting in surprise – it was only eight o'clock on a Sunday – I seized up the receiver. Had something happened to Emma and Giles? A plane crash? A sudden illness?

A voice I didn't at first recognise filtered over the airwaves, increasing my impending sense of horror. 'Is that Jo, Katja's daughter?'

'Yes,' I replied, cautiously, my heart in my mouth, 'it is. Who's speaking, please?'

'It's her neighbour from Bayham Street,' the voice said.

Immediately, I realised it was Mrs Patel, who lived downstairs from my mother in the flats. Relief flooded through me – it was nothing to do with Emma and Giles – and was then replaced by a different dread as Mrs Patel explained why she was calling.

'There's been a flood,' she said. 'I think a pipe must have burst or something. The water's pouring down. You need to get the plumber over as quickly as possible.'

I slapped my hand to my mouth. 'Oh no,' I uttered. 'I'm so sorry. I'll get right onto it. And I'll come down now and do what I can until the plumber arrives.'

As I dialled the plumber's number, I shook my head sorrowfully at Springer, who was waiting by the bedroom door, tail wagging eagerly.

'Sorry, old boy,' I muttered, 'you'll have to wait.'

Leaving Katja still sleeping, I sped down to Bayham Street, where Ed and Evan arrived before the plumber. I hadn't known who else to call when at first the tradesman didn't answer. I knew that as soon as the divorce came through, I'd have to finally cut the cord that tied me to Ed after twenty-five years together. The last thing I wanted was to be reliant on him – but who else was there? I was going to have to find those other people, I supposed.

Ed looked at the devastation that was my mother's new kitchen with a grim frown. 'This does not look good,' he said, in the understatement of the century.

Evan, always the optimist, shook his head. 'No, it's fine, it'll be OK. We just need to find the leak and bung it up. Once we've cleared all the water and everything's dried out, I don't think there's too much real damage.'

'But then there's Mrs Patel's place as well,' I reminded him.

I'd already popped in to take a look. The water had somehow found its way to the wall between the kitchen and sitting room and was running down there to the flat below. Mrs Patel had put down towels and buckets to soak it up, but everything would need redecorating.

Eventually, the plumber arrived and diagnosed the problem. One of the attachments on the pipe to the kitchen sink had been tightened too hard and caused a hairline crack which had then split further and caused the flood. The damage would be covered by the building firm's insurance, but it would delay my mother's move back in.

I sighed. I felt tearful, but knew it was because I was so tired after my sleepless night and the surfeit of emotion – a wedding followed by a totally unexpected revelation.

Ed left, saying he had to get himself cleaned up before lunch with Annabelle's parents.

'Thanks for helping out,' I said, 'it was really kind of you.' In truth, he hadn't done much, but he'd offered moral support and that was valuable enough. I turned to Evan. 'What about you? We could go to Lisboa Patisserie for a coffee and a cake, if you've time.' It had always been our treat, whenever we came shopping in Camden Town, to stop off at the Portuguese bakery for a *pastel de nata*. And then, as an afterthought, I added, 'And Josey could join us, if she's up for it?'

Evan thought for a moment. 'Great idea, Mum. Do you mind if it's quite a quick one, though? Josey wants to go down to the West End for some shopping, and then we're meeting friends for a late lunch.'

A wave of grief flooded over me like a tsunami. Ed had Annabelle, Emma had Giles and Evan Josey. I had no one. Tears pricked behind my eyes.

Dropping my head to make sure Evan didn't see, I pretended to search in my bag for my car keys until I had blinked them away.

'Of course, love,' I said, forcing a lightness to my tone that I didn't feel. 'Whatever time you can manage would be lovely.'

'We've still got our dinner tonight to look forward to,' Evan replied. I could tell he was doing his best not to make me feel left out. He was so kind, so thoughtful; I was lucky to have such a lovely son and daughter and that, I tried hard to convince myself, would have to be enough.

Evan headed for the door and I followed, unable to keep up with him as he took the stairs two at a time as always.

On reaching the ground floor, Evan waited for a moment as I quickly put my head around Mrs Patel's door again to let her know that the builders would start the redecoration in her place in a week's time, when the water had dried out.

'I'm so sorry,' I concluded again. 'I really can't apologise enough.'

'Don't mention it,' Mrs Patel smiled. 'These things happen, don't they? We're looking forward to your mum being back, anyway.'

'Yes,' I concurred, 'yes, we're all looking forward to that.'

In the café, Evan and I had a delicious *pastel de nata* each while reminiscing about all the hours we had spent in the café over the years. When he left to meet Josey at the tube station, I went home. My head swam and felt fuzzy and light with fatigue. But I had to talk to Mum. She took the news of the flood better than I expected, mainly expressing her concern about the impact on Mrs Patel, though she was also worried about how much it was going to cost to fix the damage. Once I had explained that the builders would sort both of those things as it was their responsibility, I saw my mother visibly relax.

I opened my mouth to broach the next subject, then shut it again abruptly. Springer came running in and I prevaricated, stroking his intelligent head and lovely, long, soft ears.

'Mum, we need to discuss something,' I said, eventually.

Really, I was too tired for this, but I knew I wouldn't be able to rest, let alone sleep, until we'd had this conversation.

She raised her face to me with a curious expression.

'You remember that envelope?' I blundered on. 'From Janez Novak?'

There was a brief pause before she nodded, slowly and deliberately. 'Of course I remember. But he is – *was* – no one important.'

I sighed. There was no easy way to go about this. Though I couldn't be sure my mother had actually lied to me – maybe she'd got muddled and really did think Janez was another POW – it was hard to truly believe it was all just an honest mistake. Especially considering what had been in the envelope Janez sent along with the letter, that seemed to preclude the possibility of my mother's innocence.

'I'm not sure about that,' I ventured, tentatively. I couldn't seem to find the right words, that would be tactful but also forthright. Was such a combination possible? 'I was curious, so I wrote to Janez,' I went on, haltingly. 'Perhaps you've forgotten after all this time, or got a bit mixed up. But Janez wasn't a prisoner of war. He didn't know my father during those years, or in fact ever. They never met.'

Taking a deep breath, I tried to quell the nausea that turned in my stomach.

'As I say, I wrote to him. And he replied. He told me that he is Lou's son. My brother.'

I saw how the news broke over my mother's face, how first shock, then disbelief, swept across her, before her expression settled into one of resignation. It confirmed to me what I was already certain of: that she was aware – had always been aware – of Janez's name, of his existence, of exactly who he was. That her suggestion that he was a fellow POW was a pretence, invented to cover up a shameful reality.

She sniffed. Her eyes were blank, no longer giving anything away.

'Along with the letter he wrote himself, Janez sent five others to me.' I had to get this over with now, so I pushed on. 'They were letters his mother had written to Lou over the years after the war ended. All had been returned to her; only one had been opened. On each one was written: "Not known at this address, return to sender".'

I paused. God, this was even harder than I had expected it to be.

'Mum, the handwriting was yours.'

A silence so deep that I was sure I could hear my own hair growing descended on the room. Time seemed to slow to a standstill, each tick and tock of the hallway clock half an hour or more apart.

'Why didn't you tell me, Mum?' I asked, my plea erupting into the quiet.

'It's not all about you, is it?'

The harshness of my mother's words shocked me, cutting me to the core. Was that true? Maybe it was. But then again – didn't I have a right to know this stuff? To know I had a brother?

'I understand that you might feel that,' I said, keeping my voice measured, cautious. 'But – it feels important to me. From where I'm sitting, it is at least a little bit about me.'

Her hands were trembling in her lap. 'I'm sorry. I didn't mean to be so rude,' she mumbled, contrite. 'You've been so good to me. I couldn't have got through this without you.' She pulled herself upright in the armchair, straightening her shoulders. 'You're right. I did know about Janez. Lou showed me the first letter that Eva wrote. I asked him to destroy it, because I knew that if he didn't, it would destroy me. Remember, Jo, that I had lost my parents at a young age, then my first husband, had a baby alone, been a refugee, lost that baby... This is not self-pity, but reality.'

There was no arguing with that. I understood, more now than I ever had before, ever could have done when I had known so little, what my mother had endured in her life. But still, this seemed massive, a huge omission in the information I should have been privy to.

My mother, wringing her hands together as she spoke, continued. 'Lou agreed that he would tear the letter up and throw it away, but then I found it in a drawer. We had a huge row. I told him he had to choose – her and Janez or me and you. Lou – well, he chose us. And all the other letters she sent, I sent straight back to her. I never told him about them. He didn't know that she sent half a dozen or more.'

A chill ran through my veins. Goosebumps peppered my skin as a well of fury opened up within me. The anger I'd been suppressing until I'd heard my mother's side of the story threatened to subsume me. All these years of being a lonely only child, I could have had a brother. Janez could have had a father. My mother knew about Janez but wanted my father to deny his existence – to deny his own flesh and blood. And he had agreed to this. It didn't make any sense. It was immoral, wrong.

I opened my mouth to speak but could hardly articulate the words. 'Why? Why, Mum? Why would you do that? I still don't understand. What threat were Eva and Janez to you? To us?'

My mother was rocking in her chair and I had a terrible thought that she was losing it, that I had pushed her too far, to insanity.

But when she spoke, she sounded perfectly sane. And incredibly, profoundly sad.

'I was jealous. I'm not proud of it, Jo. I despise myself sometimes. I... I thought if he met up again with Eva, a woman he'd had some passionate, illicit affair with, who then became a brave fighter with the Partisans, a noble warrior who would have her place in the history books, he'd choose her over me.'

As she finished speaking, my mother began to weep, not

quietly but great guttural sobs that seemed to rise up from the depth of her being.

'After all – who wouldn't? I was just a poor broken girl from Berlin, nothing special about me. And I couldn't bear that. Hans was dead and gone. I had you to think about, your future, your survival. In my eyes, that depended on Lou always being with us. I couldn't lose Lou as well as everything else. I couldn't lose you.'

I couldn't speak, had nothing to say. My mother's confession, incoherent and muddled as it was, was pitiful and astounding in equal measure. It had robbed me of all words.

'You're wondering if I regret it,' she continued. 'Of course I do. If I feel shame. Deep, crippling, enduring shame. You have tried to understand where my shame came from. Now, finally, perhaps you do. It comes from the many bad things that happened – that I did – and then this – a final dishonourable act that I am ashamed of.'

I regarded my mother in the big armchair. She looked tiny; fragile and vulnerable. A wave of compassion washed over me. What right had I to judge my mother, who had suffered so much?

'Oh Mum,' I said, my voice stronger now, 'I know you didn't do it maliciously. It's just... well, all these years thinking I had no living siblings and then to find that I have a half-brother, a blood relative.' I stood up suddenly and walked to the window. Springer jumped to his feet and followed me. Outside, the garden was rain soaked; a drenching summer downpour had painted leaves and flowers with glistening moisture that glowed in the evening sun. I turned back to Mum. 'Janez told me his mother is dead and that neither she nor he bear you any ill will. Dad is no longer with us. There's nothing to be scared of anymore, Mum,' I reassured her. I took my mother's hand. 'You've no need to be ashamed.'

CHAPTER FIFTY-THREE

Hampstead Heath had always seemed big enough before, its rolling acres, all seven-hundred and ninety of them, capacious enough to absorb any problem, offer a solution to any dilemma.

But today, it wasn't so.

My mother and I had talked for hours.

'But surely you could have let Janez into Dad's life,' I had asked her, pleadingly. 'You repeatedly say how great he was, what a fantastic man, a wonderful husband, how in love the two of you were. Surely you knew that she was no threat, that he wouldn't leave you for Eva, a woman he'd only known for a week?'

I simply couldn't get my head around the whole episode, my mother's jealousy and insecurity, her deceit. It wasn't that I judged her for it – I just didn't understand.

'You don't understand,' she had replied to me stubbornly, as if reading my mind. And so it went on.

After the conversation, I had to come out and walk, on my own, with only Springer for company. I couldn't face even Sue, just needed solitude, the chance to commune with my own thoughts, to try to bring some calm to my fevered mind. Springer and I strode and strode, all the way to the Hill Garden, where a woman, dressed in a glorious silk sari of the brightest turquoise, was posing for photographs. She sat beneath the pergola, amongst the pastel-coloured blooms that fizzed with insects, the most eye-catching flower of them all. Her youth and beauty made me want to cry; she seemed full of all the hope and promise I felt had been denied to my mother, and that had slipped through my own fingers. I wished I could know her future and that it was a good one, so that the happiness of her smile would never fade.

Eventually, there was nowhere further to walk and we turned back, towards Kite Hill where we had spread my father's ashes. By now, I was ready for company and I popped by Sue's house to tell her the news.

Sue was speechless.

'Gosh. Wow,' was all she could say after hearing the story, and only that after moments of stunned silence.

'I've been really struggling with it all,' I confessed, those dratted tears threatening again. 'With finding out how Mum essentially denied Janez's existence. And that Dad went along with it.'

Sue thought for a while. 'I think the whole scenario was not uncommon at the time,' she said, eventually. I could tell she was treading carefully, conscious of protecting me, of not wanting to say anything that might upset me. 'There were so many illegitimate children – born abroad, or born here. Think of all the GI babies. Times were so different then, attitudes to unplanned pregnancies so different.' She paused to take my hands in hers. 'You know this only too well,' she continued. 'We have to remember what your parents had both gone through in the war, in addition to how society has changed since then.'

I nodded. 'You're right, I know you're right. My logical,

rational mind tells me that. And I do forgive her. What would be the point in not? We can't change the past.'

'I think that's the right way to look at it,' Sue responded, decisively.

Wearily, I headed home. All this emotion was draining me and I felt nearly ninety rather than nearly fifty.

At home, my mother had another surprise waiting for me. We had already discussed that she would have to postpone her move back to her own flat. But when I took her a cup of tea, she landed something totally unexpected on me.

'I'd like to go,' she said.

I eyed her suspiciously. 'Go where?' I asked.

Frowning, she ran her hands over the rug that covered her knees. 'To Berlin. And the Sudetenland.'

Words failed me. My mother had never mentioned wanting to return and it was the last thing I expected.

When I finally regained the power of speech, I couldn't actually think of what to say.

'Will you take me?' my mother continued, quietly.

Slowly, the fog lifted from my brain. 'I-I suppose so,' I stuttered. 'I mean, of course I will.' I paused, took a deep breath. 'But, why do you want to go? Why now, after so many years?'

My mother shrugged. 'We've talked so much. I've had to remember things I'd long since tried to forget, things I wanted to forget. When I left Germany on that Dakota, with you in my arms, I didn't think I'd ever go back. But now, since we've been doing all this talking...' She paused, waving her hand in a dismissive gesture, as if to dispel our hours of chat, 'It's brought so much back that I think I ought to go. That I *need* to go.'

The thought that came immediately into my head was 'closure', but I didn't say it, knowing that my mother would hate such a word.

'Well,' I said, matter-of-factly, 'I better book us some plane tickets then.'

· · ·

WALKING through the glass doors of the travel bureau the next day, I was still trying to get my head around exactly what I was doing. It was all very well for my mother to decide a trip to the continent was necessary, but how did I feel about it? In the past, because of the bullying, I had done my best to dissociate myself from anything to do with Germany. Even now, so much older and hopefully a little wiser, I struggled to formulate my opinion and couldn't possibly have put it into words. It was an odd mixture of excitement, apprehension, fear of the unknown and a kind of certainty. A certainty that, however painful, this had to be done.

Forcing myself out of my reverie, I looked around me. There was an empty seat at one of the desks and, as I caught the travel consultant's eye, she gestured to me to sit down.

'So let me just get this absolutely clear,' said the agent, whose name badge declared her as Debs, when I had finished my somewhat incoherent explanation. 'You want to fly to Berlin and then hire a car and drive to the Czech Republic?' She peered at me over her computer screen. 'You're brave.' She sniffed and then started tapping with the utmost efficiency at her keyboard.

No I'm not, I thought, *so not brave, not brave at all. But this is necessity.* And the way this Debs regarded me, as if it was all very unwise and she doubted that I was up to it, was annoying enough to spur me on.

'I always get my husband to drive when we go to France,' Debs confided.

Lucky you, I thought. In truth, that's exactly what I had always done too, when Ed and I had been together. In France, Spain, Portugal, Ed took the wheel. That was in the past now. I had to take control, stop being such a pathetic wimp.

'I'm divorced,' I said, with a sweet smile. It was funny the reaction that word had. For women, it seemed to denote failure, an inability to please and keep hold of a man, whereas for men, it more often equated to freedom, a new beginning. Well, I was going to claim that new beginning for myself. It was about time. And it started right here. 'I'm happy to drive, it's not a problem for me,' I continued breezily, crossing my fingers under Debs' desk. And then, 'It's just great on those German autobahns, no speed limit... you can really let rip.'

Debs' eyes widened in horror.

I smiled to myself. I'd never realised before how much fun lying was.

I gave Debs the dates I was aiming for and she tapped at her keyboard anew, her heavily lacquered fingernails clacking on the tabs. She pressed a button and then turned to a printer, pulling off a long piece of paper with a flourish.

'Take a look at the itinerary here,' she said, 'and if you're happy with the details, I can go ahead and make the booking for you.'

I'd told Sue of the plan over the phone, while I'd still been trying to make sense of it myself. When I met her by the boating lake that afternoon, I pulled the tickets from my pocket with panache. The many branches of the overhanging trees dappled the sunshine as it painted patterns upon the cardboard rectangles.

'Voilà,' I said, triumphantly.

'You've done it?' Sue could not keep the astonishment and delight out of her voice.

'I'm not entirely sure what to expect from the trip,' I told her. 'But I think it's important. So, for once, I didn't procrastinate, I just got on and did it. Even Ed would be proud of me.'

Sue laughed. 'We're all proud of you. Your mum most of all.'

When I showed my mother the tickets, she also seemed inexplicably surprised. As well as something else, something I couldn't quite fathom. But as she studied the cardboard oblongs, I had a sudden premonition. This story had had so many unexpected twists and turns. But it wasn't over yet. Something told me there was more to come. And that perhaps it would be the biggest revelation of all.

CHAPTER FIFTY-FOUR

GERMANY, AUGUST 1994

In Charlottenburg, I asked my mother to show me the house where I had lived for the first three years of my life.

She took me there and was surprised to see that the shop no longer existed. The building must have been recently renovated, since the wall came down, and the shop removed, with the space converted to residential use. My mother stood on the pavement looking around her as if trying to get her bearings, turning her head this way and that, bemused.

'They were here,' she said eventually, pointing to a stretch of road opposite, 'and here.' There was a break in the buildings, a wide paved area with a magnificent linden tree, gnarled old roots clawing through the sandy soil and erupting between the slabs like the knuckles of desperate hands clutching for the sky.

'Who?' I asked, even though I was sure I knew.

'The Russians.' She wheeled around with the sudden energy and agility of a woman half her age. 'They had a fire here, where I smelt the bacon cooking. And the ponies were tied up over there, to that lamp post.'

I inspected the scene. It was just a city street, a very nice one, but nothing extraordinary, nothing particularly noteworthy. It was difficult to imagine how it must have been, fifty years previously.

'How do you feel being here?' I asked, and then immediately regretted it. Such a question made me sound like one of those news reporters on the television, finding some victim of disaster, either natural or manmade, and asking them how they felt about their dead relative, the destruction of their home, their life-threatening injuries. How would anyone feel?

But my mother didn't seem offended. She just shrugged. 'I don't know,' she said. 'I don't feel anything very much. It's all so different now.' She moved backwards, into the shade. It was a burning-hot day in the city. 'I'm so different. And now I've lived in London for so long, I've realised that Berlin was never really home. I came here because I had to find work when my grandparents died. Horst was good and kind, but, as I've said before, it was a marriage of convenience, not love. Nothing like what Lou and I had, at all.'

'So was it here, Mum,' I asked, pointing up at the first-floor flat with its large, long windows. 'Was I born here?'

For a few moments, she did not respond. Just continued staring at the place where the Russians had camped and their ponies had rattled their tethers and neighed in the mornings.

'Yes,' she said, eventually, in a dull monotone. 'Yes, that's right. Up there, in my flat.'

I continued staring upwards, imagining my baby self under one of the windows, being cradled by my mother or father. It was a nice thought. Comforting. By the time I looked back down, my mother was halfway along the road, heading in the direction of the hotel.

. . .

FOR THE REMAINDER of our days in Berlin, my mother pronounced herself too tired to traipse around a city she knew like the back of her hand. She stayed in the hotel, sitting on the balcony or in the small garden at the back, while I explored. I visited the Charlottenburg Palace, Tiergarten and the ruins of the Kaiser Wilhelm Church, the bombing of which had prompted my mother to take up the offer of escaping to the Sudetenland. I even went to the Charité hospital in honour of Hans' death. But the building bore no sign of what it must have looked like in 1945, when it had already been badly bomb-damaged, and I left. The sense of disappointment followed me for the rest of the day, though I had no idea what I had actually thought I would find there.

On our last afternoon in Berlin, I went to the car hire office. Feigning confidence about taking the keys, I recalled my conversation with the terribly superior Debs who had doubted my driving ability. What was that horrible phrase? Fake it till you make it? That's what I would do.

And, in the event, it was fine. I ignored the few beeps and hoots that let rip when I stalled trying to find the entrance to the hotel car park, which, though very narrow, I managed to negotiate without mishap. Nevertheless, I was glad the majority of the driving, once we'd left the city the next morning, would be on rather bigger and more forgiving roads.

'Let's go out for a last drink on the Kurfürstendamm,' I suggested.

My mother, somewhat reluctantly, agreed. She had already pointed out Cumberland House to me, the historic building that had served as the Control Commission's headquarters during my father's term in Berlin, and I liked the idea of being close to where he had worked.

Comfortably ensconced in a pavement bar, I ordered wine for myself. To my astonishment, my mother chose a small beer.

After a couple of sips, I plucked up the courage to make my confession.

'Mum, there's something I need to tell you,' I began. 'The thing is – I've arranged to meet Janez. He's coming to Meindorf at the same time as us.'

My mother's face fell like a stone.

'What?' I questioned, anxiously. 'What's the matter? It's not that bad, is it? He won't blame you, Mum, for anything, I'm sure of it. I know it – he's told me so. And now we have the chance to make amends. We'll get... Well, it'll be a good thing.' I resisted mentioning the dreaded word 'closure', knowing that it would not resonate with my mother. But, nevertheless, I felt so strongly that we needed to do this – both of us needed it.

My mother gripped her glass, upon which the beads of condensation shone in the twilight. Her lips were moving as if she were talking, but no sound was coming out. Until suddenly, her voice became audible.

'There's something I haven't told you.' The words blurted out as if they had become uncontainable. My mother's eyes swam with tears.

I bit my lip. Perhaps the beer hadn't been a good idea; my mother so rarely drank alcohol.

'There's something you need to know. I thought I could keep it from you. But being back here, you finding out about Janez. Now I realise that I can't. I wanted to come, I thought it would clear my head, make everything make sense. But now I see that only the truth will do that.'

Silently, I drained my glass and indicated to the waiter to bring another. My mother was talking in riddles and I felt an indefinable sense of dread about what was coming. Was this what I'd had such a feeling of foreboding about? I needed some Dutch courage, something to fortify myself with.

'When Lou got onto my bus that day during his first week in

Berlin,' she murmured, gazing at a bus that was itself passing along on the other side of the road, 'he recognised me.'

My head whirled. How could he have recognised someone he'd never met before? What was my mother talking about?

'I don't know how he knew me, because I must have looked quite different by then. A lot cleaner, dressed in my conductor's uniform rather than rags. But recognise me he did. Later, he told me it was because I always looked different to all the other *Flüchtlinge*. I hadn't given up and I still had my pride.'

'What do you mean?' I couldn't understand what she was talking about.

She clicked her tongue against her teeth. 'I'm getting there,' she said. 'I didn't recognise him straightaway, as I say, but I was preoccupied – partly with what I was doing, dispensing advice, selling tickets to the public – and partly with everything else that was going on in my life. I was still grieving Hans, and we were all constantly hungry, worried about where the next meal would come from. But Lou knew at once.'

'Knew what.'

Again, my mother looked irritated. 'That we'd met before.'

'But... when?' My mind was coming up with a plethora of scenarios, none of which made any sense. When could my father and mother have met previously? Earlier in his time in Berlin? But he had only just arrived, my mother had just said as much. 'Had he been on your bus already, from the airport or whatever?'

My mother shook her head. Her face was shadowy again, overcast with distant memories. 'We had met outside the camp he was being held in, waiting for repatriation. He gave me food from the Red Cross. And he picked a flower for my baby and tucked it into her blanket, with a note. These things were so precious to me that I kept them. I pressed the flower and wrapped the note around it. I kept the little package for a long time, but when we moved to London, I lost it. Until you found it again, behind the fire surround.'

My mouth fell open in gaping astonishment. I searched through my memory of my father's recently finished notes. 'So the woman – the brunette he talks about giving the food parcel to,' I hesitated, scarcely able to believe it, 'that woman was you.'

My mother nodded, her eyes downcast, not meeting my gaze.

I looked down at the ground as if the answer to the puzzle might lie in the evenly spaced, well-ordered paving slabs. 'But then – the baby? You said "her" so a girl, not Hans, and he wasn't a newborn anyway. Did someone give you an infant to look after?' My voice was urgent now, croaky with some unfathomable fear. 'Mum, who was the baby?'

And then, watching my mother's body language, the stillness of her head with the navy-blue evening sky behind, I understood.

'No, whoa... Mum, no, is this...'

'You.' The single word cut across my ramblings, silencing me. My mother looked defiantly upwards, towards the heavens, and then lowered her eyes and fixed them upon me. 'The baby was you.'

CHAPTER FIFTY-FIVE

GERMANY, 1945

It was a still night, the sky clear, the stars bright. The day had been balmy, but it was chilly now, and getting colder. Katja, recognising the early stages of labour, pulled her cardigan more tightly around her, but the scant warmth it gave was not enough. She shivered, and then let out an involuntary moan. Gerta looked across at her. They'd crept close to the fire another group of refugees had built, but the wood was wet, giving forth choking fumes rather than heat.

'Are you all right?' asked Gerta. She scrutinised Katja in the half-light. 'Actually, you don't look too good. Do you need water?'

Katja shook her head. She'd been sitting on the ground but found herself rolling over, onto all fours, then resting her fore-head on the grass that was already wet with dew. The dull, aching pains she'd had all day had suddenly intensified. She'd thought they might make it to Berlin, which was only a few miles away now, to her house if it were still there, but it was not to be.

She felt movement beside her, and then a hand on her shoulder, Gerta's voice in her ear.

'Is it the time?' Gerta sounded panicked. 'Is it now?'

Unable to speak, Katja nodded. She'd told Gerta she was pregnant weeks ago, long before they'd had to flee the Sudetenland. Gerta hadn't judged, or even asked too many questions. She'd just accepted it, and told Katja she'd stand by her through it all. They hadn't told any of the others, though. It had seemed easier not to. So it had been Katja and Gerta's secret throughout the long walk to Berlin, though Katja was sure Lilli had guessed, and possibly Maria and Alice too, even though, not being mothers, they were less likely to have spotted the signs.

Katja groaned as a contraction swept through her body. They were coming thick and fast now. She remembered that feeling, of being ripped apart from the inside out, from having Hans. People said the second child was easier. God willing, that would be the case.

Gerta was stroking her filthy hair, pulling it back from where it had fallen across her face. Katja tried to concentrate on that rather than on her agony. She became aware of a kerfuffle around her, of people coming and going, shouting in the distance. She didn't care about any of it, just about the ripping, tearing pains that kept coming and coming.

'Someone help! Please help!' she heard Gerta calling. 'Is anyone a doctor? Does anyone know...' Her words tailed off.

As if it was all happening very far away, Katja vaguely absorbed Gerta's frenzied conversations with those around them. Of course there was no doctor, nor a nurse. What would either one of those be doing in a muddy field close to a burning city? Katja was on her own and well she knew it. If she died here, from loss of blood or infection, it would all have been pointless. The walk, the struggle to survive, the constant fear. The horrors she had witnessed. The losing, then finding, of Hans. Maybe he'd have been better off staying with Monika in

Cottbus than waking up in the morning to find his mother dead.

Katja didn't want to scream, but she had to. It was the only release from the torment of labour. Writhing and rolling, she howled at the starlit sky and it watched on, silently.

Thankfully, though no less agonising, this second labour was at least shorter. Six hours after it had begun, the baby was born. Gerta had managed to get someone to give her a piece of cloth and a tatty blanket, and she wrapped the tiny little girl in them before handing her to Katja.

'Precious angel,' she whispered as she did so, and Katja, too exhausted to speak, nodded in mute agreement. Gerta held her hand, soothed her brow and then went to fetch water for her. While she was gone, Katja thought about how this was the second of her children that the surrogate grandma had helped into the world, and was as grateful for her help as she had been the first time around. Gerta wasn't perfect, but then most certainly neither was she. And for all their faults, they had stood by each other. Neither would have got through it all without the other.

As Hans slept in the cart, bundled up in all their clothes and jackets, Katja cradled the newborn little girl. It wasn't going to be easy, that was for sure. But she was here now, for better or for worse. And Katja knew one thing, and one thing only.

She would love her to the end of the world and back.

GERMANY, AUGUST 1994

I sank back into my chair, deflated, all the air knocked out of me. Overhead, the lights along the awnings had come on and they twinkled as if nothing had happened. As if someone beneath them had not found out that everything they thought they knew about themselves was not true. I recalled having had that very same thought, all the way back at the start of all this, when I had

had to completely re-evaluate my mother, what she had known about the bullying, what she had suffered but never told me.

But this. This was on another scale altogether.

'Bloody hell, Mum.' I rubbed my eyes with the backs of my hands. 'I mean, really. Bloody flipping hell.' I never usually swore, but it felt good. Appropriate. In that moment, expletives seemed to be the only words that could tackle a situation such as this. I shook my head in disbelief. 'But how on earth? The baby in my dad's diary was newborn. But I didn't arrive until March 1946.'

'No,' she replied. 'That's not the case. You were born in May 1945.'

'But you weren't pregnant. On the walk. All these hours we've spent talking, you never mentioned being pregnant.'

She gave a lopsided grimace. 'I just left it out of the story.'

Lights danced behind my eyes as I squeezed them shut, struggling to absorb the information my mother was giving me. I thought of the number of times when, during the telling of her story, she had stumbled over the word 'child'. Now I understood why. Because she'd been about to say 'children' and then had to hurriedly cover up her inadvertent mistake. And with this realisation came another. Suddenly, it hit me with the full, unstoppable force of a tsunami, that my whole life had been a lie. That I wasn't who I thought I was. My father wasn't who I thought he was. I wasn't even the age I thought I was. That small fact, which for most people was beyond doubt, for me was a lie.

I needed to have it confirmed, to hear my mother say it.

'So Lou isn't my father?'

Katja grimaced sorrowfully. 'No. Lou is not your father.'

My head reeled. 'And... that means that Janez isn't my brother?'

'Janez is not your brother. I'm sorry, Jo. I'm so, so sorry.'

But I wasn't ready for apologies yet. There was still too much to clarify, to understand. 'But when you were telling me about Berlin when you first got back there, about the Russians, about the constant struggle for survival – you never mentioned a baby.'

My mother shrugged. 'As I said, I just left that bit out. When I agreed to talk to you – I made a pact with myself that I'd tell you everything but this. I didn't want to take Lou away from you.'

The waiter came past again and I waved him away. This was no time for interruptions.

'I didn't plan to tell you. It was going to be my secret, to take to the grave. But being here, in Berlin, reliving that time – I realised that it had to be full disclosure. That I – *we* – couldn't live with secrets anymore.'

I gave a great, heaving sigh. Call it sixth sense, whatever you want, but I had known something was missing. I had just had no idea it was something of this magnitude.

My mother was continuing to elaborate. 'When Lou and I met again, on that bus, he asked if he could come and visit, bring me food and extras from his rations. He asked after the baby – you were in the flat, being looked after by Gerta while I worked. He was so relieved to hear you had survived your terrible start. I couldn't believe his thoughtfulness, and his kindness, when he could have hated us, like lots of people at the time hated all Germans. I also couldn't believe that he had remembered, that he cared. So I agreed that he could come by, not really believing he'd do it, thinking that, in all likelihood, I'd never hear from him again. But he came, that very evening.

'And I found that I liked him – he was so thoughtful, so big-hearted. Of course, I didn't have romance or a relationship in my head. I was worried about you all the time – you were such a frail, sickly little thing – no surprise, I suppose, given the circumstances of your birth. Apart from anything else, you were at least a month, maybe as much as six weeks premature. That was probably inevitable, given the lack of food I'd had during the pregnancy, and all the stress and worry. I was desperate, as any mother would be, for you to survive. Once Hans – well, when Hans passed, I became even more obsessed with keeping you alive. Lou appeared like a guardian angel out of the darkness. I wanted a father for you and he wanted to be that father. I knew we could make it work.'

My forehead was creased in puzzlement. 'But I don't understand – how did you manage to change my birthdate by a full ten months? To fool everyone?'

'Oh!' Katja gave a dismissive snort. 'That was easy. No one was interested. I'd given birth alone, amidst the mud and the flies and the dirt, with no one but Gerta to help. She cut your cord with our old kitchen knife that she held in the flames of the fire to sterilise. That's all the help I had.' She exhaled harshly. 'Later – well, Berlin, Germany, was in chaos. I didn't register your birth at the time because there was nowhere to do so. But a baby here or there was nothing, anyway. Children were being born out of wedlock all over the place; the Russian rapes alone led to hundreds of babies. Lou had access to Control Commission supplies, so I could get by without a ration book for you. When we made the decision to come to England, I got a birth certificate for you and just gave a false date. You were a tiny little thing, you easily passed for a child ten months younger.'

'Oh my God, Mum.' A tide of horrified disbelief, denial, distress, swept over me again, engulfing me. 'Truly. I could never have imagined.'

'Lou and I – we agreed it would be much easier for you if we arranged everything so that Lou really was your father. There would be enough stigma for you being German without piling illegitimacy on top of it. He wanted it that way. He loved you like his own, from that very first time he lay eyes on you the day after you were born, at the end of our long walk and his long march. That's why he gave you a flower, a hardy dog rose, plucked from a bush that was also struggling to survive in the harshest conditions.'

The pressed flower, and the note. I'd known my mother had recognised them when I found them behind the fireplace, and I'd known that they were precious, that they meant something. I had been right.

Pressing my fingertips against my closed eyelids, I struggled to take it all in. My mother fell quiet and we sat together for a long time, saying nothing. I sensed our patient waiter hovering and then discreetly fading away.

'Coming to England was the chance to start over,' pronounced my mother all of a sudden. Her demeanour was almost trance-like. 'So we did.'

A profound silence settled on the café table, despite the noise all around, music, voices, traffic. The dancing fairy lights made a mockery of the heaviness of my heart.

'What else could I do?' my mother burst out, as if reading the quietude as an admonishment, a judgement. I felt that she had been asking this question, defensively, for weeks now, after almost every chapter of her story. But I wasn't judging her. Not anymore. 'What would you have done? This wasn't a choice, Jo, this was life and death. This was survival. You fought or you died. That's how it was.'

Understanding that was possible, I told myself. Of course it was. But the biggest question of all still hovered between us. Somehow, I had to ask it.

'So who is my real dad, Mum? Who was my dad?' The questions took so much effort to ask that I could only whisper them, coaxing the words out like you would try to encourage a small animal to come forward to be petted. Even asking made me feel so disloyal to Lou. But I had to do it.

My mother's lips narrowed and she exhaled a puff of air.

'It was Karl Hausmann, the injured Waffen-SS officer I met at the convalescent home in Stahlbach.' She clenched her fists defiantly. 'Well, it must have been. He was the only person I... It couldn't have been anyone else.'

Pulling the chair cushion out from behind my back, I held it in front of me like a shield. Karl Hausmann had been a Nazi. But, then again, he hadn't, because he'd been sending messages to the Allies. My mother had helped him. He had died in battle, but he'd been trying to end that battle. So was he good or was he bad? Collaborator or resistor? The words revolved around my mind, dizzying me. I couldn't work it out. And, anyway, did it really matter? Lou was not my father. Karl Hausmann was.

BACK AT THE HOTEL, my mother went to bed. I supposed that was possible for her. She had always known the truth. It was only me who had found out something of such great magnitude, something I had never so much as suspected, not even when I started delving into the past. My mother's world had not come crashing down around her as mine had done.

Utterly disorientated, I had no idea what to do with myself. Sleep was not an option. I knew it wouldn't happen. In my bedroom, I dialled Sue's number. Phoning from the hotel room and paying the connection charges would likely cost an arm and a leg, but I didn't care. I needed to speak to someone and Sue was the only option. She was the only one who knew the story so far. Even if Emma and Evan had known, I could not have called them. Emma was still on honeymoon and Evan somewhere on his whirlwind tour of Europe, both with their partners, and this was the sort of news that had to be imparted in person.

As I waited for the call to go through, I didn't think I'd ever felt so alone, partner-less, almost homeless, rudderless. Sue and I were both on our own, two middle-aged women for the world, if it could be bothered, to feel sorry for. And to cap it all, my father was not my father.

Sue didn't answer. I checked my watch. It was life-drawing night. She would be there, sketching and shading, toning and blocking, oblivious to what had happened to me. Afterwards, she'd probably go to the pub with the other attendees of the session for a quick drink before home and bed.

I went back out to wander the streets. Berlin, like London, was as alive at night as by day, but I felt dead inside. No wonder all those years on the hippy trail hadn't led me to myself. I wasn't who I thought I was. I hadn't been there to find.

CHAPTER FIFTY-SIX

THE CZECH REPUBLIC, AUGUST 1994

I thought about putting off our trip to Meindorf, worried about driving after a sleepless night. But I wanted to get out of Berlin, where my world had been turned so monumentally upside down so, after a couple of cups of strong coffee, we set off. With great concentration, I remembered to keep to the right and had no trouble changing gear with a different hand. By the time we were on the autobahn, I felt like an old pro.

At first, it seemed as if my mother was behaving completely as normal, with no hint of the bombshell she had dropped the night before. She did not mention anything about it. Neither did I, finding the whole thing still utterly overwhelming. I could not have articulated my feelings if I had wanted to.

It was only after the first hour or so of the drive that I realised that actually my mother wasn't quite the same. Usually hard to impress, today she seemed to be going out of her way to find things to compliment me on.

'You drive very nicely,' she remarked, as I negotiated a hairy roundabout. 'Very nicely indeed. Well done.' And then, later, as we sailed past a labouring truck on a slow uphill incline, 'Good girl. Very smooth driving.'

Like many women of her generation, my mother had never learnt to drive. Normally, that didn't stop her criticising the driving of others and I was glad she wasn't doing that now. My frazzled nerves wouldn't take it. Today, I preferred the compliments, even if they were unusual and unexpected.

The journey was easier than I had anticipated, probably because in the light of what I'd found out the night before, anything else that life could throw at me seemed insignificant. The car ate up the miles, effortlessly. As I drove, I tried to imagine my mother, Hans and Gerta's tortuous progress along this route in the opposite direction, on foot, my mother pregnant, weighed down by the burden of being with child, as well as feeling responsible for the whole debilitated entourage walking with her.

Signposts whizzed by for towns and cities, which, in the car, we could reach in minutes or hours, not the days it had taken my mother and her weary band. As well as places, country names flew past; Poland this way, Austria in that direction, Switzerland over here. It was always fascinating being on the continent, I mused, where so many sovereign nations were just a drive away. Not like the little island of Great Britain, where to get anywhere meant crossing the sea. The Eurotunnel had just opened, earlier in the year, in May, and soon, in November they said, train services would start running under the English Channel. I thought this was amazing and exciting, a new start for Britain, joining it closer to Europe, tightening the ties that already bound the two parts of the continent.

'What do you think of Eurotunnel?' I asked my mother, realising that we had never discussed it.

My mother gave her special disapproving sniff. 'No need for it,' she snapped. 'Load of money for nothing. What's wrong with a boat if you want to cross the water?'

I giggled inwardly despite everything. My mother had her opinions and wouldn't change them for anyone's money.

'Let's get off the motorway,' I suggested. 'See a bit more of the countryside.' I wanted to get a better sense of the terrain my mother had passed through on her epic journey so long ago.

We meandered through back roads and lanes, surrounded by meadows of grazing cattle or horses, and cultivated fields growing wheat, sugar beet, potatoes and cabbages. I tried to imagine these thoroughfares and *waldwege*, forest paths, crowded with *Flüchtlinge*, dragging with them their worldly possessions, no idea when, or if, they would reach their destinations, many not even knowing what that destination was. They'd been eagerly cast out, but few places wanted to welcome them in.

My mother was mostly silent, gazing out of the car window, lost in her own private world. I left her alone with her thoughts, not wanting to disturb her. It was so hard to tell what she was thinking. She might be recalling her young self, thrust so unwittingly into a role of leadership more demanding than she could ever have imagined. But, knowing my mother, I thought it just as likely that, if I asked, she would deny that she was pondering the past, say she was wondering what she'd like to have for tea or whether the hotel would have the sheets, blanket and eiderdown that she liked, rather than one of these modern continental duvets.

Having stopped for lunch, and because we'd taken the slow road, it was late afternoon when we arrived in Meindorf. The summer sun gleamed off the mountaintops and bathed the picture-perfect town in a gentle, buttery light. Even if I hadn't known it was the place, I would have recognised it from my mother's descriptions. We drove down the wide main street and here were the houses with their picket fences, and the shops, and at either end the churches with their steeply pitched shingle roofs, just as she had described them. Stalled at some traffic lights, I stole a covert glance at my mother's face. She was staring out of the windscreen as if transfixed by what she saw, engrossed in a world she'd long left behind.

Once we'd checked into our hotel, I asked my mother if she'd like to go out exploring now, or leave it until the morning. She stifled a yawn, but waved her hand to dismiss the suggestion that we should take the latter option.

'I want to go to the house,' she insisted. 'To Herr Wagner's house by the edge of the forest, at the foot of the mountain.'

I wondered if she'd be able to find the way there; memory plays tricks on the most acute of minds and it had been fifty years. But her feet seemed to automatically know the route, only faltering momentarily at a couple of turnings and intersections.

When I saw the house, I knew it immediately. The gabled roof, the garden leading to the hill country, the heavy wooden door that would bang shut on my mother when she went out to hang Hans' nappies up to dry.

We walked all around the property in silent contemplation. At the garden fence, my mother pointed to a tree. 'So, it's still here,' she murmured. 'The tree where the old boy buried his silver. It's much bigger now, of course. Taller. But that's definitely the tree.'

'So the linden survives,' I said. 'What about the treasure?'

My mother shook her head. 'I don't know. I doubt it. Who'd want it now, anyway? Ugly old things he had, only he liked them because they were family, you know...' Her voice tailed off as words failed her. 'Heirlooms, that's it. They were heirlooms, but they weren't pretty things.'

We walked a little way up the track towards the forest.

'Mum,' I ventured, tentatively, 'I've got to ask. Why didn't you and Lou have any children?'

Her lips trembled, her papery skin suddenly seeming more than thin, transparent almost. 'I was... I couldn't...' she faltered, taking time to regain her composure before continuing. 'I was so badly torn when I gave birth and I had no medical care. The Russians – they did more damage that was never treated. There were no GPs and I was never setting foot in that hospital that killed Hans again. They'd have killed me, too, and then what would have happened to you? The simple fact is I never got pregnant again – and I think the hysterectomy was the result of those problems that never got fixed.'

It was a terrible thought, but I was glad I'd asked. For this whole process to have been worthwhile, everything needed to be out in the open, however difficult to hear.

We went back to the hotel and had dinner.

When the meal was over, I plucked up the courage to broach the subject that had been niggling at me all day. 'Janez will be in Meindorf tomorrow. Just to let you know.'

Instantaneously, tears began to roll down my mother's cheeks. Wordlessly, she put down her napkin, stood up from the table and left the dining room.

Propping my elbows on the table, I let my head fall into my hands. I hated making my mother cry but I knew better than to go after her right now. She needed some time to absorb what I had said. And I wasn't going to change my mind on meeting Janez. I had to keep reminding myself that this was my story, too, that my need to know my history was important, vital even, especially with the latest bombshell revelation. Though it might be hard at times, it had to be done.

After I'd been sitting like that for a while, I became aware of the nervous waiter hovering around me. I sat back up, smiled, waved my hand across the table and said, 'So sorry, please do clear everything away. We've finished.' The waiter leaned forward and began to scoop up plates and cutlery. 'When you're done, no hurry, I'll have a cognac,' I added. 'Could you leave it here? I'll be right back.'

In my bedroom, I cleaned my teeth and washed my face.

Thank goodness I wasn't bothering with make-up on this trip; I'd have mascara down to my jowls by this point.

I went back to the dining room. The glass of cognac stood on the table, the burnt umber liquid reflecting the room back at me, the stags' heads and flying ducks on the wall distorted by the curvature of the glass. I eyed the drink. This wasn't a good idea, when I was wallowing in self-pity anyway. But what the hell. I'd thought I had a father and I didn't. Janez thought he had a sister and he didn't. It was all a mess, and apart from anything else, I hated the prospect of letting him down.

Picking up the glass, I took it back to my bedroom, where I sat in bed, drinking and crying.

WHEN MY MOTHER joined me at the breakfast table the next morning, she looked contrite. 'I'm sorry,' she said, staring into her cup of steaming coffee. 'For keeping the truth from you. It wasn't right. But I hope you can understand why I did it.'

I stirred milk into my coffee. 'I'm not sure that I do. Not completely.' I wondered momentarily if I should say the next thing and then decided that I would. If we were ever going to move on, everything needed to be out in the open. 'You prevented me from knowing about my real father and Janez from knowing his. Yet I feel more for Janez than for myself. And I find your denial of him harder to comprehend. Maybe because he told me that Eva had never married and had brought him up alone, so, unlike me, he didn't benefit from a father figure in his life at all.' I realised as I spoke that I bore a heavy burden of guilt that I had had Lou's paternal love when his real son had not.

My mother's head was still bowed over the table. 'I've done wrong, Jo. So many wrong things.' She looked up and I saw she was crying again, silently weeping. 'Can you ever forgive me?'

A rush of love for my mother stronger than I had ever felt

before surged through me. She was so flawed, so vulnerable. So many of her decisions had been the right ones, but there had also been many that were wrong. Wasn't that true of all of us? Just that Mum, thrust into an apocalyptic world war and a continent torn apart, had had the opportunity to make bigger rights but also bigger wrongs than those who'd lived their life in peacetime could ever imagine.

I smiled softly. 'Of course I can forgive you,' I said. 'I already have. It's just – well, it was a shock. A huge shock. But I'll come to terms with it. As for Janez – we shall see. But he doesn't seem like the grudge-holding type.'

The waiter came with scrambled eggs on black rye bread, which I eyed greedily before diving in. This was just what my hangover needed.

'All wounds can be healed,' I added, between delicious, comforting mouthfuls. 'It will all be all right.'

My mother regarded me with a gaze of unalloyed relief. 'Thank you,' she muttered. 'You can't know how good those words sound. So often, during the war, the walk, I wished that someone would say those words to me and take care of it all and that it would, indeed, be all right. When Lou did – I would have sold my soul for the relief it brought me.'

Her words silenced me. I had also spent years wanting to hear those words, years when the bullying had sapped my spirit, when I had not been able to see the way out, or through. It will all be all right. How powerful was that one short phrase. Yes, it was true, I hadn't heard it when I'd needed to. But neither had my mother and I had the opportunity to put that right.

'Everything is still OK, Mum,' I reassured her, laying my knife and fork on my plate. 'You don't need to worry anymore. There's nothing for you to worry about.'

.   .   .

I HAD ARRANGED to meet Janez at a restaurant near Herr Wagner's house for lunch, thinking that if we only had enough conversation for the duration of the meal, then once over, our ways could part. But if we were getting on, we could take a walk in the forest or even get the restored funicular up the mountain.

Waiting just outside the front door of the hotel for my mother, I began to get impatient. I didn't want to keep Janez waiting. He might think we weren't coming and leave and I didn't know where he was staying so wouldn't be able to contact him.

After a couple more anxious minutes, I went back inside and knocked on my mother's door. When summoned inside, I found her sitting on her bed, head in hands.

'What's the matter? Mum, are you OK? What's happened?'

Slowly, she removed her hands from her face. She shook her head. 'I can't do it, Jo. I'm too old for this, it's been too long. I can't bear to face Janez, for him to know what I did. It's been hard enough facing you.'

Her face was stricken, her distress obvious.

I plumped down onto the bed next to her and put my arms around her. 'OK, Mum, that's fine. It's not a problem if you really can't manage it. But I don't think he's come to judge you. He just wants to meet us.'

She shook her head again. 'I can't do it,' she repeated. 'Jo, you'll have to go alone. I'm not coming.'

CHAPTER FIFTY-SEVEN

Walking into the restaurant, I kept my eyes peeled. Janez and I had exchanged photographs by post, so we knew what each other looked like. Scanning the room, I saw him sitting in the window, a broad-set man with short, curly brown hair. Immediately, I recognised in him a distinct air of Lou, the same easy friendliness of demeanour, the same kind eyes. The same, I noticed as I drew near, sticking-out ears. A flash of realisation struck me. I'd commented on those ears, in the picture of Lou in his RAF uniform, and my mother had stumbled over her response, almost seeming surprised that I should imagine I might have inherited any of Lou's features. I had brushed it off at the time, but now I understood its significance. Of course I didn't look like Lou. I was no relation to him at all.

This recollection threatened to broadside me so completely that I'd be unable to go through with the meeting. Taking a deep breath and squaring my shoulders, I forced myself to focus on Janez and banish all the other things my mind was full of.

As I took another step towards him, Janez turned around, recognised me and smiled the broadest, most beguiling smile of greeting I had ever seen.

'Jo!' he cried, leaping up and enveloping me in a hug.

'Janez,' I responded, and hugged him back.

He already had a bottle of local spring water on the table and he poured us both a glass as I apologised for my mother's absence. I wittered on a bit about the lovely location, and how had his journey been, and wasn't the weather glorious, all means of prevarication from the crucial thing I needed to share with him.

'Janez, it's so good of you to have come all this way,' I finally began.

He held up his hand in a gesture of repudiation. 'No, please, it's not far at all – much further for you than for me. And I would have travelled any distance for this meeting. I've been waiting for it all of my life. Who wouldn't want to meet their sister?'

I gulped. Janez's politeness, together with his expectations, was not making this any easier. I felt terrible for letting him down. But he had to know the truth, just as I had had to.

'Janez,' I intoned, watching the bubbles in my water glass rise slowly and inexorably to the surface. 'The thing is, there's no easy way to go about this. But – well, I'm not your sister. Lou was your father, but it turns out that he was not mine.' I took a large swig of water to buy some time, felt it fizz its way down my throat. 'We are not related. I'm sorry.'

Why was I apologising for not being a relation of a man I'd never met before? It made no sense, except that I felt it was a disappointment I had to mitigate in some way.

Janez frowned in puzzlement. 'Oh,' he said. 'Well, that's... I mean, it's fine. It's not what I expected when I got your letter but...'

'It's all a bit of a mess,' I replied with a sigh. 'When I wrote a reply to the address on that old envelope I had found, I thought I was Lou's daughter. Since then, my mother has revealed to me that I'm not. The day before yesterday, in fact. So it turns out we are absolutely no relation to each other at all. It was a shock to me, too.'

Janez grimaced sympathetically. 'Well, it would be,' he agreed. 'Absolutely it would be.'

The waiter came and we ordered lunch. It felt so strange to be choosing between boiled or chipped potatoes at a time like this, in the midst of such a conversation, I nearly laughed.

'I suppose it's quite a long story,' Janez suggested, once the man had departed.

I gave a short laugh of acknowledgement. 'Both long and short. Which version would you like?'

With a chuckle, Janez responded, 'You choose.'

It took the rest of the meal for me to tell Janez everything I had learned, and I was surprised by how easy I found it to talk to him. I'd never bonded so immediately with a complete stranger before. Usually I was shy until I'd met someone many times, wary I suppose, wanting to know how they perceived me before letting my guard down. But with Janez, I felt completely at ease from the very beginning.

At the end of the tale, he sat back in his chair and narrowed his eyes in contemplation. 'It's a compelling story,' he said. 'Your mother is clearly one very strong woman. It's good that you've had the chance to hear it all from her directly.'

My heart went out to my not-brother. He had never had that chance. He had not been able to speak to Lou.

'I'm sorry for what my mother denied to you,' I said. We'd left the restaurant now and were walking towards the woods, green and still in the hot summer air. The verges billowed with wild flowers and white-tailed rabbits darted out of sight as we approached. There was no one else around.

Much though I didn't want to blame my mother – and didn't feel that Janez wanted to blame her either, the truth was that it was her fault. As we strolled, I tried to explain why she had behaved as she had. I had no need to make excuses on my mother's behalf – but couldn't help feeling I ought to.

'If it's any consolation, she feels deep remorse for what she did.'

We had paused at the brow of hill and were looking back down at the valley. At least the scenery, beautiful, majestic, timeless, suited the magnitude of the occasion.

Janez rolled a stone beneath the toe of his shoe, lost in thought. 'I understand,' he mused. 'I can see it from your mother's point of view. From what I gathered, Lou and Eva had a very intense love affair. They packed into a few short days what other relationships might take years over, and then were suddenly and violently torn apart. The idea of them meeting again, rekindling those levels of emotion, must have felt very threatening to Katja. Please understand that I don't hold it against her. There would be no point in that, would there?'

Silently, I shook my head. It felt overwhelming again. Every new revelation had taken me by surprise and now here I was, walking in a Czech forest with Lou's son. He had found a father and I had lost one. I could hardly get my head around what was happening to me. To us.

'The past is a shambles, isn't it?' I muttered, and as I did so I thought of how my mother, a young widow and mother, had walked on these very paths through winter's silvery glades, drinking brandy with the woodcutters, knowing but not knowing that the world as she knew it was about to end.

Janez smiled thoughtfully. 'But we can make a better future, no? Look at what this country has achieved for a start. The Velvet Revolution and the first president a writer.'

Janez' optimism, his lack of bitterness, was as refreshing as it was admirable. It made me feel a bit better about everything, about opening such a Pandora's box of emotions.

After our walk, we parted company, agreeing to meet for a drink later. Janez would come to our hotel at eight.

I went back to my mother.

'He's a lovely man,' I told her. 'He's not at all angry. But he'd like to meet you. He's coming over later this evening – will you have a drink with us?'

Her nod, though almost imperceptible, told me that my mother would try her best.

WHEN JANEZ APPEARED at the door of the hotel bar, my mother and I were waiting. She had surprised me by turning up without any further cajoling. Looked down upon by the heads of once majestic stags that adorned the walls, my mother came face to face with the person whose existence had scared her so much for so long.

At first, the conversation was awkward, stilted. Questions such as 'how are you, what have you been doing for the last fifty years?' were hardly appropriate. It was all so big, the kind of experience that no has any preparation for. But gradually we all relaxed and the atmosphere lightened.

Janez was an illustrator and cartoonist and he drew caricatures of us both that were so comically accurate they had us in fits of giggles.

'They're wonderful, thank you!' I laughed. 'I'll frame those.'

My sitting room had a whole wall of pictures – photos, drawings the children had done, cards and postcards that meant something. I would add Janez's pictures to the collection, I thought, and then my breath caught in my throat at the sudden realisation that this would never be possible as I would not be in the house much longer. I might not have a picture wall in my next place.

Even as that thought occurred to me, I could hear Emma's voice of reason echoing in my ears. 'Mum, all houses have walls,' she'd say, practical as ever. Which was absolutely true.

How I wished Emma were here now, with her no-nonsense

approach to everything. She never dwelt on things, just got on with them, always optimistic, always looking on the bright side. At least I must have done something right, I reflected, to have such happy, cheerful children.

When Janez left, I escorted my mother up to her bedroom.

'Well,' I said, as she sat down on her bed to take off her shoes. 'How was that?'

She shrugged non-committally. 'He seems like a very nice young man.'

I had to laugh. Janez was fifty-one, older than me. The idea that either of us was young was ridiculous – but, at the same time, appealing.

Bidding my mother goodnight, I crossed the corridor to my own room. Sitting on the bed, I contemplated everything that had happened over the last couple of months. It had all occurred at such speed that I had hardly been able to process one revelation before another came along. Here, far from home and the stresses of everyday life, work, renovations and all the rest of it, I had some distance to think about it all.

I went to the window and looked out, breathing in deeply of the cool mountain air, fresh and clean-smelling, nothing like that of London, always thick with pollution. As I stood there, I tracked the course of my life, from my first memories as a small girl in London, stepping off that noisy Dakota into a strange new land, trailing behind my mother as we went shopping on Camden High Street or to feed the ducks in Regent's Park, to the terrible experience of school.

And then my protest years, travelling, always moving on, never alighting anywhere for longer than a few weeks. I had long been aware of how fruitless that search for myself had been. Perhaps I had always known, deep inside, that something was missing, that there was a piece of the jigsaw that didn't quite fit. For the first time in my life, I had all the bits, but I felt that I was still working without the picture, the image on the front of the box that showed what the finished product should look like.

In the calm stillness of the summer night, I tried to think about it rationally. Who did I want to be? And whoever that was, was it anything to do with the man who had fathered me, Karl Hausmann, or with the man who, to all intents and purposes had been my father, Lou?

However long I stood at the window, studying the star-studded sky and the nearly full moon, the answers did not come.

THE NEXT DAY was the start of our last twenty-four hours in the area before we had to drive back to Berlin, to the airport and thence to home. We went to Stahlbach, to the convalescent home. It was a hotel now, and we could have gone in. But my mother didn't want to, so instead we stood on the drive and contemplated it, both lost in our own thoughts. My heart turned over in my chest as I imagined how my mother had laughed and danced and sung, whirling in romantic waltzes with the handsome, charming, entrancing Karl Hausmann in those last carefree days before everything began to unravel.

I thought of my own conception, a snatched moment in Karl's bedroom, I supposed, his Waffen-SS uniform hanging on the back of a chair, none of the other inmates or staff any the wiser. These short-lived but impassioned affairs happen in wartime; it is an age-old story, the desire for intimacy, connection, closeness, in a world that's falling apart. At least, I consoled myself, I had been conceived through love and desire. That, at least, was something.

Driving out of town, we passed the railway station and my mother cried out, asking me to stop. Inside the little terminal building, she marvelled at how little it had changed. She could almost still see the soot on the walls, hear the subdued chatter of the *Flüchtlinge*, ordered there to face an uncertain fate.

'We had no idea,' she said to me, as we watched a train pull in, deposit some passengers and move off again. 'We simply did not know what was in store for us.'

We had arranged to have dinner with Janez again, as it was the last opportunity to see him. I felt disproportionately pleased that he wanted to come. It must mean that he liked us, I reckoned, and that was a pleasant feeling. The meal went well, with free-flowing conversation and no awkward pauses. Even my mother seemed to have relaxed. By nine thirty, she was tired and took herself off to bed, leaving Janez and me chatting. We were still sitting in the hotel bar when the waiter clocked off at midnight.

Janez told me about his experiences of growing up in communist Yugoslavia. Unlike other Eastern European countries, it didn't sound so bad. But he had always chafed at the bit, and the fall of communism had allowed him to surge forward in his career, permitted for the first time to use his cartoons to poke fun at political leaders and government policies. His love of art was all-consuming and he avidly averred that my talent for gardening was really an artistic one.

'You draw with plants and vistas and different heights and levels,' he pronounced, waving his arm expansively across the table. Discreetly, I moved the bottle of wine that was perilously close to being swept over. 'That is just as much art as using paint or charcoal or watercolours. And it is in 3D.'

'I suppose so,' I agreed. Then, for some reason that I could not fathom, I told him about the life-drawing classes. 'I'm so bad,' I confessed, 'but I'm going to carry on with the classes. Philippa – the tutor – says everyone can improve. Even me!' I hoped Janez wouldn't think me pathetic, a middle-aged woman pretending to be an art student.

But he was entranced. 'That's wonderful!' he said. 'I'm so

impressed. It's never too late to learn a new skill, is it? I myself have taken up the guitar. I'm not very good. I do a version of "Stairway to Heaven" that would horrify Jimmy Page, but – it amuses me.'

'I'd love to hear it,' I laughed, and realised that I really meant it. Janez was starting to creep under my skin; his intelligence, his kindness, his grace towards my mother. I was, I suddenly understood, in danger of becoming a little too fond of him. Perhaps it was a good thing he wasn't my brother, after all.

The conversation concluded with Janez's exhortation that I should come to visit him. His small town was within easy reach of the capital Ljubljana and he'd love to show me around. 'And one day,' he added, 'it is my intention to come to London, to visit the Tate, the National Gallery, the Wallace Collection.'

'Well,' I said, jokily, trying not to give away how much I meant it, 'then to London you must come.'

It was 2 a.m. when we finally decided to call it a night.

'I feel so privileged to have met you,' Janez said. 'Truly it's been wonderful.'

'No!' I exclaimed, overly quickly and loudly. The moment was full of emotion, which I felt ill-equipped to handle. 'The privilege is all mine.'

Something hovered between us, unseen, unsaid. And then in the same instant we came together, flinging our arms around each other and hugging tightly.

'Come to London,' I said, my voice muffled from my mouth being wedged in his shoulder, 'but come soon! My house is being sold and I don't know where I'll be living.'

As we released each other, Janez looked down at me, his kind brown eyes soft and mellow. 'I might just do that. I really might.'

CHAPTER FIFTY-EIGHT

In London, my mother's flat was ready, the flood damage repaired. She wanted to move back, so, immediately on our return from Europe, I went to Sainsbury's to do a big shop for her and then left her to settle in. She looked exhausted. I had the feeling that the trip had taken more of an emotional toll on her than she wanted to admit, and there had undoubtedly been a physical one.

Driving off up the high street, a deep sadness subsumed me. I'd enjoyed this time with my mother, and felt close to her in a way I never had before. I guessed it was due to the breadth of the revelations we had shared. This was good. But it left me regretting that it had taken so many years to get to this place. I tried to think of what Janez would say – don't dwell on the past – or Emma – Mum, you always take things too much to heart. Lighten up! Perhaps that was exactly what I needed to do. Not dwell on the past and lighten up.

While I'd been away, Springer had been staying at what Sue and I jokingly referred to as Sue's holiday camp. We arranged to meet by the lido to hand him back over, combining it with a long walk and ploughman's lunch at the Old Bull and Bush. By the time we reached the pub, I had pretty much told Sue everything that had happened in Germany and the Czech Republic, ending with the news that Lou was not, in fact, my father.

'Goodness.' Sue seemed lost for words. 'That's... well, that's pretty major. How do you feel about it now?'

I sighed lengthily. 'I'm still mulling it over, really, trying to work it all out. But truthfully – after the initial shock, I'm not sure I feel anything very much. On the one hand, it's changed my whole life. But, on the other, it's changed nothing. Katja's still Katja and Lou's still Lou and my own family are still what they've always been.'

'I think we need a drink,' stated Sue, flabbergasted.

'Later,' I laughed, 'or I won't make it home.'

It was six o'clock before I left the pub, Sue and I had spent so much time talking. I had a sudden urge to check up on my mother, to make sure she was all right on her own after so long with me always on hand. When I got to her place, I found her comfortably ensconced in front of the television. Her face lit up when I entered. The flat looked marvellous, and right somehow, now she was back in situ.

I made tea and sat down next to her on the sofa.

'I want to give you something,' she said, blurting the words out as if they had been ready and waiting for some time. 'A couple of things actually.'

'Oh, Mum,' I replied, 'that's kind, but you don't need to give me anything. There's nothing I need.' Since the trip, my mother had seemed lighter and freer, as if sloughing off the lies and deceptions of the past had done her a world of good.

'But there is,' she interjected, cutting in sharply. 'There's something you need very badly indeed. And that is the money for the house. So that you can keep it, buy Ed out. I want to give you the money.'

I gasped. 'Mum! You can't do that. Anyway, where are you going to get thirty thousand pounds from?'

She gave a small, thoughtful smile. 'I've been saving all my life. That's what my generation did. A shilling here, a Deutschmark there. I've received a war widow's pension from the German government ever since Horst died and I put it all away in a separate account that I've never touched. You know the saying: if you look after the pennies, the pounds look after themselves. We never had much money when you were small and you never complained if you couldn't have what the other children had. Now – well, I've got the money just sitting there and I've nothing to spend it on. My flat's all finished' – she waved her hand around at the immaculate space – 'and what I have will see me out. I can't take the money with me. I want you to have it. It's the least I can do.'

I was struggling to take it in. 'Well, thank you. I really appreciate it.' And then I remembered that she had said there were a couple of things. 'Was there something else you mentioned?'

My mother nodded. She reached out her hand to the table beside her chair, where an envelope lay, small and faded with age. 'I would like you to have this letter. It's from Lou, after we met for the second time in Berlin. It gives a bit more background, I suppose, an explanation. I've always kept it safe, a personal treasure. But now I want you to have it – it goes with his notebook, and the dried flower.'

Gingerly, I accepted the proffered letter.

'Shall I read it now?' I asked.

A small incline of my mother's head indicated yes.

My dear, darling Katja, the letter began.

I can't believe that I have found you. That so soon after returning to Berlin, I've achieved what I set out to do. I came back for you. You are the only thing I wanted after all those years of death and destruction. That's why I signed up with the Control Commission. I hoped it would give me the opportunity to seek you out, wherever you were in Berlin.

After that first encounter, I couldn't forget you – your beauty, your dignity, your determination to survive. And I couldn't forget your baby, that tiny, perfect, blue-veined child, who I first saw on the day she was born, during her first few hours on this planet. The flower I gave her was because I could not tear out my own heart and gift her that. I knew you would do everything in your power to save her, to nurture her despite the difficulties. And I wanted to save you, both of you. I'm sorry I didn't get there soon enough to save your son.

I'll never be able to explain how I felt when I laid eyes on you on that bus. It was a miracle. It told me, without any doubt, that you and I were meant to be. Thank you for giving me the opportunity to be part of your lives, to be a father to your child.

I love you both with all my heart and always will.

All my love from your true love,

Lou

Long after I'd finished reading, I lowered the thin paper from my eyes. Tears were flowing, faster and stronger than at any time in this process of discovery.

'Don't get it wet!' my mother exclaimed. 'The ink will run!' She smiled a soft, sweet smile of memory. 'It's the only love letter I've ever had,' she added.

And suddenly we were both laughing because everything was out in the open now and the past was exactly where it should be – behind us. My mother's hardness, her prickliness, her sensitivity to talking about her history – it all made sense. She had been hiding something, concealing a huge secret that had dogged her life and that she had felt she could never reveal. The weight of that secret, after fifty years, had finally become too much to bear. It could no longer be hidden away, pushed under the carpet. It needed the fresh air of confession, divulgence, to temper its debilitating power.

'The shame, the guilt, the blame – all those things I heaped upon myself for so many years – I feel that they are gone now, Jo,' she said, simply, as she handed me a cheque for £30,000. 'Not because I'm giving you money – it's not that banal. But because you know the things you should have known all your life. And I hope, and believe, it's not too late for you to benefit from the knowing.'

I shook my head. 'It's not too late, Mum. It's never too late to put things right, is it?'

CHAPTER FIFTY-NINE

A couple of days later, when I'd had more time to digest it all, Sue and I got together for that drink.

'Mum's given me the money for the house,' I told her. 'And I'm so grateful because keeping the house means everything to me. But I feel bad – she never spends anything on herself.'

Sue twirled her glass of wine in her hand so the liquid ballooned up and down the sides. 'She doesn't have the spending habit, does she? Which is understandable, given where she's come from. But you're not exactly a spendthrift yourself. It's not your fault that you can't stump up what Ed wants. And your mother's not donating it to you so you can go on a world cruise or fritter it away on baubles – it's to secure your future. Take it and be happy, I say. After all, there are no pockets in a shroud.'

I smiled. 'That's pretty much what Mum said. And you're right. I mean, it's the answer to my prayers, I can't really believe it.' I drank a sip of wine and grinned wickedly. 'I can't imagine what Ed's going to say when I tell him. He'll be miffed. He'll wish he'd hung around to be the beneficiary of Mum's unexpected largesse.'

We both fell about laughing. It was unfair really – Ed was entitled to want his share of our worldly goods. But he hadn't taken any consideration of what it meant to me as the deserted party to also lose my home. And I was still sure he'd been dishonest about when his relationship with Annabelle became physical. It felt good to have a little piece of vengeance.

My laughter ended abruptly with a heartfelt sigh.

'What's up?' asked Sue. 'Not more to wrestle with?'

I shook my head. 'It's stupid really,' I mused. 'I've been trying to make the most of my life, not to dwell on being alone but to fill every day with new and challenging and wholesome and mind-improving activities. I promised I'd get on with being the new Jo when Mum was back home and the house was sorted. Now both of those things have happened and I'm feeling exhausted at the prospect of the goals I've set myself. Far from being more meteor, I feel like being more of a couch potato. I'd like to do very little for a while. But the guilt that engenders is too much.' I pushed my empty glass of wine a few inches away from me. 'How are you doing it? You set out on much the same course after your cancer scare and you're putting me to shame. Waterskiing, hot-air ballooning, life drawing, plus your running and swimming...'

Sue grimaced and rolled her eyes heavenward. 'OK,' she began, 'time to come clean. I've realised that trying to be like that – living every day as if it's your last – what you're supposed to do when you've nearly died – is impossible. Exhausting and unsustainable, putting me under so much pressure it would likely make me ill again. I can't keep it up and I can't believe many people can. Of course I'm so grateful that I didn't die – but I can't be glad every minute of every day to the exclusion of all else.'

I was listening intently, frowning.

'So,' continued Sue, 'I've decided to kick back, stop pushing myself. Just take things as they come. Chill out. I've been given a second go and I have to approach it on my own terms, not do what some lifestyle guru or other overpaid celebrity tells me to. Anything else will drive me mad.'

I was silent for a while. Then, 'Wow,' I said. 'Double-wow. Um – I'm getting more wine. I think we need it.'

When I returned with two more glasses of the house white, I proposed a toast. 'Here's to us. And to a life where we make all our own compromises!'

Sue laughed delightedly as we chinked glasses. 'Absolutely right. Here's to us.'

SHORTLY AFTER THIS, Emma returned from honeymoon, tanned and glowing, smelling of coconut shampoo and happiness. I had to tell the whole story again and, then once more to Evan. I found that every time I recounted it, it cut a little less deeply, was a little easier to articulate. I didn't cry when I told my son and daughter about Lou.

Emma, who at least I could speak to in person rather than over the phone, was dumbfounded, lost for words for the first time in her life. Finally, she recovered enough to speak. 'Shit, Mum, you're nearly a year older than you think you are!'

I nearly fell off my chair laughing. 'Trust you to focus on the least important part of this!'

Emma snickered. 'No wonder you look forty-nine not forty-eight,' she added and then immediately, louder, 'Joke! You don't even look forty, let alone approaching fifty.'

'Well, that's sweet of you to say,' I smiled.

We went through to the sitting room, where I gave Emma the letter that Lou had sent to Katja after finding her in Berlin.

'Wow, that is so, so romantic,' she said, once she'd finished reading. 'Who would have thought it? Wait until I tell G. He won't believe it.' She put the paper carefully back into the envelope. 'What do you think, Mum? Are you going to try to find your...' she faltered, unable to say the words 'your father' about someone who wasn't Lou – 'this Karl Hausmann bloke? Would you like to track him down?'

I shook my head. 'No. No I wouldn't and I'm not going to try. Mum's fairly sure he didn't survive the war and, as far as she knows, he didn't have much family – only parents who would be long gone by now.' I paused to look out at the garden, where the second flush of summer roses billowed in the breeze.

Emma's forehead creased and her mouth narrowed to a quizzical frown. 'I can sense a "but"...'

I sighed. 'I'm worried. Karl fought for the Nazis. Have I been tainted by his bad blood?' This thought had been plaguing me since our return from Germany.

Emma gave an incredulous hoot. 'Oh Mum! How could you think such a thing? Karl turned good in the end, didn't he, however he started out – and you're the kindest, fairest, truest person I know.' She got up, came to me, threw her arms around my neck. 'And we love you – Evan and I – so much.'

I sniffed and wiped my eyes with the back of my hand. 'Thank you,' I spluttered. 'That's the nicest thing anyone's ever said to me.'

Emma smiled. 'And it's true.'

I went to my desk and fumbled in the drawer for something. I brought it over to Emma.

'What's this?' she asked, as I handed her the sheets of paper.

'It's the contents of the last letters Karl gave to your grandmother to pass on to the Resistance. Before she burnt them, she memorised what was written, and the maps. In case she had the opportunity to give them to someone who could make use of them. She had no idea who that could be, but she wanted to finish the task. She copied it all down for the history project.'

Emma picked up the papers I handed to her and scrutinised them. 'Wow, go Grandma!' she breathed, astonished. 'That's amazing that she could remember it all.'

'Well, in all fairness,' I joked, 'we wouldn't have a clue whether these copies are accurate or a load of nonsense, would we?'

Emma laughed with me, then folded up the papers and placed them down on the side table, before looking back at me with an air of expectancy. 'So – what now?' she demanded, with characteristic forthrightness.

I ran my hands through my hair. 'The last few weeks have been a rollercoaster ride, if I'm honest. But now – I'm done with the past. I want to look to the future.'

'Agreed,' said Emma, emphatically. 'Good plan. Out with the old, in with new. Shall I pour more tea?'

Nodding my assent, I contemplated the one last thing I needed to tell Emma. Delaying it would only make her more suspicious when she did find out.

'By the way,' I began, airily, 'Janez is coming for a visit. He's never been to London. He's coming in a couple of weeks. He might stay awhile. He thinks a new environment will inspire his art.'

Emma, at first preoccupied with stirring the tea in the pot ummed in response, not paying much attention. And then the reality of what I'd said dawned on her. 'Really? Huh, Mum, really? A man, coming to stay, for a while?'

A grin spread unstoppably across my face. My mentions of Janez had passed completely beneath Sue's radar. But Emma was another matter.

'We like each other. That's all.'

'You hardly know each other!' Emma retorted. 'How many conversations have you even had? Go on, how many?'

'Well,' I countered, evenly, 'we spent quite a few hours together in Meindorf, and we've been talking a lot on the phone since then, so—'

'Oh!' Emma almost shouted, 'so suddenly phone calls aren't so killingly expensive, hmmm?' She paused and her mock indignation turned to a bellow of delighted laughter. 'But a male visitor – I'm not sure if I approve. Who'll be your chaperone?'

'Emma! Really!' I smiled primly. 'As I said, we like each other. We get along. We're both free agents, but that's as far as it goes right now.'

Emma gave an elaborate sigh and poured the tea, holding the pot ostentatiously high above the cups. 'Well, it's your life. Nothing to do with me.'

I had a sudden feeling of déjà vu. The children not liking my attention to be elsewhere, always wanting me all for themselves.

'You're right. It is. And it isn't.'

Emma plonked the mugs of tea on the coffee table. Then immediately got up again, leaned towards me and gave me a hug. 'I'm delighted for you, really I am. If this is a thing – then let it be a good thing,' she cried joyously. She raised the teapot high and brandished it like a trophy, 'I declare my mother to be on to a good thing.'

I gave a wry snort of laughter. 'Emma, you are so melodramatic. Always have been, always will be.'

We drank tea in silence for a while. The truth was that I didn't know exactly what was going on between Janez and me. Maybe it was something, maybe it was nothing. What was important at that moment was having the chance to find out and, freed from a need for the outcome to go any particular way, I relished the thought of the adventure. It would be fun, and fun had been in short supply for some time.

'But about Lou,' Emma started up, eventually, her brow creased in thought, her voice low, 'it doesn't change anything, does it? He was your dad to all intents and purposes. He loved you like a dad. He probably saved both your lives by giving Grandma that food parcel. And think of it this way. I read in a magazine once that about ten per cent of all children, their father isn't who they think it is. And think of all the step-families, and the sperm-donor children. Being a biological father is pretty irrelevant, when you think about it.' She closed her eyes in concentration, then opened them again to conclude, 'Grandad was there for you all your life. Nothing else matters, does it?'

My eyes fell on my picture wall, where Janez's caricatures of my mother and I now hung alongside a frame containing a single pressed flower that was once a pale pink dog rose growing on a hedgerow near Berlin. Maybe I'd add one of my life drawings, if I ever progressed beyond unrecognisable daubings. It would be nice if I did, but if not, so be it. I would be happy either way. The point of any of these things was the journey, not the getting there. I understood that now, in a way I never had before.

I reached out and held my daughter's hands, feeling the hard, cool metal of her wedding band, rubbing my thumb over the diamond of her engagement ring, feeling their solidity, their realness. 'You're right, Emma, my love. Absolutely right. Nothing else matters at all.'

A LETTER FROM ROSE

Dear reader,

I want to say a huge thank you for choosing to read *The Lost Diary*. If you enjoyed it, and want to keep up to date with all my latest releases, just sign up at the following link. Your email address will never be shared and you can unsubscribe at any time.

www.bookouture.com/rose-alexander

Writing this book was a labour of love and very personal because it is based on the true stories of members of my family. In bringing Katja, Lou and Jo's incredible experiences to the page, it felt really important to get their voices right. I hope that I've done that and that you feel that you know these people as well as I do. While what they went through was so challenging, I wanted the book to feel uplifting at the end.

If you liked *The Lost Diary*, and I really hope you did, I would be so grateful if you could spare the time to write a review. I'd love to hear what you think – it really helps new readers to find my books for the first time.

I love hearing from my readers – you can get in touch through Twitter, Goodreads or my website.

Thanks,

Rose Alexander

www.rosealexander.co.uk

 twitter.com/RoseA_writer

Printed in Great Britain
by Amazon